VANESSA NELSON

THE HUNDRED - BOOK 1

THE GATHERING

The Hundred - Book 1

Vanessa Nelson

Copyright © 2019 Vanessa Nelson

All rights reserved. This is a work of fiction.

All characters and events in this publication are fictitious and any resemblance to any real person, living or dead, is purely coincidental.

Reproduction in whole or in part of this publication without express written consent is strictly prohibited.

To find out more about Vanessa Nelson or her books, please visit: http://www.taellaneth.com

For Mum and Dad

With love.

Contents

1. CHAPTER ONE — 1
2. CHAPTER TWO — 12
3. CHAPTER THREE — 22
4. CHAPTER FOUR — 33
5. CHAPTER FIVE — 39
6. CHAPTER SIX — 47
7. CHAPTER SEVEN — 53
8. CHAPTER EIGHT — 66
9. CHAPTER NINE — 74
10. CHAPTER TEN — 85
11. CHAPTER ELEVEN — 96
12. CHAPTER TWELVE — 107
13. CHAPTER THIRTEEN — 118
14. CHAPTER FOURTEEN — 125
15. CHAPTER FIFTEEN — 130
16. CHAPTER SIXTEEN — 140
17. CHAPTER SEVENTEEN — 149
18. CHAPTER EIGHTEEN — 157
19. CHAPTER NINETEEN — 165

20.	CHAPTER TWENTY	174
21.	CHAPTER TWENTY-ONE	183
22.	CHAPTER TWENTY-TWO	199
23.	CHAPTER TWENTY-THREE	212
24.	CHAPTER TWENTY-FOUR	220
25.	CHAPTER TWENTY-FIVE	230
26.	CHAPTER TWENTY-SIX	243
27.	CHAPTER TWENTY-SEVEN	256
28.	CHAPTER TWENTY-EIGHT	267
29.	CHAPTER TWENTY-NINE	274
30.	CHAPTER THIRTY	286
	THANK YOU	291
	CHARACTER LIST	292
	PLACES	294
	ALSO BY THE AUTHOR	295
	ABOUT THE AUTHOR	297

Chapter One

A SORCERESS AND TWO wulfkin walked into a tavern.

It sounded like the start of a bad joke, but Yvonne couldn't think of a good punchline. Nor did she think anyone would believe that she was a sorceress. Sorceresses rode on prancing white steeds, clothed in gem-encrusted robes, and were so extraordinarily beautiful that ordinary mortals were bewitched at first glance.

At least, that was what the stories told.

There were no stories that she knew of where the sorceress rode an old warhorse, long past his prime. Or where the sorceress wore threadbare clothes and boots that were leaking, again. She had always thought that gem-encrusted robes would be both impractical and uncomfortable, but right now she would very much like to have some gems. Particularly when the next step reminded her that her boots were soaked through from walking beside her horse for part of the morning, heavy woollen socks saturated, cold damp between her toes.

She could not remember the last time her feet had been dry. It seemed to have been raining for the entire journey. It had been a panicked rush to leave their last home, and then twenty days of hard travel, moving as fast as they could, fear dulling to exhaustion on the way.

And now they were nearly at journey's end. The Tavern's door was open in front of her, the tantalising smell of food drifting out, curling through her senses, and reminding her stomach that it had been a long time since she had eaten well.

Still, she could not move forward, her damp feet fixed to the ground. Another unfamiliar place. More strangers. More questions. Good reasons to stay still, she thought, even if they weren't the real reason.

"Kalla?" Kinswoman, in an ancient language that few people spoke anymore. It snagged her attention away from her thoughts.

For a moment she wasn't sure which of the children had spoken. A bad sign. She had not realised she was so tired. Some of it was hunger. And she hated having wet feet.

She blinked, shook her head slightly, forced a smile to her face, and found the pair of them standing shoulder-to-shoulder nearby, waiting for her. Joel, tall and broad with a shock of fair hair and bright blue eyes, watchful and a little wary. Mariah, delicate next to her brother, barely reaching his shoulder, with dark skin and startling blue eyes, looking around her with curiosity and anticipation, even after so long a journey.

They looked human, to a casual glance. A closer look at either would show the slightly more prominent brow and bone structure of a wulf, and the faint hint of something other in their eyes, the predator never far from the surface.

Right now, they were simply waiting. Yvonne had an impulse to turn and go back to the horses, who were doubtless now happily munching feed in The Tavern's stables, under the watchful eyes of the pair of grooms who seemed far more competent than the ones she was used to dealing with. The horses were warm, dry, and having their lunch. They did not have to deal with the stares of strangers and the inevitable questions, many of them rude. She envied the horses.

But she and the children had not eaten properly for a couple of days, after their travel rations had been raided overnight by some desperate forest creature, and the smell drifting out of The Tavern was wonderful. Someone inside was an excellent cook.

Her mind sharpened, taking stock of their surroundings. She had been dangerously distracted.

Tipping her head back, she saw that the sign had been replaced since she was last here, before the winter. It was a plain wooden board, understated. Beautifully crafted, though. A simple tankard, for those who could not read. Plain words, for those that could. The Tavern.

It might seem like a humble name. Yvonne had met the owner, though, and there was very little humble about him. Subtle and clever. Far more so than any other wulf she had met. The Tavern. As though there could be no other taverns in this town. In the same way as he was the cerro. The leader for all wulfkin in the town, in charge of the local range.

He was attempting to hide in plain sight, operating this large, busy, prosperous tavern in a large, busy, prosperous town. Her sword hand twitched at the idea of a wulf being subtle, and she forced it still. He might be watching, and she needed his acceptance of the children.

Joel and Mariah were still waiting.

"We are expected?" Joel asked, a subtle tension in his voice and body that someone who didn't know him would have missed. It was not the first time he had asked that question on the way here. She had answered the question each time, and would answer it as many times as he needed to hear it.

"Yes," she confirmed, keeping to the one word this time, conscious there might be others listening, and gave them a single nod, letting them go first into the building. She resisted the urge to lift a hand and check her neck. Her scars were covered. They always were.

The old fear still crawled over her skin, making her sword hand twitch again. It had been years. It did not matter. She was walking into a wulf's territory. The memories were still there, ready to come to the surface if she let them. She willed them back, drew a breath, and straightened her spine. She wasn't a frightened child anymore. Had not been for years. She was a sorceress. And she was armed.

They came into The Tavern's common room, a surprisingly high-ceilinged room with large windows, full of daylight and rows of tables and benches set at odd angles. Wulfkin were highly social by nature, but did not always like to be in each others' pockets. So, the room was designed with tables and chairs that could be moved around quickly, as needed, but would give the patrons an illusion of privacy and personal space when they wanted it. It was clever. Much like The Tavern's owner.

It was also quite busy. She easily identified the merchants, who must be travelling on one of the river barges that regularly passed through the town. A group of dark-skinned men and women clad in loose, flowing garments that told her their home land was far warmer and drier than this one. There were a few mercenaries with them, hard-edged and keen-eyed, who took a careful look at Yvonne and her companions as they came through the door.

Most of the rest of the patrons were wulfkin. Yvonne did not need her nose to tell her that, the way they moved was evidence enough. Quick, lithe, graceful. Deadly predators when they wanted to be. Her sword hand twitched again, but she stilled it with the ease of long practice.

She found a table that wasn't too close to everyone else, but not so far away that they would look antisocial. It was a fine balance to strike.

A petite wulf, dark hair pulled back from her face, cheeks flushed with effort, came up a moment later with a bright smile.

"Greetings, strangers. Be welcome to The Tavern. What can I get you?"

"What's for lunch?" Mariah asked, eyes gleaming. There had been little time for cooking and good meals on the road. Just enough food to keep them going, fuel for their bodies, and not even that for the last two days. Mariah and Joel were used to far better fare.

"We've got stew," the girl began answering, then tilted her head, nostrils widening. "I'm sorry. I did not notice at first. What range are you from?"

It was an innocent question, and Yvonne saw the way that both Mariah and Joel tensed, an unhappy pull to Joel's mouth.

"My children," she told the girl. That should set tongues wagging, but stop any further questions.

There was no word for wulfkin without a range. Every wulf knew where they belonged, even if they did not like it. Apart from her children and one other, older wulf she knew, powerful enough that he did not care what others thought of him.

"Oh. I'm sorry. I didn't mean to be rude." The girl's face had flushed more deeply. Yvonne wondered how long this girl had been working. She looked barely old enough to be in here, as patron or server, and clearly not used to using her senses properly or she would have recognised fellow wulfkin sooner.

"That's all right." Some of Mariah's brightness had faded, but Yvonne could almost sense her shame. Appearances mattered to Mariah, after too long moving from place to place. Wulfkin without a range, but apparently with a human mother who looked too ragged to be of much use.

"It's my first week here," the girl said, as though reading Yvonne's thoughts, tucking a loose strand of hair behind her ear. Her skin was pale enough to suggest a northern heritage, still flushed with embarrassment. "I'm still getting used to things. The stew is really very good."

"We'll have stew and small beer for all of us," Yvonne said.

The girl might be new, but she was quick. They had barely settled in their seats and exchanged a few words, Mariah complaining about her wet feet, before bowls of stew and wooden tankards of small beer were in front of them. Mariah and Joel nearly buried their heads in the bowls, barely remembering to use their spoons.

"This is really good," Mariah told her between mouthfuls. "You want yours?" she asked, seeing Yvonne had barely touched hers. Years of table manners being drilled into her, the hard rap of a wooden rod across her knuckles when she erred, and she was always careful to eat slowly no matter how hungry she was. She had tried to teach her children, although the lessons had not involved a wooden rod. She could not bring herself to hurt them. And table manners were far less important among wulfkin than among humans.

"Yes. But you can order more if you want," Yvonne told them, hiding a smile with another mouthful. Wulfkin required a lot more food than humans, and hungry wulfkin were dangerous.

Given permission, they lost no time in ordering more stew. The serving girl brought it with the same quick efficiency and bright smile. She was walking with a slight limp, Yvonne saw. She frowned at her back, watching the girl walk away. The Tavern's owner did not strike her as someone to permit harassment or injury to his people, and that limp had to be a recent injury as wulfkin healed extremely quickly.

"What are you staring at?"

The belligerent tone and the beer fumes that accompanied the question gave her a fairly good picture of the man before she turned to look. One of the few humans in the place, he was middle-aged with a paunch, the front of his tunic bearing beer and food stains.

"Good day to you," Yvonne said, keeping her voice even and pleasant, and staying settled on the stool. She was a tall woman, and a lot of drunk men had taken exception to that over the years. She could sense Mariah and Joel tensing up. They had been through variations of this many times over the years.

"You were staring at Willa."

"Are you her father?" Yvonne asked. It was a provocative question, but her tongue had run away with her before she knew what she was saying. It was one of her most serious flaws.

To her surprise, the man seemed to find this hilarious, laughing loudly. "No. No children. But she's a good girl."

Yvonne's opinion of the man rose. "She seems so."

"And who are these?" the man asked. Nosy, Yvonne thought. Probably harmless.

"These are my children," she answered.

"You don't seem old enough to have children that age," the man answered, with what he probably thought was a charming smile. The leer sent another blast of beer fumes across her face.

She wasn't old enough. Not in any culture. Barely past thirty herself. And the relationship she claimed wasn't quite right, either, but it was the easiest explanation. They weren't tied by blood, but by legal agreement that made her guardian of two wulfkin until they reached age eighteen. She had never been able to bring herself to say she was their mother, but she could say they were her children. Her wards.

She watched as the man's eyes travelled over them. Joel, with the fair hair and pale skin of the far north, Mariah with the dark skin of the far south. And her, last of all. Somewhere in the middle. Taller than Joel, and not as broad. Pale skin and black hair from her mother, her eyes, darker than Joel's, lighter than Mariah's, from her father. The only thing she, Joel and Mariah shared was blue eyes, of varying shades, and that was a coincidence more than anything else, although she did not see the need to tell the man that.

Before she could speak, a heavy hand landed on her shoulder. There was no warning, just a hand landing on her person.

She moved. Grabbed hold of the wrist, pulled the arm forward. Locked the arm and the wrist with one hand as she rose from the stool, then turned and moved her weight through her hip and leg, throwing the man onto the floor.

Only then did her mind catch up with her body, heart thudding in her chest, mouth dry.

A wulf. Young, by the looks of him. Flushed with fury and embarrassment. Probably hadn't expected a woman to react like that, or to be able to throw him. She took a steadying breath, stomach twisting. She would not be able to do that again, she knew, not when he was prepared.

He gathered himself on the floor, eyes lighting with the beginnings of the change, an eerie glow that always sent shivers down Yvonne's spine, remembering the first time she had seen it. The predator that lived in all wulfkin coming to the surface. She pushed the memories away. Again.

She stayed on her feet, waiting, one hand going to her sword hilt. The symbol on her left shoulder glowed faintly with green light. A symbol anyone in the lands would know, even if they did not believe it.

"You bitch. No one does that to me." The wulf's words were distorted by the fangs springing into his mouth with the beginnings of the change.

"And you should know better than to lay your hands on anyone without their permission," Yvonne told him, voice even and calm. Her heart was still racing. The older wulfkin, the ones with more sense, would be aware of her pulse. She could not do anything about that. But she could face down this young thing, all bluster and fury. He could kill her. She was quite aware of that. But she had faced down a lot of creatures who could kill her, and held her ground.

He gathered himself to crouch on the floor, fingers lengthening as claws sprang out from his fingertips. Her hand tightened on the sword hilt. She could also kill him. One clean sweep of the fine edge of her sword, tempered by a master at his craft and honed with magic, would slice through skin and muscle and bone. She had done it before, and her stomach tightened as the memory resurfaced for a moment.

"You'll pay for that," the wulf growled, body tensing, ready to spring.

Wait, she told herself, coming to her toes, ready to move. Wait.

"Stop."

The one word, quiet, but carrying a world of authority, stilled everyone in the room. A wulf's power shimmered in the air with none of the eerie glow of a change.

"Sephenamin." She greeted the newcomer without turning around. The young thing in front of her was still crouched low to the ground, still lethal. And she had met The Tavern's owner before, when she had scouted out the town as a possible home for her and her children.

"Hunar." The word carried the same level of authority as the previous one, and had a quite different response in the room. A ripple of shock carried around the space, everyone straightening a fraction.

The symbol at her shoulder shimmered in response to her title. The symbol that everyone would recognise, even if they didn't believe it. The stylised outline of a great bird, wings spread, head lifted in a defiant shriek. The first Hunar's legendary companion, the Firebird, bringer of justice.

Oath-sworn to help those in need, Hunar were trained in magic, and weapons. And outside the reach of any ruler's influence.

Hunar were also rare. A bare legend in some places, they were so rare, origins told like ghost stories on dark nights, gathered around fires.

Very few people alive had met Hunar, although everyone had a story about their aunt, or grandfather, or cousin, or some more ancient ancestor, who had spoken with Hunar once, who had requested their aid, and often found the result wasn't quite what they had expected.

She turned her head slightly, to track his progress across the floor. Tavern owner. Shrewd businessman. And, far more importantly, cerro of this range. Perhaps the most powerful wulf she had ever met in her life, and she had met a great variety of wulfkin, one way or another. He was not much older than her, or so it seemed. Ageing in wulfkin was difficult to pin down, even for someone with her skills. What she did know about him was that he ran The Tavern, and his range, with absolute power and authority. A young wulf of his range, in The Tavern, should never have put a hand on one of the guests. She was not the one in trouble here.

"I am sorry that you have been so disturbed," he said. Another ripple around the room. Some surprise, perhaps from those who did not know him well. A grim acknowledgement from those who did know him, and knew the rules of this range.

"It is of little consequence," she answered. Another place, another time, another wulf, and she might have made more of it. But all she saw was a hot-headed young thing, too close in age to her children for her to be truly cruel.

"An apology," Sephenamin said, his eyes changing from their normal pale grey, brightening to almost white with power as his gaze moved past Yvonne to the young wulf still crouched on the floor.

The youngster's pride had all gone and he was pale, almost trembling. Not dangerous anymore. She released the grip on her sword hilt and saw the youngster's eyes track the movement, skin paling further. He had not realised she was armed, and ready to defend herself. Fool.

"Will that suffice?" Sephenamin asked, turning his attention back to Yvonne. An apology. A slender thread of civilised behaviour against a potentially lethal attack. One of them would not have survived.

"Perfectly well, thank you," she answered. Civility was important to wulfkin, helping to keep their predatory natures intact. A lesson she had tried to instill into her children over and over.

The apology was delivered in a stuttering voice, far different from the fury that he had shown a few minutes ago, and Sephenamin dispatched the wulf, sending him out of The Tavern with a flick of his fingers and promising to deal with him later. From the little she knew of him, Yvonne suspected that Sephenamin's punishment for the young wulf would be something like mucking out the stables, on his own, for several days to come. From the sideways glance that the young wulf gave his cerro as he scuttled away, she thought the youngster was imagining any number of torments.

"I am pleased to see that you have arrived, Hunar," Sephenamin said, turning his attention completely towards her. "Will you introduce me?"

It was a polite, almost deferential request. Yvonne was not fooled. Unlike many powerful men, Sephenamin saw no need to demonstrate his power at every turn. In the holding back, he demonstrated his perfect restraint and control, traits which, like civilised behaviour, were much admired among wulfkin.

"I should be pleased to. Joel, Mariah, this is Sephenamin, cerro of this range. Sephenamin, these are my children, Joel and Mariah."

The pair were on their feet, wide-eyed and, Yvonne hoped, on their best behaviour. Best behaviour would not last long, of course, but she could only hope they would try and make a good first impression.

"I am pleased and honoured to meet you both," Sephenamin said. As cerro, it was his role to speak first.

Joel looked Sephenamin in the eye. There was no challenge there, just a wary assessment, one wulf to another. A few months away from leaving her guardianship, he was already showing signs of growing into significant power. She was glad she had been so candid with Sephenamin when they had met before. Very few cerro would want another budding cerro on their territory. But she trusted Joel, to the depths of her being. Despite the fight that had led to their headlong flight from their previous home, there was not a bad bone in his body, and he had no desire whatsoever to lead his own range. At least not yet. Perhaps in twenty or thirty years. Not now, not with recent events so vivid and raw in his mind.

Mariah was making her own assessment. A little younger than Joel, she had a tendency to see the best in most people. And if she did not see the best in them, it was almost impossible to change her mind. She was not subtle. It was a trait that Yvonne admired, even if it was exasperating at times.

"We are pleased to be here," Joel said. Wulf protocol put him ahead of Mariah. Not by much, in terms of age, but by a significant margin in terms of their power.

"Please sit and finish your meal." Sephenamin waved a hand, settling himself on the stool at the end of the table as they took their places again. Willa brought him a tankard without being asked to, and moved away to the kitchens. Yvonne found her eyes following Willa's movements. She wanted to ask Sephenamin about the injury, but now was hardly the right time.

"Willa's brother did not like the way she looked at another wulf," Sephenamin volunteered, following Yvonne's gaze. "The brother is no longer welcome here." It was a quiet, emphatic statement. Nobody would breach that order, not if they wanted to stay in this range. "Her hip was broken. She will heal completely in a few days."

"I am glad to hear it," Yvonne answered, conscious of the wide eyes and listening ears of her children. They had lived with a few different ranges over the years, one way or another. Yvonne could count on the fingers of one hand the number of cerro that they had met who would have cared enough to do what Sephenamin had done, to protect a vulnerable member of his range. Sephenamin's mouth quirked up in an unexpected smile, but he said nothing.

The children finished their stew in silence while Sephenamin and Yvonne exchanged little bits and pieces of information, and watched, still with wide eyes, as Sephenamin waved away Yvonne's coins. Sephenamin's domain. His rules. She made a polite protest, which was ignored, and accepted the free lunch, hoping that none of her relief showed on her face. The journey, at short notice, had been expensive. There had been no time to gather in provisions and make her own travel rations, and buying on the road was never cheap. Her small hoard of coins was even smaller just now. She would need to take paying work again soon, or they would end up hunting and foraging for their food.

Chapter Two

It was still dry when they left The Tavern. Sephenamin had offered them an escort the rest of the way in a casual demonstration of his local knowledge. He had not pressed the matter when Yvonne had, politely, turned him down.

Even if the offer had been selfless, they had ridden far on their own and she did not think that there were any dangers between here and their final destination that two wulfkin and a sorceress would be unable to deal with. Before they left, he insisted that they should visit again soon. It was all very polite and, judging by the expressions on Joel's and Mariah's faces when they recovered their horses, not at all what they had been expecting, no matter how much reassurance Yvonne had tried to give them on the way here.

Yvonne thanked the stable hands, left them with generous tips, and they rode away from The Tavern in silence, weaving through the streets of the town.

It was only when they reached the outskirts and green fields lay ahead of them, with the occasional copse of trees dotted around, that the children spoke.

"He is not what I was expecting," Joel said.

"He seems nice," Mariah added. She sounded bemused. "He seemed genuinely happy that we were here."

Yvonne could understand the confusion. None of the previous cerros had been all that pleased to see them, or particularly welcoming, even the nice ones. And none of the previous cerros had been all that sorry to see them go, when they had needed to move on for one reason or another.

She looked across at them. Mariah was examining everything around her with interest, eyes bright, taking in the details of the well-kept fields, well-fed livestock, and the fresh air that surrounded them. A far cry from their last home.

Joel's shoulders had relaxed for the first time that Yvonne could remember on this entire journey, and probably for some time before then.

"He's a cerro," she said, too many words cramming up in her throat to get out in good order. Sephenamin was what she thought a proper cerro should be. Utterly ruthless in the defence of his people. Demanding the highest standards from his range. Caring of those within his range, and with more than enough power to defend those who needed it. She opened her mouth to try and express some of that, and then shook her head slightly. "I hope we'll be able to stay here for a while," she told them instead. "And I hope you had enough food, because there is work to do."

Familiar grins crossed their faces. They rolled their eyes, but it was a genuine tease. There was always work to do.

A little while later they rode around a bend of the small river they had been following and, ahead of them, an old stone bridge spanned the water. Not high enough for any but the smallest boats to get under, it led across the river to a property that sat on its own. There was a good-sized house, outbuildings and a few fields, all enclosed with a low fence that looked like it had not been tended in years, wooden slats broken and missing in places. The fields were big enough to hold the horses, and some other livestock if they chose. The two-storey house was made of the pale grey stone native to the area and, to Yvonne's relief, looked whole. No obvious sagging in the roof and no broken windows.

"Is this it?" Mariah asked.

"Yes."

"I can't believe the tiny rent they're charging," Joel added. "It's huge. And fields as well."

"I told you. It's haunted."

They had discussed this a lot on the journey here. It had been the only property for rent in Fir Tree Crossing, and nobody local wanted it.

"Well, they had better move out," Mariah said, baring her teeth for a moment. "I don't want to share my house with a haunting."

As they moved closer to the house, Yvonne could see signs of neglect. The windows might be intact, but the window frames were desperately in need of some paint, as was the front door, slightly warped with the weather, black paint almost turned to grey. The door of the nearest outbuilding was hanging half open, one of the hinges gone, paint almost all peeled away. There were stables beyond that, though, which looked weatherproof, doors open and flapping slightly in the breeze. Grass and weeds were taking over what had once been the bare, packed earth of a well-used stable yard, the plants vivid green next to the grey stone of the buildings and dark earth.

The breeze, cool against her face, brought with it the faint scent of herbs. There might be a kitchen garden, though it would doubtless have run wild with neglect.

The horses' heads lifted as they drew closer and Yvonne's horse, Lothar, an old warhorse that had carried her safely for more years than she cared to remember, gave a low, huffing sound. He recognised a stable when he saw one. Yvonne took that as a good sign. The horses, and Lothar in particular, had a knack for spotting when things were wrong.

Joel and Mariah might dismiss the idea of a haunting, but she had seen too many things and experienced too much to wave it away. It might be nothing more than an odd wind through the house overnight, or there might be something more sinister afoot. The children were confident that between them they could deal with it. She hoped they were right.

"Chores," she said, breaking into their chatter as they looked around. There were no rolled eyes, and no groans. For once.

Leaving Mariah to settle the horses and draw water for them from the well, she and Joel went into the house, armed with the cleaning supplies that she had insisted they carry on their spare horse. The children had not believed her when she had decided that they needed to carry brooms and buckets with them. One look inside, and Joel nodded his head once, seeing what she had meant.

The interior was dusty but in reasonable condition. Better than she had expected. By some miracle, the pump tap in the kitchen produced clear water after a few tries. The floors all seemed intact, although a few floorboards creaked. The entire place was thick with a layer of dust, and there were impressive cobwebs in some of the rooms.

"Kitchen first, then bedrooms," she told Joel. He looked around, half-opening his mouth with the obvious question, and then closed it again, nodding. And they set to work.

Sorceresses were supposed to be able to conjure miracles, she thought, as she brushed another cobweb aside. They should certainly be capable of cleaning a neglected house. But what the legends failed to mention was that magic required energy, and one of the prices paid for being a Hunar was that using magic for selfish reasons required a far higher price. Some years before, she had used magic rather than complete a day's housework. The magic had rebounded on her and she had not been able to get out of bed for days. Brooms and buckets and soap and cloths were not glamorous, and required physical effort. But it was far less effort than magic, in this case.

Mariah joined them when they had moved upstairs, cleaning the stairs as they went, and were half-way round the first bedroom.

When the first room was done, she left them arguing over who would have which bedroom. It did not really matter to her, and they would clean three for them all to use. She was more interested in one of the outbuildings at the back, which was the real reason she had been prepared to overlook the haunting.

On her way to the outbuilding, she set a cook pot on the kitchen fire, using the last of their vegetables for a basic soup and finding an odd comfort and delight in having a hearth to cook with and knowing it was hers, for as long as she wanted.

When the sun was fading, she went to check on the horses. They were quiet, dozing happily. Mariah had left them with enough feed and water for the night, but they flicked their ears towards her, accepting a pat from her before she left them.

Joel and Mariah were in the kitchen, eyes on the cook pot.

They were all covered in dust and bits of cobweb, but they had clean bedrooms and a clean kitchen. A good place to start. The rest of the house could wait.

"Come with me. There is something else that you might like."

Intrigued, the children followed her round the side of the house to one of the outbuildings at the back. She had started a fire there and the air was warm when she opened the door.

"A bathhouse?" Joel was astonished. As well he might be. An innocuous farmhouse, not that far from a trading town, was an unlikely place to have its own bathhouse. Particularly one which provided heated water, from the furnace in the corner.

"Now I know why we got this house," Mariah said, smiling.

"Who wants to go first?" Yvonne asked.

The children argued. Eventually Mariah won, as Yvonne thought she might.

"Let's go and set the ward stones while Mariah has a bath," Yvonne suggested.

The ward stones, set at intervals of no more than six paces all the way around the house's immediate surroundings, were dormant, the spells in them old and degraded. Even a Hunar needed protection, and her magic rose to her command. Still, it took a considerable amount of energy and effort to restore each spell so that the ward stones gleamed faintly in the fading light, and she was truly worn out by the time they came back to the house.

Mariah had finished her bath and was tidying the kitchen. Yvonne sent Joel off for his bath, and helped Mariah sort through and wash out the crockery and cutlery stores.

"It's like they just left everything," Mariah said.

"I think they did."

"I know. But there's cupboards full of sheets upstairs. There were some old housekeeping spells. No rats." Mariah's nose wrinkled. She did not like rats.

"Well, we'll see," Yvonne said. The more she looked around the house, the more she wondered just what had driven successive families out of the place. And whether the property agent, who she had thought had been honest, had actually not told her the whole truth. The house was theirs as long as they needed it, a dizzying prospect after so much uncertainty. If they survived the night, of course.

Meal over, Yvonne went to have her bath, sinking into warm, fresh water with a sigh of relief that echoed around the tiled room. There had been no baths on the road, and she wanted to scrub her skin until it was pink and clean.

She closed her eyes and rested her head back against the edge of the bath, feeling the warmth seep all the way into her bones. She felt like she had been cold for weeks.

Ever since that awful afternoon in Ilfton when she had come back towards their house, diverted by the unmistakable, near-silent sounds of wulfkin fighting, and turned a corner to find most of the range gathered around two wulfkin, in their animal forms. A little larger than wild wolves, coats a mix of greys and browns that blended into shadow, eyes full of the sheen of wulfkin power, with fangs as long as her fingers. Predators. And this pair were Joel and Brias, the second in command of the range.

Brias was one of the most unpleasant wulfkin she had ever met. A bully, through and through, making no secret that he thought all females were beneath him, constantly making remarks to Yvonne or Mariah that they had little chance of defending against if they wanted to stay within that range, making threats to teach Mariah a lesson, out of Mariah's hearing but designed to get a reaction from Joel.

Yvonne did not know then what had finally provoked Joel into fighting with Brias. But she did know that Joel was, by some way, the more powerful wulf.

Still warm in the bath, the fight between the two played out in colour and detail behind her closed eyes, and, moments later, she heard again the sharp and unmistakable crack as Brias' neck broke. Joel's first kill. The pain in her chest was as sharp now as it had been then. A first kill. In a fight that should never have happened.

The other wulfkin had been too shocked to do anything at the time, but Yvonne had known that at least one of them would run for the cerro. She and her children had gathered everything together in a frantic rush, Joel still hollow-eyed and shocked from the fight, bloodied from various minor wounds that Brias had inflicted.

They had been on their horses and riding out of the city within the hour, Yvonne not wanting to risk any retaliation. Or, worse, risk a fight between Joel and the cerro. Joel would win that fight, too, and she had not wanted that burden for him.

It was strange waking up in a bed, covers warm around her, in the middle of the night and not hearing any sounds from outside. There were no carriages rattling past, wheels loud against cobblestones. There were no drunks singing their way home. There were no couples arguing, often fuelled by beer and spirits.

It was quite different to being on the road. The horses were always close by when they camped and if she woke during the night she would often hear a soft sound from Lothar, reassuring her that all was well.

Even in the country, there should still be sounds. There had been birds, earlier. She had left the window of her room slightly open to catch sound, and some fresh air over the smell of soap. And with the fields around having been neglected, she was sure that there should be wildlife rustling through the grasses and the trees. Something had sent the night predators to ground, hiding until the greater threat had passed.

She got out of bed, not bothering with her boots, and settled her sword at her hip. She had put on clean clothes after her bath and not bothered getting undressed for bed, knowing she was likely to be up and about during the night.

She might not have believed the property agent that the place was haunted, but there was something wrong, for so many families to have been driven away.

The children were still sleeping as she crept past their rooms. She could hear Mariah's faint snore and wondered what odd position she was sleeping in tonight. She had chosen the oddest places to sleep in as a young child and as a near-adult she might sleep in a bed, but she rarely slept straight and calm. Joel was silent, of course. He slept the same way as he did most things, with quiet and careful determination. If she needed them, they would both be alert within moments.

She went down the creaking stairs, the sounds loud in the silence. As she made her way down the stairs, another sound emerged. A child sobbing. A quiet, desperate sound. The sound of a young thing whose world had ended, utterly, and they did not know how to make sense of it. It was a sound to pull anyone's heart, to make them rush forward, wanting to help. And completely out of place in this old, neglected house.

She traced the sound, the sobs growing louder as she walked, to the long corridor that ran through the spine of the house. There was very little light here. She was sure they had left the doors open, to let the moonlight through into the corridor, but all the doors were shut now. The only thing she could see was a blur that looked like white cloth at the end of the corridor, and pitch black before it.

She murmured a spell for light, magic coming easily to her command, and sent it out ahead of her, faint sparks like miniature candles carrying in the air before her, showing a few feet of floor boards in front of her, and then nothing. The ordinary house faded into black, with that white cloth bundled ahead of her, where she thought the end of the corridor would lie.

The sobbing died. The cloth moved, becoming a small child. Girl or boy, she could not tell at this distance and with the faint light.

"Will you help me?" The voice was singsong, a child's plea for aid.

A plea for aid made to a Hunar would normally pull the magic in them, an invisible tug that told her that there was someone in need. Work to be done. This plea did nothing apart from prickle the skin across her body.

Yvonne stopped where she was, the miniature candles gathered around her, and set her hand on her sword hilt.

"I know what you are," she told the creature ahead of her. "I've met your kind before."

"Will you help me, then?" It was still a child's voice, layered with something else.

"Let me see your true face," Yvonne asked. She did not order or command. Not yet. If she was right about what this thing was, there would be time for that later.

"This is my face." The child's body in the white nightgown straightened at the end of the corridor, light gathering around it so she could see it more clearly. A small child. Perhaps five or six years old, thin, and malnourished with eyes bulging in a hollow face. It did not look threatening. Unpleasant, perhaps, but not threatening.

"I don't believe you." One hand on her sword hilt, the other hooked into her belt. She had spells tucked in a pouch at her belt, including a powerful counter-agent to most hauntings. The spell should work. If this thing was what she thought it was. There were a few evil spirits that disguised themselves as children, knowing that humans, in particular, found a child in distress almost impossible to resist.

"Don't believe me," the voice answered. The child's veneer was fading, replaced by a mocking tone she knew well. It was, indeed, what she thought it was. Deadly and vicious. Lethal, at close quarters. The trick was not to let it into close quarters.

She slid the spell out of the pouch, a stealthy movement perfected over the years, the slender bit of parchment crackling between her fingers. It needed only a bit of power to ignite it, like one of the miniature candles hovering around her head, and for the banishment to take effect. The problem was, this kind of spell needed close quarters, and she did not want to move closer.

"Let me." Joel's voice sounded just behind her. She did not start. She may not have heard him approach, but she trusted her children. She put her hand behind her back, without looking at him, and felt the little bit of parchment leave her fingers. She called down one of the miniature candles, and sent it behind her and heard, and felt, the slight puff of air as the candle lit the spell parchment. A moment later, an arrow flew past her shoulder, striking the white nightgown dead centre, catching fire.

The creature screamed. The veneer of a child fell away, revealing a twisted beast. Not the most hideous thing she had seen in her life, but close to it. Vaguely human in shape, it had blackened skin that was scored with years of hard living, and huge, reddened eyes. Fangs as long as her fingers, and claws to match. The spell took hold of it, burning through its flesh and bone, and it screamed again. It fell forward, towards them, across the pitch-black space in between. Forgetting the trap it had laid.

Another one of Joel's arrows shot it straight through the eye. He was an excellent shot. It shrieked again and fell, down into the pitch dark, the flames of its burning body revealing the deadly trap it had set. The floor had been taken away and there were iron spikes on the bottom, coated with old blood and tangled with the bare bones of previous victims. These sorts of creatures liked to eat their kills.

Joel moved to stand next to her shoulder, watching as the thing burned down to ash.

"We'll need to get that out," he said, voice calm. It was not the most hideous thing that he had seen in his life, either.

"I have some ideas about that," she answered.

"You think this is all there is?"

It was a reasonable question. A more than reasonable question, and a sign of how difficult their lives had been up till this point. She pulled another spell from the belt pouch and sent it out, with another spark of power from the candles. There was nothing else magical in the whole house, no other spells apart from hers, and nothing had come past the ward stones.

"That's all there is. All I can find, anyway. We'll need to be careful a few more nights. But if you don't know what they are, that thing would have been deadly."

"Everything is returning to normal outside," he told her. His sense of hearing, like his sense of smell, were far superior to hers.

"Good."

"It's going to be morning soon," he observed.

"There's some hot chocolate in the supplies," she answered. She had no desire to go back to bed, either. The thing was dead, and she knew some would call it foolish, but she did not want to go back to sleep, knowing that there was this open pit full of old blood and bones in her house.

"The landowner will probably charge us more rent now," Joel said, humour brightening his eyes.

"Not without a lot of cost for him. We have a binding contract. Five year lease, money paid upfront. If we remove the haunting, we can still stay on the same terms. If we don't want it, they get the house back at the end of five years, and they can get more rent after that."

"Five years?" Joel was startled. She had told them they could be here a while, just not how long. It was the longest time they had planned to stay in one place, and she could understand why he was surprised.

"This is a good place," she told him, walking with him to the kitchen. "Sephenamin is a good cerro. The town is peaceful. I did my research."

"I trust you, Kalla," he assured her. "It will be nice to be in one place for a while."

"Yes. Or, at least, have a base to come back to," she added, thinking of the small hoard of coins that were tucked into her bags upstairs. Work was needed.

"Did someone say hot chocolate?" Mariah asked, voice full of sleep. Yvonne turned and was not surprised to see her daughter armed, eyes alert despite her tousled hair. "What did I miss?"

Not sorry to miss the haunting, but Mariah would have been annoyed to miss the hot chocolate, Yvonne thought, hiding a smile. She knew her children well.

Chapter Three

With the grisly task of clearing the bone pit done, and the hole filled in with a use of magic that had left her weak for a while, the house was returned to an ordinary building again. They had opened all the windows to let fresh air in, chasing away the last possible remnants of the haunting, breeze drifting through the rooms, around the staircase, and along the corridors. Yvonne followed the breeze through the house for a while, making sure there was nothing else. She didn't find anything and came back downstairs with a lighter step. The building was now truly theirs, a place to settle for a while.

Satisfied the haunting was dealt with, she left the children with a list of chores when the sun was fully up, saddled Lothar and rode into town.

They needed more chocolate, according to Mariah. More practically, Yvonne knew, they needed basic supplies, now that they were in one place for a while. And, just as importantly, she needed to make herself known to the local dignitaries. Bitter previous experience told her that many of them would not be pleased to find there was a Hunar within the town limits that they had not been told about. Their short stay in Ilfton had been challenging for her as well as her children.

It was a beautiful morning, with fresh blue skies above, the slightest bite of cold in the air and birdsong around as she rode. Once over the small stone bridge there was farmland to the town's edge, the fields well-maintained, a mix of fields full of crops or healthy-looking livestock grazing on lush grass. It had all the hallmarks of a prosperous farming area, even though she knew that was not where the real wealth came from. The town was a calm mooring point along the Great River, a stopping place for merchants bound for the Royal City to the north, or for the glorious city of Abar al Endell to the south, the last city before the desert and the Forbidden Lands.

The river was the thing that made the town prosperous. Just beyond the town, as she got closer to it, she could see the flat marshland that stretched for miles, preventing direct overland travel further north. Travelling overland added days to any journey, compared to river travel.

Fir Tree Crossing, seen in sunshine after the grey skies from the day before, looked like a large, prosperous town. The houses were well-maintained, streets clear of debris, and the townsfolk she saw were all adequately dressed for the weather. Some of the householders had even planted flowers in front of their houses, adding some colour and cheer as she rode past.

The groom at The Tavern was pleased to see her again, and happy to take a horse for a few hours. It was a common arrangement with town or city centre taverns and she left Lothar, knowing he would be spoiled rotten, and probably not want to leave when she got back.

On foot, and with the clear skies meaning her feet were warm and dry, she made her way to the biggest building in town, which was the residence of the town's mayor and the offices of whatever local governance there was. She had not met the mayor on her previous visit, not wanting to alert him to her presence before she had to. Now she was here and could not avoid it.

The building itself had a grand exterior, lots of carved stone and intricate banding around the windows. It was well-maintained, with no cracked glass or peeling paint that she could see. Based on the outside, and previous mayor's buildings she had visited, she expected a grand interior, full of treasures of art, thick rugs under foot and richly dressed officials.

Instead, when she went through the open doors of the building, she found an almost austere interior. It could have been grand. There were niches around the entrance hall where statues had probably once stood and, in the blank spaces between the niches, rods fixed to the wall that would hold tapestries or other art. But there were no tapestries, no statues and no other art. Instead, there was a large, imposing desk, a plainly dressed middle-aged woman sat behind it with a stack of papers that she was methodically sorting through, and a series of small handbells within reach.

"Good morning," Yvonne said.

"Good day to you," the woman said, looking up. Her eyes widened. She rose to her feet and bowed slightly. "Hunar, it is a pleasure to welcome you."

It was not quite the greeting that Yvonne had been expecting.

"I am newly arrived in town, and wanted to introduce myself to the mayor," she said.

"Of course. He will be delighted to meet you," the woman said, a smile transforming her face from austere and stern to warm and welcoming. "It has been years since we had a Hunar visit."

There was no waiting, or checking to see if the mayor would be free to see her or telling her that she should come back in a day or two's time when the very important official she had come to see might be able to squeeze her into his calendar. Instead, the woman led Yvonne along one of the side corridors, also bare of any art or statues, and opened a plain wooden door, beckoning Yvonne inside.

The door opened onto a functional office. There were desks, and shelves, and piles of parchment and ledgers on the desks and shelves. A pair of young people, clerks by the look of them, were busy working at two of the desks. The biggest desk in the room was piled highest with the papers and ledgers and behind it was a small, slender man who Yvonne thought might be related to the woman she had met, judging by a similar cast to their features. He was dressed as plainly as the rest of them, with no ornate robes, any badge of office or gold chains around his neck. He looked up when she approached him, eyes widening slightly in surprise. Definitely related to the woman, Yvonne thought.

"Priadan, this is the Hunar, wanting to meet you," the woman said, with no formality, bow or curtsy.

"Oh, a good morning indeed." The man's voice was calm and mellow, his face breaking into a smile as warm as the woman's. "I am delighted to meet you, Hunar."

He came around the desk and made a small bow before offering his hand. Yvonne took the hand and he gave her a firm but not overwhelming handshake. He was shorter than she was, the top of his head barely reaching her shoulder, and looked up at her with bright, interested eyes. Not one trace of resentment or avarice. A mayor who did not surround himself with sycophants, who did not dress in the elaborate robes of office that were probably hanging in a cupboard somewhere. A mayor who worked just as hard as everybody else around him.

She was beginning to understand why Fir Tree Crossing was so wealthy, and so peaceful, and found her mouth curving up in an unexpected smile.

"I'm newly arrived in town," she repeated, "and wanted to let you know I was here."

"Yes. Thank you. I am Priadan. This is my sister, Orla. You are most welcome. Please, have a seat. Has my sister offered you any refreshment?"

"It is not necessary," Yvonne began, taking the seat indicated. It put her opposite the mayor, and he had artfully arranged his desk so that anyone sitting in the chair would have a clear view of him between stacks of paper and ledgers.

"Tea, I think," he said to Orla, who nodded once and left the room. "We have not had a Hunar in town before. The last one passed through before my time. More than ten, perhaps even twenty years ago. All stories say that she was very kind."

"A small woman with red hair?" Yvonne asked, pain searing through her heart. There were no other Hunar who she would have described as very kind. It had been her very first impression of Elinor. Yvonne had been broken when they met, terrified of her own shadow and wounded in ways she had not understood, trying to protect the pair of wulfkin children who had been clinging to her as though she was their only hope. And Elinor had made them all tea, even the youngsters, speaking to them in a calm, matter-of-fact tone. It was only later that Yvonne had learned that Elinor was as fierce and stubborn as she was kind.

"Yes. You knew her?"

"Elinor. She was my mentor."

"Was? I am sorry."

"Thank you." The polite words were an automatic response, Yvonne holding herself still and breathing through the fresh wave of grief. Mentor was a poor, shallow description of what Elinor had been. Teacher. Friend. Confidante. A place of safety and refuge.

Orla returned with a tea tray, interrupting further conversation. There were plain, beautifully made mugs and a similarly plain, well-made tea pot, which did not drip when the drink was poured.

Locally made, the mayor was happy to tell her. There was a pair of skilled potters in the town, great rivals, and he had a tea set from each, used on alternate days.

There was a bright gleam in his eyes when he said that, and Yvonne found herself smiling in turn, grief fading once more.

After a pleasant round of tea and conversation with the mayor and his sister, at least as well-informed and involved in the running of the town as he was, Yvonne went back into the sunshine with a lighter heart. Mayors did not always run their towns. The weak ones tended to give way to criminal gangs, or the local cerro, often a bully. Even the good ones were quite often more concerned with keeping up relations with the merchants, who paid hefty taxes, than with actually running the town for the benefit of townspeople and mundane matters such as road repairs. She had the distinct impression, from the little she had seen, that Fir Tree Crossing was quite different and she found herself, for the first time in a very long while, looking ahead with a little bit of hope. She might have signed a five year lease, but that did not mean that they had to stay that long. Now, she was considering it. Daring to think that this might be a place to settle for a while.

A place for all of them. Somewhere, finally, that Joel and Mariah could settle and flourish, form friendships that might last longer than a year or two. Somewhere with enough people in the town and passing through that a Hunar might be kept reasonably busy. The tentative and tantalising possibility of somewhere to call home, after so long displaced.

She shook her head slightly. All possibilities. There was a long way to go still, and one more place she needed to go today, before anywhere else.

The law keepers' office was not far from the mayor's building, the purpose of the squat, stone building shown by the stylised metal gates hanging in place of a sign. She paused for a moment, looking at the sign. It was a miniature portcullis, exquisitely made. As well as excellent potters, the town must boast an excellent blacksmith. She wondered how many other fine craftsmen were to be found.

She went to the open door of the building, pleased again to find that the town's offices were holding to a long tradition of open doors, allowing townsfolk to come and go as they needed, rather than having to make an appointment or, worse still, hunt out the people they needed.

The inside of the building was simple. A set of stairs ahead led down to what she imagined was a basement, possibly with some cells. To one side there was an open door into what looked like an office, with an imposing desk, the wall behind it covered with an array of weapons. It was an intimidating display, enough to make many people pause. To the other side of the entranceway was an open archway leading into a refectory, full of low benches and tables and the tantalising smell of food. There were about half a dozen people in the room. Men and women both. They were not in any particularly rigid uniform but, dressed in dark, serviceable clothing, a few with arm braces, a couple with the glimpse of chain mail under their over tunics. They also had the air of soldiers waiting for the next battle. A lot of them were still, settled in deliberately relaxed postures on the benches, idly playing dice. Others were tending their weapons. It was the sort of idle busywork that she had seen before, in mercenary groups or king's armies, when they were between duties or skirmishes.

It was also an odd thought to have in a town's law keepers' office. Law keepers were traditionally drawn from the townsfolk, given a badge and a cudgel, and not much more training than that.

"How can we help?"

The voice was male, low, cultured and not at all what she had expected. Almost accent-less.

She turned to find the speaker was a tall male, a fraction taller than she was, dressed in the same nondescript, serviceable clothing as the others she could see, a loosely knotted black scarf around his neck hiding what she was sure must be a mail vest under his black over-shirt. He had arm braces and a sword at his side. Not a casual sword, either. It had a plain, serviceable hilt similar to hers, and the little she could see of the scabbard had seen a lot of use.

"Good day to you," she answered, noticing that his eyes were inspecting her as keenly as she was inspecting him. "I'm newly arrived in town, and wanted to introduce myself, in case of need."

"Hunar," he said, lips twitching. He made a shallow bow that no ordinary soldier would do. He was older than she had thought at first. There was grey sprinkled in his dark hair, lines around his eyes, and a slight pull to his mouth that suggested a long and hard life. "We had heard rumours," he added. "I am Grayling, law keeper of this town."

"Yvonne," she answered, with a slight bow, unable to help her gaze drifting again to the other law keepers settled around the refectory.

"Won't you come and sit for a while. Tea?"

Tea was a rare treat for common folk and law keepers. She was surprised, for a moment, that it was so readily available, and then remembered the wide river, with its barges. It was possible that every house in the town had access to tea. She gladly accepted a mug and was amused to see that it came from the same pottery as the set the mayor had used, commenting on the same.

"Oh, yes. The great rivalry. We have two sets of everything as well." It was said with a sort of weary amusement that suggested that the law keepers had been involved in the great rivalry more than once, and regarded it as a mildly amusing diversion rather than a serious threat. Yvonne was quite sure that this man, who was not the simple law keeper he appeared to be, would treat a serious threat quite differently.

They exchanged idle conversation, about the weather, about the number of barges, about the merchants passing through town. By then the tea was drunk and Yvonne hesitated before raising another, far more serious matter. No one had asked for her help yet, but it was not in her nature to simply do nothing while people suffered.

"I have come from Ilfton. There were stories on the road. Young people going missing. As young as ten, as old as twenty-five. Girls and boys."

All the idle amusement had vanished from his face and he was now as focused and intent as she had imagined he would be.

"Yes. We have heard rumours too. We arrived just before winter. Nothing in Fir Tree Crossing yet, but we have doubled our patrols and we are keeping an eye out. What have you heard?"

They exchanged information, Yvonne not surprised to find that he knew almost as much as she did. News travelled slowly across most of the lands but this was a trading town, and merchants paid attention to anything that might affect their business.

Still, neither of them had any first-hand, eyewitness accounts. Just second-hand information, rumours, innuendo and speculation that followed familiar patterns. In some of the smaller, more outlying villages, some of it was attributed to superstition or monsters in the night. In the larger cities, speculation concerned pleasure houses, and individuals catering for specific tastes. None of it was proven.

She left a short while later, satisfied that Fir Tree Crossing was in as good hands as it possibly could be, between the mayor and the law keepers. She wondered if the mayor knew that he had a group of Antonine Rangers posing as law keepers. It was no wonder that the town was peaceful. She also wondered what had happened to make the Rangers leave their home, far in the northern reaches, and busy themselves in a small trading town where, she was quite sure, not much of significance happened. There were no vettr here, the stone creatures able to decimate entire towns, their only effective enemy the powerful Rangers. And there were no wars here, either, that threatened the population. It was possible that the Rangers were tired of war. Tired of fighting near-indestructible creatures. Perhaps they, like her, were looking for somewhere to settle and call home.

That little glimmer of hope she had felt leaving the mayor's office resurfaced, unwilling to fade. She tried to quash it, at least for now. There had been too much false hope over the years. But she had never encountered this before. An honest mayor. Law keepers who were Antonine Rangers, with oaths like hers. A cerro who held to the old ways, protecting his range. The hope surged up again. This could be somewhere to settle.

The town had its own market square. She got what she needed, enduring the curious stares from the traders and passers-by. The symbol of the Hunar was there for all to see on her shoulder, the green outline of the Firebird unmistakable, even if many people still believed the Hunar to be as much of a legend as the Firebird herself.

Taking a different street, she made her way back towards The Tavern, pausing in her stride as she saw that, ahead of her, there was a thick white line painted along the precise centre of the street, across the uneven cobblestones.

Curiosity spiked, she continued forward, seeing as she drew closer that there were shop fronts on either side of the street across from the line. Both selling pottery. She remembered the carefully maintained sets of pottery both the mayor and Grayling had commented on.

Some instinct made her walk onto the white line, and not to one side or the other. It was more than wide enough to act as a path.

She glanced to one side and then the other and saw that each shop had an almost identical display at the windows, and through the open doorways she could see a short, slender man in one and a tall, burly man in the other, standing with folded arms staring across the street at each other.

She briefly considered stopping and asking them why they hated each other so much, forcing herself to keep walking until she reached the end of the white line. In the shadows ahead, a figure moved, raising a hand to his head in a brief acknowledgement. One of Grayling's men. The town's law-keeper was keeping watch on the potters.

After the misery of the journey and the night's encounter with the haunting, unexpected and welcome laughter bubbled up. She hastily put a hand across her mouth, covering a fake cough, and nodding in response to the Ranger as she passed. His eyes were dancing with amusement. So, she was not the only one that found the situation ridiculous. She wondered how long the mayor had been trying to get one or other of the potters to take different premises.

Movement further along the street drew her attention away. A beautifully crafted fabric banner was fluttering slightly in the breeze.

Her feet took her there without any thought and she found herself outside a clothier's shop, the window full of a life-size man made of straw clothed in plain, serviceable clothing that nonetheless was beautifully made.

The door to the shop was open, a tall, slender lady sweeping imaginary dust into the street. One glance and Yvonne knew that this was the owner.

"Good day to you, Hunar."

"Good day, mistress," Yvonne answered. "You do excellent work."

"Thank you," the woman answered, dipping her chin. There was no false modesty. She knew her own worth. "Newly arrived?"

"Indeed. Just yesterday."

"Old man Sanderson's place, isn't it? Haunted, they say."

"Not anymore," Yvonne answered, hiding another smile. She had found the centre of the town's information network, quite by accident. She wondered how many items of clothing the mayor and his sister had purchased here, all in the name of getting information. "Would you tell me, mistress, about that white line?" It seemed an entirely safe topic of conversation. Something very unusual.

"Name's Frida. Everyone calls me that," the woman answered, then looked down the street to the potters' shops, shaking her head slightly. "Idiots. Too long a tale for just now. Another time. You must come and have tea."

Curiosity roused, Yvonne accepted. She thought she might enjoy the tale, and had a feeling that Frida knew she had already had plenty of tea that day. The woman glanced past her shoulder again to the silent potters.

"It doesn't help that Handerson," Frida nodded her head towards the shop with the slight man, "has a rather beautiful daughter that Keffle's son," she tilted her head towards the burly man's shop, "is smitten with. And definitely not that Keffle's son is a lovely lad but nothing special to look at."

"A kind heart will take you far, though," Yvonne put in, fascinated.

"That it will. And the children are as kind hearted as you could wish." Frida eyed her up and down. "I could fix that for you," she offered, nodding to Yvonne's sleeve.

Yvonne looked down and sighed. There was a small tear in the sleeve. She didn't remember catching it, and yet there was an unmistakable tear.

"That is kind of you, but my daughter loves to sew."

"She did the rest of the repairs?" Frida asked. It was not a mean-spirited question. Instead, it was a professional one, her eyes keen and assessing as they moved over Yvonne's person.

Yvonne could not remember precisely how many repairs Mariah had needed to make over the years. A lot.

"Yes. She taught herself."

"Self-taught?" Frida's eyes narrowed further. "I would like to meet your daughter. She'd never be short of work here."

"I will tell her so," Yvonne promised, smiling. Mariah loved to sew, and loved to talk. There had never been anywhere that she was accepted where she had been able to do both. Yvonne continued on her way with a lighter step, that little bit of hope, most dangerous of emotions, spreading further in her chest.

Chapter Four

That little bit of hope was warming her through by the time she reached the small bridge that crossed the river near the house. She drew Lothar to a halt at the summit of the bridge, looking at the scene ahead of her. The haunting was gone. There was just a large, square house, the grounds around it gone wild with neglect. There might have been a vegetable garden once. And a hen coop. The fields were more than enough for four horses, once the fences were repaired.

The warmth grew. This could be, finally, a place to settle. A dressmaker who wanted to speak with Mariah. A variety of trades in the town which might suit Joel. Somewhere they could have some time, and space, to work out what they wanted after so long moving around, and after so long feeling unwelcome. They knew they would always have a home with her, however long they wanted. She was not ready for them to move to homes of their own. Not yet.

As well as places for her children, there should be more than enough passing trade to keep a Hunar moderately busy. There were people she would like to get to know better, to work with. An honest mayor, and an equally hard-working sister. Law keepers with a background as complicated as hers. A dressmaker who, she was sure, would hold all the town's secrets. And that was just on her first day here.

It was enough. It was more than enough. Even though she could see, in her mind's eye, the tilt of Elinor's head and the disappointment in her mentor's face. Elinor had said, more than once, she could not live without love and passion. Elinor's very different lovers had each brought different things. Yvonne had not been able to imagine, then or now, sharing her life with anyone in that way.

Seeing her children grow. Interesting work. Friendships. A house that was hers, that could become familiar over time, a place where old memories had no place.

It was a life. A comfortable, safe life that she wanted to try. At least for a while.

"I hate you!"

The scream, at full volume, carried faintly to Yvonne's ears, cutting across her pleasant imaginings. Lothar merely flicked an ear. He had heard Mariah in a temper before.

He did not want to move on when she asked him. More sensible than she was, perhaps, but she knew she needed to be there when Mariah said something unforgivable, or Joel punched through another wall because he had just enough restraint not to punch his sister, no matter how furious she made him.

"You've ruined our lives!" Mariah was shrieking as Yvonne dismounted in front of the open front door. There was an old bell there, doubtless designed for visitors to summon the householder from about the property. Yvonne picked up the striker, a rusted bit of metal that had fallen to the ground, and hit the bell as hard as she could. One strike and the bell rang through her, a clear, deep note that would be heard throughout the entire property.

Scrambling footsteps inside the house told her that it had been heard.

She leant back against Lothar, waiting. He turned his head towards her and sighed, warm breath stirring her hair. She scratched behind his ear.

Moments later Joel and Mariah burst out of the house, both armed, eyes shimmering with wulf power. They were flushed with anger and too close to the edge of the change.

"I could hear you screaming from the bridge, Mariah," Yvonne said, keeping her voice mild and calm. No matter how she might want to shout, it always went better when she could stay calm.

"He's an idiot," Mariah answered, turning her shoulder on her brother. "Did you get chocolate?"

"Never mind that. What in the name of reason has happened?"

"Mariah's mirror broke," Joel answered.

Yvonne had to think for a moment what he meant. A small, handheld mirror with a plain wooden surround, it had been a gift long ago from Elinor.

"You broke it," Mariah growled.

"Show me," Yvonne ordered. When neither of the children moved, she did, lifting the heavy saddlebags from Lothar's shoulder, settling them across her own shoulder and trying not to grimace at the weight before flicking the reins over his head and handing them to Joel. "Rub him down and make sure he has feed and water. Mariah, go and fetch the mirror and meet me in the kitchen. Joel, come to the kitchen when you're done."

Slightly to her surprise, they did as she asked.

She walked through the house, noticing that they had done most of the chores she had asked for. The hallway from the front door to the kitchen had been washed and the cobwebs cleared. The kitchen smelled of fresh air and soap, a far better fragrance than the dust and neglect from the day before.

Expecting both her children to be gone for a few moments, she unpacked her saddlebags, setting them empty near the back door to take to the stables later and then starting to put away the food she had bought.

"You did get chocolate!" Mariah said, fury all gone into delight.

"A little. Enough for each of us." She had almost no coins left now.

"See. He broke it."

Mariah put the mirror down on the table, face up. The glass had cracked across the face.

Yvonne glanced at it, and then took a stew pot from one of the shelves, fetching a chopping block and knife before coming back to the table, rolling her sleeves up. Only when she was cutting into a carrot did she answer.

"Do you remember when your horse slipped, about three days into the journey?"

"That was horrible," Mariah answered, sitting at the other side of the table, near her broken mirror. "I thought we were going to get swept away."

"You bumped against a tree," Yvonne prompted.

"Yes. I had a bruise for days. Oh." Mariah straightened, her expression changing lightning-fast. "And there was a crack. I couldn't work out where it had come from."

"You insisted on carrying that mirror with you," Yvonne said gently, "rather than putting it with the luggage." The luggage that had been carefully packed and loaded on to the spare horse.

Mariah's brows drew together and she glared up at her guardian. It was a front, Yvonne knew. Her daughter was not stupid. She might have a temper that lit like a forest fire, but she was not stupid.

"Joel didn't break it," she said softly, fingertip tracing the mirror's edge. "It has been broken for days."

"Make me some tea," Yvonne told her.

"We've got tea?" Joel asked, coming into the kitchen through the back door. He stumbled back as Mariah launched herself at him, hugging him tight.

"You didn't break it. I'm sorry. You didn't break it."

"I know I didn't, silly." Joel gave her an absent-minded hug back. "Tea?" he said to Yvonne.

"Blue packet." She nodded to the end of the table. "It's not that expensive here, with the river trade. Still not cheap," she added, mostly to herself. Wulfkin had exceptional hearing, to add to their other exceptional senses.

"Is there milk?" Mariah asked wistfully, coming back to sit at the table, watching her brother move around the room. He lifted the metal can in silent answer.

Mariah was sad now, Yvonne saw. It was a familiar after-effect of her fury. Sad, and not yet forgiven.

"When was the last time you got into a fight, Mariah?" Yvonne asked. She had moved on from the carrots to the onions. She saw Joel tense, shoulders stiff under his shirt. Which was nearly too tight for him. He had grown. Again.

Neither of them was looking at Mariah, though.

"Fight?" Mariah's voice carried her disgust. "Never. Not since I was young."

"And why is that?"

"Fights are boring."

"Sewing is boring," Yvonne countered, dropping the onion into the stew pot with the carrots and starting on the potatoes.

"Sewing is not boring. It requires skill and patience."

"And you are good at it," Yvonne said, keeping to the same, even tone.

"I am. Very good."

"But you are not good at fighting," Yvonne added. She looked up and met her daughter's eyes. "The last fight you got into was about two years ago. You wanted ribbons from one of the younger girls in the range. And she would not give them to you. So, you challenged her to a fight. And she won. Because she might be younger, but she is a good fighter. You do not like fighting because you are not good at it." She kept her tone calm, each word clear and spaced. Mariah had been seething with Joel since their flight from Ilfton, never getting beyond her anger to think about why it might have happened. "You cannot defend yourself within a range."

Mariah was white-faced, fury and shame mixed together, her eyes shimmering with wulf power.

"And I cannot defend you," Yvonne added, the guilt twisting her stomach again. If she had intervened, on any of the occasions her children had got themselves into trouble, she would have been facing the entire range. And she had judged badly in choosing their last town, not spending nearly enough time with the cerro before she moved her small family there.

"It is the duty and honour of the more powerful wulfkin to protect the less strong," Joel said, voice harsh. He was still looking at the tea pot.

"Yes. And you did that," Yvonne told his back. He had nothing to feel guilty about. His shoulders were a little less stiff.

"He was fighting for me?" Mariah asked, not really believing.

"Of course he was," Yvonne said briskly, throwing the potatoes into the pot as well.

"No one else would," Mariah went on, voice small. She would be crying soon, Yvonne knew.

"It was not a good place," Joel said, moving across the room to give his sister's shoulder a squeeze. "And I am glad we are not there anymore."

"Me, too," Yvonne answered. The guilt twisted. She kept her lips firmly closed. The guilt was hers to carry, that she had made a bad choice for them and that Joel had paid the price.

Very few ranges would take in orphan wulfkin, let alone take the time to teach them what they needed to know. Things their human guardian could not understand. After several settled years in one place, the death of the elderly cerro had forced them to move. She had been pointed towards Ilfton and discovered no one else would take them. There had not been another choice that she could see. Still, the guilt twisted in her gut.

"It's not your fault, Kalla," Joel said, surprising her. "There wasn't anywhere else for us to go." Sometimes he was a lot wiser than she was, particularly in the ways of his kind.

"I am still proud of you," she told him directly. She might not be able to hug them as often as they needed, but she could give them words.

His shoulders eased a little more.

"You need a new shirt," she commented, reaching for the rest of the stew's ingredients.

"I can make that." Mariah lifted her head, tears drying. "I can. And sew that tear on your sleeve."

"There's a dressmaker in town who you should speak to," Yvonne said over her shoulder, taking the stew pot to the fire. "She was impressed with your work."

"She was?" Mariah's face was brighter as Yvonne turned back, the fury and the tears forgotten. She would settle over the next few years, Yvonne knew. That warm heart and fiery spirit would have slightly softer edges but still burn brightly.

"Did you find a job for me, too?" Joel asked, laughing. He set the tea pot onto the table along with three mismatched mugs and the milk can. "I saw biscuits."

"Indeed," Yvonne answered, distracted by the mugs. "I didn't find a job for you just yet. There's plenty to do, if you want, though. But let me tell you about the potters."

And as quickly as that the fury and the hate were gone, the three of them settled at the table with mugs of tea and biscuits, stew cooking gently in the background, none of them thinking about missing children, lack of funds or what the next day might bring.

Chapter Five

Yvonne carefully stepped around another puddle. There had been no time, or money, to get her boots re-proofed and she did not want to spoil the day by going through it with wet feet. After an early morning downpour, the sky above was a pale blue, with a few strings of white clouds. Hopefully there would be no more rain today.

She was, for once, early to meet her children. She was usually running late, something which they had all got used to over the years. But today there had been no last-minute requests and she had not been asked to judge anyone's pottery. She was walking with loose, brisk strides, trying to avoid catching anyone's eye. The magic would alert her if there was anyone in desperate need. It always did. Until then, she wanted to get back to the house, with her children, and get on with the long list of chores that they had to deal with.

She came into The Tavern and found the common room unusually noisy for the number of people inside. Something had stirred people up. She glanced, by reflex, to the large window at the side, which overlooked the mooring point on the river. There was a barge there. A merchant vessel, she thought. It wasn't particularly ornate, but well-maintained. She thought she had seen it before, but couldn't place it just now. Not the cause of the excitement, then.

"Good morning, Hunar." Willa's voice was bright. Yvonne was pleased to see that her steps were completely even now, no sign of the limp she had first observed. "You want lunch?"

"Not yet. I'm waiting for Joel and Mariah. Is Sephenamin in?"

"He's back at his office. I can take you there?" From the keen interest in Willa's eyes, Yvonne wondered if she was looking for an excuse.

It would be useful to have a conversation with Sephenamin away from the watchful eyes of The Tavern's patrons, so Yvonne agreed, and followed the girl past the well-stocked bar and down a wide corridor that led to a part of The Tavern she had only been to once before, when she had first come here, to meet Sephenamin.

Then, he had been curious and not-quite hostile to the strange woman turning up wanting to speak with him. The fact she was a Hunar had got her a private meeting, last of a long line of awkward meetings with new cerros over the course of her life.

Her hand went to her throat on reflex, remembering the sharpening of Sephenamin's attention as she had shown him the scars there, the only real proof she had of where she had been and how she had come to be guardian to two wulfkin children. He had stayed behind his desk, though, unlike other cerro who had wanted to inspect her scars more closely. And she had felt the first, faint glimmer of hope that she might have found somewhere that her children would be safe.

Today, her fingers closed around the scarf. Her scars were covered, as always, and she forced her hand away before Willa could notice.

The door at the end of the corridor was half-open, sunlight flooding through and lighting up the dark wood floor and pale painted walls of the corridor. Sephenamin did not believe in unnecessary decoration.

There was a murmur of voices coming out of the room and Yvonne's spine stiffened, hesitating. She thought she recognised both voices. Sephenamin, of course. And another that she had thought was many, many miles away.

Willa knocked and pushed the door fully open. Yvonne's view of the room was blocked by the back of a tall male figure. Sleek black hair fell, completely straight, below his shoulders over a deep, midnight blue greatcoat that almost met the top of glossy black, polished leather boots. She knew that coat. Mariah had mended it once. And she knew that voice. It was one of the most beautiful things in the world, that voice. And she knew that when he turned, she would be faced with the smooth grey skin, bright green eyes, and even features of a high-ranking goblin.

"Hunar," Sephenamin acknowledged her, waving Willa away. The young wulf left slowly, reluctance clear. "You are in good time. This gentleman was just asking about trackers."

Gentleman. Yvonne bit her lip to hide a smile. She knew, and she was confident that Sephenamin knew, that his visitor was not, exactly, a gentleman. Rather, Guise was a member of the Karoan'shae, the corona of goblin houses that ruled their lands. And not just a minor second cousin. He was very close to the heart of the Karoan'shae. In some countries he would be considered a prince. But a gentleman was a disguise he used often.

"The Hunar and I have met before," the voice said. He turned towards her and made a small bow, a sign of respect. "I am delighted to find you here, mristrian."

"My lord," Yvonne acknowledged, reverting to formality, still standing in the doorway, the different parts of her in conflict. Out of all the people she had met in the world, he was the only one who had this effect on her, making her feel unsettled and content at the same time. Partly it was his voice, but partly it was his presence in a room where, like now, he seemed to take up far more space than he needed to, even with a powerful cerro beside him.

"You know each other?" Sephenamin asked, curiosity brightening his eyes. Yvonne did not blame him; they were an extremely unusual combination. Goblins generally wanted nothing to do with Hunar, managing their own affairs without outside interference. And Hunar, for their part, did not want much do with goblins, either. The few times that goblins had requested the aid of a Hunar had not ended well, for either the goblin or the Hunar involved. So much so that Hunar were given an exception for goblins. No Hunar could be compelled to aid a goblin.

"Indeed," Guise said, a small smile tugging his mouth. "The Hunar and her children were kind enough to take me in a while ago. A minor disagreement," he explained, as an aside, to Sephenamin.

Sephenamin nodded, face grave, expressing his understanding.

Yvonne resisted the urge to roll her eyes. It had been nothing like a minor disagreement. Guise had turned up at her house in the middle of the night, clothes soaked through with blood, including the greatcoat he was currently wearing, and requested her aid. She remembered, vividly, the sense of dread even as she let him into the house. Goblins were far more powerful than she was, and she had feared what would happen if Guise's attackers caught up with him. What they might do to her, or to Mariah or Joel.

A few almost sleepless nights later, and he had been restored to health, leaving them with a fat purse of coins that she had, somehow, been unable to reject. For the trouble, he had said, with a dark undertone that suggested he knew just exactly how much danger he had placed her family in by his presence. That heavily-disguised gratitude was one of his few redeeming features and, she told herself, the main reason she ended up spending too much time in his company. Along with that voice. Whatever he was, whatever he did, however much danger he had brought to her and the children, he always paid his debts.

"I do hope that matter is settled," Yvonne said, some streak of mischief prompting the comment. He did not like to discuss his business.

"Quite satisfactorily, I assure you." The gleam in his eyes suggested that the other parties involved may have a different story to tell, if they were still alive and able to tell it.

"Sephenamin said you are looking for a tracker?" Yvonne prompted. Wulfkin made excellent trackers, thanks to their superior senses. It was completely logical that Guise should be here, in the office of the local cerro, seeking a tracker. And yet, Yvonne did not think that was the whole story. She thought she never got the full story with him, which she found both frustrating and oddly fascinating. He was never boring.

"I am concerned about a business associate who has gone missing. A merchant by the name of Ubel," Guise told her. From the expression on Sephenamin's face, he had heard the story already and was not sure he believed a word of it. Yvonne did not blame him. She had never been entirely clear just what it was that Guise did but she had her suspicions, and very little of it was on the right side of the law, even in some of the more liberal countries.

"Sephenamin has some excellent trackers among his range," Yvonne commented. It was the absolute truth. A bare few days in Fir Tree Crossing and she already knew that the senior most female in his range, Ella, was renowned as an outstanding tracker.

"Sadly, it seems that something has been used to obscure the trail," Guise told her.

"Ella tried," Sephenamin told Yvonne. "She got so far, and lost the trail. She is not pleased about it."

Yvonne could imagine. Wulfkin rarely took defeat lightly.

"I need someone who can track with magic," Guise said. "I was just asking Sephenamin if he knew of anyone."

"You mentioned that you had done some tracking," Sephenamin prompted. She had mentioned it. Once, in their first meeting, when she had come to see if he would accept her children. A passing comment. She was not surprised he remembered. Sephenamin liked information as much as Guise.

"Where did your associate go missing from?"

"One of the barges on the river. It seems to have belonged to him."

Her ears sharpened at the careful phrasing. It sounded like the barge might have, in fact, belonged to someone else.

"Ella picked up the trail from the barge, but lost it as it crossed into the marshland," Sephenamin added.

The marshland stretched for miles, an effective barrier to one side of the town, alongside the Great River, with little solid ground for paths through it. Yvonne had spent the morning there the day before, getting a little bit familiar with the lay of the land. She had made sure to take a guide with her, one the mayor's office had been happy to recommend, and to mark in her mind some secure places of refuge. The marshland was an excellent place to hide a body, and, from the slightly grim expressions on Sephenamin and Guise's faces, she thought they had already imagined that scenario.

"I should be very glad of your assistance," Guise prompted.

She thought about her leaking boots, the constant demand of feeding two teenage wulfkin, the worn leather on Lothar's bridle, the new shirts that Joel needed, and the many repairs that needed doing around the house and grounds, that were her responsibility as tenant. Money was needed.

And there was Guise. He might make her uneasy in all manner of ways, but as well as being an excellent and generous client to work for, he was also an oddly comfortable companion. The tasks he had for her were always interesting, varied and, importantly for her, on the right side of the law.

"Very well," she tilted her head. "I have some things to deal with today. Tomorrow?"

"That would be acceptable, thank you. Shall we meet here at first light?"

"Very well. Pack for a few days?"

"Yes. I think that would be wise."

She saw Sephenamin's eyes widening slightly and realised that she and Guise had fallen into the easy back-and-forth that they used on the road, the few journeys they had taken together. It was all business. All professional. And clearly not what he had been expecting.

A burst of laughter from the common room caught her attention.

"I think my children have arrived." She hesitated, turning back to Sephenamin and Guise. "Sephenamin, if I may have a moment?"

"We will look after Mariah and Joel," Sephenamin said, unprompted, accurately guessing her question. "They are friends of the range, and no harm will come to them from my people."

It was an extraordinarily generous gesture, from a powerful cerro to unknown wulfkin. She inclined her head in respect and acknowledgement.

"I am more grateful than I can say," she told him. There were limits on his protection, naturally. He only had command over the range. But he had just guaranteed Joel and Mariah's safety within his range. "I hope they will not be too much trouble."

Sephenamin's face lit with genuine amusement. "We have a number of youngsters in the range. None are as well-mannered as your two. We will manage."

Yvonne's mouth curved in an answering smile. She had met some of the youngsters, almost killed one the first day here. The range would manage. Another burst of laughter and she turned her head back to the common room. "If you will excuse me."

To her surprise, and a little dismay, they followed her to The Tavern's main room. Mariah and Joel were engaged in lively conversation with a few of the younger wulfkin in Sephenamin's range. Yvonne felt her mouth lift in a smile again, a bit of tension easing from her shoulders, as she watched. There had been very little lively conversation, or laughter, for quite some time.

The change when they turned and saw Guise was almost comical. Joel's eyes widened slightly, but he did not say anything, schooling his expression into something like polite attention.

Mariah, naturally, was much less discreet. Her eyes widened, her nose wrinkled in disgust, and she shook her head slightly.

"I see he's found us again," she said to Yvonne. "Can we go home now?"

"You don't want lunch?" Yvonne asked, surprised. It was a rare day indeed that either of her children turned down a hot meal.

"We went to the bakeries," Joel said. "I think we have enough." He patted the saddlebag over his shoulder and Yvonne's eyes widened. It looked full. There were six bakeries in the town that she had found so far. She wondered how many her children had gone to, and how they had managed to make the small amount of coins she had given them stretch so far.

"Very well." She half-turned to Guise, wondering if she should apologise for her children's rudeness, and saw that he was, in fact, quite amused. Perhaps thinking that if they had been in goblin society, they would both be facing severe punishment. While he did not generally make much of his high status among goblin society, the innate arrogance of his station crept out now and then.

"Until tomorrow, then," Yvonne told him, then gathered up her children, leaving The Tavern for the bright sunshine.

"How did he find us?" Mariah hissed the moment they were out of the doorway, crossing the yard. "We've only been here a few days."

"Manners," Yvonne answered, voice calm. She had long ago learned to appear calm on the outside while anything but on the inside, a necessary skill for a Hunar. And a parent.

"He does seem to turn up a lot," Joel added, sending a frowning, sideways glance to Yvonne. "Apart from Ilfton," he said, still with that crease between his brows.

"That is true." Yvonne kept walking, feeling heat in her face. She was not sure why she was embarrassed by Guise's behaviour, the discomfort of that twisting with the renewed guilt at their stay in Ilfton.

"Are you alright, Kalla?" he asked.

"Perfectly fine, thank you," she answered, and proved that a lie a bare heartbeat later by walking through one of the puddles lying across the yard. She bit her lip to stop a curse. She would spend the rest of the day with wet feet. At least there would be something to distract her from guilt, or the fact that Guise was back and she would be spending at least a few days in his company, with the now-familiar push and pull of his presence.

Chapter Six

She soon forgot about her wet feet, and Guise's presence in the town, as she, Mariah and Joel set to work repairing the fence of one of the small fields that lay around the house. After the long winter, spring was taking over and bright, new green grass was peeking up, plants shaking off their winter sleep. The whole world seemed poised on the edge of bursting into life and greenery. The horses had been patient, kept indoors or out on long tethers, but would be far happier with the freedom to roam and eat the new grass.

There were definite advantages to having wulfkin around, Yvonne thought. Two human teenagers, even with her help, would have taken a day or more to fix the fence. It wasn't difficult, just tiring. Whoever had built the fences had meant for them to last, and the wooden bars were heavy. They were all worn out and sticky with sweat by the time the last piece was fixed. Still, the field was secured in one afternoon's work. And Joel had cleverly saved some of the bakery goods, so that would be a treat to look forward to later.

With the fence done, and the day still dry, they let the horses out and leant on the fence, laughing as four fully-grown horses cavorted about the field as though they were month-old foals. They might have been polite, but the horses had definitely missed the freedom.

"Someone's coming, Kalla," Mariah said, turning her head in the direction of the road that led to town.

"Pair of ponies, I think," Joel added. "They're not moving very fast."

Moments later, Yvonne saw the pair. Round, hairy ponies bearing a couple that even at this distance she could tell were of middle years and not used to riding. Here to see the Hunar.

She rolled down her sleeves, brushing bits of grass and dirt off her forearms. She had her weapons on her, as always. No need to say anything to Mariah and Joel. They had all been through this numerous times before.

"I'll bring some water," Mariah said, and went back to the house, strides loose and unhurried.

"I'll keep an eye on the horses," Joel said. Any excuse to remain out of doors, she thought. Unlike her and Mariah, he did not seem to mind wet feet.

She made her way at a steady pace, not too fast and not too slow, to the boundary of the property where there was a small area of flagstones and a pair of benches set up. The first chores she had set her children, and they had surpassed themselves. As usual. An outdoor consulting room for the Hunar. She did not like strangers in her personal space and here, with the fields around, no one would overhear them. Joel had promised to build a cover of some sort to protect her and the supplicants in bad weather.

Supplicants rarely came to visit Hunar in an orderly fashion. So Elinor had said, and so she had found to be true. Weeks, sometimes months, could go by without a single visit, and then several over the course of a few days. Everything got done. The trick, though, was working out what needed to be done first.

By the time she reached the benches, the couple had done so as well. They were clearly not used to riding, sitting too straight and stiff on the ponies. They had the lean, focused look of skilled craftsmen of some kind. And in some distress, tension clear across their shoulders and in their faces.

"I am the Hunar. Be welcome."

They did not so much dismount from the ponies as fall off them, legs shaking as they met firm ground. The ponies stood, untroubled by their riders' weakness. Hired ponies. She wondered where the couple had come from and suspected she would soon find out.

"Good day to you, Hunar," the man began, voice higher than it should be.

"Please, sit down for a moment. I'll tend to the ponies. Catch your breath."

Yvonne took the reins of the ponies and led them to the trough that Joel and Mariah had carried from one of the outbuildings, then filled with buckets drawn from the well. Joel had suggested a water barrel here, too, for any horses or ponies.

These ponies stuck their noses in quite happily, letting her tie them loosely to the hitching post where they were in reach of the water and some grass.

By the time she returned to the benches, the couple had sat down and Mariah had been and gone. There was a pitcher of water and three glasses sitting at the end of one of the benches. Yvonne served them without asking, took a glass, and settled on the bench, hoping that she was downwind from them. The afternoon's work had left her sticky and in need of a bath.

"We're sorry to come. We're sorry to have to come. But we couldn't think what else to do. The law keepers won't do anything." The wife stumbled into speech.

"We're not from here," the husband continued, clearly feeling that some explanation was needed. "We're from Silverton. Upriver. Name's Cressin," he added, as though the name might mean something to her. "We know Grayling. We know he would help, if he could."

Silverton was outside Grayling's jurisdiction, Yvonne knew, a small, isolated village upriver, towards Hogsmarthen and the Royal City.

"We do business here sometimes," Mistress Cressin took up the tale again, "in the market. We heard about you today." And had immediately sought out a pair of ponies to hire, and then ridden out of the town in search of the Hunar. Yvonne's focus sharpened.

"What would you ask of me?" It was a question Hunar had been asking of their supplicants for generations. The oaths she had taken bound her to serve those in need.

"Our son is missing."

Yvonne felt a chill run through her, despite the sun still overhead. A son missing. And not an old one, judging by their age, and the fear in their voices.

The magic in her stirred, responding to their need. The ritual words weren't always needed to trigger the Hunar's magic. And particularly not where family ties were involved. Perhaps because, legend said, the first Hunar's greatest battle had been against his own brother, the two of them opposites in many ways, the brother using his power for his own gain, the Hunar for the good of others.

Whatever the reason, the magic had stirred and she knew that she would do what she could to help this couple.

A missing child. To add to the other rumours she had heard along the road. Guise would understand, she thought, if she needed to put him off a few days. Goblins might appear disinterested in their young, but they understood the value of family. And legacy.

Keeping her voice calm and gentle, she asked them to tell her everything.

The sun had all but gone by the time they were finished. Silverton was a small enough place that the Cressins knew everyone there, though still large enough to have three taverns.

There was not much to tell about his disappearance, in truth. He had gone to meet friends in one of the town's taverns. Had not made it home. No one else was missing a child in the town. They had searched. Their neighbours had searched. Yvonne had the impression that the whole village had turned out to help. The Cressins had gone to the law keepers, based at a larger town upriver, finding the law keepers not interested in looking for a young lad who, they said, might just have found a girl to chase after.

The parents were sure that had not happened. And all the searching they had done had not helped. Nothing. Not a single trace.

Yvonne made a mental note of where they had looked, and where she might start her search. It was helpful.

Far more important was what they told her about their son, Alexander.

Fully sixteen years old. Older than she had expected, given the way his parents talked about him. Considered an adult in many lands but Yvonne knew, from her own experience with Mariah and Joel, that they were really still children. She had not been ready to let them go at sixteen, and it seemed neither were the Cressins ready to let go of their son, or consider him an adult.

They held each other's hand as they talked to her, the affection between them clear. From time to time, Yvonne had found herself wondering what that would be like. To have a life partner. And then the memories would creep back, her skin would crawl, and the half-formed wish would die. A half-life, Elinor had called it more than once. At least it was a life, Yvonne had replied.

Watching the couple talk to her, she knew that there were no bad memories between them, no violence, nothing but a long life together.

And they had raised their son in a house with that affection all around him. Yvonne could not imagine what that felt like, but she was sure that the son had not known how lucky he was.

Alexander was full of mischief. The parents did not say it so bluntly, but Yvonne gathered that from what they let slip and what they did not say. He was apprenticed to them. They were leather workers, a craft much in demand. Skilled and prosperous, too, she guessed, unable to help a glance at their boots, which were beautifully made and fitted.

An only child, she had the impression of a bright, generous young man, slightly spoiled, a little careless with his time keeping, and too trusting, in his mother's eyes. Too flighty, in his father's eyes.

She gathered all the impressions in, along with the contradicting physical descriptions they gave her. Tall for his age. But average height. Curling brown hair. Blue eyes, the father said, like his mother's. Grey eyes, the mother said, like his father's. They both agreed on his smile, and the freckles.

The weight of responsibility settled on her shoulders and in her middle, along with the gathered impressions of the boy. Alexander. She had a picture of him in her mind, and an impression of him in her chest.

Task accepted, she sent them on their way back to the town for a night's rest, promising to start looking as soon as she could.

She wanted to start looking immediately, forcing herself to stay still for a moment, to think.

There was the Cressins' child, and the pull of a Hunar's obligation to find the child. A missing child that she could find, thanks to the magic she carried. As well as the impressions of the child, she rang with echoes of the parents' shock and grief. A loving family, and their imaginations turning to the worst possible explanations.

And then there was Guise's request, with too many questions just now, not least what his associate might have been involved in. However terrible a missing child was, it was possible that finding Guise's associate was more urgent.

She did not have enough information. She needed to go to Silverton, the last place Alexander had been seen, to start looking for him.

Guise might understand if she needed to delay, put her task as Hunar first. More than likely he would. But she should find out more from him before deciding which path to take.

Chapter Seven

Hammering at the front door brought her awake and out of bed before she registered the unease in the ward stones. Whoever was at the door had been moving quickly.

Even as she pulled on clothes, winding the scarf around her neck, she could hear Joel descending the stairs.

By the time she was coming down, in the travelling clothes she had laid out before bed, Joel had their guest in the hallway, the scene lit by a single candle. The law keeper, Grayling, was grim-faced, expression telling her that whatever reason had brought him here was not a happy one. It rarely was. Not in the middle of the night, anyway.

"What's the trouble?" she asked, by way of greeting. Careless of manners, she sat on one of the bottom steps and pulled on her boots, lacing them quickly.

"I need your help. There's a child missing."

He had her full attention now, the magic of the Hundred stirring in response to his request, senses sharpening. She looked up from the bootlaces and met his eyes. Not just missing, she realised. Taken. At least, that was what he suspected.

She remembered their first conversation. The exchange of information. No children missing from Fir Tree Crossing since his arrival in the winter but the law keepers had been taking no chances, with extra patrols and vigilance. Despite that, this news. A child missing.

"We've been out looking, but there is no trace of her."

"How old?"

"Nine." His voice fractured slightly on that one word. Antonine Rangers were not known for their family commitments but it did happen. She wondered if he had left behind a sister, or even a daughter.

"I'll saddle Lothar," Joel said, and padded off into the depths of the house towards the kitchen, which led to the outbuildings.

"I'll pack some travel rations," Mariah added, slipping past Yvonne.

Grayling watched her disappear into the depths of the house, a slightly bemused expression on his face.

"They seem very calm," he commented.

"You're not the first law keeper to come to me in the middle of the night with a missing child," Yvonne told him.

"Tell me you found the others."

"All of them." Her throat tightened, memories threatening to surface. "Not all alive, though."

"I'll keep hoping." He did not sound hopeful, though.

By the time Yvonne had her boots done up and cloak in place Mariah was back with saddlebags, and the soft sound of hooves outside the front door told her that Joel had brought Lothar round.

She and Grayling were on their way moments later, Lothar striding out despite the poor light. He could always sense when something was wrong. Grayling's horse danced sideways as they crossed the bridge, picking up the urgency.

They didn't need to speak as they made their way to where the girl had last been seen, in her parents' house.

The house was easy to find. Even without escort, Yvonne would have found it. It was the one fully lit, lamps or candles burning in every single room and torches set outside. There were law keepers milling about as well, horses ready. Weapons ready. All of them as grim faced as Grayling. And from inside the house came hysterical sobbing. A frantic mother, doubtless feeling helpless that there was nothing she could do.

"I need to see her room. Talk to the parents." Yvonne dismounted. One of Grayling's deputies offered to take the reins but she shook her head. "He'll stay until he's needed."

The law keeper took another, closer look at the dull brown horse and nodded, eyes widening in surprise. Not many people had met a Hunar. And those that did, didn't expect her to have a warhorse to ride.

Inside the house was as bad as she thought it might be. Memories of other nights, of other frantic, desperate parents. Of other grim-faced law keepers, few of them as competent as she knew Grayling was.

The girl's room was upstairs, under the eaves. There was a small window that opened out over the river and a large, mature tree growing up beside the house. The window was open. A quick glance at Grayling told her that the window had been open when they came to the house, and that he suspected that was how the girl had left. It was easily big enough for a nine-year-old girl, and might be big enough for a slim, determined adult.

That was the easy part.

Talking with the parents was always hard. Their friends and neighbours were there, too. Most of them in their night clothes, coats and cloaks hastily pulled on. There was a pair of women, perhaps more, making tea for everyone and, it seemed, baking bread. An unusual activity for the middle of the night, but there was nothing normal about this night and Yvonne understood the impulse to do something with their hands, something familiar and soothing.

The parents had little to tell her about the disappearance. There was a small soft toy missing along with the girl but she hadn't taken any of her clothes. Only her slippers. Yvonne took a description of the girl's nightclothes, slippers and soft toy. Out of the corner of her eye, she saw Grayling listening intently. He would have taken the same descriptions already, but was making sure he hadn't forgotten anything or if the parents remembered some further detail that would help.

And as they talked, she gathered impressions. Cheeky nine-year-old. Talking back to her mother, as many nine-year-olds did. Bossing around her little brother. Wanting ribbons in her hair every day, not just for special occasions. Popular with the other children at the local school. Their teacher was one of the neighbours, as white-faced and shaken as everyone else.

Nobody in the house knew anyone that might have taken her. The parents were adamant that she would not go out alone. The tree was too far away for her to reach from her window. They had checked. Careful, conscientious parents. Everything building a picture of a close, loving home. The husband as distraught as his wife, as they held on to each other. The son, a few years younger than his sister, was being cuddled in a corner by neighbours. No reason that Yvonne could see, or could sense, that the girl would have left on her own.

By the time she and Grayling left the house she had a hard, painful knot in her stomach. Happy, contented children did not just leave home. The parents, and the neighbours who were in earshot, had not known of any new friends or any changes in the child's behaviour. She could see from their faces as she asked the question that the same, awful thought had occurred to a few of them.

"We have boats ready," Grayling told her as they left the house. "And some local guides for the marsh, if we need them."

That last stopped Yvonne in her tracks. She had not realised, in the journey to get here, just how close they were to the edge of the town and to the marshland. The hard knot in her stomach tightened.

Without speaking, by mutual agreement, they went around the side of the house to the back of it where the girl's window was still open. The parents had been right. The tree was a little bit too far away for the girl to get to. Any adult trying to climb that high would have broken the branches. But there were other ways of getting a child out of an upstairs window. Too worried to really care what others thought, Yvonne called up a quick spell, sending sparks of light ahead of her, the small candles providing enough light for her to see better without ruining her night vision.

The better light showed which she had feared. There, in the soft ground underneath the girl's window, were clear indentations in the mud. There had been a ladder placed here and not that long ago.

"Taken." Grayling's voice was heavy. There were no good reasons to take a child from her parents' house in the dead of night.

"Anyone spring to mind?" Yvonne asked, not looking at him. He had been in the town far longer than she had and, she suspected, with the stories that they had both heard, would have made it his business to know and identify those who might be a danger.

"Only one or two. It's a peaceful town. And the one or two know we're looking at them. I don't think they'd risk it."

"Well, let's see where she went."

Yvonne's method of tracking wasn't something she could explain to anyone else, not even her children. But then, she had asked them to explain to her how they tracked using their nose, and they had run into similar difficulties. There were no precise, exact words to describe the set of impressions she had gathered from looking at the girl's room and from talking to her parents. But she had gathered enough impressions to form a trace in her mind, the vaguest shape of a small, lively girl. Enough bits and pieces, fragments gathered together, to let her find a trace of the girl in the air.

"Not in the river. Not yet," she told Grayling, almost absently, finding the girl's trail in the air. She started following the trail, trusting him to follow.

Whoever it was who had taken the girl, they had also left an impression on the world. The girl was bright and carefree. The other was darker, leaving traces of anxiety and a desperate kind of longing in the air as they moved. The girl had been willing, excited to be out on an adventure.

"We'll need horses, I think," Yvonne said, staring ahead. She could see the faintest wisp of the two trails, twined together, heading off out into the marshes. "They were on foot, but they are hours ahead of us."

"They?"

"The girl was with someone. An adult. I can't tell more at the moment."

It was a matter of moments to get the horses, Lothar coming to her low-voiced call, and ride out into the marsh. One of the guides went ahead of them, to make sure that they were on solid ground, with Yvonne directing him to adjust his path and direction.

She could sense the tension from the guide the further they rode.

"What is it? What's ahead of us?"

"There's a nasty bit," he told her. "Most of the marshland is flat and calm. But there's a bit, just ahead, where it sucks under. We've dragged plenty of bodies out of it over the years."

"Straight ahead?"

"Yes."

That hard knot in her stomach tightened still further until she could barely breathe from it, the trails of the girl and her adult companion stretching out in front.

"We need to leave the horses here. There's not enough ground for them ahead." The guide's voice was grim. He sounded as defeated as Grayling had.

They left the horses in the dark, with one of Grayling's deputies to look after them, and went forward. Yvonne, slightly ahead as the trace pulled her forward, spotted it first. A splash of white.

The group moved forward with quick, careful strides. The splash of white grew larger, rippling with the water. Something in the black water beneath them.

The guide stood at the edge of the path, looking down, shoulders slumped. Yvonne could not see his expression fully in the uncertain light, but the slumped shoulders told their own tale. She went to stand beside him and felt that hard knot jam up into her throat. It was a child's nightgown. Floating in the water, rippling with the surface as it responded to some deep current underneath. Worse, far worse, it was not just the nightgown. There was a long plait of dark hair, tied off with a red ribbon, and the pale outline of a hand against the water.

"Let me," she said, stepping forward. She crouched, cautiously, at the edge of the path. The ground here was soft under her feet and she could feel it sliding away from her toes even as she reached forward, gently taking hold of that pale hand and tugging, carefully and slowly, until she had the girl, in her perfect white nightgown, at her feet.

The face that turned up to her in the uncertain light was peaceful. Sleeping. Or so it seemed.

"Gone." Grayling's voice was harsh.

A clean wash of fury had Yvonne putting her hand on the girl's chest. Cold, but there was the faintest trace of warmth. Nine years old. Taken from safety into this dark night, into the cold water.

She murmured a healing spell, her hand shimmering with magic for a moment before the spell coursed into the girl's body. It didn't always work.

The body shuddered and she moved, quickly turning the girl on her side, patting the small back.

A spew of dark water came out of the girl's mouth.

"Blankets," Yvonne said, relief making her voice shake. "Lots of blankets."

Shouts went up all around them, blankets handed to her one after the other. She used the first two to rub the girl down, drying her off as the small body continued to spasm, coughing up more water than seemed possible. Then she used the next several blankets to wrap the girl up into a tight cocoon, layering carefully to preserve warmth.

"Anything to drink? Not hot, it will burn her."

Several flasks appeared in her vision.

"This one. Lukewarm tea," Grayling said, taking one of the flasks and waving the others away. He knelt by her, tipping the flask to the girl's mouth as Yvonne held her up. "I thought she was gone."

"So did I," Yvonne said, shivering now that the worst was over. The girl coughed up the first mouthful of tea, spilling onto the blanket. Yvonne did not think the owner would mind. The girl swallowed the next, and a few after that. "She needs to go back to her parents. And a healer. There are no marks on her," she added, seeing his face grim again, "I don't think whoever took her had her long enough to hurt her. But she was nearly gone, and she's still cold. She should live, but she needs care. At once."

Grayling turned away and was issuing orders that had a quartet of his men stripping off their cloaks, leaving them on the ground, and taking vials of something out of their belt pouches. Antonine Rangers were famed for their ability to move through any terrain, and find their way in near-dark. There had been rumours that they used magic, but no one had ever been able to confirm it until now.

She watched as the chosen men swallowed the contents of the vials and their eyes shimmered with an eerie light, similar to a wulf near the change. Wulfkin could see in the dark as well as they could in daylight.

"They'll take her as fast as they can."

The first of the four came forward and knelt nearby, holding his arms out for the girl.

"She's sleepy, and wrapped tight, but she might be frightened if she wakes," Yvonne told the Ranger, handing over the bundle.

"We'll be quick," he promised, voice rough, whether from magic or feeling she could not tell. He was away as quickly as he had approached, rising to his feet and turning back into the night with no further word.

The quartet set off at a flat run, heedless of the territory, one in front, and two behind the one carrying the girl. Four of them. They would be able to swap the girl between them as they ran.

"No need for horses," Yvonne commented, mostly to herself.

"Faster to run in the marshes," Grayling confirmed. Another one of his men was gathering up the discarded cloaks and empty vials. "And we've a kidnapper to find."

Yvonne looked ahead into the marshland, the inky dark water and tufts of reeds that she could see, and the trail that went on ahead. There was nothing more of the girl's trail. Naturally. The bright, young life was on her way back to her family. But there was something else. The other trail, the companion. Anxiety and grief and longing all twisted up inside her.

It wasn't the trace she would expect from a kidnapper. From someone who would coolly place a ladder under a child's window and take her out of her home. Something else had happened. Something that her instincts told her was almost as important as rescuing the girl had been. They needed to go on.

"What's up ahead?" she asked.

"Barely a path. Almost no one comes here."

Yvonne could understand why. Without the guide finding the firm ground for them, they could all have drowned in the cold black water around them. The guide made a small sound, as though he was holding something in, and then continued.

"There's a herbalist's hut. A bit further on, towards the edge of the marsh." The guide looked ahead, shoulder squaring. "Nice woman. Viola. Had a daughter a few years older than the one we found."

"What happened to the daughter?" Yvonne asked, her feet moving her forward before her mind could catch up with her.

"Don't know," the guide said, voice heavy. That was what he had been holding in, Yvonne thought, trusting her instinct. "Haven't seen her for a while."

"We need to go there," she said.

The guide didn't say anything, just started walking, back stiff. Something about the herbalist upset him. Or maybe it was that her daughter had gone missing and he didn't know when.

Yvonne followed him, Grayling with her, his men spreading out behind them.

Something caught her eye as they walked and she stopped, crouched by the side of the path again. A slipper. A child's slipper. Just under the surface of the water, and just out of reach of her fingers.

"Be careful, Hunar," the guide said. "It doesn't look like much, but that is deadly."

"It looks like she went in there," Yvonne said, pointing to the slipper. "Would the current take her back?"

"Yes. It could. It's chancy underneath."

The guide moved, using the long staff he held to fetch the slipper out of the water. There was no obvious damage, no blood, no sign of a struggle. Just a child's slipper, mired now with water and mud. Yvonne felt her chest tighten, thinking of what might have been, if they had been a little later.

Grayling handed the slipper to one of his men, who tucked it away to give back to the family.

They kept walking and, into the eerie silence of the marshland, another sound emerged. The high-pitched wailing of a woman in distress. Yvonne had heard that sound before. Too many times.

"You may want to stay here," she told the others.

Past the dangerous part of the marsh, the path had widened a little so that they could all walk side-by-side comfortably, if they needed to. Ahead of them, a dark blot in the night, was a small, low building. A cottage. The scent of herbs carried on the slight breeze. Marshlands were not obvious places for herbalists to gather and work. But then, there was little free land around the town, and most herbalists that Yvonne had met preferred solitude and quiet.

There was a lighter patch outside the building. A figure, huddled against the wall, sobbing quietly, not moving as Yvonne approached. A woman, dressed in plain, serviceable clothing, dark hair framing a pale face that was mottled with tears and grief, clutching something to her chest. A child's toy. The one that had been described, with much care and attention, by the girl's parents.

The trail of anxiety and grief and longing led to this woman, who barely reacted as Yvonne, the Rangers and the guide reached her.

Yvonne crouched down near the woman. Close enough to get a better look at her, even with the poor light, but far enough away to give the woman the illusion of privacy and space.

"Viola. What happened to your girl?" Yvonne asked.

"Gone." The woman's voice was harsh, hoarse with grief. Not grief that was mere hours old. This grief had been building for a while.

"What happened?"

"Men on horses. Grabbed her up. I ran after them. Screamed at them. No one cared. No one listened to me. Law keepers didn't care. Nobody. Nobody cared. And she's gone."

"When was this?"

"First day of spring. Beautiful spring day. She had flowers in her hair."

Last year. Yvonne felt a stab of sympathetic pain run through her. Last year. Viola's daughter had been taken. Before Grayling had arrived in the town. He would not have ignored a claim of a missing child.

"What about tonight? There was another girl. What happened?"

"The men were back. With horses. I got her away. Had to save her." Viola looked up at Yvonne, mouth trembling. "And now she's gone." The last word was a wail that turned into a wrenching sob.

"No, she's not," Yvonne said softly. "She's on her way back to her family."

"You're lying. I saw her. Saw her face."

"I am Hunar. We do not lie."

The herbalist stared at Yvonne for a long moment before her face collapsed and she started crying in earnest, whole body shaking. Relief. Old grief at the surface again.

"What happened to her?" Yvonne asked, voice soft.

"Tripped. Lost her slipper. Wanted to go in after it. Wouldn't listen when I told her no. Pulled away from me. I thought she was gone."

"An accident," Grayling said, voice heavy. "A stupid accident."

"You need to take her," Yvonne said.

"There is no crime here," Grayling said. "She was trying to protect the girl."

"Men with horses, she said. She's seen them twice. They've seen her, too. This poor woman needs somewhere safe," Yvonne told him.

Grayling did not like it, but did not argue.

"Where did you get the ladder?" Yvonne asked Viola. She was still huddled against the side of her hut, but she did not look like a large woman, and a ladder big enough to reach to the girl's room would have been big and heavy.

"What ladder?"

"How did you get the girl out of her room?"

"I didn't. I told you. The men with horses. They were taking her. Managed to get away from them. Just for a moment. We ran."

Yvonne looked at her. There was not a scrap of deceit, not even the faintest hint of a lie. Behind her, there was a sharp intake of breath as Grayling followed Viola's words and understood what had happened.

"They're in my town," he said, fury in his voice. "A year ago and now. No more. I need descriptions."

"Take her in," Yvonne said, "and get her safe passage somewhere else." She hesitated, looking back at the woman. "I can help with that."

"I can tell everybody what I've heard," the guide said, unexpectedly. "An accident. People trying to kidnap the girl."

No ill intent. Nothing for frightened parents to take their revenge over. Although, Yvonne hoped the parents would be so relieved to have their daughter home that they would not be thinking about the herbalist for a while.

"We don't want to scare them off. Not until I've had a chance to meet them," Grayling said. The hard, tight knot of hurt in her middle loosened into a warm wish that Grayling got to meet them. She was quite confident that the men on horses would not enjoy the experience.

Before they could do anything else, Viola moved, grabbing hold of Yvonne's wrist, grip stronger than seemed possible, fingers hard enough to bruise.

Her lips moved for a moment, face white, eyes unfocused.

"Is she –?"

"Leave her," Yvonne interrupted Grayling. "It's the sight."

The law keeper shifted on his feet, uncomfortable. Yvonne did not look round, sure he would have one hand on a weapon hilt. The sight was unsettling, particularly the first time. She kept her attention on Viola. Whatever sight had taken hold of her had terrified the woman, tears beginning to fall again down her face.

Her lips moved again, soundless, Yvonne trying to make out the words.

"He is coming."

The words were spoken in the same harsh voice Yvonne had heard before from people in the grip of the sight. Nothing like the ordinary voice of the person.

"Who is?" she asked, keeping her voice as calm as possible. She did not really expect an answer.

"He. Is. Coming."

Viola's face twisted and she screamed, a silent sound that was almost worse than a full-throated cry. Then she slumped forward, releasing Yvonne's wrist.

"What was that?" Grayling asked. Yvonne glanced up to find him pale and white-lipped in the dark, knuckles white on his sword hilt.

"It's the sight. Some people have it."

"She looked like she was being tortured," he said.

"It's never good news," Yvonne answered, turning back to Viola. "Is there some tea? Or something stronger? She'll need something to warm her." She gently put her hands on the herbalist's shoulders and pressed her back, so she was leaning against the side of the hut. Viola's face was slack, eyes half-open, unaware of anything until the guide knelt beside her and gave her a drink out of his flask.

"What …" Viola shook her head, grimacing. "Oh. The sight?" she asked.

"Yes. Do you remember any of it?"

"No. I never do. Hate it." Viola's hands were shaking as she reached for the flask again.

They waited while she took another long drink, and brushed tears from her face. Yvonne could see the guide and Grayling bursting with questions. Now was not the time, though.

And Yvonne did not think that the answers would do them any good. The sight was a chancy thing, but seemed to deliver its grim news to the right person in all cases.

He is coming.

For a moment, Yvonne wondered if that meant Guise. But he was already here. Someone else, then. And someone powerful enough that the sight had warned a Hunar.

She would have to ask her fellow Hunar about other warnings. There was never just one. And the sight, whatever mysterious power drove it, tended to warn the Hundred. Obscure, oblique warnings that nonetheless put the Hundred on alert.

He is coming.

"We'll go back towards town now," Yvonne told Viola. "On the way, will you tell me about your daughter?"

"Caroline," Viola said, straightening away from the wall, voice stronger than it had been. "Her name is Caroline and she was fourteen last summer."

The magic of the Hundred stirred. Another missing child. Another obligation to carry until it was fulfilled, one way or another.

Chapter Eight

It was daylight by the time she got back to the house. The awful night had given way to a bright, fresh morning. It felt like spring. She remembered the herbalist, voice raw with grief, and the daughter who had gone missing on the first day of spring. The impressions she had gathered of Caroline, vivid memories of a loving mother, rested inside along with the impressions of another missing child. Alexander, the Cressins' son.

Every part of her was heavy. Her eyes were hot and sore though she did not think she had been crying. Not tonight, anyway. Even though there had been one happy result, she was still heartsick.

Mariah and Joel were up and about already, she saw, the curtains upstairs drawn back, windows open to let in some air. It was a little earlier than normal, but nothing about the night had been normal.

She rode Lothar to the stables and found them both there, going over the saddles and bridles. It was a task they usually hated and she felt an odd stab of pain. They were waiting for her.

Joel took one look at her face. "Rough night."

"The girl is safe. But there's another missing. For a year. And no one was looking for her."

"But you are now," he said.

"Yes." Along with Alexander. And Guise's associate. The twist of competing obligations held her still for a moment, mind refusing to unpick them and work out what she should do first.

"Who has been missing so long?" Mariah asked.

"The herbalist's daughter." Yvonne leant on Lothar for a moment, feeling him shift his weight slightly to hers, weary to her bones. She remembered the feel of that cold hand in hers, and the dread that she was holding another dead child, before she had found some life in the small body. Children were the worst. Small, fragile bodies and a lifetime of potential.

"The herbalist," Mariah repeated slowly, frowning. She was making friends in the town, settling in far faster than she ever had before.

"Out on the marsh," Joel told his sister.

"Oh, Viola." Trust Mariah to know the name. She had only spent one morning at the dressmakers' so far. "Frida was saying she keeps to herself, but seemed sad."

"No one noticed her daughter was missing," Yvonne said, shaking her head. It was almost unbelievable, except that she could understand how it had happened. A single mother, living outside the town, visiting rarely. The rest of the town caught up in their own business, not noticing time passing.

"Would you like a hug, Kalla?" Mariah asked.

She had them well trained. They knew better than to touch her without warning. It had been a struggle, raising them. Wulfkin were often very tactile and she had worried that they would suffer because she could not give them all they needed.

She nodded, once, and was immediately surrounded by her children. Warm, familiar bodies. Fresh scents. They had both bathed that morning, something else that was unusual. But it meant that she was not surrounded by the overwhelming scent of wulf. It meant that she could stand, hold them back, and simply be still, surrounded by her family, for a full five breaths. Even as the last breath left her and she could feel her heart skip, the panic threatening to rise, both of them were releasing her, stepping back. Five full breaths. That was the limit that they had discovered over the years. All she could stand. Not enough for them, almost too much for her.

Any longer and the memories came back. The suffocation of being held against her will. Unable to move. Unable to free herself. Fingers biting into her arms hard enough to bruise.

There had been no affection in her house growing up. All her memories of being held, before her children, were unpleasant. Years of raising her children had helped but not cured that.

But this morning, she was not drowned in bad memories, simply left with the warmth of her children around her, and the faint scent of soap and wulf.

"Guise was here," Mariah told her, taking Lothar's reins. "He said he will meet you tomorrow, instead, outside The Tavern."

"He was here?" Yvonne's brows rose. That might explain a few things.

"He stopped at the gate," Joel answered, tilting his head towards the benches and the horse trough that had been set up for the Hunar's supplicants. "Waited for one of us to go to him." He sent a sideways glance to his sister.

"Well, I wasn't going to let you go alone." Mariah's tone was sulky. Yvonne could imagine the whispered argument behind the door, trying to decide who would go out, and indeed if they would go out.

Still, Yvonne was grateful for the reprieve. She could have a day to gather herself, get some sleep, decide which trail she needed to follow. Which was most urgent. Alexander. Caroline. Guise's associate. Her mind snagged on that last one. She didn't know enough. Not yet.

"Sephenamin sent some stew," Joel added. "Ella brought it." There was something in his voice as he said that that caught Yvonne's attention. Female wulfkin were generally jealously guarded by the males in their range, often relegated to the bottom of the pack. But this was not a normal range, and Sephenamin was not a normal cerro. Ella was by far the strongest female wolf, strong enough to be the cerro's second, although that position was currently held by a much older wulf, one the rest of the range respected with a deep, quiet affection. From a brief glimpse of Ella, across The Tavern's common room, Yvonne suspected she was not that much older than Joel.

Yvonne opened her mouth to make some comment, then thought better of it. In most places, Joel would be considered an adult. He was only a few months away from being free of her legal guardianship; he could make his own mistakes, and his own explorations.

Besides which, she realised that she was hungry. Despite the awful night, her body needed fuel. Tracking always made her hungry, no matter what the end result was.

So, she took her saddlebags, with the uneaten food that Mariah had given her the night before, and went into the kitchen to find it full of the scent of The Tavern's best cooking and remains of freshly baked bread, raggedly cut.

An unexpected bubble of laughter rose up. Fresh bread was a rare, and special, treat. She could imagine how carefully the children had measured out that portion of bread, that they would leave for her.

Not long after she was bathed, fed and fractionally rested, and riding back towards town on the spare horse. More used to carrying luggage than people, he was slightly skittish in the late morning, requiring more concentration than she was used to when she was riding. It was no bad thing, not letting her mind go back through new memories.

Mariah and Joel had gone ahead, each with business of their own. Joel was, apparently, going to return the stew pot to The Tavern. Yvonne had a feeling she might not see him again that day, if Ella was around. Mariah, she thought, did not want to be alone and there were enough girls of her age in the town that she would always find some company. Frida, the dressmaker, had a daughter roughly the same age, who was also friends with the potter's daughter.

She was not entirely sure what she wanted. She needed sleep, but was not willing to lie down just yet, with the memories quite so fresh, hollowed out with everything from the night before. The urgency of the track through the marshes. The relief of that first breath from the girl. The echo of Viola's despair ringing through her. Another lost child. And the harsh sound of the warning. He is coming.

She shivered in the sun, a chill running over her. No, she could not stay still.

And she had an instinct that she needed to talk to Guise before the next day, before they headed off in pursuit of his associate. If, indeed, that was where she should go. She had virtually no information from Guise, and the traces of two other missing children had settled inside her, trails that she needed to follow.

The atmosphere in town was odd. Calm and measured. Not at all what she had expected. The near-death of a child, however accidental, would usually have groups gathered in the street and an ugly mood developing as people looked for someone to blame. Here, the townspeople were quiet, going about their business, talk more muted than normal.

She left the horse at The Tavern's stables then let her feet go where they wanted, finding herself on the way to the law keeper's offices. In the square outside the offices she saw the first sign that the town may not be as peaceful as it seemed. There was a group of perhaps ten people. They did not appear angry. There were no weapons evident. But there was a pair of law keepers outside the open doors to their offices. They were fully armed, carefully keeping their hands away from their weapons and standing in the most casual guard position she had ever seen. Rangers were not the most polished unit in any army, but they did have some basic discipline and she was quite certain that, had they been wearing their normal uniforms, the casual posture would not have been permitted. But they were trying to be in disguise here and she did not think that Grayling would discipline either of his men for their sloppy appearance.

There was nothing sloppy about the glances they gave her as she put her foot on the bottom step up to the building.

"He's at the wine bar," one of them said. "With the goblin."

Her brows lifted, almost to her hairline. Grayling and Guise in the same place? This, she had to see. About to turn around and go and find them, her brain caught up with the other piece of startling information.

"A wine bar? There's a wine bar in this town?"

The muffled snort from the junior of the pair was quelled at once by a sharp glance from the senior.

"One of those barges that arrived. At the dock. It's got red drapes."

Red drapes was an understatement. The entire barge was actually painted red, and it had a fancy awning draped over the front deck, sheltering the patrons from any excessive sun or rain. The awning was made of brilliant red fabric and, as she approached, she could see that the underside had been liberally painted with what looked like glitter so the effect for the patrons underneath must be something quite extraordinary. She could also sense a small fizz of magic as she approached and took time, engaging her senses, to see where that might be coming from. It seemed nothing more harmful than a little bit of extra glamour in the glitter. Probably making them appear like stars, although she had never seen stars on a bright red background.

There were people wandering about the barge itself and the intrepid owner had also set up a series of small tables and chairs on the dockside. Normally used for packing crates and whatever other goods the barges were due to carry, this particular section of the dock now looked like an outdoor tavern. She had seen something similar in some of the larger cities, in summer, where the cafes would take over part of the street outside. Judging by the number of locals standing around, eyeing up the scene, she did not think that Fir Tree Crossing had ever seen anything like it. A few people, mostly other merchants, were taking advantage of the fine day, so quite a number of tables were occupied.

To one side of the open-air common room, Grayling was sitting, apparently entirely relaxed, at a table with Guise. To look at them, they were two acquaintances catching up on news. There was no hint of the bloody battles fought between the Rangers and goblins in the past.

There was a tall bottle of pitch-dark glass and two glasses on the table, partly filled with deep red liquid. Yvonne's brows rose again. That was not cheap wine. In fact, it was extremely costly wine. Guise had expensive tastes, and the means to indulge them. She wondered if Grayling had also developed a taste for the finer things in his travels.

Guise saw her first, coming to his feet with easy grace. He could have had one bottle to himself, or three, and his movement would not be impaired. Goblins had a notoriously high tolerance for alcohol.

Grayling rose a moment later, movements as easy as ever. She suspected that they had been talking more than they had been drinking.

"Hunar," Grayling said.

"Mristrian," Guise added, inclining his head. She still did not fully understand what that meant. A goblin term of respect, was all he had said, and somehow managed to not explain further when she had asked. She had given up trying to get more out of him. For now. "Were you looking for me or the law keeper?"

"Both of you, I suppose. Mainly you," she told Guise.

Of course, he insisted that she sit down. With a wave of his hand one of the serving staff appeared with a fresh glass for her and, moments later, a dish of savouries that made her eyes widen again.

"A very well-resourced merchant," she commented. She let Guise pour her a glass of wine, and set it in front of her. She knotted her hands together, out of sight under the table, for a moment before she took the glass, exchanging a brief toast with them.

The wine was like drinking a small piece of heaven. She so rarely got a chance to drink good wine, or indeed any wine at all. Taverns served beer and locally made spirits, neither of which she particularly enjoyed. This, though, was full of flavour and sang in her senses.

"Viola is still in our building," Grayling said, posture still casual. "And Guise here was making an extraordinary offer."

"I simply indicated that I know a place where she may find refuge," Guise said, eyebrows lifting in evidently fake surprise.

"With the Sisters in the Stone Walls?" Yvonne asked.

Grayling's brows shot up in unfeigned surprise, then he shook his head slightly. A connection between the Hunar and the Sisters was far less remarkable. "Indeed. He has also offered to pay for her passage there."

Yvonne's brows rose in turn, startled for a moment. Just when she thought she had figured Guise out, he did something like this.

Her first impressions had been of a spoilt, overindulged lord, very high ranking in the Karoan'shae, the complex network of houses that ran goblin society. She still thought he was spoilt and high-ranking. She no longer thought he was quite as selfish, or self-absorbed, as he pretended to be. There were too many instances like this over the years where he would step out of his way to help an absolute stranger. Always in circumstances where the stranger was in peril or grieving. And the herbalist was both.

"I can write a letter for her as well," Yvonne said, turning back to Grayling. No need to tell him, or Guise, how well she knew the Sisters, or that, many years before, she had been one of the strangers they had taken in and put back together. The Sisters took in anyone in need, and did not demand answers. "A skilled herbalist is always in demand there."

She did not need to elaborate. The Sisters were renowned, almost as much as Hunar were, and far more numerous and accessible. They mostly lived behind the stone walls that gave the sisterhood their name, practising advanced healing and advanced medicine on anyone who travelled to see them. Like the Hundred, though, the results were not always what the petitioners expected.

Yvonne clearly remembered the first time she had heard of the sisterhood taking in, and healing, a known murderer. There had been utter outrage from the victims' families, that their loved ones' killer should be restored to health. Outrage had turned to bewilderment when the Sisters themselves had delivered the cured murderer into the hands of the law keepers who had been looking for him. Last Yvonne had heard, the murderer, with his newly healed body, was working in the prison mines, notorious for being an actual death sentence for a kingdom that did not have a gallows or an executioner's block.

"Let me know when arrangements have been made," Grayling said, cutting into her thoughts. He finished the wine in his glass with one slow, careful swallow. "I have not had wine this good for many years. Thank you."

Guise tilted his head in acknowledgement and Grayling left, doubtless to check on the small crowd outside the law keeper's offices. Yvonne watched his back for a moment, finding she envied his simple task. Keep the law-abiding people of this town in safety. It seemed far easier than the tasks she faced.

Chapter Nine

"Have some more," Guise suggested, pouring more wine into her glass.

"That's plenty, thank you. I did not get much sleep last night." She drew the wineglass closer and assessed the amount in her glass. Enough to enjoy. Not enough to compromise her senses.

"A bad business," Guise said. His tone was idle, almost casual. If she had not known him, she might have been fooled.

As it was, she did not want to discuss it. She could still feel the cold skin against hers as she pulled the girl out of the water. Still see the bright ribbon tangled in wet hair. Still feel the stop of her heart as she thought the girl was dead.

She took another sip of wine, the flavour of it lifting the memory long enough for her to remember why she was here, why she had sought him out.

"Can you give me more information about your business associate? Ubel. A northerner, I assume?" The name was a common one in the mountains. The northerners were renowned for their bartering skills, making good merchants when they chose to travel. "The wulfkin traced him to the marshes?"

Guise's eyes flared, their normal green shimmering a moment with a tinge of something else. Not red, not in this public place, but enough of a shift to make Yvonne hold herself very still and mentally review the weapons on her. Guise would not hurt her. It was simply prudent to know how well she was armed.

"The marshes, yes. They went out again this morning." After the girl was back home, Yvonne would bet. The range might have been holding themselves ready in case their skills were needed, and would have been glad of something to do with all that restless energy. Guise's careful, relaxed poise was a mask. A very good one. Goblins could be as savage as wulfkin. "He went into the marshes and came back."

"What was he doing in the marshes?" Yvonne was proud of her voice. Even and calm, the question perfectly reasonable. She could wear a mask, too.

Guise's lip lifted, showing the barest hint of a gleaming white fang. Goblins had teeth as long as wulfkin.

Yvonne's heart sped up, and her fingers twitched, wanting a weapon. Involuntary reactions. Triggered by the chill touch of old, old fear. She kept herself still, though. They were in a public space. In daylight. Guise was not annoyed with her. And he would not hurt her.

"He went to the herbalist's hut and then back."

"Did he now." She tilted her head slightly, staring into middle distance as she considered that. The impressions she had of Viola were of an honest person, grieving for the loss of her child. She could not imagine what a herbalist might have to do with one of Guise's associates. Or why Guise's associate might have sought out Viola.

"There's a marsh plant that's valuable in the southern cities," Guise said. He'd clearly also been wondering what a herbalist and his associate might have in common.

"Really?" Yvonne cast her mind over the plants and herbs she knew about for use in medicine or cooking, and could not think of a single one valuable enough to harvest and transport all the way to the southern cities.

"It is said to stop unwanted pregnancy," Guise told her, lip curling slightly.

"Oh. That one. It doesn't work," she told him, shaking her head. "Might as well use common grass."

"Indeed."

"Was your associate in the habit of peddling false medicines?" she asked, curious. It might explain why he had disappeared.

"Not in his dealings with me," he answered, a low, dark tone to his voice. Very few people would be stupid or desperate enough to try and fool a goblin. Goblin society had very direct ideas of punishment. "Other than that, I do not know."

"Well, what can you tell me about him?" It wasn't like Guise to have so little information. She wondered how long he had been doing business with this particular individual, and why.

"We can do better than my description. That's his barge, along there," Guise told her, inclining his head slightly. "The grey one, with the yellow painted name." His voice was low, and there was no one within easy earshot. He did not want people to realise his keen interest in the barge, Yvonne saw, although he had placed himself in a position where he could easily see it. She would bet money, that she did not have much of, that he had paid others to watch the barge for him as well. There were always people glad of a few extra coins.

"Did he paint it himself?" Yvonne asked after one casual look around. The paintwork was dreadful. Even at this distance, she could see the uneven depth of colour, and the garish yellow did not sit well against the more modest grey background.

"I believe he did. He may have been trying to hide from me." Guise's lip curled. His fangs were still partly extended. "He has been avoiding me for a while."

"I am not a debt collector," she told him, matching his easy, light tone. She had said that to him before, more than once. It never hurt to remind him, though.

A small smile and a tilt of his head was all the acknowledgement she had for that. He did not volunteer more information, and she did not ask.

They finished their wine at a civilised pace, Yvonne setting her empty glass down with some regret. She had eaten some of the savouries as well. For a moment, she could not remember if she had eaten properly at the house before she left, then remembered the stew and carefully measured portion of bread. That seemed a distant memory, a far-away place from the expensive wine and delicate food.

Guise rose to his feet in a graceful move she knew she would never match, and they made their way along the dockside to the grey painted barge.

Closer up, the paintwork was even worse than Yvonne had thought. It looked like the barge's original colour had been blue. There were gaps between the brush strokes of grey paint where a vivid blue was shining through. Merchants and barge masters were notorious for painting their barges bright, gaudy colours, to deter thieves. It did not always work. But it did take many hours, if not days, to paint over the vivid colours, so any thieves had to be well-resourced to disguise the stolen craft.

She wondered what Ubel had done, or not done, that had led him to try and hide from Guise, painting the barge so it would not be recognised. Wondered, too, if this really had belonged to Ubel.

This particular barge sat tall out of the water, a simple design with a sturdy wooden top where cargo could be carried and which lifted off in sections to give access to the larger cargo hold underneath. With the wooden sections in place, the cargo hold was just tall enough for Yvonne to walk upright. Guise had to crouch, or tilt his head at an uncomfortable-looking angle, which he did with the same grace as he did everything else. There were a few small cabins towards the rear of the vessel, and the usual steering platform. No room for oarsmen on this barge. He would have needed draft animals to tow the barge upstream and relied on the current to travel downstream, steering from the platform at the rear. Not the best arrangement.

Whoever had owned this barge, whether it was Ubel or someone else, had not believed in comforts for the barge crew, or anyone travelling on it. The shoddy paintwork and the absence of any crew made Yvonne suspicious that the barge had been used for illegal purposes. At first glance, it did not look anything like a smuggler's vessel. The cargo hold seemed entirely open, marked off by iron rings in the floor and walls, with a large pile of thick, coiled ropes in one corner. She could easily trace, by the marks on the floor and the wear pattern on the iron rings, where the cargo was usually secured by the ropes. Simple and cheap. Not carrying delicate cargo, then. Glass merchants used specially created fixed partitions and a lot of soft packing material.

The whole space, empty of cargo or people, was also almost void of any trace of its crew, or anyone else who may have been on board, even when she enhanced her senses with a quick spell.

The only personal item that they found which had any resonance to it was a small ledger, tucked underneath the thin, hard mattress in one of the sleeping quarters. Guise's face tightened as he saw it and he flicked through the pages, but made no comment as he passed it to her.

"Is this his?" she asked. She was more interested in whether she could pick up anything of the owner's personality from the book, rather than trying to work out the code that had been used to write in it. She had seen a number of merchant's ledgers over the years. They all had slightly different ways of writing things down, and she knew enough not to trust the apparently innocuous column headings describing the goods that had apparently been shipped on this barge. She was quite sure that there had been no horses on this barge. Not ever. Despite the ledger claiming that there had been at least a half-dozen on one of the previous journeys.

"Yes. I've seen him writing in it before."

"Horses," Yvonne murmured, something she had seen in the cargo hold demanding her attention, although she did not know what. Not just yet.

She handed the ledger back to Guise and went back to the cargo hold, pacing the length of it, tracing the wear patterns on the floor, the iron rings worn smooth by ropes being passed through them.

There.

That was what her eyes had seen, and her conscious mind had not noticed the first time. There were traces of a row of heavy boxes near one side of the barge. And a gap between that row and the side of the barge. With the boxes in place, that gap would not have been visible to any inspection or casual glance. A gap where there was a series of newer-looking iron rings that could be used to secure smaller objects.

"He did not have my permission for this," Guise told her. He was crouching down by the iron rings, a hint of fang at his mouth as he spoke. He was angry. And keeping himself under control. She was able to stay still and breathe. He would not hurt her.

"There's no trace that I can sense," she told him. "Do you know what was here?" Her earlier spell had faded and his senses were sharper than hers.

"Something living. That's all I can tell." His nose wrinkled. "Too small for horses, I think." So, he had noticed the ledger entry as well. For a moment she was tempted to ask him what he had authorised, and decided against it. Some things she did not wish to know, not when she was committed to spending more time in his company to find out what had happened to his associate.

There was nothing else to learn here.

"You'll need to describe him to me," Yvonne told Guise. "I can't get any trace of him here, and the impressions on the ledger are too faint." She hesitated a moment. "I don't think he was here for long. He didn't live here."

"Interesting. Certainly not his property, then," Guise answered, eyes unfocused for a moment before he inclined his head. "Yes, I can describe him. But not here."

They left the barge and Guise turned them to walk a little distance along the dock towards the ferry point where a large, flat raft would take paying passengers from one side of the river to the other. There were no bridges in the town, the river too wide for any non-magical structure to survive. The nearest bridge was a half-day's ride downriver, carrying the King's Highway from one side to the other. The king could afford to have one or more of his Court magicians attend the bridges from time to time.

It was mid-afternoon now and the town was relatively quiet, the raft point deserted. As they walked, careful to make sure no one was in earshot, he gave her a brief description of Ubel. Human male, shorter than she was, stocky in the manner of the northern people, with blond hair and a scar on his face.

As with every time she gathered impressions, it was not so much what he said but the images it left in her mind that she used to build the faintest echo and trace of the person.

By the time they had walked to the ferry point, far away from the bustle of the working docks, turned and come back, she had a reasonable impression of the missing merchant to begin tracking him. There was just one problem.

"There are two kidnapped children that I know of," she said, without warning. "One on the first day of spring last year. From this town. And one a few weeks ago, from Silverton."

"And you have promised the parents that you will find them," Guise said. He was not surprised. "This barge was in Silverton before it was here. It may be that he has gone back there."

"So we can start there," she said. The uneasy feeling in the pit of her stomach settled. Just a little. She would not need to delay looking for the children.

She blew out a breath, looking over the river, the different parts of her dancing in their usual conflict. The guilt that she would need to leave Mariah and Joel again, for however long the tasks took and however necessary it was. She had taken them with her, more than once, when it was too chancy to leave them and there had been no willing housekeepers to look after them. They were old enough to be left alone now and, particularly with Sephenamin's word, this town was a safe place to leave them.

Along with the old, familiar guilt was the almost equally familiar push and pull of Guise's task for her and the need to look for the missing children.

Apart from finding him unsettling, she enjoyed working with Guise. He was a surprisingly easy companion and always paid well.

The tradition for Hunar was that supplicants would offer gifts, whatever they could spare or afford. In Yvonne's experience this was most often food or drink, rarely coins. She accepted what she was offered, and was glad of it, but the reality of life was that money was required. At some point over the coming year, with the house and grounds to settle in, they would be able to grow or forage for at least some of their own food. For now, they were dependent on the dwindling supply of coins and the occasional gifts that she might get for completing tasks as a Hunar.

She felt guilty about enjoying the glass of wine now, thinking about the likely cost of that bottle, and how many meals it could have provided in her household. Then she shook her head. She could hardly have demanded the coins instead of the wine. It had been a casual offer from Guise, and he could more than afford it.

Having arranged to meet Guise at first light the next morning, Yvonne made her way back to The Tavern to collect her horse and go home. The day was fast fading and her limbs were heavy. Lack of sleep was beginning to tell.

As she crossed down the side of the mayor's building, she saw that the small group was still there, not sure what to do with themselves. Shocked by the brazenness of kidnappers in their town, relieved by the return of the girl. She hoped to pass by unnoticed, simply wanting to get home and get some sleep before the journey began the next day.

As with so many things she wanted, this was not to be.

A couple detached themselves from the crowd and moved slowly across the square towards her. She stopped at the corner of the law keeper's building and waited for them to join her. The parents. Both pale, eyes red-rimmed. Their daughter might be back with them, but they had spent horrible hours thinking the worst. They would be a handsome couple in normal circumstances, she thought, but she had never seen them in normal circumstances.

"Hunar," the man said, coming to a halt nearby. He had his arm around his wife, and even as Yvonne watched, she tucked herself into her husband's side. A strong couple.

"I am sorry for what happened. How is your daughter today?"

"She's sleeping a lot. The healers said it might be a few days before she's back to normal. We wanted to stay with her," the husband said, glancing down at his wife.

"Our neighbours chased us out. Said we needed some air," his wife added, more tears in her eyes.

"We can never thank you enough," the husband began.

"No thanks is required. I am glad she is safe home," Yvonne said, preparing to move on.

"We do not have much to give you," the wife said, voice shaking.

"Nothing is required." Yvonne made her voice calm, firm and as kind as she could. She had taken things from grieving parents in the past, and hated it. But gifts, freely offered, were difficult to turn down and Elinor had counselled her to accept them. It helped the grieving, Elinor had said. And this couple, even with their daughter sleeping at home, were still grieving.

"But you found her. If you had not looked, we would have lost her, and may still be wondering," the husband said, voice choked.

They were good people. She could only imagine their confusion and bewilderment. Someone had taken their little girl.

"I have a touch of sight," the woman said, her bottom lip trembling. "I knew something was wrong. Badly wrong. Even before we knew she was missing."

She would make an excellent witch, Yvonne thought. In other circumstances, this young, grieving mother and the herbalist might well have been friends. The gift of sight, the gift of medicine, the gift of using the powers of nature were all extraordinarily rare and, in Yvonne's estimation, to be treasured. From the clasp of her husband's arm around her, he felt the same.

"It is a difficult gift," Yvonne said, remembering Viola's words from the night before. *He is coming.* "It almost never shows you what you really need to know," she added, more to herself than for their benefit.

"Grayling says that Viola will go to the Sisters in the Stone Walls. We're glad there's somewhere she can go," the man said.

"We'd like you to have this," the wife said, holding her hands out. Yvonne felt the knot in her stomach return, hard and painful, but she put her hands out, palms up, and closed them around whatever the wife put in them, barely glancing at the offering. A small, leather pouch. It was heavier than she had expected, and clinked slightly as she drew it back towards her. Coins, she thought.

"The Hundred thank you. I am sorry for your trouble." Partly ritual words, partly heartfelt.

They exchanged clumsy, silent bows and by some unspoken mutual consent parted ways, Yvonne continuing on her way back to The Tavern, the couple returning to their friends and their odd vigil outside the law keeper's offices.

She did not look in the pouch until she was safely back in the rented house, in the kitchen surrounded by Joel and Mariah's good-natured bickering. Mariah had noticed Joel's interest in Ella and was making a number of pointed comments about female wulfkin that had Joel blushing and grinning like an idiot. It was a perfect antidote to the grim night before.

Before they set the table to eat, she put the leather pouch on the scarred surface and opened it. And froze. She had expected coins, but not this.

The purse was about half-full. She could imagine the parents measuring it out. The price of a returned life. Retaining some for their daughter's future. Considering if it was payment enough for a Hunar's service.

"Is that gold?" Mariah whispered, coming to look over Yvonne's shoulder.

"Yes." The tight feeling in her stomach intensified. She did not want this. She emphatically did not want this. She wanted to get up, go out into the night air, and throw the coins into the nearest river. A kidnapped child. The cold hand, too-still body, the bright coloured ribbon. And the surge of air into small lungs, the heaving cough ejecting dark water onto the ground.

"It's half a bride price, isn't it? For the girl?" Joel said. "Fifteen pieces of gold."

"Yes. I think so."

"They could have kept it," Mariah said. "It's a fortune."

"They are kind people. Honest. I don't think they would have felt right keeping it all, knowing she nearly didn't come back," Yvonne said. She remembered the impressions of the young girl, the bright, mischievous soul. She could imagine the parents carefully hoarding their wealth, adding a coin now and then. It took most families longer to save up, and some never managed. This family was wealthy. A healthy daughter, a healthy son, and means enough to set aside a full bride price before the daughter's tenth birthday.

Depending on where the parents were from, this was either the price of her admission into her husband's family or a gift from loving parents. A secret treasure for the bride that she could take with her, enough to buy her independence in future, if she wanted. If the man she ended up with was not quite who she thought he was. From the secret way it had been passed over to her, Yvonne thought it was the latter. And she could not imagine, from the little she had seen of the house, that they would sell their daughter, unwillingly, into marriage. So, this was a parent's gift, a wish of joy for the future. And their gift to the Hunar, now, for returning that joy to them.

"The Sisters would like to have it, I am sure," Joel said. "I know we need money," he added, seeing her surprise, "but there's work here. The farrier is always looking for labour, and the docks. Honest work." Shifting heavy loads around. Something that Joel, with his wulf-gifted strength, would find much easier than humans.

"The dressmaker has offered me work," Mariah said, voice high and excited, eyes shining. "I wasn't going to mention it, not just yet."

"Only if you both want to," Yvonne said, feeling her throat close. None of them were strangers to struggles with money.

She remembered, vividly, the summer that Mariah had turned thirteen and had decided to sell her hair. It had been sleek, thick, black, hanging down to her hips.

She had walked out of the house in the morning with it curled in a thick plait under a headscarf, and returned later that day with the same headscarf on, settled oddly around her head, pulling the headscarf off with her chin tipped up and jaw set, a light in her eyes Yvonne knew well. There had been barely a finger's width of hair left all around her head. The coins from Mariah's hair had kept them all fed and housed for a full three months. Mariah had been completely unrepentant, as well.

Yvonne's stomach tightened again and she repeated, in the quiet of her mind, that it had been Mariah's choice. One that had been made freely. They had not been starving, not by a long way. No one had forced Mariah to sell her hair, or have it cut off her head. A free choice, Yvonne reminded herself for the hundredth time. One that Mariah had never regretted.

"We could forage if we needed to," she heard her voice saying. "There's enough land about." The itching sensation over her skin faded. Money was short. It usually was. But they had clothes, food in the pantry and open land around them that hadn't been available in the towns they'd lived in previously. They would not starve.

"Good," Mariah said now, the reality of here and now sending Yvonne's memories back where they belonged. "We'll manage, Kalla."

"I know you will." Yvonne gathered the coins up and tied off the pouch with a slightly lighter heart, the traces of the two missing children settled inside her. "But please be careful."

"Always," Joel promised, quiet and serious.

"Always," Mariah said, eyes dancing with mischief.

She could only hope that the house would be in one piece when she got back.

Chapter Ten

Yvonne didn't know quite how Guise had managed it, or what promises he had made, but he had managed to get them and their horses places on a barge going upriver the next day. He had even persuaded the barge master to put in at Silverton to drop them off, so they could start the search for Guise's associate and the Cressins' child.

Which meant rather than a day or more riding through the country, skirting around the vast marshland, they were less than half a day on the river, travelling at a soothing, sedate pace.

And, in another miracle, Grayling, or Guise, had managed to procure spaces for two of the law keeper's deputies and Viola on the same barge. The barge would keep going upriver until it reached Hogsmarthen, the nearest town to the Sisters in the Stone Walls.

Grayling had accepted the heavy, tied off pouch without question or comment and passed it into the keeping of one of the deputies on the barge along with Yvonne's hastily-written letter of introduction for Viola. The herbalist herself still seemed shaken, barely speaking and staying huddled in her cloak. The deputies were concerned about her, but Yvonne thought that a few days' working behind the Stone Walls, with the Sisters' briskness, would draw the woman out of herself more. And then the tears would start again. The old grief of her lost child. The fright of nearly losing another.

Yvonne knew it was selfish, but she felt her step lighten as they left the barge at Silverton. The weight of another's grief stayed on the barge and she was moving forward to a new challenge.

Lothar snorted in disgust when he saw the narrow, flimsy pier that he needed to jump onto. He did jump, though, with little fuss, and picked up his heels to move briskly onto dry land, tail twitching.

Unlike Guise's horse, who took one look at the pier and jumped off the barge into the river, swimming downstream for a distance before finding a spot where he could wade onto solid ground.

The deputies were openly grinning as the horse, dripping with river water, came back to his rider, the saddle and Guise's luggage not only wet but coated with leaves from the plants choking the river banks.

Guise just shook his head slightly, picked up the nearest rein, and lifted an eyebrow to Yvonne.

"Shall we go?"

Yvonne bade farewell to the deputies and Viola and followed Guise along the packed earth road that led from the small pier to the town itself.

The ground here, near the river, was mostly marshland and fairly flat, giving them a good view of the town, which was actually more of a village. From a quick look around, perhaps half a hundred houses in total.

And it was a prosperous village. Every one of the houses that she could see had glass in the windows and a neatly maintained roof. There were no loose shutters, no boarded-up windows, no doors hanging by one hinge. Everything was well-maintained. She remembered the impressions she had got from the Cressins. Everyone knew each other. That did not mean that they liked each other. There would be strong rivalries and resentments running under the surface. On the face of it, it would be a pleasant place, somewhere peaceful to settle and live. Too small an environment for her, and her children. She would bet money that everyone in the town was fully human.

"The taverns here are small," Guise told her. "They don't cater well for overnight guests."

"There's a larger tavern about a half day's ride away," Yvonne answered, although she was quite sure he knew that already.

Half a day's ride, a short distance along the King's Highway, which was not far from here. On the road that led, eventually, to Hogsmarthen and the Sisters. She would like to see the Sisters again, but had a feeling that their trail would not go that way. Hogsmarthen was an orderly, law-abiding city. The kidnapping of children, and whatever had happened to Guise's associate, seemed lawless.

"The larger tavern here is also the marketplace," Guise added. He was extremely well-informed, which no longer had the power to surprise her. Either the missing Ubel, or someone else he did business with, had kept him advised. It was unlikely that he had been through this town himself. Purely human towns tended to have very long memories and a goblin lord, travelling alone, would draw a lot of attention.

As luck would have it, the first people that she saw when they arrived at the main street were the Cressins. They were walking, slowly, towards the largest building in the village, which Yvonne assumed was the main tavern. They checked in their strides when they saw her and she could see the tension in their bodies, even from the distance. Torn between hope for news, and fear of what that news might be.

She held up a hand in a brief greeting and excused herself from Guise's company, leading Lothar ahead to meet the couple even as Guise made his way to the tavern.

"I have no news for you yet," she told them at once. "Good or bad. We've business here as well as looking for your son."

"Hunar," the man said, and stopped, expression blank.

"We ... well, we have a message for you. There was an old woman. Herbalist. Lived on the edge of the town. Died a day after we got back. She was rambling toward the end."

"Not now, the Hunar won't want to be bothered," the man said, shushing his wife, face turning red.

"No, now. When else are we going to see her? And it might be important."

"A herbalist," Yvonne repeated, stomach tightening for a moment. "Did she have the sight?"

"How did you know?" the wife asked, astonished.

"Never mind that," the man shook his head. He had aged since they had come to visit her in Fir Tree Crossing. They both had. Worry had that effect.

"Oh, right. You know all sorts of things. Where was I?"

"The old woman was dying, and she gave you a message for me?" Yvonne prompted.

"He is coming. That's what she said. Over and over. Like it was important. Gave me the chills, I can tell you."

Yvonne did not blame her. Her skin was crawling with ice spiders. He is coming. She remembered Viola's sightless gaze and the harsh voice in the dark of a long and grim night. He. Is. Coming.

Her mind spun on the possibilities for a moment. He. There were any number of war-hungry rulers anxious for more land, more conquest, and more bloodshed. There was a particularly savage warlord who claimed to be a descendant of a darkin mother and goblin father, which was an unlikely but lethal combination. There were legends and stories and half-truths and self-proclaimed prophets whose entire purpose seemed to be to stir up trouble. And, in the far distant past, there was the first enemy of the Hundred, the first Hunar's brother. They had almost torn the world apart in their battles. Both long dead.

She shook her head. He is coming. It could be any one of a dozen or so people.

"Thank you for telling me," she said.

"Is it important?"

"It might be. The sight is a difficult burden to carry, and the messages not always clear."

The man nodded, in complete agreement, his embarrassment fading.

"Do you need to see his room?" his wife asked, in an abrupt change of subject.

The son had not gone missing from her house, or from his room, and Yvonne had a very clear impression of the boy from his parents' description. Sometimes it helped the parents if she came into their house, looked in the child's room. In this case, the subtle tension between them suggested that they did not want strangers in their house. They were used to living here, where everyone was familiar.

"It is not necessary, thank you," she said. "But can you tell me if there is a regular stop for the barges here? For correspondence and the like?" Now that she had seen the town, she realised how isolated it was. Not on the King's Highway. Extensive marshland blocking it from its nearest neighbour, Fir Tree Crossing. And although it was on the main river, the pier was not used to heavy traffic, and not built to withstand it.

Isolated. Everyone familiar with each other. Which made her wonder just how the boy had gone missing.

"Usually a couple of times a week. The trade guilds have offices in Hogsmarthen, and the clerks there send messages on when they can. When there's a barge." The husband had straightened slightly, become more focused, answering a simple question about how he got his post.

"It can take a few days to reach us," the wife added.

Isolated, Yvonne thought again. Although even as she thought that she realised just how spoilt she had become. Living in bigger cities and bigger towns she had become used to hearing the major news of the lands almost as soon as it happened. Nearly all of the ruling cities had message towers and relay towers set up to make sure that they heard about significant events as soon as possible. Humans with skill in magic could make a decent living relaying messages. And where that was not possible, the king's riders were never delayed, no matter how busy the road was or who else wanted to use it.

"We won't be here for long," she told them, "and then moving on, following any trail. I will have a look around the town just now, see if I can find anything."

"We couldn't find anything," the husband said, colour rising in his face.

"Don't be daft," his wife told him, sliding her hand into his elbow, "the Hunar has methods that we don't."

Yvonne left them and returned to Guise, to see what he had learned. From the slight frown, she did not think the news had been good. And it was not. Ubel had been here briefly, then got back on his ugly barge, heading for Fir Tree Crossing. He had done nothing apart from selling some of his goods in the tavern, from a full barge. And make a purchase or two.

"The barge was empty," Yvonne remembered.

"It seemed legitimate cargo," Guise said, lips thin for a moment. "But there were no coins on the barge."

"So he was here, then at Fir Tree Crossing. Sold his goods, and then left Fir Tree Crossing, leaving his barge? That's a big thing to leave," Yvonne said slowly, trying to map out the man's movements in her mind. "But he didn't come back here?"

"Not that the people in the tavern could say," Guise answered, a hint of frustration in his voice. "But the ground is flat. He could have ridden around the town and not been seen."

"We're going to need to look around for a bit," Yvonne said, a sinking feeling in her stomach. Even for a small place, riding the perimeter was still a fair distance.

"I'll come with you," he said, and then eyed his horse, still damp with river water. The air was not warm enough to dry him off, or dry off his saddle. The horse gave Guise a sour look, still unrepentant.

"Let me," Yvonne suggested, and stepped towards the horse with one hand outstretched. Goblin horses were beautiful creatures, but could be as vicious as their riders, and she had no wish to lose any fingers, or her hand. The horse watched her approach with wide, dark eyes and did not move as Yvonne placed a hand on its neck, making a soothing noise, before sending a low-level spell across the horse's skin, chasing away the moisture, and drying out the horse's harness. A little bit of magic that pulled energy from her, but would leave the horse and rider more comfortable. And not smelling as the river water and leaves dried during the afternoon. She hoped.

The horse, and its saddle, were dry when she had finished. She had left Guise's saddlebags alone. She had not checked, but she expected that he had ward spells crawling all over them. Goblin magic was as fierce as their horses.

Guise's brows lifted, but he merely said a polite thank you, brushing off dried leaves, before they got on their horses and set off for the perimeter of the town.

For a village so isolated, there had been a significant amount of traffic around the place over the past few weeks, and perhaps longer. There was only one real road that led through the town. She suspected that one end of it led, eventually, to Fir Tree Crossing and the other end, which she and Guise would follow later, led to the King's Highway.

As well as the actual road there were numerous paths, of course. Not everyone would live in the cluster of houses, and she could see traces of small buildings among the trees that surrounded the village and at least a couple of farms with livestock in the fields. There was plenty of room for an enterprising and lively child to go missing, or for Guise's business associate to come to a bad end.

They made a slow, careful circuit of the village, the horses happy to plod along on loose reins.

The only significant trace that Yvonne found, of the missing boy and of Guise's business associate, was at the other end of town, on the road that led to the King's Highway. There were faint traces of the boy around town, naturally, but nothing recent and she knew, from experience that her magic would only pick up the most recent trail, the one that she needed to follow. She had long since given up trying to make sense of it. It simply was what it was.

"We need to go this way," she told Guise.

"Good. Because that's where I wanted to go."

She shook her head slightly, saying nothing. With no further business in the town, by mutual agreement, they turned their horses down the road and set a faster pace. Guise's horse threw his head up in protest and snorted, once, letting his rider know that he was not at all happy with the treatment he had endured that day. Lothar simply flowed into a faster pace, a steady trot that he could keep up for hours, if needed.

Night had fallen by the time they reached the tavern on the King's Highway. It was not that far from the junction to Silverton, and brightly lit with torches outside and candles inside. It looked like there was a caravan of merchants stopping there as well.

Yvonne had lost the trails when they joined the King's Highway. Not that surprising, with the amount of traffic. They would need to ride off the highway in the morning to see if she could find the trails again.

"If you see to the horses, I'll get some rooms for us." Guise dismounted from his horse and collected his saddlebags, slinging them over his shoulder.

It was their usual arrangement on the road. Yvonne took the reins of the goblin horse and rode round to the stables. Lothar's ears flicked forward. He had stayed here before and was, by those forward-pointing ears, quite happy to be here again. The goblin horse did not look impressed. It seemed to be his usual expression.

The head groom himself came out to greet her, which she was not at all used to, then she realised he had recognised the goblin horse. Goblins might be tricky to deal with, but those of them that spent any time in the human world tended to pay well. Guise had commented once that it was easier to pay than to fight.

She took her saddlebags and was making her way to the tavern when the trace of something in the air caught her attention. Not the boy. Older. Adult. Male. Possibly Guise's associate.

She hesitated, torn for a moment between going to look for Guise and following the trail. It was so faint she was not sure she could find it again, so she turned to follow it, securing the saddlebag more comfortably across her shoulder as she walked.

A short while later and she was regretting not going to get Guise or, at least, leaving her saddlebags behind. They seemed to have acquired more weight with each step she took, and the ground underneath was rough, giving way occasionally to puddles that she could not see in the dark. It must have rained earlier in the day. And she still hadn't had her boots waterproofed, so her feet were now getting wet.

She was tired, burdened with her travel pack, and had wet feet. She was close to giving up on the trail when it abruptly folded back on itself, coming to rest at a suspiciously rounded piece of ground underneath one of the large trees. She stared at the disturbed earth for a moment, the scene lit only by the faint stars and moon overhead flickering through the trees, and the spell she had murmured on the way here, sending miniature candles around her. She was far enough away from the tavern now that none of the lights and noise had carried here. She was also away from the King's Highway, away from casual passers-by.

"What is it about forests and dead bodies?" she muttered to herself, partly for reassurance and partly to focus herself.

A slight sound behind her was all the warning she had before another voice spoke.

"Well, the forest is quite large, and useful to hide things in."

She had managed not to scream. Not this time, anyway. Guise, unlike anyone else, had the ability to sneak up on her, even when she was paying attention to her surroundings, and seemed to take great delight in doing so. He was several paces away, outside stabbing distance and, she saw with a scowl, had managed to offload his saddlebags before following her into the forest.

"It does not normally take you so long to settle the horses," he explained. "I caught a glimpse of you disappearing into the forest when I came outside." It was possible. Maybe. Perhaps. She had accused him, several times, of having some kind of tracking spell on her. But none of her skills in magic had been able to detect such a spell and her children had reassured her, more than once, that they could not sense any active magic on her, and no goblin magic in particular. He still managed to find her. Whether in this forest, or Fir Tree Crossing, or elsewhere.

It had been a long day and she thought there was more work to do, so she accepted his explanation, for now.

"I don't suppose you brought your own shovel, did you?" she asked, putting her saddlebags down.

"No. But I am sure that the tavern keeper will have at least one. And a pair of grooms willing to earn some extra coin."

"That sounds like an excellent idea," Yvonne said slowly, "except that we don't know, quite, who was buried here, or how they died."

"Indeed. Perhaps you could ..." He waved his fingers in an imitation of the method some human magicians used to cast a spell.

"I don't want to destroy what we might find," she told him, kneeling beside her saddlebags. She had a small shovel in her pack, with a folding handle. A cunning design by one of Elinor's friends, it had come in useful more than once on her travels, including being used as a make-shift club to knock out a would-be thief.

They took it in turns to move the soil off the rounded bit of earth, gradually exposing a cloth-wrapped bundle. Definitely a corpse.

When the bundle was fully exposed to the night air, and Guise had added some of his magic to Yvonne's lights, he carefully peeled back the cloth and made a low sound in his throat. It was, indeed, his associate. Ubel's eyes were still open, glazed over with death, mouth half open in what looked like a final protest. Underneath his open mouth, his throat had been cut.

"A clean, quick cut," Yvonne noted, crouching by the body. "He was not expecting it."

"Killed from behind," Guise observed, crouching at the other side of the body. "Left handed. A long blade."

"Someone he turned his back on. He didn't see a threat. Perhaps someone he knew? Do any of your other associates use a long blade with their left hand?"

Guise gave a muffled laugh. "A few. I do, from time to time."

"You did not do this," she said, staring down at the corpse.

"I am honoured by your faith in me, mristrian."

"It's not really faith. He was hiding from you. He would not have turned his back on you. And there's no trace of you here, before tonight."

"Still," he said, and made a small bow in her direction. It doubtless had some profound meaning among the Karoan'shae. In an unnamed bit of forest next to a corpse, she took it as an expression of gratitude. She did not believe he was a cold-blooded killer. She wondered how he would react if she did voice some of her other suspicions.

They quickly and carefully searched the body, finding nothing. No coin. No papers. Not even a comb, which he had surely had, judging by the long hair around his head. And the barest trace of someone else in Yvonne's senses. Not quite enough for a trail, but she might recognise them again. Definitely not Guise.

By the time they were finished, the scene was disturbed with their footprints and presence. Guise frowned slightly as he looked around.

"The nearest law keepers are a day's ride from here."

"We can't leave him here," Yvonne pointed out, nose wrinkling.

"No," Guise agreed. "Will you wait while I fetch the tavern keeper?"

"Yes." As little as she wanted to stay in the forest with a corpse, there were night predators which would welcome a meal. She also knew that the tavern keeper would believe Guise more readily. Not to mention, she thought as he disappeared into the night, that Guise had a knack for getting people to do his bidding. Which was why she was standing, tired and cold and covered in grave dirt, with wet feet, in a forest rather than enjoying one of the tavern's splendid baths. And no closer to finding the missing children.

Chapter Eleven

Two days later and Yvonne was deeply regretting her decision to remain travelling with Guise. She could have simply demanded payment from him for her service so far and carried on alone, looking for the missing children. Instead, she had agreed to his suggestion that they go on to the last place Ubel had done business before he had travelled to Fir Tree Crossing. They might have found his body, but they had no real clues as to why he had ended up in a shallow grave not far from the King's Highway.

Tired, her skin itching with the need for a bath after dealing with Ubel's corpse, Yvonne had agreed without too much thought. It was only afterwards, when she was soaking in the bath to get rid of the grave dirt, that she realised that Guise had not said where his associate had last been. But it was too late by then, because she had agreed. A Hunar did not go back on their word.

As she had suspected, the omission of the place name was completely deliberate. Which was how she found herself in Three Falls.

It should have been a beautiful place. High in the hills, it was situated at the convergence of three larger rivers that cascaded over cliff faces outside the city, the waterfalls giving the city its name. It should have been a place of fresh, clear air, plentiful running water, lush greenery and splendid architecture.

Instead, it was closer to a cesspit of human desperation and vice.

The city around her was a cacophony of sounds, and a clash to her other senses as well. She was half-deaf with the noise. There were bands of musicians or single performers on street corners, sometimes beautiful, more often out of tune and grating her ears. At least a dozen different languages were spoken. Arguments were taking place in many of the languages. There were also shrieks of laughter, the occasional scream of pain and nervous bleats and whinnies from livestock and horses in the marketplace. An unceasing babble.

Then there were the smells. Scents from every part of the known world. Exotic spices that she could not name. The tantalising scent of fresh bread, reminding her that she had not eaten much that day. The vibrant colours of wealthy merchants, with their hard-eyed mercenaries around them, protecting them from the many pickpockets.

It was a city like no other. And it was a trap for the unwary.

Despite the lingering bite of winter in the air, she had pushed her cloak back off her shoulder so that the mark of the Hunar was clear to anyone who cared to look, and she walked with loose, easy strides, shoulders back and one hand on her weapon. She did not have that much of value to steal, but for some of the thieves in this city even her well-worn knives would be enough to feed them, and their families. She understood the desperation that drove them. And the fear. Fear of reporting back to the gang bosses with nothing to show for the day, with the ever-present threat of violence, or being sold, or taken to one of the beautifully decorated houses that dotted the city, catering for all sorts of tastes.

There were, sadly, too many children bred in the city who did not make it to adulthood. And a lot of tradesmen trapped as well. Not enough money to leave, struggling to make ends meet as it was. It was a hard life for an honest person, far outnumbered by the cheats.

Impossible to stay here for long. Impossible to relax while she was here.

Guise had found them somewhere to stay. As usual. The hotel was one she hadn't seen before, a plain-walled, discreet building that had its own small stables and garden, in a city where land was at a premium. It did not look like much on the outside, and the inside was apparently plain. She was not fooled. Every single item she could see was beautifully made. The plainness was the sort that only the very wealthy could afford. If she had been on her own, without Guise, the hotel owner would have turned her away without a second thought, no matter the Hunar's emblem on her shoulder.

Guise had been greeted with enthusiasm by the hotel owner, the entire hotel placed at his disposal if he wished. Yvonne had tried not to roll her eyes. Only the best for a lord of the Karoan'shae, no matter that he was travelling in disguise, still pretending to be a gentleman of business. He had arranged with the hotel owner that their horses and belongings would be guarded in their absence. Yvonne didn't have much concern. Anyone trying to steal Lothar would find out just how sharp his hooves could be. And anyone trying to go through her saddlebags would find themselves on the receiving end of a nasty shock. Hunar training in magic was extensive and varied.

But no matter how good her training, the press of wants and needs of the people of the city would not let her rest, and she could feel them even within the hotel's walls. And so she had left the hotel, without thinking too clearly about where she wanted to go, just needing to move and to be away from Guise for now, annoyed that she was here.

She hated the city. She hated the cynical trading that went on, not just in livestock and goods, but in people as well. It was no place for an honest person, and no place for a Hunar. Oath-sworn to help those in need. Everywhere she looked she could see people in need. Almost every single person she saw was a potential supplicant. She could spend the rest of her extended life in this place and never run out of supplicants.

She knew that was unlikely, though. It took a great deal of courage to approach a Hunar in a place like this. There were watchers everywhere, and as many people listening. No such thing as an anonymous petition here.

In the middle of the marketplaces and the smells and the sounds and the sights and the press of all the despair and struggle, she picked up something she did not expect. The faintest trace. A trail. Someone she was supposed to follow. A young boy. Alexander. The Cressins' son.

She followed. Along one of the side streets, away from the main marketplaces, a part of the city she had only been in once or twice, and then only with other people around her. Even with the symbol at her shoulder, her weapons and her magic, she still felt vulnerable. There was an itch between her shoulder blades. For a moment she considered going back to see if Guise would come with her. But this was not his task. It was hers. And she was not sure she wanted to speak to him just now, anyway.

She ducked into a side alley and checked that it was clear of any watching eyes or listening ears before rearranging her cloak so that the symbol was hidden, then pulling the hood over her head. The cloak was nothing remarkable. A dull, serviceable fabric. Not wealthy enough to attract attention. Not threadbare enough to look desperate. Just an anonymous traveller, one of many in this city. As well as the gaudy outfits of the merchants, and the armour of their mercenaries, there were a lot of people walking with hoods tugged far forward, hiding their faces. She pulled on gloves, making her truly anonymous.

The alley led, at length, onto a small square surrounded by warehouses. She stopped in the shadows of one of the buildings, sending her senses out with a spell that all Hunar learned early in their training. A few watchers. The cluster of wagons in the square were empty, the oxen harnessed to them dozing.

Hunar also learned to work with shadow and she drew some of it around her, moving within the shelter of the buildings, following the trail to one of the warehouses. The sides of the warehouses were high enough that not much sunlight was getting into the square, leaving it gloomy even in the bright afternoon light.

Sending her senses out into the warehouse, she recoiled against it, hitting her head with a thump that rattled her teeth. It was full of misery. Too many different personalities for her to count, and almost all of them hopeless and lost. A few, dotted around, with a quite different outlook. Angry, bored, with violence held back by a hair's breadth.

The pulse was beating hard and fast in her neck, throat tight and mouth dry. She knew what this was. It was one of the many reasons why she hated the city. Slavery. And the boy's trail led to the warehouse. She could feel him, among the other souls. He was as lost and bewildered as all the other ones.

And then she found something else, another familiar trail. Ubel. Guise's associate had been here, too, before he had been in Silverton. The trail was faint, but she had stood over the man's corpse and had enough to identify him. Ubel had been here. Where slaves were kept.

Before she quite knew what she was doing, she was striding back along the alley, uncaring of who might see her or what they might think.

She made it back to the hotel in about a quarter of the time it had taken her to find the warehouse, careless of watchers. Far from the fear she had felt earlier, she was now angry.

Guise was sitting, apparently at his ease, at a table on his own. He had bundles of letters in front of him and was sorting through each, making notes in a ledger of his own. He looked up as she came into the room. It was the hotel's main dining room, and empty at the moment apart from him. He took one look at her face and gathered all his papers up, shoving them in the satchel and rising to meet her.

"You seem angry, mristrian. What's wrong?"

"I need an advance on my wages," she told him, words clipped off, fury still riding her.

"As you wish. May I ask why?"

"Your dead friend was trading in flesh. A lot of it," she told him. "I found a warehouse full, including one of the children I was looking for."

He went very still. She had never seen a living being go that still before. Not even wulfkin on a hunt. Only his eyes moved, their normal green darkening, tinges of red appearing. Normally it was a warning sign that any healthy person should be backing away, very slowly, and making soothing noises, hoping that the goblin's rage would not come out.

She stood her ground. She was still furious, her heart thumping in her throat and there was a tight knot of fear inside her. There would have been watchers around the warehouse. Her presence would have been noted. The slavers would not know who she had been there to look for, but they would know that somebody had been there and, if they'd followed her, they would have seen the Hunar's symbol on her shoulder.

"Modig." The word was soft, spoken with the quiet calm before the storm.

She was not sure how he had heard it, but the hotel's owner appeared at once. And, with the odd given name, she realised that, like Guise and like his hotel, the owner was not quite what he appeared to be. He looked human. The slight glimmer in his eyes suggested another heritage.

"My lord?"

"I need your funds. All of them. Now."

"Of course, my lord."

It said something for Guise's authority that a hotel owner in Three Falls emptied his safe out for him, without question and without hesitation. Several purses, all of them round and clinking with the unmistakable sound of high-value coins, were brought to him in moments. Moments that Guise used to tidy his satchel, sealing it with a word and spark of magic that hurt Yvonne's senses. Goblin magic and Hunar magic did not get on well together. He was already armed. Goblins did not go anywhere without being armed. Rumour was that they even slept with their weapons. They were not the only ones.

Guise took the pouches of coins as though they weighed nothing and meant less. He tucked them into various pockets around his person, and it said something for his tailor's skill that his coat did not look the least bit burdened.

"Look after this until I return," he said to Modig, handing across the satchel. "Do not open it, and guard it with your life."

"Always, my lord." Modig made another low bow and, when he straightened, Yvonne realised that the not-human part of his heritage was almost certainly goblin. A human–goblin pairing was unusual, to say the least. "Good hunting, my lord."

"Show me," Guise said to Yvonne.

He had surprised her again. She should be getting used to it by now, the fact that she never really understood his motivation or why he did things. But for now, with the possibility of losing the child's trail, she did not question it and did not speak, simply striding out of the hotel and back through the streets of the city. He kept pace with her, shoulder to shoulder, seemingly careless of the fortune he was carrying about his person. No one approached him. In fact, Yvonne saw one of the pickpockets she had spied earlier glance in their direction, turn pale and then run away. Actually run. She looked across at Guise and saw why. His eyes were still tinged red, and there were hints of fang at his mouth.

"You're scaring everyone," she commented in a mild voice, turning down another street. They were getting close.

"Good. They should be scared," he said. "Are we there yet?"

"Along the end of this alley, there is a square. There are warehouses around the square and it is the warehouse on the right-hand side of the square," she told him. "There are guards."

"Good," he said again. "Some exercise would be welcome." He strode ahead.

Yvonne felt her mouth open, and shut it with a snap. That did not sound like the preparation for a business transaction, of buying the boy's freedom, which was what she had intended. It sounded far more like the prelude to war.

She was nearly running to keep up with him as he used his slightly longer stride, and his superior strength, to draw ahead of her. He was not in the least out of breath, perfectly in command of himself, as he walked across the square without hesitation and kicked in the doors of the warehouse. They yielded to that single kick, breaking into pieces that flew into the darker interior.

Yvonne arrived on his heels to see that the inside of the warehouse had been fitted out with a series of cages. All of them were full.

The world spun for a moment, her stomach twisting but not rising as she remembered other cages, in other circumstances, and the feel of badly formed metal against her skin.

Then a shout of anger snapped her back to the here and now, and a half-dozen armed guards surging towards the door, doubtless drawn by the sound of splintering wood.

"Ubel was inside. Before Silverton," Yvonne told Guise.

"You neglected to mention that earlier," he said, voice perfectly calm and controlled.

"I did tell you he was involved," she pointed out, refusing to apologise. "I only mention it now because you may want to leave one alive for questioning." She took a deliberate step back.

"You aren't going to help?" He sounded more amused than anything else. The amusement, and possibly the red tinged eyes, made the guards pause in their tracks, only a few paces away.

"It's barely a fair fight as it is," she told him. And she did not like to fight if she did not have to. Whereas, for goblins, fighting was an art form. "I take it we're not going to buy their freedom?"

"I despise slavery," he said, calmness sliding away into icy fury. "People are not things to be bought and sold."

He had surprised her again.

There was no time for more conversation as the guards were on him, surging forward with their weapons already drawn and ugly expressions on their faces.

Perhaps thinking that a beautifully dressed goblin lord was no match for six of them.

But, as Yvonne had observed, it was barely a fair fight. He probably would not actually class this as a decent workout. Five of the guards were dead within as many heartbeats, and the sixth was pinned to the ground by one of the swords Guise had about his person, the tip of the other one resting just underneath the guard's eye.

"I think he's ready to talk," Guise said. "Why don't you free the children?"

It was only then that Yvonne realised what Guise must have seen as soon as he entered the warehouse. The cages were full, yes. Full of children. Some as young as ten, the oldest perhaps in their late teens. Children. She felt her hands shaking and rage of her own rising up.

She remembered the narrow space left on Ubel's barge, the small gap between the heavy crates and the side of the barge, where living things had been kept. Children. The half dozen horses that Ubel had so carefully recorded in his ledger had been children, sold to slavery.

For a moment she was frozen with rage, wanting to go back along the King's Highway, dig up the corpse and kill him again. However irrational that was. A clean, quick death. One slice of a blade. It was far less than he had deserved.

"Hunar, help us," someone said from the nearest cage, breaking into her fury.

The paralysis lifted at once, the Hunar's magic kicking her in the stomach. She had a task to complete. She searched the guards' bodies and found several sets of keys, going to the nearest cage.

"Tell them to wait for a little bit," Guise said, not looking up from the guard. "I have something to give them."

She gave murmured instructions to the children that she released to go and stand by one of the side doors, away from the sight of blood and whatever it was that Guise was doing to the remaining guard. In the middle of the second cage she found her quarry.

"Alexander," she said. The boy looked at her. Freckles, standing out starkly on a white face that was far too thin, underneath hair that was longer than it should have been, if his mother had anything to say about it, and matted with dirt. "Your parents asked me to find you."

He let out a single, heartfelt sob, clapped his hands over his mouth to hold in any further sound, and tears rolled in silence down his face.

She stepped forward, put her hands gently on his wrists and pulled his hands away from his mouth. "You don't need to be quiet anymore." She looked around the listening children. They were all far too quiet, all wide-eyed, terrified and too thin. And absolutely filthy. "None of you need to be quiet anymore."

Two of the older children stepped forward and held out their hands, asking for sets of keys. Between them they went to open the rest of the cages. Six cages in all, each holding perhaps a dozen children. Far too many. Far too many that nobody in the surrounding area had noticed. Even with children terrified into silence, there was the smell of so many bodies in such a small area with no bathing facilities. The comings and goings of the guards had to have been noticed. And even though the children were thin, they had been fed and given water.

She left the children huddled against the wall, all of them eyeing the door with longing, and told them, again, to wait.

"We are ready," she told Guise, going back towards him.

The guard on the ground was dead. It had been a quick, easy kill and, from the expression on Guise's face, nothing that he had learned had improved his mood.

"Good," he said. "We need to arrange safe passage for them, and distribute this," he said, digging into one of his pockets and producing one of the pouches of coins. "I didn't realise there would be so many, but it's the best I could do at short notice."

He strode forward, towards the children, and a few of them gave muffled cries, backing against the wall.

"You may want to put your sword away," Yvonne commented, going with him. "And calm down a bit."

He sent her a sideways glance, his eyes still tinged with red, and lifted an eyebrow. "I am not calm," he said, words very precise.

"Well, you're scaring them. Could you pretend?"

"That, I can do."

A moment later, the furious goblin was gone, replaced with the polite facade that she was familiar with. There was no red left in his eyes, no hint of fang at his mouth.

The children were still wary, of course. They had seen the red, and the white tips of his fangs.

The sight of coins drew many of them forward, listening intently as he gave them instructions. The older ones should pretend to be guards, with the younger ones hiding in the wagons outside. They would need to be very quiet through the streets. One last time being quiet. Merchant caravans left the city all the time, and at all hours. They could sneak out after dark.

Yvonne saw the determination settling on their faces. No one needed to spell out the dangers for them. Children were vulnerable in Three Falls in ways it did not bear thinking about. And there might be others involved in this set up. The cages, and the guards, suggested a level of organisation. Best for the children if they could escape the city unnoticed.

It was a well-thought-through plan at short notice, Yvonne thought, eyes narrowing in suspicion, particularly when he gave them specific instructions on where to go. A place not that far from here, where friends of his would help them get back to their homes, if that's what they wanted, or find somewhere else to go.

Then he divided the coins up, asking each one their name and where they were from as he gave them their share.

All over. They were from all over. The rumours that she had heard, and shared with Grayling, had not covered the extent of it. So many taken.

And then one of the older ones offered more information. There had been a wagon full of older ones taken away the day before. The people who had collected them hadn't been interested in what they looked like, one of the girls said, just that they stood up straight and seemed strong. Guise and Yvonne exchanged glances, making sure each other had noticed that information, before they sent the children on their way, packed into the wagons that had been waiting in the square, the oxen making no fuss at the change of drivers.

Yvonne watched them go with her jaw clamped shut. One child found. Alexander was tucked among the others, on his way back to his family. One other missing, the impression of Caroline bright inside her. And all those others, far more than she had imagined possible. Gathered together like cattle for market. She wished for a moment that she had joined Guise in fighting the guards earlier, rage coursing through her.

Somewhere, there was a leader. Someone responsible for all of this. And she was going to find them.

Chapter Twelve

As they watched the wagons leave the square, Yvonne had the urge to follow them, make sure they were safe. She was too noticeable, though, even in this city.

She was relieved when Guise said he would follow them. The people of Three Falls were used to seeing goblins, and he had even brought a disguise of sorts, producing a hair tie and hat from his coat pockets. With his hair bound, and hat pulled low, he became just one more well-dressed goblin. He hesitated a moment, glancing at her.

"You don't want me with you," she guessed, mouth twitching into a smile at his expression. "I will be perfectly content to go back to the hotel."

"Thank you," he said gravely, as though she had done him a tremendous service.

"It would have been useful to look around here a bit more, though," she said, walking with him to the side door.

"It will be taken care of," he told her. She believed him.

So it was not really a surprise when, several hours later, Guise came back to the hotel, requested her presence in the dining room, and put several ledgers out onto the table. He did not need to worry about them being overheard. She was not quite sure what he had done, or said, to Modig. She was sure that she had seen at least a few other guests in the hotel earlier in the day, but it was now empty apart from them.

She was freshly bathed with the faintest trace of the flowery perfume in the hotel's soap teasing her nose, the hair at the nape of her neck still slightly damp from the bath, confined to its usual single braid straight down her back.

Looking across at Guise as he settled into a chair, she knew that, outwardly, there was no reason for her to have bothered with her appearance. No matter how much soap she used, and how carefully she braided her hair, she would never match even his most casual appearance. He did not look like someone who had been creeping around the city streets, ensuring the safety of freed slaves. He was dressed with his usual understated elegance, the quality of his clothing evident even in the soft light of the dining room.

"You have not eaten," he commented. "Aren't you hungry?"

She was starving. Her stomach had been making gurgling noises for quite some time. Without even having to look at the menu, she knew that nothing in this restaurant was within her means. Guise had not given her an advance from her wages, and the few coins she had she needed to preserve. He often paid for meals when they travelled together, but she could not take that for granted.

She had been waiting to make sure he was back, and the children were safe, before venturing out again. This was Three Falls, and there were food stalls open virtually the night through in the market places. And she was hungry enough to risk going out again into the press of people.

"Modig," Guise called. He barely raised his voice but, as with earlier in the day, the owner was there in a moment with a shallow bow.

"The bank delivered the replacement funds as you requested, thank you, my lord," Modig said. If he was surprised or relieved by the turn of events, he gave no sign of it. The thank you was sincere but matter-of-fact. "I have your papers safe, whenever you wish."

"Later. For now, I find myself rather hungry, and I am sure the Hunar is, too. You are still doing your tasting menu?"

Yvonne put a hand over her stomach as it made a small, desperate sound. Tasting menus were legendary in this city. It might be corrupt, and she might hate being here, but the food was superb. Apparently, liars, cheats and thieves liked to eat well.

Neither Modig nor Guise paid any attention to her abrupt move, the hotel owner disappearing silently into the depths of the hotel. He was replaced moments later by a pair of waiters, one carrying a tray with a bottle of wine and two glasses, and the other a tray with an array of small savouries that made Yvonne's stomach gurgle again.

"The menu here is superb," Guise told her casually, pushing one of the dishes of savouries across to her. "You will want to give it most of your attention."

She bit her lip to hide a smile. They were worlds apart in their upbringing and life experiences.

Instead of answering him directly, she took the topmost ledger from the pile he had put on the table, and began reading.

If she were not so hungry she might have lost her appetite, despite the promise of a tasting menu. The ledger went back months, recording a series of apparently innocuous transactions. Horses. Cattle. Pigs, of various varieties. Sheep. Not one single mention of humans, or any of the other races. And yet the prices were oddly consistent across the different breeds of animal.

"There's some code here," she commented after a while. Guise had another one of the ledgers open in front of him.

"Yes. I think horses must be the younger children," he said, lip curling and showing a glimpse of white teeth for a moment. No fangs. Not now. "They are the highest price."

"There were horses on Ubel's ledger," she remembered.

"Yes." There was fury in his voice. Not directed at her. He lifted his eyes a moment, red pinpricks visible. "No wonder he was hiding from me."

"Too quick a death," she agreed.

"Much too quick." He smiled, fangs very white against his skin, then turned his attention back to the ledger.

She took a hasty sip of wine, not wanting to think about that, and was distracted for a moment. Another superb vintage, and another bottle the cost of which would keep her family fed for the better part of the year.

"Did they get away?" She thought to ask him, finally. She had assumed so, from his return.

"Yes. All of them are out of the city. My friends will see the boy safely home to his parents."

Her ears snagged on that word again. Friends. She had, for some reason, not expected Guise to have friends. Associates, yes. He had those aplenty. Business transactions. People that were useful to him, but friends? That was something rare.

There was no more time for talk as the waiters returned, bearing what looked like an entire month's worth of food, the scents curling through Yvonne and making her mouth water even before she had set eyes on the dishes.

Guise cleared the table with swift, casual movements, tucking the ledgers into another satchel he had brought with him.

By the time he had tidied up, the table was covered with dishes, most of which Yvonne had difficulty identifying. There was fish, and chicken, and some kind of roasted meat with an aroma that drew her full attention from anything else.

"If you will allow me?" Guise said. She nodded, and moments later was presented with a plate with about half a dozen different foods on it.

"This is just the first course," he told her. "Have as much as you like."

The one area where they were equal, Yvonne had noticed before, with much inner amusement, was in their table manners. She might be from a humble background, but her mother in particular had insisted on good table manners. Her knuckles ached for a moment in memory of that wooden rod being brought down with force as she made yet another mistake. The echo faded, chased away by the tantalising scents, the manners she had learned standing her in good stead now, settled across from a member of the Karoan'shae.

If the first course had been mouth-watering and delicious, the second was finer still. She did not think that her stomach could take any more, and found herself in the extraordinary position of turning down food as she was offered a second helping.

Apparently, there was also a dessert course, the thought of which made her groan. She loved desserts.

"They will package the leftovers up for us, if we want," Guise said. "They have access to some decent preservation spells. Perhaps your children would like some?"

Yvonne tilted her head, considering the offer. It was generous, and out of character. In their business dealings, Guise was usually direct.

"If I was given leftovers, I'm not sure that they would survive to reach my children," she told him with a smile.

"Probably just as well. I doubt that they would appreciate the kitchen's work as it should be enjoyed." Guise turned and gave some low-voiced instructions to the waiters, who cleared the table with the same silent efficiency as they had set the course.

"I'd still like to go back to the warehouse," Yvonne said. "I'm sure we've missed something."

Now that she was completely full of food, clean and pleasantly relaxed with half a glass of wine inside her, she had the nagging feeling that she had missed something. Something important.

"We can go back there tomorrow. I want to see if we can trace that other wagon," Guise said. He must have seen the surprise on her face. "It may not have been in your ledger, but it is clear from the one I was looking at that several wagons have been sent already. Many of the sales were of individuals, to individuals. But it seems there was more than one wagon sold to the same buyer, and they always wanted the older children."

"The ones who are strong," Yvonne commented, feeling the food inside her churn a little.

"Matters for tomorrow," Guise said firmly. "Today's children are safely away. If you will excuse me, I have matters to attend to." He rose to his feet, inclined his head with the manners ingrained in him, and left.

As he left, Yvonne realised that she was warm, fully fed and safe, and with nothing to do and no demands on her time. The children were safe, as Guise had said. Her limbs were weighted, pleasantly tired. There was also a bed upstairs for her use, and it seemed like an excellent idea to see just how comfortable it was.

By the time they got back to the scene the next day, fuelled by what Modig had termed a casual breakfast but which rivalled the meal from the night before in variety and taste, the warehouse had been completely emptied. It was frustrating, but neither of them were surprised. Whoever had done the cleaning had done a reasonably thorough job, removing the cages, and making a cursory effort to sweep the floor, replacing the shattered doors. They had not managed to get rid of the smell, though, and Yvonne's nose wrinkled as she walked with Guise through the large, empty space.

"This had not been their base for long," she commented, rubbing a toe along one of the marks on the floor. The cages had simply been set on the floor, weighted down and pinned at each corner. A more permanent arrangement would have been more secure. "How long ago do we think Ubel was here?"

Guise tilted his head, considering. "I lost track of him maybe ten days ago. So perhaps around then?"

"Not as long, I think," Yvonne said, her eyes on the scuff marks. Barely worn. Ten days at the absolute most. She opened her mouth to ask Guise how he had been keeping track of his associate, but he had other things on his mind.

"They would not want to stay in one place for long. Slavery is illegal, even here," Guise commented, lip curling in disgust.

"If there's anyone to enforce it," Yvonne countered. She suspected there might well be law keepers somewhere in the city. She had never seen them, or any evidence that crimes were, in fact, punished. With such liberal laws as the city had, she was not sure how busy a law keeper would be.

"There isn't," Guise acknowledged. "The city does have some official law keepers, but they are poorly paid and vulnerable to incentives." It sounded to Yvonne like he had personal experience of delivering those incentives. She did not enquire further.

"Those ledgers were vast. More than ten days old. There was somewhere before this. And they probably have somewhere else set up again." Disgust was fast being replaced by anger. She remembered the sea of faces from the day before, behind bars. Small children, utterly bewildered and terrified. Older children, who may have had a good idea of what could happen to them when they were taken out of the cages. None of them deserved it.

And they had been gathered from so many different places. This was not a simple kidnapping operation, taking targets of opportunity. This was organised and planned. Widespread, with surprisingly few rumours about it, from the little she had heard. And that meant that there was a mastermind somewhere. Someone had put this plan in motion. Someone was deliberately, systematically, cynically gathering in children and young people and selling them on. Slavery might be technically illegal in this city, but it was lawful in other places and, once sold, slaves were usually subject to such harsh treatment that they did not speak out against their owners, even when a Hunar asked them if they were all right.

She could not breathe for a moment, throat tightening, memories rising to the surface. She had far too many bad memories.

"The handwriting on the ledgers belongs to three different people," Guise said unexpectedly. He was standing more or less in the centre of the warehouse, hands folded behind him as he looked around, a shaft of sunlight from a gap in the roof overhead catching his hair, turning it to shimmering obsidian. Today's coat was the same deep blue greatcoat that Mariah had mended, she noted.

"It's unlikely that they would hire clerks in for the work," Yvonne said, catching the line of his thinking. She thought back to the ledger she had reviewed the day before. The writing had been uneven, with the occasional spelling mistake. Mistakes that a clerk would not make. She had seen many merchants' ledgers properly prepared, with the handwriting perfectly even and not one mistake or smudge on pages and pages of detailed notes. "Not a trained clerk. Someone educated, though, and used to writing."

"I agree."

Most people in the city were virtually illiterate. They did not need to read and write to go about their daily lives. Even quite a few of the mercenaries could not read or write. Yvonne frowned, trying to think of what sort of person might keep the ledgers for a slave trading operation. Even in this city, there might be some punishment if they were caught, and punishment tended to be severe.

"Do we inspect all the warehouses in the city and look for people going in and out with ink on their fingers?" she speculated. It was not the most ridiculous idea that she had thought of.

"That will take a long time," Guise said. He was not dismissing the idea, though. In a city this big, and with limited information available, it would take a long time no matter how they managed their search.

A soft sound outside the warehouse drew their attention.

"Or, we can wait for someone to turn up here, and question them," Yvonne said, voice as soft as she could make it. They had left their horses at the hotel, so there was no sign outside the building that it was occupied.

Moving as silently as she could, she followed Guise to the wall nearest the sound, and held her breath for a moment as someone fiddled with the lock of the door before opening it, stepping quickly inside from daylight to the comparative gloom of the warehouse's interior, and shutting the door behind them.

Guise was on the newcomer before they could take a step into the building, pushing them back against the wall, one hand over their mouth to stop them from crying out.

The newcomer wriggled and let out a muffled squeal that drew Yvonne's sharp attention. For some reason, she had not expected there to be any women involved in the operation. She was annoyed with herself immediately for that assumption.

Guise, who had surely been brought up to treat women with respect in the Karoan'shae, apparently had no difficulty in forgetting his manners when it came to somebody potentially involved in slavery. There was a red tinge to his eyes, again, and the faintest tips of fangs showing at his mouth.

The woman that he had held up against the wall was wide-eyed, face pale. She had also stopped struggling, completely still underneath his hand across her mouth.

"I'm going to take my hand away. You're going to be silent. Then you are going to answer our questions. Fully, completely and quickly. Do you understand?"

The woman nodded her head, as much as she was able to under Guise's grip.

"A moment," Yvonne requested, and said a quick spell, sending a shower of white sparks into the air around them. The woman's eyes grew wider still. "We won't be overheard within the spell, but we can still hear other sounds," she told Guise.

"Good." He measured the extent of the white sparks before he released the woman.

"They made me do it," she said in a high, rapid voice. "I didn't want to. They made me. I just kept the books."

Guise and Yvonne exchanged glances. One of the clerks who had recorded the goods and sales so meticulously in the ledgers.

"What's your name?" Yvonne asked. Guise would not care, but it would help settle the woman.

"Rebecca," the woman answered, voice steadying a fraction. "Rebecca of Hogsmarthen."

Yvonne's eyes narrowed. Hogsmarthen was known for its law-abiding citizens, and its utter disgust of slavery.

"How did you come to be here?" Guise asked, clearly thinking along the same lines as Yvonne.

"I came looking for my brother," she said, a catch in her voice. "They said they would let him go. If I paid off his price by working for them. Too old for one of the brothels, they said. But I can read and write, so they made me do this," Rebecca's voice was choked and bitter by the time she finished, and her eyes travelled around the room. "They didn't tell me they were moving, though."

"They didn't know they were moving," Guise told her, a hint of satisfaction in his voice.

"Where is your brother?" Yvonne asked. The woman was, she thought, somewhere in her late twenties, possibly early thirties. That meant her brother was likely a few years younger. Too old to be one of the children that they had seen in the slave pens here, and very few slave owners had much use for mature men. They preferred them young, while they were still vulnerable.

"He's not here," Rebecca said, voice full of pain and frustration. "It was months before they told me. But by then, I knew too much. They weren't going to let me go. Said I was too useful for them."

"You keep saying they," Guise said. "We need descriptions."

"I can't," she said, shaking her head, her eyes going wide with fear again. "They'll kill me."

"Rebecca," Yvonne said, voice firm, "they didn't tell you they had moved. You turned up here for work as normal. They don't care about you anymore. If you go and find them again, you're probably dead anyway. Tell us what we need to know, and we can get you out of the city."

"And what about my brother?"

"I will help him if I can. If you ask me to," Yvonne said, feeling the weight of more expectation on her shoulders. There was another missing girl to find. And she wanted to find the people behind this slave trade as much as Guise did.

"I think he might be dead," Rebecca said, her voice catching. "I looked for him, when I had some free time. No one has seen him. Nobody knew his name, or where he might be."

"Tell him what he wants to know," Yvonne said, tilting her head to Guise, "and then tell me about your brother."

Rebecca drew a breath and her shoulders eased back, strain lifting from her face. It made her look younger, all at once, and Yvonne wondered if her estimate of age had been off. Grief and strain could add years to someone's appearance.

"You are Hunar," Rebecca said, voice cracking. "I thought they were just legends." She stared at the Firebird's symbol, biting her lip, before a question rushed out of her, words tumbling over each other. "Is it true that the first Hunar died to save the world by killing his own brother?"

"So the legends tell us," Yvonne answered. It was the story told to children. That the first Hunar, and his hundred followers, had battled his brother, and that they had both died, the first Hunar's followers forming the Hundred in his name. Like all good stories, there was some truth in it.

"I thought it was all just stories," Rebecca said, voice shaking.

"The Hundred are quite real," Guise said, shifting his weight slightly to draw Rebecca's attention, "and you will have the Hunar's full attention when you have told me what I need to know."

Once the original shock and strain had worn off, Rebecca proved highly informative. She had a quick mind to go with a keen eye, and was able to give descriptions of everyone she had interacted with in the slave trading operation, her descriptions carrying enough emotion that Yvonne was able to pick up faint traces to follow from her words, and her reactions. She was also able to tell them which warehouses around the city had already been used to house the cages, and give them three options for the next place that she had overheard being discussed.

It was only when Guise commented how much she knew about the operation that she stopped talking, going chalk white, her eyes wide again. Yvonne thought that was probably the first time she had really, truly realised just how deeply embedded she had become. She knew far too much. The slavers had been over-confident in their hold on her, that she would be too frightened to say anything against them. But then, Yvonne thought, the slavers probably believed Hunar were legends as well, and the last thing anyone would expect would be a lord of the Karoan'shae working with a Hunar.

Once Guise was satisfied he had extracted all the information he could, Yvonne asked about her brother. She had to wait some time while Rebecca cried, partly relief from stress and partly the knowledge that her brother may be long dead, or not even in the city.

When Rebecca had given them all the information she had, Yvonne's head was spinning with the new information and new traces that she would be able to follow. The brother's strongest of all, of course, because Rebecca knew him best.

Questioning over, they took Rebecca back to the small room she had rented, waited while she packed her belongings into a small bag, and then took her back to the hotel. Guise explained, at Yvonne's lifted brow, that he couldn't guarantee her safe passage from the city just now. And Modig would look after her.

With the clerk safely stowed away, Guise decided that they should go looking for the slavers. It was an insane idea, but one Yvonne agreed with.

Chapter Thirteen

The new operation was at the second warehouse on Rebecca's list. There were a few watchers scattered in the alleyways and at the corners of nearby buildings. Not very well trained, or well armed. Yvonne kept watch while Guise took care of them, slightly surprised when he simply disabled most of them, leaving them securely tied in places where no one would think to look. It was a potent message, though. He managed to disable the entire set of watchers without raising the alarm, or needing to kill any of them.

They paused in the shadows of the alleyway closest to the warehouse. There were guards outside the doors this time. Inside the building, Yvonne could sense a dozen or so terrified people and perhaps another dozen guards.

"I think we made an impression yesterday," she said to him. "There are at least a dozen guards inside. And about a dozen new slaves."

"They are replacing their stock very quickly," Guise commented. She glanced across and saw that the red tint was back in his eyes, and white tips of fangs were showing at his lips. His voice might be casual, almost bored, but it was a complete lie.

"The children yesterday were from all over the lands," Yvonne said, stomach twisting. "They must have a supply line of some kind."

"We'll see to that," Guise said.

She watched as he simply walked out of the alleyway, heading towards the doors. It would not be long before the guards discovered that the watchers were not there anymore. Guise had clearly decided that he had had enough of skulking around alleyways. Or perhaps he was concerned about the damage it would do to his coat, Yvonne thought, following him. The alleyways were filthy.

The pair of guards outside the door of the warehouse reached for their weapons as soon as they saw him coming towards them. There was nothing very threatening about Guise at the moment. He did not have a weapon in his hands, he was simply walking with brisk, clipped strides. But Yvonne had seen the red in his eyes and suspected the guards could, too.

They made the mistake of attacking him together, both at once, neither of them holding back. He blocked the first attack with a casual swipe of his arm, the guard's club connecting with Guise's forearm with a thump that made Yvonne wince in sympathy. The blow would have shattered her arm. It did not seem to have any impact on Guise. He tore the club out of the guard's hands and used it to deliver a sharp blow to the first guard's skull before turning, in one smooth movement, to the other guard. Both were on the ground, unconscious or dead, in moments.

"As I recall, you can conjure fireballs," Guise said, eyeing the wooden doors of the warehouse.

Yvonne choked on an unexpected laugh, then dug in her belt pouch for the necessary spell, wrapped it around a pebble from the ground and threw it, igniting the spell with a word as it struck the doors.

The wooden doors exploded into flame. Magic fire burned hotter than normal fire. The doors would be ash in moments.

Guise did not wait for the fire to die down, going into the building through a ring of flame as the doors burned. There were cries of alarm inside, and a few screams.

Yvonne followed him in, her weapons ready, and found that the warehouse was almost identically laid out to the one they had seen the day before with a series of cages around the warehouse floor, only two of which had any occupants. And there were the dozen guards that she had sensed from outside. They were a little better trained than the ones they had encountered outside, or at least a little more wary, having the sense to approach Guise in ones and twos rather than rushing him all at once.

Yvonne knew that there was not much she could do, and she did not want to get in his way. So she stayed near the doors, watching as he cut through the first four or five guards, barely pausing for breath. The rest grew more cautious, holding back. Guise had no intention of letting them get away, though, and paced forward.

Movement at the corner of her eye was her only warning and she cried out as a shadow detached itself from the wall at the other side of the building, raising a weapon which her eyes did not make sense of at first. It was only when an arrow flew through the air that she realised it was a bow and arrow, her heart missing a beat. An efficient and deadly weapon, and one of the few that were effective against goblins. Close quarter combat tended to be lethal for the attacker.

Guise made a low, grunting sound as the arrow struck home. Yvonne was already moving forward, towards the archer, speaking a fire spell as she moved, that caught the next two arrows that flew from the archer's bow towards her. And then she was on the archer, catching the bow with one of her blades, ripping it out of the archer's hands.

She had a moment to register that the archer was dressed head to toe in black, with a black wrap around their face, and then she was committed to the attack.

The archer was quick. Much quicker than the other guards. A raised arm blocked the flat of Yvonne's blade with the sound of steel against armour. Armour under dark clothing that she now saw was loose around the archer's body. Then the archer wriggled away, tumbling backwards in a graceful, coordinated move, before running for one of the doors at the side of the warehouse. The bow was still there, apparently carelessly discarded.

There was no time to look at that, or to follow the archer. Guise had been hit and, even for a goblin, an arrow strike was dangerous.

She turned back to the fight to find that there were three guards left. All the others were dead. The three that were left were wiser, coordinating their efforts, spread out around Guise, trying to tire him out. He was down to one weapon now, the arrow sticking out of his shoulder, and that arm hanging uselessly by his side. He was still deadly.

Yvonne bent and picked up one of the clubs discarded by the fallen guards and swung it, as hard as she could, at the head of one of Guise's attackers. He fell with almost no sound, drawing the attention of the other two. The moment's distraction was all Guise needed to kill one of the remaining pair, arterial spray from his throat spreading far and wide.

That left one remaining guard, and both Yvonne and Guise to deal with him.

The guard looked between Guise and Yvonne, face pale, and then clearly decided that Yvonne was the weaker target, approaching her with his blade up. She might not be as deadly as Guise. Very few people were. Still, Hunar were trained to stand against attackers and she had him disarmed and unconscious on the ground moments later.

"It's not like you to leave me the last one," she commented to Guise, trying to ignore the liberal splatters of blood.

"Damned assassins," he answered her. He did not sound himself. Turning, she saw that he was leaning against the wall of the warehouse, his skin paler than normal, eyes dull. The arrow was still in his shoulder, black fletched end rippling as he breathed. Too fast and too hard for the fight that they had been in.

"Poison?" Putting her weapons away, she moved towards him, held off by a slight shake of his head, and nod behind her. The cages.

Trusting that he would keep breathing while she rescued the slaves, she got the cages open and the slaves out. They were not quite as worn out as the ones from the day before. A fresh batch.

She had no coins to give them, but she sent them off in the wagon parked outside with the directions and instructions that Guise had given the children from the other warehouse.

She came back to him to find him watching her with a slightly surprised expression.

"I had no idea you paid so much attention to me," he commented, trying to keep his voice light. It was not working. He was paler than he had been and she could hear each breath.

"When it comes to rescuing children and others from slavery, I pay very close attention," she told him. "I suppose you'd like me to look at that wound?"

"Just like old times," he answered.

"Mariah's sewing skills are far better than mine. I can't fix your coat."

"The arrow needs to come out," he said, grimacing, "and before too long. Whatever is in this is strong."

It took some persuading, but she got him to sit on the warehouse's floor, back against the wall, before drawing a small, very sharp knife from her boot. Digging arrows out of bodies was also part of a Hunar's training.

She had rarely had a patient as compliant as Guise, though. He stayed as still as he possibly could, flinching only when she, very carefully, began to pull the arrow out and the barbs on the arrowhead dug further into his flesh.

With the arrow out, she pulled clean cloths from a bag at her waist and a small jar of salve, plastering the salve on the open wound before packing the cloth into the wound, beneath his shirt and coat, murmuring a quick spell to keep the cloth in place.

Luckily, with the arrow blocking the wound, he had not bled that much and she was able to disguise the hole in his coat, more or less, by teasing the ends of the fabric together. It would not pass close inspection, but would hopefully get them back to the hotel.

"We need to leave," he said. "It's going to take some time for me to heal, and we have created quite a noise."

"Understatement," she answered. She looked at the arrow again. An assassin's tool, as Guise had said.

It looked like one of the tools used by the Abar al Endell assassins. A desert people, they had access to all manner of exotic poisons not normally found in this part of the world.

"I don't think the assassin was working with the slaveowners," she told Guise. "Looked like he was here for you." She tilted her head, remembering the loose clothing, and trying to feel if she had a trace of the assassin. It was almost familiar. "I think he might have been the one to kill Ubel," she speculated aloud. Although the body disposal had been careless, easily found.

"She," Guise answered with a grunt as he sat forward and got to his feet, carefully and much more slowly than normal. He was also moving with none of his usual grace. Almost like a human. "And, yes, she might well have killed Ubel. Left him for me to find. It would be very like her."

"You know her?" Yvonne asked, and then bit her lip. Of course he knew an assassin. He probably counted several as associates. Guise's business dealings took him to all sorts of areas, and it was hardly surprising that he would have drawn the attention of an Abar al Endell assassin.

"From a long time ago."

"Nice of her to keep in touch." Her mouth ran ahead of her mind. Not for the first time.

His mouth twitched in what looked like the beginning of a smile.

Yvonne clamped her lips shut, going with him to the door of the warehouse. They were in luck. The carnage in the warehouse, and the escape of the children, had not yet been noticed.

By mutual agreement, they left the warehouse as silently and quickly as possible, keeping their pace brisk and business-like.

They arrived back at the hotel to find Rebecca in a panic, Modig physically barring her way out of the hotel. She had become convinced that they were going to lead the slavers to her, for some reason.

Modig's eyes widened as he looked at Guise, paler than normal and swaying on his feet now that they were away from the watching eyes on the streets. The hotel owner shoved his patron into the nearest chair, sending one of the servants for a healer, before issuing more orders for their rooms to be cleared and their horses readied, including an extra one for Rebecca.

Yvonne did not blame Modig for wanting them gone. He had to live here and, however powerful Guise was, he would not be able to protect the hotel owner forever.

The healer turned out to be a mostly competent, although extremely drunk, human male who looked like he was elderly but who, she suspected, was actually barely older than her, and aged early by the amount of alcohol he had consumed.

Despite his trembling hands and the smell from his breath, he managed to draw some of the poison out of Guise's shoulder and re-bandage it.

By the time that was done, their bags were packed and the horses were ready. Modig was unable to stand still, moving from foot to foot. Worried by their presence, Yvonne thought. Or perhaps he was worried about Guise, who was paler than she had ever seen him, held upright and conscious by will alone at this point. A knot of worry formed in her stomach. Goblins were hard to kill, but they could be killed.

Modig insisted that Yvonne should go to an address in Kelton. Her brows lifted in surprise. Kelton was a thoroughly cosmopolitan place, full of artists and master craftsmen and women, welcoming anyone within its limits. Not the sort of place you would expect a part-bred goblin to send a wounded lord of the Karoan'shae.

Still, it was a plan, and for some reason she trusted Modig, wondering again what connection he had to Guise, and what they would find at the address he had given them.

Chapter Fourteen

Kelton was just as Yvonne remembered it. Despite the circumstances, she could feel a smile tugging her mouth as they rode past the outer limits of the town. The air was full of a rich mix of scents. Spices from afar, common herbs that were grown anywhere and expensive perfumes that were made here. The population was just as varied as in Three Falls though everything here moved at a softer, gentler pace.

Modig's directions took her to a large property on the edge of the town, an unusual sight even in this varied town. A desert dwelling, with the property surrounded by a high wall into which several ornate gates had been set, giving a glimpse of lush gardens beyond. In the middle of the gardens was a two-storey building that, she knew, would be a series of rooms set around a central courtyard. There would be a fountain in the courtyard, and many of the walls would be decorated with exotic and beautiful ceramic tiles. They were not far enough south to make this sort of dwelling commonplace, and it stood out among its more ordinary neighbours. Her curiosity spiked, wondering who lived here and why Modig had sent her here, with Guise injured.

His condition had worsened over the ride, to the point where she and Rebecca had to take turns in watching him carefully in case he slid off his horse. He had only done that once, landing on the packed earth road with a thump that made Yvonne wince in sympathy. He had barely felt it, despite the fact that he landed on his injured shoulder. He was only half-conscious now and mostly unresponsive. On her own, Yvonne would have stopped at least for a night and tried a healing spell. But Rebecca was terrified of the slavers catching up with them, so they had stopped only a few times for short breaks, pressing on to the address Modig had supplied.

Yvonne slid off Lothar near one of the gates, not sure whether she or the horse was more relieved. It had been an exhausting journey. There was a beautifully made bell hanging by the gate. She rang it once and waited.

Moments later, a small group appeared from the central building. A man and a woman at the front, another, younger woman behind them. Yvonne blinked in surprise. The trio might be dressed in the loose, flowing garments of the desert people, but they were goblins. A family, she thought.

As they drew closer, she could see that they were not just goblins, but high caste goblins. They had the slightly paler skin and more refined features she associated with the Karoan'shae. And all of them were armed.

"Hunar," the first woman said, surprise in her voice. "What brings you ..." Her eyes travelled past Yvonne to the two people still on their horses. "Guise."

"He is injured. A poisoned arrow two days ago. We were in Three Falls and Modig sent us here." The words came out in a rush. Goblins and Hunar did not normally mix. "This is Rebecca," Yvonne added, "she was forced to work for slavers."

It was a terrible introduction, as introductions went, but the trio in front of her accepted it without a blink, the man opening the gate and the older woman coming forward, taking the reins of Guise's horse.

"I am Brea, this is my husband, Thort, and our daughter, Jesset. You are welcome in our home. Come in, come in, all of you. Jesset will take the horses. Thort, take Guise up to the blue room. Hunar, would you and Rebecca like to sit in the courtyard for a bit, while we make Guise comfortable? Jesset will bring you some refreshments when the horses are settled."

Yvonne was not used to being organised, let alone in so competent a fashion. Brea did not raise her voice, or exude any air of authority or command. She was simply calm and utterly in control.

It was not long before Yvonne and Rebecca were settled on wrought iron chairs in the courtyard in the centre of the building, iron offset by brightly coloured cushions. It did, indeed, have a fountain and the painted ceramic tiles on the walls around them were among the finest she had ever seen.

"What kind of building is this?" Rebecca asked. "I've never seen anything like it."

"It's designed to cope with the desert heat," Yvonne told her. "It's very common in the southern reaches. Very few are as fine as this, though."

"My parents would be delighted to hear you say so," Jesset said, coming into the courtyard on silent feet. She was carrying a large tray, laden with what looked like a glass teapot, small cups, and enough food to feed all of them. She set it down on the larger of the low, iron tables. "Our neighbours think we are mad," she added with a slight smile, looking around, "but Mama met Papa in the desert, and she has always wanted a home like this."

"It's beautiful," Rebecca said. "Did you live in the desert?"

"Not me," Jesset answered, her face closing slightly. There was definitely some story there, Yvonne thought. "Come, Mama would be annoyed with me if you did not take some refreshment. The tea can be an acquired taste, so if it's not to your liking, I can make ordinary tea instead."

"Liquorice tea," Yvonne told Rebecca, identifying it from its scent. "I would be very happy with plain water," she told Jesset.

Jesset's face split into an unexpected grin. "It really isn't to everyone's tastes," she answered. "If you wait, I'll make some ordinary tea. Rebecca, if you want to try some, please do."

Rebecca's face, when she took a sip of liquorice tea, was enough to make Yvonne choke on a laugh.

"What is this?" Rebecca said, nose wrinkling.

"Liquorice," Yvonne reminded her. "It is a highly prized tea. In some desert cultures, it is a deadly insult to refuse it, and it is generally only brought out for the most honoured guests."

"But we do not take offence if you do not like it," Brea said, coming into the courtyard on feet as silent as her daughter's. "I don't know why Jesset just made you the liquorice tea. We usually offer our guests more choice," she said, frowning as she saw the tray.

"She is making ordinary, as well," Yvonne said.

Brea still seemed dissatisfied but didn't say anything more about it, settling into a nearby bench.

"A nasty wound," she commented to Yvonne. "Although the arrow was expertly cut out. Thort is making Guise comfortable just now, and giving something to help him sleep. He won't be up today."

"The healer in Three Falls said he needed rest," Yvonne commented.

"That drunken sot," Brea dismissed the healer with the wave of her hand, glancing across as her daughter came back into the courtyard with another tray with a more ordinary teapot and mugs and, Yvonne was relieved to see, a milk jug. She had never acquired the taste for black tea.

"Did you see who shot him?" Brea asked, not even pretending that the question was a casual one.

"An assassin from Abar al Endell. Her face was hidden, but Guise knew her."

"Oh. Her." Brea's lips thinned. "Yes. That would fit."

Yvonne hesitated, but decided Brea needed the information. "It is possible she also killed one of Guise's associates. A merchant called Ubel."

"That one." Brea's lips tightened into a thin line for a moment, fine lines spreading around her face that told Yvonne she was far older than she had first appeared. "Nothing but trouble. Both of them." She shook her head slightly, and rose to her feet again. "If you will excuse me, I need to add some precautions."

"An assassin?" Rebecca said, eyes wide. "Really? One of the desert killers?"

"Assassins," Yvonne corrected absently, curiosity spiked by Brea's reaction. It seemed that Guise wasn't the only one who knew the assassin. Or Ubel.

"Aren't they killers?" Rebecca asked, curious.

Yvonne laughed softly, turning her attention back to Rebecca and seeing that Jesset was just as interested. "Yes, some would call them so. But anyone can kill, with a weapon or some luck. Abar al Endell assassins train for years before they can call themselves such."

"A school for assassins?" Rebecca's eyes were wide again.

"Indeed."

Before Yvonne could say more, Brea was back, looking as unruffled as she had before, settling with her guests and joined moments later by Thort who simply said that Guise was sleeping and comfortable. The calm competence with which they had dealt with their unexpected guests suggested this wasn't the first time Guise had turned up wounded.

Yvonne looked at the surface of her tea, the steam lazily curling up, and sent out a wish that the friends Guise had sent the slaves to were even half as competent as Brea and Thort. The children would be in safe hands.

Brea and Thort were excellent hosts, making sure that their guests had plenty of tea and refreshments. Even with the addition of three people to their house, the whole atmosphere remained serene, Thort going so far as to promise Yvonne and Rebecca a feast to remember that evening.

As they sat in the quiet courtyard, listening to the sound of water in the fountain, exchanging idle conversation, Yvonne found herself going restless. It was a nagging sensation, like something she had noticed, or something she had forgotten to do. Something she had missed. It became increasingly difficult to sit still.

Before her hosts could notice, she sat forward.

"My children are particularly fond of some of the confectionery made here," she told Brea and Thort. "If you would not think me very rude, I should like to see if I can find some to take home."

It would take almost all her remaining coins to get the treats for Mariah and Joel, but she had a strong conviction that she needed to be out of this house, and somewhere else within the town.

Brea and Thort exchanged glances that she could not interpret, but the response was perfectly polite, encouraging her to go.

As she rose, they promised to look after Rebecca, who did not look like she wanted to move ever again.

"You may find some things have changed in the town since you were last here," Brea added. She shook her head and would not say anything more when Yvonne lifted a brow.

Yvonne checked her weapons as she left the house. A Hunar, skilled in magic and weapons. And in Kelton, a place of peace and beauty. She wondered what she might find that had changed so much.

Chapter Fifteen

Yvonne left the house on foot, leaving Lothar to the comfort of the stables. After the fast-paced journey to get here, with Guise so ill and Rebecca doing what she could but clearly not used to hard, rapid travel, it was good to be on her own, moving at her own pace, and somewhere familiar, even though she had never lived here.

After the first relief of moving, her unease crept back again, growing the further she moved among the buildings. Something was not right here. Something she had not consciously noticed on the way through, too intent on keeping Rebecca safe and getting Guise to their destination.

She let her feet go where they would, trailing through well-kept streets, exchanging polite greetings from time to time with people out and about. This had always been a friendly place, welcoming of newcomers, tolerant of all races. The atmosphere of the town seemed the same, and not. There were a few uneasy glances at her weapons, and eyes sliding away from the Hunar's symbol, which she did not remember from her previous visits.

And then, after she had been walking for a while and not really identified the source of her unease, something else rippled across her senses. A trace. Someone that she had been asked to look for. The herbalist's daughter. Caroline.

Recognition of that trace stopped her in her tracks, in the middle of the street. The person behind her had to take a swift sideways step to move around her. She murmured an apology, and waved off the woman's concern. Alone again, she stood under the overhang of a trade building of some kind, trying to work out if she had just imagined it or if the daughter was, indeed, within range of her senses.

There. The faintest trace. Caroline had been here.

Puzzled, and bearing Brea's warning in mind, she set off to follow the trail. Once again, the peculiar magic that she carried in her took her the right way along the trail, tracing it from oldest to newest.

She had been in the centre of the town, where various trades and crafts were carried out, shop fronts displaying as wide a range of goods as in any city across the lands. As she followed the trail, she moved out of the centre towards the old trading district, when the town had been known for its animal market. It led her past the old market itself, now transformed into a cleverly designed public garden surrounded by modest, prosperous homes, each with their own small garden.

The houses all seemed empty, which surprised her. The last time she had been here, the houses had been full and there had been children playing in the public garden. Now the windows of the houses were blank, the garden empty. And her skin was prickling with unease.

Beyond the old market was the edge of the town, the final set of buildings an old stable block before lush grass plains stretched as far as her eyes could see.

The stables were built in the traditional way, of red brick, formed in a large rectangle around an open yard in the middle, and entrances to either side of the long arms of the rectangle. Caroline's trace led there.

As she took another step towards the stables, moving out of the boundary of the public garden, her body seized, an all-too-familiar ripple coursing over her. Magic residue. Wulfkin. The kind of residue created when a group of them congregated. It had a savage edge to it, a wildness that Sephenamin would not have tolerated. The edge brought old, unwanted memories to the surface and she had to shake her head to clear it. That many wulfkin, creating that sort of effect, were dangerous.

A moment later and she was glad she had stopped, seeing that there was a pair of wulfkin on watch at the main entrance to the stables. They were lounging against the wall, not trying to hide, looking bored. As the residue had already told her, these were not the civilised, well-mannered wulfkin that were usually found in this town. They had a feral edge to them, hair uncombed, a glint of power in their eyes that should have been kept hidden, and even from this distance she could tell they had not washed for some time.

Her stomach clenched, old fear creeping up her spine. She began to have a very bad feeling about what might be inside the stable block. And why the herbalist's daughter was in there.

The wulfkin did not appear to have seen her, or paid any attention to her, and she forced herself to move, keeping an easy pace, not going any closer to the stables, moving slightly away until she was among the houses. The houses followed the perimeter of the stables, and she was able to stay in their shadows until she came across a side-entrance. Too narrow for horses, it had likely been for stable hands and looked like it had not been used for years, with peeling paint and, as she moved closer, hinges caked with rust. There were no guards here.

The door eased open with some gentle coaxing and a murmured spell, the hinges silent as they obeyed her will.

She stepped inside the building, the door closing behind her, and stilled, throat closing, stomach twisting, heart thudding in her ears. The residue was much stronger inside. And there was more. Quiet, desperate sounds. Crying. Whimpers of pain.

Memories rushed back, none of them good. The unwashed scent of wulf. The brutal fights. The ripping of teeth into her flesh.

Her worst fears realised.

This was a quarrel.

Wulfkin had set up a quarrel. Grabbing up young women and girls, using them for their own pleasure, discarding the bodies when they were done.

In this peaceful town, where there was no meaningful law enforcement to keep them away, or to keep their excesses in check.

Even in Three Falls, quarrels were frowned on and shut down quickly.

A scream scraped her ears, stirring old memories she did not want to think about. The all-too familiar sound of a woman, or a girl, who cried out again moments later, in fear and in pain. Yvonne knew the sound. She had made it herself, more than once. Many years ago.

The hilt of her sword bit into her palm, the minor discomfort anchoring her. She was not that scared girl anymore. Hunar. She was Hunar. And somewhere in this awful building there was a daughter. Caroline. Whose mother had asked for a Hunar's aid.

The magic of the Hundred coursed across her skin, welcome and warm.

Yvonne took a step forward. She was in a narrow passageway between brick walls, hidden in shadows as she edged forward, staying as still and quiet as she could as she looked around.

The stables had been re-purposed. Rather than the simple ropes at each entrance, more than enough to contain a well-trained horse, metal gates had been installed instead. Behind the gates were women and girls. Most of them bleeding, huddled against the back walls, as far away from the gates and the inner courtyard as possible. The stables were partitioned on each side by high stone walls, so the girls could not see their neighbours. But they could see across the courtyard, to the stables on the other side. And they could see the centre of the space where a fighting ring had been set up and a half-dozen wulfkin were pitting their strength against each other, watched by other wulfkin. Most of the fighters were bleeding, stripped down to their waists, partly shifted out of their human forms so they had their longer fangs and claws visible.

She froze again at the sight. Partially-shifted wulfkin always triggered the worst memories.

A quiet, desperate sob nearby drew her attention. It was the source of the trace. Yvonne edged forward, put her head around the wall. The herbalist's daughter. She was huddled in the nearest stable, filthy blankets held around her, face turned away. Not wanting to look. Not wanting to listen. Hoping that it would just end. Yvonne remembered that feeling, too.

"Caroline," Yvonne whispered. "Your mother sent me. Viola."

"She's dead," the girl answered, between sobs. "They told me."

"She's not dead," Yvonne said, throat tight. The wulfkin had told her the same thing, all those years before. And that her family wouldn't want her back even if she did escape. They had been right about that. But Caroline's mother definitely wanted her daughter back. "She wanted me to find you, and to bring you back to her."

"What have we here?"

It was a young wulf who spoke. Perhaps the same age as Joel. Not nearly as powerful. He strutted across the courtyard to her, chest puffed out, scratch marks across the bare skin, trickles of blood running down his stomach. Either from a fight with one of his brothers, or from one of the women attempting to defend herself, Yvonne was not sure. He was eyeing her up and down as though she were fresh meat. "Bit old for my taste, but I'll make do."

Fear faded, welcome heat of fury rushing to take its place, filling every part of her. She took a step forward, away from the wall, straightening her spine. She was a good head or so taller than him, and could tell he had noticed as his lip curled.

"I am Hunar," Yvonne said, proud that her voice did not shake. "And I'm here to take the girls."

The wulf laughed. "One puny little human girl. Against all of us. I don't think so."

There had been a change in atmosphere, though. Yvonne took another careful step forward, so that she could be seen from all the stables around the square. The symbol at her shoulder was shining, vivid in the sunshine, clearly visible to everyone.

She lifted her voice, speaking so everybody could hear her.

"I am Hunar. I will help you if you ask."

"We don't need any help," one of the other wulfkin said, teeth bared.

"I was not speaking to you," she told him, dismissing him.

From around the stables came soft sounds. Bare feet moving forward on matted straw. Sobs quieting.

And then, the sound that she had hoped for.

"Help me, Hunar."

The simple words, repeated over and over around the courtyard. With each request, with each plea, the symbol at her shoulder deepened, until it had shifted from its normal pale grass green to a blazing, endless shade that was the heart of pure emerald.

The power of the Hundred gathered, coursing across her skin, lifting the hair at the nape of her neck, crackling in the air around her, catching the breath in her throat.

"If you leave now. If you promise never to do anything like this again. If you do that, then you may live," she told the gathered wulfkin. She almost did not recognise her voice. She'd rarely carried this much power. Power that didn't need a spell. The full authority and gift of the Hunar.

Disbelieving laughter met her offer.

"You don't scare me," the young one in front of her said. Other wulfkin joined him in agreement.

The power was there. Her entire body was humming with the intensity of it, static brushing the backs of her hands, sparks of energy at her fingertips. It was there. It just wanted to be released.

"One last chance. Leave now. You will not get another offer."

They laughed again, with slightly less assurance this time, but then a few of the younger ones surged forward, teeth bared, claws ready.

Lightning crackled from her fingers, cutting them down more swiftly than any sword could manage. More lightning spat out across the ground, catching more of them. They burned to ash, the scent of wulfkin replaced with burning.

She took another step forward. There were still some wulfkin standing. They were looking at her with disbelief. So confident and self-assured in their own power, in their own selfishness. And so stupid. They had not realised that their reign had come to an end. That their pleasure, taken at the expense of others' pain, was at an end.

The lightning died. That much power was hard to contain for any length of time. She drew her sword instead and met the first attack with an easy sweep of her blade.

She lost track of time. She lost track of who she was, of where she was, of anything apart from the sweep of her blade and the anticipation of the next attacker's move. Placing her foot just so, body moving smoothly. Hours and hours and hours of practice. Foot forward, knee bent, elbow bent, sword just so. Blade sweeping forward, meeting minor resistance. Turn. Blade up. Deflect. Move again. Blade down, cut and bite.

Over and over. Until there were no more attackers.

She paused, sword held ready, length steady. Dimly she was aware of her lungs burning with effort, rib cage heaving as she tried to get enough air in, her body coated with sweat under her clothes, and the sticky, cloying smell of blood in the air.

She looked around. There were severed limbs, and other body parts, scattered around her along with dark piles of ash where the lightning had struck. They were all dead. Every single wulf. There had been no mercy for them.

And in the cages around the courtyard a dozen, perhaps more, women and girls were looking at her with pale, solemn faces. Another set of bad memories to add to the ones they already had.

A soft sound behind her. She whirled, sword up, and checked the move with an exercise of will that jarred her teeth in her skull.

Jesset, still dressed in the flowing desert clothes, was standing a few paces away, her mouth open, her skin paler than normal. She looked around her, mouth working silently.

"Mama wanted me to keep an eye on you," Jesset said. "I don't think it was needed."

She looked back at Yvonne, shock fading from her face, replaced with something that looked like awe. Her eyes began to clear, lips curving upwards. "You have done what all of us have been wanting to do for a long time. A few people tried. The wulfkin just cut them down."

"I despise bullies," Yvonne said, lowering her sword. Now that the fight was done, the reaction was setting in. She was standing in a quarrel. A place that she had sworn never to go again. She wanted to move, to run, to escape, to scrub her skin until it was raw to get the stench away.

All around her were pale, silent faces. Wulfkin victims. She could not run. She owed them that. She flicked her sword, sending the last spots of blood onto the ground, murmured a quick spell to clean it thoroughly, and then put it back in its place. It settled against her hip again, seeming to murmur in contentment. She knew it was not alive, but there were times, like now, when it seemed to be.

"Are there healers in town?" Yvonne asked.

"Yes. I will go and get them," Jesset answered, and sped away in a swirl of colour. Yvonne went to the nearest cage and glared at the crude lock. She turned her head slightly, looking at the bits and pieces of wulfkin on the ground, and decided it would take too long to find the keys. She called more magic, another murmured spell, and yanked the door open, letting the girl out. Not much older than she had been, Yvonne saw, with the pain through her chest. And not quite as badly damaged.

There were others, though, that made her heart constrict and her throat close. Women who had been here for too long. A day was too long. But, from the scarring on their necks and shoulders, some had been here for months.

She took them out of the stables to the public garden, surrounded by the modest houses with their blank windows. This early in the year there were no flowers. But there was some grass on the ground, some benches for them to rest on, although many of them simply flopped down on the grass and did not want to move.

"We have nothing to give you," one of the women said, tilting her head up. She had been beautiful once, with symmetrical features that were now distorted by a jagged scar across her face. She had been a fighter, Yvonne thought.

"No payment is needed. Nothing is needed." Yvonne hesitated and then reached up, her fingers unsteady, and loosened the scarf that was always around her neck, taking it away so that they could see the scars that she bore. Years old, but they were still vivid.

Exposing the scars to the air, to the gaze of others, brought back the memories again. Of being helpless. Of pain. Of feeling there would never be an end to it.

There were a few gasps from the crowd around her, and the girls gathered closer.

"How did you survive?"

"Does it get better?"

Questions tumbled out of them, one after the other.

Yvonne tied the scarf back around her neck, tucking the ends under her shirt, her fingers still trembling, and thought carefully before she spoke.

"Very few people survive a quarrel," she told them. "That makes us lucky."

It was something she had to tell herself often. In the beginning, she had needed to repeat that several times, every hour of every day. Now, she needed the reminder much less frequently.

She told them that. She told them about waking up in a cold sweat from time to time, but she also told them about the friends she had made. About the joys that could be found in simple, everyday things. About the fact that there was wonder and life to be found, even when it did not seem possible just now.

By the time she had finished speaking, Jesset was back, a dozen or so healers, mostly male, gathered with her. The healers were all pale, and more than a few of them shaded green with nausea. Jesset had taken them to the stable courtyard first, with the carnage. From the glint in her eye, Jesset had enjoyed making them face the death in there.

She told Caroline where her mother was. Caroline had not been here long, it was clear. She had been a house slave in a grand lady's house, she murmured, until a passing wulf saw her and brought her here. Not as long as some of the others, but too long.

Caroline was shaking with relief and pain and the terrible beginnings of hope, Yvonne thought. Alive and out of the horror of the quarrel. And with her mother to go to.

As soon as she mentioned the Sisters in the Stone Walls, she could sense attention from the others. It was a hard life, with the Sisters. But she suspected most of these women and girls would take a hard life for the one that they had left.

It was growing dark by the time the healers, and the town's mayor, had arranged for accommodation for all the women. Brea had appeared at some point in the long afternoon and had, in her calm and understated manner, organised clothes for all of them, and bathing facilities to be made available.

Yvonne's own skin itched at the mention of a bath. She could feel the stickiness under her clothes and the scent of wulf was all around her, saturated into the fabric. Some of the women had been rubbing their skin, trying to get the dirt out, scrubbing their hands across their heads.

The sight of the crudely shaved heads sparked more memories, Yvonne unable to stop herself reaching up and tangling her fingers into the length of her own braid. Most of the victims here had been shaved as she had been, their hair growing back in odd tufts. More than one girl in a quarrel had hung herself from her own hair, or tried to strangle her attacker. The wulfkin took no chances. Yvonne could still remember the crawling, itching sensation of her too-short hair on her scalp, and the scrape of dirt across every part of her body. She needed a bath.

She was also exhausted. She was barely standing by the time all the girls had been found clothes and places to rest. One more missing child found. Viola would want her daughter back, Yvonne knew. Unlike her own family.

But her work was not done. Not yet. There were too many children missing, and a mastermind to hunt. Tomorrow. She would start tomorrow.

Chapter Sixteen

She could barely remember the walk back to Brea's house, mother and daughter on either side of her. They did not touch her, and did not speak to her. Perhaps they understood more deeply than she did how much she needed the quiet.

Brea showed her to the house's bathing room and left her there with a glass of wine and a dish piled high with food.

She came out of the bathing room sometime later, dressed in the ornate robes that had been left for her, her hair loose around her shoulders. Her clothes had been cleansed, but the memory of the blood was too fresh and she could not bear to put them on just yet. The robes had a high neck and Brea had left a scarf for her as well, so her scars were covered.

She came into the courtyard to find Thort settled, cross-legged, on the ground, whittling something with his knife, shavings gathering in a pile around him. Brea, Jesset and Rebecca were settled on the chairs. The air was full of the sweet scent of the plants in the garden, many of them evening flowering, releasing something beautiful into the night air. There was also a large pile of boxes setting a somewhat jarring note in the peaceful domestic scene.

"Your hair is so long," Rebecca commented, unguarded.

Yvonne lifted a hand self-consciously. Her hair was most of the way down her back now, kept above her waist by regular trims. It had taken years to grow after the wulfkin had forcibly shaved her head.

"It is beautiful," Jesset said. "Why do you keep it tied up in a plait all the time?"

"Jesset," Brea scolded. "Long hair is beautiful, but it is hardly practical day-to-day to have it flowing about," the goblin lady said with a flick of her own loose hair. "Hunar, please sit and take your ease. Our meal is almost ready. There is no meat in it," she added.

Yvonne felt her mouth curving into an unexpected smile as she sat down. "Thank you."

"And these are all for you," Brea added, almost casually, waving her hand towards the boxes, "from the people of Kelton."

"Cowards. All of them," Thort added, not looking up from whatever it was he was carving. Yvonne was glad he kept his eyes down. His tone was savage, the knife biting hard on his next pass. "And these gifts are penance for their cowardice."

Yvonne was familiar with penance. She looked at the boxes and thought of the terrified girls, wounded and bleeding, and the many dead wulfkin in the courtyard, and wondered if there was enough penance in the world to make up for all of that.

Still, she had to be a realist.

"May I look at them tomorrow?" she asked, suddenly weary. A pleasant dinner, with no meat in it, and a night's sleep were badly needed.

"Of course. Although there have been more arriving."

"We've stopped answering the gates," Jesset said. "I've put a sign up."

"Everything will still be there tomorrow," Brea added, lips twitching. "No one wants to steal from someone who can fire lightning from her hands."

Yvonne gave a hollow laugh.

"I had no idea the Hunar were so powerful," Rebecca said, eyes wide again.

"Not all of them are." Brea tipped her head to Yvonne. "This one is exceptional in more ways than one."

By some trick of the light, Yvonne met Brea's eyes in the fading day. Whatever the goblin saw made her lower her eyes hastily and bow her head, a gesture of contrition and respect that was rare indeed among the Karoan'shae.

Without looking up, Thort freed one hand from his carving and reached up, curling his fingers through his wife's where they had rested on her knee, holding her for a moment before letting go and returning to his carving. Some kind of animal, Yvonne thought. Not a wulf, though.

The next morning, she was awake and up, it seemed, before anyone else. The sun had barely crept above the horizon. She performed another cleansing spell on her clothes, wanting every possible trace of wulf out of the fabric, and bound her hair in its usual single plait before going down to the courtyard, wanting to move but not to disturb the whole house. All the windows that faced onto the courtyard were shuttered, so she was not overlooked, and had the illusion of privacy.

The first rays of sun were catching the pile of boxes in the courtyard. Gifts. From townspeople who had not intervened as a quarrel was set up in their midst, and girls taken into it. She remembered the terrified faces from the day before, the scars and the bleeding. Gifts would not cancel out those memories. Not for her, not for the girls.

But gifts might feed her family, even as the townspeople had taken the rescued girls into their homes, clothed and fed them. If the town had offered her coins, she would have taken them. Her skin would have felt sticky, her stomach uneasy, but she would have taken the coins. Her family needed to eat. Joel and Mariah both needed new clothes. So did she, for that matter. And Lothar, after years of loyal service, was growing a little too old for the journeys she needed to make. She did not want to think of that, another crack in her heart waiting in her near future as she left him behind for the first time.

She put her hand on the first box, seeking distraction, still reluctant to open it. She knew that she would open it, that she would look inside. And she would either keep whatever it was, or sell it. Somewhere else, though. She was not ill-mannered enough to sell gifts in the town where they had been given.

"You made an impression, I see, mristrian."

Guise was standing in one of the doorways. She had not heard his arrival, as usual. He moved as quietly as a wulf. He was more casually dressed than she was used to seeing him, having left off his tailored coat, and his hair was not quite as straight and sleek as she was used to seeing it. He must have borrowed one of Thort's shirts. The one he was wearing did not have an arrow hole in it.

"I see you're better," she commented. She still had her hand on the top box of the pile.

"Much better, thank you. And I thank you, and Rebecca, for your care of me." He made a shallow bow. Finely calculated. Acknowledging her service, as an equal. It was a high honour. The Karoan'shae bowed to very few. "I do not think I would have made it here on my own."

Yvonne felt her mouth turn up in an unexpected smile.

"I'm sure you would have managed," she said.

"I owe you more than I can repay." The sincerity of his words took her by surprise, far more than the bow. She shook her head slightly, not meeting his eyes, words tangling in her mouth, and then felt her lips curve again.

"Perhaps you could assist me with ideas. I've just realised that I'm going to need a means of transporting all these items back to the house," she said, voice light. "And I believe that there are more at the gate."

"Easily done," he answered, waving a hand in a familiar gesture. A small matter, for him and his resources. An impossible task, with her tiny hoard of coins. This was not Hunar business. She could not commandeer a barge, or afford to pay the fare. Depending what was in the boxes, of course.

She moved to pick the first box up and then stopped. Receiving presents was a rare and treasured event for Joel and Mariah. She measured the extent of the boxes here and smiled again, thinking that, perhaps, they would enjoy opening these far more than she ever would. And the pile at the gate outside. And they would know, after a lifetime spent with her, that they could not keep everything.

"I will make arrangements for transport," Guise promised her, and disappeared back into the house. She half-opened her mouth to call him back. She had not meant for him to take that on, not really. She closed her lips firmly together. If he thought her aid was worth the cost of transporting the boxes, she was not going to argue.

With the issue of the boxes resolved, she made her way out of the house with a lighter step, heading towards the stables. Lothar would have been well cared for, she knew, but she wanted to stroke his nose and tangle her fingers in his mane.

Just for a moment. There would not be many more mornings like this, out on the road.

He and a group of other horses were grazing in a small field inside the boundary walls of the property. Not just any horses. Apart from her horse, and the one that Rebecca had ridden, the rest were all goblin-bred horses. Beautiful, and tricky.

Jesset came out of the stables, pitchfork in hand, and wished her a brisk, cheerful good morning. Yvonne hesitated, wondering if she should offer to help with mucking out, then Lothar made a low sound, recognising her. He was capable of making a much louder sound if he did not get his head scratched, so she waved to Jesset and went on to the field, receiving a hard shove of his nose in her chest by way of greeting.

At length, he had been petted enough and she was calmer. Jesset had finished her tasks, and Yvonne's stomach was informing her that breakfast would be an excellent idea. Despite the generous feast from the night before.

She made her way back up to the house, on the path she had taken to get there, which took her close to the house's kitchens. It was a huge house, but she had not seen any signs of servants or hired help. Unusual for members of the Karoan'shae, but not unheard of.

The kitchen door was open, the double doors propped wide to let the heat of the kitchen out into the rest of the house. At the kitchen table Brea, Thort and Guise were settled in conversation. And not any idle conversation, either. Yvonne knew business dealings when she saw them. She lifted a brow, then took a deliberate, noisy step forward to let them know that she was there.

They had all known she was there, of course. Goblin hearing was far more acute than hers. Brea looked across and smiled a greeting. As she moved, Yvonne could see there was a map on the table between them. Definitely not an idle conversation. They might be friends, but Brea and Thort were heavily involved in whatever business Guise carried on.

"I am sorry to disturb you," Yvonne said.

"Nonsense," Brea said, rising to her feet. "Would you like some tea?"

"That would be welcome."

"We were just trying to plot the reports of disappearing children," Thort told her, nodding to the map. Curious, Yvonne looked more closely. It was beautifully detailed, the clear lines of the map overlaid with what she took to be finer paper, on which they had marked various crosses and question marks.

A closer look and her breath caught. It was not paper, but magic. Goblin magic. So finely detailed and complex that her mind could not take it all in at once. The magic was layered. The basic map. The crosses and question marks on another layer.

"This is extraordinary," she said.

"Thank you," Guise said, with no false modesty. She met his eyes across the table, startled. She had known he was powerful, but had not expected this.

She took a mug of tea from Brea and settled at the table, following the marks with her eyes.

"I think you have more information than I do," she told them. "Although there have been no reports of missing children around Hogsmarthen."

"The Sisters would see to it," Thort commented, mouth lifting for a moment.

And they had not known about the disappearance in Fir Tree Crossing, Yvonne thought. Not until men with horses had tried to abduct a nine-year-old girl from her bedroom. And Caroline had ended up first at a grand house and then stolen into a quarrel, not wherever the wagon loads of children had been taken. Those taking wagon loads had wanted strong youngsters, not pretty, delicate ones like Caroline.

"It's always possible that the mastermind is simply gathering in goods," she speculated, glad that she had nothing but tea in her stomach as it curdled.

"And then simply selling them to the highest bidder?" Guise finished for her, lips curling for a moment in disgust.

"We'll keep our ears open," Brea promised.

There was more to that than simple words. Yvonne cradled her tea between her hands and looked around the table, at the serious expressions, then at the map. Finely made. It must have taken an extraordinary amount of effort and magic to make it. And few people would need a map with layers. She had the odd certainty that there were more layers that she was not being shown. And Brea and Thort took the detailed magic in their stride, had combined their knowledge with Guise's. Friends was a poor word to describe their relationship.

"You let the quarrel be," Yvonne heard herself saying, voice matter-of-fact, "to avoid drawing attention to yourselves. So you could keep gathering information."

A shadow crossed Brea's face, confirming her suspicion. Thort reached for and took his wife's hand again.

"It has been hard," Thort said, his voice harsh with an emotion Yvonne could not identify at first. He shook his head slightly, turning to Brea, his eyes shading to a colour Yvonne had never seen before among goblins. A soft, melting gold.

"We had another daughter," Brea told Yvonne, her voice as rasping as her husband's. "She was taken."

"She died before Jesset was born," Thort added. The echo of their loss and grief rang around the peaceful room. Goblins, like Hunar, lived long lives. The grief was decades old, and still fresh in their minds.

"Sold," Guise added, voice soft. Looking at him, Yvonne saw the echo of Brea and Thort's grief in his face. He rarely showed emotion. His eyes were blazing green, tinted with red. A childhood friend, Yvonne guessed. Perhaps something more. And her capture and death had left Guise a life-long enemy of slavers.

"I am sorry for your loss," Yvonne told the room.

"We were close to acting," Brea said, turning to meet Thort's eyes. "However dangerous it was. Even if we would need to move on from here." She shook her head slightly, swallowing. "To know that the quarrel was there. And to do nothing." A tear made its way down her cheek. "All those other daughters."

"Safe now," Yvonne said, throat tight. All those other daughters. The ones from this quarrel were alive. Not whole. Many of them would never be whole again. But there were other daughters who had not been saved. Too many of them, and too many of their screams echoed in her head.

"We will take them to the Sisters," Brea announced, as though there had been a discussion and agreement leading up to that statement. "And Rebecca, too, if she wishes to come."

"Good." Yvonne sipped her tea, finding she was cold and the tea's slight warmth created a welcome burning through her. The Sisters never turned anyone away, and they had past experience of healing those rescued from a quarrel. "When?"

"Tomorrow," Thort answered, and untangled his hand from his wife's. He picked something from the pocket of his coat and handed it across to her. "To remember."

The carving from the night before.

Yvonne set her tea down and took the carving with both hands, cupping it in her palms.

A Firebird. A creature of legend. A protector. A mythical being that could level whole cities with one sweep of its great, flame-encrusted wings. Thort had carved the bird with her great, spreading wings half-open, head lifted in defiance, mouth open in a furious cry. Yvonne could almost hear the shriek, feel the heat from those magnificent wings, and see the fury in the burning eyes.

"It is exquisite," she said, voice hushed. "Thank you."

"It is the least we could offer," Thort answered, bowing his head.

She turned the creature in her hands, wondering how much Thort, Brea and Guise knew. The Firebird was the legendary companion of the first Hunar, a loyal and lifelong companion who despised injustice as much as the first Hunar had. There were crude drawings in story books, and painted on walls of old temples.

The only place she had seen a more detailed depiction was a place she had thought only the Hundred knew about. The final test that they all had to pass to be accepted as one of the Hundred.

For a moment she was back there, bare feet on sun-warmed stone, her whole body heavy with exhaustion, staring up at the wall that rose high above her head, plaster still fresh after all the years, and the giant painting of the Firebird, shimmering slightly with the gold leaf used to outline her wings, her head back, beak open in a silent scream that Yvonne could feel ringing through her soul as she looked at the wall. The first Hunar's legendary companion, as formidable as he had been.

She closed her fingers, gently and carefully, around the carving, imagining that she could feel the flutter of feathers against her skin and the burn of the bird's anger.

It did not matter where Thort had got the idea from, she told herself. It was simply beautiful, and one of the best gifts of her life.

"I have made a sort of nest for it," Thort added, "so you may take it safely."

"Thank you," she said again, opening her hands. "You have an extraordinary gift."

"That he does," Brea agreed, proud of her husband.

Yvonne looked back at Guise's map, the Firebird in her hands. She could almost feel those wings twitching, wanting to rise into the air, to soar over the land, searching for those responsible for all this. All those children taken.

The map. A bird's eye view. Underneath the crosses and question marks were the black lines that mankind had made. Borders. Patches of territory. Things that a bird did not care about, but which mattered to humans. Mattered a great deal.

The mastermind had not cared about the borders. But the rulers did, and kept their attention focused on their own lands. Their own interests. And, if they were good rulers, their own people. She wondered how many of the leaders were aware of the missing, and how many of them would care, even if they did know.

Chapter Seventeen

Yvonne did not know what kind of money Guise had needed to spend, but somehow he had arranged transport for her and the vast quantity of gifts the townspeople had left for her that same day. He regretted he could not come with her, he said. But he would send word to her at Fir Tree Crossing. Meantime, she had transport back to Fir Tree Crossing.

There was a mastermind to hunt. But, before then, she needed to see her children. Wanted to listen to Mariah's laugh, see Joel's smile. Wanted to be surrounded by familiar things for a while, to set aside the memory of the quarrel.

And she needed time to think. To prepare. Caroline and Alexander were found, the girl badly wounded but heading to the best place to heal her, and a mother who loved her. Ubel's corpse was with law keepers, his killer still at large. But Guise had not asked her to track Ubel's killer.

Rebecca was on her way to the Sisters, too, and Yvonne had a sketchy impression of her brother, although some instinct told her that was not an urgent matter.

She and Lothar were carried in style on a barge which she was quite sure was meant for more commercial service but which had been given over to her exclusive use. She was given her own cabin, a small but adequate room, and as much privacy as could be managed on a river barge, but chose to sit outside, wrapped in the down-soft blankets the barge captain had insisted on fetching for her, protected against the slight chill in the air.

As they travelled, she remembered Guise's map, with the marks made for each missing child he and his friends had learned of. With those black lines depicting borders. Law keepers might search high and low in their own territories. Very, very few of them crossed borders. And even smaller numbers of rulers welcomed outside interference in their lands.

It was likely that no one else knew the full extent of the slavers' operation.

For several long breaths she felt overwhelmed by the task she had set herself. The mastermind could be anywhere across those lands, in any of those countries marked by the black lines of the borders.

Very few people could cross borders at will, and have their authority respected. A Hunar could.

The Hundred were outside the reach of rulers, their only purpose to help those in need.

Her breathing settled, stomach calming. She knew what she needed to do.

With the smooth passage of the vessel across the water, she pulled out the parchment and pens she always had in her travel pack. The barge captain saw her preparations and had his own writing desk brought from his cabin, a beautifully crafted wooden box with a sloping top covered in fine leather. It needed two of his crew to lift it.

Settled like a grand lady, in blankets, and with a beautifully crafted writing surface to use, she picked up the pen and began writing.

I call for a Gathering.

The barge moored at Fir Tree Crossing at dusk the day after they had left Kelton and, in more evidence of Guise's influence, as if she had needed it, wagons were waiting to take the goods to her house.

She arrived home in early dark, to Mariah and Joel's evident astonishment, at the head of the train of three wagons whose drivers cheerfully helped to unload the boxes from the wagons and take them into the house's largest room.

It had once been a grand dining room, complete with an elaborate chandelier at odds with the plain outward appearance of the house. The room had seemed huge when Yvonne had first seen it. By the time the wagoneers were done, boxes were piled high against every wall, and there was barely any room to walk around the table and chairs. Some of the boxes smelled divine, with delicious scents that she thought she knew. Mariah and Joel were not the only ones who loved the confectionery that came from Kelton. Not only that, but she still had the discreetly labelled box that the hotel manager had somehow smuggled onto Lothar when they had left Three Falls. The preservation spell was still intact and she knew that, when she opened it, it would be full of the desserts that had belonged with the superb tasting menu from the hotel. It seemed a lifetime ago.

The wagoneers left with the same efficiency with which they had arrived, and refused her offer of coins as an extra tip for them, her small hoard of coins much larger thanks to the heavy purse Guise had insisted she take. She wondered, not for the first time, just how vast Guise's resources were.

"The horses are settled," Joel told her, coming into the dining room. "Mariah is warming the stew." He read her expression and laughed, softly. "Don't worry, it's very good. We got it from The Tavern."

She trusted his judgement, and put the hotel's box on the table. "We'll need side plates and forks, as well."

His eyes lit up. Side plates and forks meant something sweet, and a rare treat. He left on silent feet, and for a few moments she was alone in the still-unfamiliar surroundings of the house's dining room, made even more strange by the towering piles of boxes all around. The children had been busy in the house while she had been away, whatever else they had been doing, and the room itself was spotless. Not one speck of dust anywhere. The table surface, scratched and pitted from years of use, was gleaming softly in the light from the candles that they had set there, in mismatched holders.

It was only a few moments of displacement before the children were back, with bowls and cutlery and plates and a pitcher which contained plain water flavoured with fruit. Her brows rose as they set the table with no fuss and no arguing, and she sat down with them for their meal.

The lack of arguing she could explain immediately, as their eyes travelled around the boxes in the room.

Even so, she stuck to their normal tradition. She asked them for news, and what they had been doing since she had been away. They were used to this, used to the departures and the returns. Elinor had stayed with them when she could, or another trusted adult, until a few years ago when Yvonne had arrived back at their house to find that the trusted adult had been thrown out by a determined-looking Mariah, having been caught going through Yvonne's belongings. There were no more adults after that, the children more than capable of looking after themselves.

But she always wanted them to tell her their news. She very rarely told them what she had been up to, even when she came home bruised and bloodied.

The meal passed quickly, with more laughter than she would have thought possible. They had both been doing some work. Mariah for the dressmaker in town, who seemed to want to hire Mariah full-time, having far more work for her than she could possibly do. Joel had done some shifts loading and unloading barges at the docks. They both reached into their pockets, in a move that they had clearly planned, and drew out piles of gleaming coins, spilling them onto the table. More than enough money to feed them all for the next month, at least, possibly beyond that.

"We were quite pleased with ourselves," Mariah commented, looking around the room again, "but you have surpassed us."

Yvonne ignored the implied question, instead opening the box from the hotel, the preservation spell flying away and releasing the scents of the food inside. She saw, with an odd pang, that the hotel had given her three of everything. Somehow the manager, and Guise, had known that she would want to share this with Mariah and Joel.

"That smells amazing," Joel said, completely distracted from the boxes. "Where does it come from?"

"Three Falls city," she answered, carefully lifting out the desserts and sharing them among their plates.

They both hesitated, looking at the food, clearly wondering at the source.

"Guise knows one of the hotel managers well. He seemed an honest man, and the food was amazing."

They still hesitated, but their eyes were wide now, as if they were not sure it was real.

"If you don't eat it, I will," she told them, not really joking.

That was more than enough.

When they were finished, and there was not even a single crumb left, Joel tilted his head to the boxes lining the room.

"These did not come from Three Falls."

The desserts, which had been an explosion of taste in her mouth, suddenly seemed leaden in her stomach. She looked around the room, and thought that they needed to know.

"No. We went to Kelton. There was a quarrel."

They both stilled. They might not have any active memories of the quarrel that they had been born in, but they knew enough. Bits and pieces of information gathered over the years, innuendo and threats from various bullying cerro.

"Was?" Mariah had picked up on that critical word.

"Yes. These," she tilted her head to the boxes, "are gifts from the townsfolk. They hadn't dealt with the matter themselves, but they were grateful that somebody did."

She rose and picked up the smallest box that she had carried with her through the journey. "And this was a gift from a master carver."

She opened the box. The nest, Thort had said, lined with cream satin. The Firebird glared out at them, as lifelike as she had been when Yvonne had first seen her, in Brea and Thort's kitchen.

From the slight intake of breath from Mariah and Joel, they were equally impressed.

"Stunning," Joel commented. "Master carver, indeed."

"May we?" Mariah asked and, at Yvonne's nod, tentatively picked the carved creature out of the box. "This is days of work."

Yvonne shook her head. "Overnight. I suspect a bit of magic went into it."

"Goblin magic, by the feel of it," Mariah noted, passing the bird to Joel. "Not Guise?" Her eyes narrowed in suspicion.

"No." Yvonne laughed. "He was recovering from a poison arrow. This was from Guise's friends. They live in Kelton."

"Guise has friends?" Mariah's brows shot up.

"Mariah," Joel chided, carefully putting the bird back into its nest. "She is beautiful," he added, to Yvonne. "I swear she would take my head off if I looked at her the wrong way."

Yvonne laughed, bringing the box slightly closer to her.

"I know what you mean."

"So, what's in the rest of the boxes?" Joel asked, eyes gleaming.

"I don't know."

"You haven't opened them? Not even one?" Mariah was astonished.

"I thought you would like to help me," she said, a welcome smile pulling her mouth, her meal settling in her stomach again. It had been the right decision.

"Where can we start?" Joel asked. He did not have the same delight in material things as his sister, but even he was looking around with eyes glinting with excitement.

"Wherever you like."

Yvonne sat back in her chair, comfortably warm, full of food, and watched her children as they grabbed the nearest boxes, bringing them back to the table to unwrap them.

Despite the abundance before them, they were, both of them, careful and meticulous in the unwrapping. Mariah demanded that all the ribbons be kept. She might be able to make use of them, she explained. And Joel was simply careful by nature.

They unwrapped each one with the same care and attention. They revealed boxes of candied fruit, marzipan, chocolates, bottles of exotic liqueur, perfumes that made Yvonne's nose itch and Joel and Mariah sneeze, luxurious soaps and other toiletries, silks, beautifully patterned blankets and rugs, swathes of fine linen and a case of good wine.

When they reached the wine, they were not even halfway through the boxes. Joel left the room for a moment and returned with a wine glass and a corkscrew, opening one of the bottles without asking and handing a glass to Yvonne.

"Thank you," she said, throat closing for a moment. It was so easy to forget how observant they were, particularly when they were squealing with delight like tiny children at each thing they unwrapped. "Why don't you open some of the confectionery?"

By design, or by coincidence, there were boxes of each of their favourites.

Not used to this much abundance, it would have been so easy for them to be greedy, and to inhale the gifts on offer. But they did not. Control was valued among the wulfkin. So they took a piece at a time, and made sure they shared with her as well.

It must have been the early hours of the morning before the last box was unwrapped. It was a deceptively simple, but beautifully carved, set of candlesticks. Without asking, Mariah immediately set them onto the table.

Yvonne took a look around the room. From being an overwhelming, orderly display of closed boxes, it was now an overwhelming, utterly disordered riot of colour and texture and scent.

"Do we have to give it all back?" Mariah asked. She was sitting on a chair, looking about her with a slightly dazed expression.

Yvonne looked around the room. She may have underestimated the townspeople, she thought. Every single item in the room, however beautifully made, or however frivolous, was one that they could use. From the excellent wine she had been sipping through the evening, to the confectionery the children had delighted in, to the leather that would make them each a good pair of shoes or boots, to the saddle blankets, to the swathes of linen that would make shirts and clothes for them. Even the perfume, overwhelming with all the other scents, was delicate and would be lovely on its own.

There was nothing in here that she did not want in her house.

"No," she said, at length. She took the last sip of wine out of her glass. Joel had topped up the glass for her through the evening, perhaps thinking she had not noticed. Her head was clear, though. And she had the rest of the case, as well as the rest of the bottle. It was a luxury she could not have imagined.

She set the glass down to find the children looking at her with identical expressions of astonishment.

"We've never had so much before," Joel said.

"I know," she answered. "Nor have I. But we can use all of it." Her mouth curved up. "We can all get new boots," she told them, and had to laugh at the relief on their faces. Joel might not care as much, but none of them liked wet feet. And perhaps the Cressins would take some work from her, now that they had their son back. "Although I am sorry, Mariah, it looks like a lot of sewing for you."

Mariah laughed, a brilliant, lovely sound.

"I love sewing," she said, and sprang out of her chair, almost dancing across the floor to a bolt of silk cloth. "Oh, this is going to be so much fun."

It was exactly what she had needed, Yvonne thought. A brief respite before the hunt began in earnest.

Chapter Eighteen

A FEW DAYS LATER and, between them, they had found a storage place, or a use, for all the gifts and the dining room had been returned to a simple, functional room. Yvonne had cast preservation spells on everything that needed to be kept fresh and the large pantry next to the kitchen was now half-full.

After Yvonne had simply put one of the fragranced candles onto the narrow table in the main entranceway, thinking that the scent would carry up the stairs, Mariah had rolled her eyes and taken over. About half of the candles had been unpacked, Joel and Mariah delicately sniffing each one to make sure it wouldn't irritate their far more sensitive senses. The single candle in the entranceway was now a display of five, artfully set among some of the ribbons used to tie the boxes. Every one of the public rooms had a set of candles, each room with its own, subtle fragrance, and Mariah had made a display of some of the empty, patterned boxes on the half-landing at the main staircase, commanding Yvonne to put a preservation spell on the pile to keep it free from dust.

Amused at being ordered about, Yvonne had complied and had to admit that, with the changes Mariah had made, the building no longer felt neglected, left empty too long because of the haunting. Instead it was, tentatively, beginning to feel like a home. It did not feel quite like her home, Yvonne thought. Not yet.

But it was a familiar and comfortable space. And theirs for years to come. A place from which Mariah and Joel could do some exploring of their own, find out what they wanted to do with their lives. A place of peace for her to come back to. A town nearby with people who might, over time, become friends.

It had been a few days of blessed peace. No middle-of-the-night-calls from the Rangers. No calls from supplicants, seeking a Hunar's aid. No more missing children.

A few days of domestic peace. A rare event. Long enough for the worst memories of the quarrel to settle in, become just one more set of bad memories, for the fresh scent of wulf blood to fade, overtaken by the fragrance around the house, for the bite of steel into flesh to be overtaken by the far more familiar noises of Mariah and Joel bickering, the steady flow of the river outside and the contented murmurs from the horses when she went to see them in the mornings.

Peace that would not last. It never did.

By the third day, her skin was prickling with the sense of coming danger. One quarrel had been destroyed. There were still many more youngsters missing, the nagging sensation in her chest of an unfulfilled promise growing more pressing with each day.

One more day, she told the promises she had made. One more day, and then she would act. The scale of the problem was bigger than she had imagined possible, based on Guise's map. And she was only one mind, one person. More was needed.

This day, she needed for planning.

The promises settled, grumbling as they faded into the background.

One more day, she told them. She could not do this alone. Help was on its way. The letters she had written on the barge, brief, blunt, to the point, sped on their way with spells behind them, had found their targets, replies sent just as swiftly. She had called for a Gathering. The Hundred had responded. Help was on its way.

The promises settled some more, the uneasy sensation of unfulfilled promise giving way to anticipation.

The house was spotless. She had cleaned every room with a dose of magic, the power co-operating with her this once, not draining her. There was a feast cooking in the kitchen. A roast big enough to feed most of Sephenamin's range, if she chose to.

She finished her final check of the upstairs and came down to the entrance hall, full of the fresh green scent of the candles Mariah had set there, to find Mariah and Joel standing together at the bottom of the stairs, for once not arguing, with identical expressions of determination on their faces.

"Who is coming to stay?" Mariah asked bluntly.

Yvonne drew in a breath, shoulders bowing. A few days of peace at an end. She had not told them everything. She never told them everything. When they had been younger she had wanted to protect them from the worst of the world, and the habit had stuck when they had grown. She still did not want to share some of the ugliness with them, wanting to shelter them a little longer. Just a little, even though they were no longer small.

"It's the Hundred, isn't it?" Joel said, eyes narrowing. "It can't be Adira, or another of the Sisters, as she would only need one room. I saw you counting the rooms," he explained, in response to her silent question.

"Oh, that's brilliant," Mariah said, determination vanished into smiles. She practically danced on the spot. "Why didn't you say so, Kalla? It's been ages since we've seen them."

Not since Elinor's funeral, in fact. The Hundred rarely gathered in one place, and never for very long. It tended to be solemn and awful occasions that drew them together. Like Elinor's funeral. Yvonne could not remember much of the funeral itself. Her chest had hurt so much that breathing had been difficult, her entire being shaken with the barely-understood knowledge that her teacher, and closest friend in the world, was no longer.

Reminded of the death, for a moment all Yvonne could do was stand and breathe, the pain coming back as it always did.

"Mariah," Joel said, his tone firm, "it must be serious." Solemn and awful occasions, Yvonne thought again, throat closing again. No funeral this time.

"It is," Yvonne said. She did not want to say anything more. They might be considered adults in some lands. Both of them old enough, or very nearly, to have their own households, their own spouses, even their own children. But they were still under her care, and she still wanted to protect them. Their lives had not been easy. They had endured a lot because of their natures, because of where they came from, and because of her. Hunar and human, mixing with wulfkin.

"They're definitely coming? And today?" Mariah asked. "How did you manage that?"

"Letters," Yvonne answered, voice dry. Mariah had teased her many times over the years for her letter writing. In rare moments of peace in the evenings, settled with bright candles around. It was one of the only ways she had to keep in touch with the rest of the Hundred, and the few other people across the lands that she counted as friends. "Replies came yesterday." Delivered by a boy from Fir Tree Crossing who had been pale and wide-eyed as he handed the letters across. Perhaps scared of coming near to the haunted house. Perhaps awed by approaching a Hunar. Or for other reasons Yvonne could not guess at.

The replies had arrived far more quickly than she had dared hope for, many of her fellow Hunar already on the way when they had sent word. The Hundred were travelling with all the resources available to them, at speeds few kings could manage, pulled by her brief letters. She did not know where they had all been, or how they were getting here, but they would all be here today.

"What we going to feed them?" Mariah asked.

It was such a practical matter to raise that Yvonne wanted to laugh.

"Use your nose. There's a huge roast on the spit. And the market cart was here earlier," Joel observed. "Haven't you been in the kitchen? It's stocked full."

"Really?"

"Will you set the dining table, please?" Yvonne asked, suddenly wanting a bit of time to herself.

The Hundred had always been kind to her children, some of them in a very distant way, and it was hardly surprising that Mariah was looking forward to the visit from her favourite aunts and uncles. Joel was more wary. And that made her heart break again. A few months ago, before the fight, before his first kill, he would have been as bright-eyed and delighted as Mariah was.

She did not wait for an answer, going past them to the kitchen, but, for once, found no peace there.

Elinor had been a very skilled cook, and had been horrified by the plain fare that Yvonne could produce, taking time to teach Yvonne some of her skill. Normally, Yvonne found cooking soothing. Occupying her hands, and at least part of her mind, preparing food was a good distraction from the many worries she carried. Today, as she moved about the kitchen, measuring out the necessary spices, she could hear Elinor's voice.

Not too much of the ground red pepper, or that's all you'll be able to taste. A little more of the rosemary – it can get overwhelmed by the pepper.

Elinor's voice was so vivid that she turned her head, expecting to see her dearest friend sitting at the table, a mug of tea in front of her, light catching her red hair, finding the streaks of white and the fine lines of age across her face. Hunar lived long lives. The years did, eventually, leave their mark.

There was no one there. Empty space. The sunlight caught a few motes of dust. The chairs were all tucked into place, the table surface clear. Her eyes burned as she turned back to the pot.

In her distraction, she had measured the ingredients wrong, and had to add even more rosemary to compensate.

Eventually, it was done.

The kitchen was full of the scent of cooking, and Mariah and Joel had been back and forth, making sure that there were enough glasses and cutlery and plates. They had not said anything to her, although she had seen their sideways glances. They pretended to be light-hearted, chattering about nonsense, even getting together pitchers of plain water and others flavoured with fruit without needing to be asked. As they carried the pitchers to the dining room, her heart ached again. Somewhere along the way, she had done something right in raising them.

When the first hoof beats sounded on the bridge, her chest didn't ache quite so much, and they were all ready.

Joel and Mariah had changed into clean clothes and, miracle of miracles, had washed their hands and faces without needing to be asked. Yvonne herself had managed a quick bath and changed into her least worn set of clothes. Even in her own house, among her family and the Hundred, she still carried her weapons. The Hundred would expect nothing less.

It was no surprise to see that first to arrive was Annabelle, with her apprentice Idal in tow.

Annabelle slid off her horse, a handsome black mare that was new since the last time Yvonne had seen her fellow Hunar, and came forward to Yvonne in a rustle of fabric, the riding dress exquisitely made and wholly impractical for hard travel, her perfume enveloping Yvonne as she gave her a quick, hard hug. Flighty and vain on the surface, Annabelle was a more than adequate Hunar, the expensive clothing hiding a warm and generous heart.

Idal was an excellent foil to her. As slender as she was, he was quiet and unassuming, exchanging polite nods with Yvonne and slightly warmer greetings with Joel and Mariah, before asking where he should take the horses and then their bags. They had an extra horse with them for their luggage. Of course they did. Annabelle would never travel with fewer than three bags, and five changes of clothes.

Leaving Joel and Idal to deal with the horses and the bags, Annabelle practically dragged Yvonne inside the house, exclaiming as she went, Mariah following them.

"Where on earth did you find this place? It's so old and antiquated. Oh, my goodness, is that an actual cobweb? How delightful. Spiders are excellent house guests. And did you say it was haunted? Actually haunted? Not one of those fanciful imaginings of the locals? How on earth do you occupy your time here? You're so far away from everything civilised. That town is charming and quaint, but surely not much can go on there. There was not a single theatre that I saw. And I can smell your cooking. How fabulous."

Annabelle drifted through the house, from the entranceway to the sitting room to the dining room, and then on to the kitchen, chattering all the way. Yvonne followed out of politeness and habit, Mariah biting her lip to hold in the occasional laugh even as she examined Annabelle's clothing for the detail of it.

Before Yvonne had time to do more than offer Annabelle a drink, in a rare pause between words, the wards shivered, closely followed by Joel coming in through the house's back door, Idal with him, to let her know that there was another group of riders on their way.

"Oh, that must be the others. I think we passed them on the road. Idal, did we pass them?"

"They had gathered at the last tavern on the highway," Idal said. "I think it was everyone else." His mouth tilted up in a mischievous smile. "You didn't want to stop, remember?"

"No, of course I didn't want to stop. I wanted to get here," Annabelle told Yvonne, giving her another, brief hug. "And see my dear friend. It has been such a long time. Too long."

Yvonne agreed, another bittersweet pang shooting through her. The Hundred were the ones she trusted most in the world, besides her children. They could not stay together long. There were too few of them, and too many people in need. Times together were rare, and precious.

She shook off the melancholy and went to the front door just in time to see the rest of the Hundred arrive in a great cavalcade.

"There are too few of us," Annabelle murmured, voice carrying her sadness.

Yvonne agreed. Far too few, for all the ill in the world. And their numbers had lessened, not grown, over the years. Far fewer now than there ever had been, since the first Hunar so many years ago. So Elinor had said.

Yvonne swallowed the returning pain. She was the youngest Hunar to bear the name. Idal showed promise, but he was not ready. A long way from ready. She remembered the final test and knew, bone-deep, that he would fail if he tried it now.

And it was not just the test. The Hundred were trained to skills few humans knew about. Magic. Healing. Weapons. They were keepers of secrets that could tear the world apart, much like the first Hunar and his brother had tried to do. The most dangerous knowledge was never revealed before the final test, when the prospective Hunar had been accepted.

And Idal was not ready for that burden yet.

More than one of the others had suggested if he had a different teacher he might progress faster. Elinor had overruled the mutterings. He was working at his own pace, she had said, voice stern, eyes hard as she looked around the group. As they all had, she reminded them. It had taken Dundac almost a decade to train, and Idal was not even half-way through that.

Yvonne missed Elinor. Missed her wisdom and her way of speaking her mind.

But she was gone, and the rest of the Hundred were far fewer than they should have been, or needed to be. Never a full Hundred, not since the time of the first Hunar. So called for those who had stood with the first Hunar against his enemy, his own brother. A hundred brave souls against an onslaught.

Hunar had always been rare. Now not even a dozen.

But they were Hunar. The magic of the Hundred had called them the same way it had called her. They had endured the same training, and the same trials, as she had. And dedicated their lives in the same way. Committed to helping others, to answering the call when somebody asked for their help.

As they got off their horses and came forward, she greeted each one with a smile, seeing a few of the others also hiding a tear or two even as they also smiled. Too few of them. And only ever gathered for solemn and awful occasions.

There was Pieris, more grey in his hair than she remembered, with his quiet smile and brief, heartfelt hug. Suanna, bending slightly to give Yvonne a swift peck on the cheek, as slender and austere as ever. Dundac, who folded her in a cinnamon-scented embrace, grown even rounder since she had last seen him. Mica, who ignored her dislike of being touched, instead lifting her up and whirling her around. Difficult to be angry with him as he laughed, setting her down as soon as she asked, and she laughed in turn when he gave Suanna the same treatment, much to the older woman's disgust. Firon, whose hug was brief and abstracted, looking as though he had acquired even more sorrows than she had. And, finally, Sillman, pure white hair as sleek as ever, a contrast to his dark, well-fitting clothes. Unofficial leader of the Hundred. Not for the first time, Yvonne thought that Sillman's taste in clothing was at least as expensive as Guise's.

Even Hunar had to deal with practical matters such as luggage. For a while the house was full of heavy footsteps as Joel and Mariah carried bags from the horses to the various rooms, chattering all the while, the bright sound of Mariah and the deeper tones of Joel's laughter mixing with voices through the house.

Yvonne retreated to the kitchen, standing with her back against the cool stone wall for a while, drawing in breaths flavoured with the scent of cooking and traces of the fragranced candles around the house. The building had transformed from a too-large residence for three of them to a too-small place full of noise and voices and the powerful personalities of the Hundred. And the waiting promises inside her curled, sensing action not far away.

Chapter Nineteen

SHE WAS STILL FEELING unsettled when they all gathered a short while later, Joel and Mariah helping her carry the food through so that everyone met in the dining room. There was no formality or ceremony here, everyone simply helping themselves from the serving dishes on the sideboard before they settled, in no particular order, into chairs around the table. Taking her usual place at the head of the table, for a moment she saw a room full of strange faces, Joel and Mariah in their midst, her chest tightening, before she blinked and saw instead the familiar faces of her fellow Hunar, Joel and Mariah chattering happily to some of their favourite people in the world.

They spent the meal catching up on trivial matters, on gossip, and there was more laughter than she could remember at their last gatherings. Not really surprising as the last gatherings had both been funerals. About a year before Elinor's death, the eldest of them had died. Not a great shock, given his age, and although they had mourned, he had been a difficult and distant character, even among other Hunar.

Elinor's death had been different. Yvonne could still feel the shock of it ringing through her, and from the occasional pauses and tightening of expressions around the room, she was not the only one who missed Elinor's presence. If Sillman was their unofficial leader, Elinor had been their openly acknowledged heart, loved by all, even when she was reprimanding them. She had died too young, the extended life span of a Hunar cut short.

It was only when the meal was done, and they were passing around a couple of the bottles of the exotic liqueurs that had been gifts from Kelton, that Sillman leant forward slightly, catching everyone's attention.

Sillman had been the unofficial leader of the Hundred even before he was the eldest of them. Decades of serving as Hunar had given him an air of calm authority that Yvonne always found soothing. Elinor had possessed something of the same manner. The unspoken assurance that, whatever the problem was, they would find a solution to it. It was what had first drawn her to Elinor, when she had still been frightened and wounded. Before she had seen the green symbol on her shoulder, and felt the first trickle of a Hunar's magic, calling her forward. It had been weeks before Elinor had told her what that sensation meant, that it was the first sign that someone had the potential to become one of the Hundred.

"Lovely as it is to gather again, and to see you, Yvonne, you did not call a Gathering simply for an excellent dinner and drinks. What is the matter?"

Mariah and Joel looked at her, eyes wide. They might not understand the full implication of a Gathering, a plea for aid to all members of the Hundred, but her children were used to being sent out of the room before any detailed discussion took place. She hesitated, on the verge of asking them to leave, and then shook her head slightly. They were both older now than she had been when she became their guardian. Old enough to be here. Besides, they would find out about it soon enough, and they might be more cautious if they knew what was going on.

"A problem too large for me to manage alone. There is an organisation of slave masters. They are gathering children and youngsters from across the lands and selling them on."

Silence met her words, a collective breath drawn in, and then Annabelle shook her head slightly. Not in disagreement but in sadness, her natural enthusiasm dimmed. "We've heard rumours. Children missing. Some of them seemed too fanciful for words. There was a young girl, perhaps nine, taken from an upstairs bedroom. Her parents swore it was fairies."

"But there were ladder marks underneath her window," Idal added.

Yvonne felt ice trickle down her spine. It was identical, in every way, to the kidnapping of the girl from the town. She saw Mariah and Joel exchanging glances, doubtless realising the same thing.

And then others of the Hunar spoke up, recounting other tales. Children being taken. And more than one story of an identical snatching of a nine-year-old girl. Other youngsters simply disappearing, vanishing while going about their daily business. The mood darkened as they exchanged glances, the others realising, perhaps for the first time, just how widespread the problem was.

When they had finished, Yvonne told them about the warehouses and Three Falls. She told them about the clerk, Rebecca, about the ledgers. She told them about the wagons, of strong and sturdy youngsters.

She told them about the sight. About the message. He is coming. She tried not to feel even more worried when no-one else reported any further messages. The sight never worked that way, directed at just one Hunar. Usually all of them would get the messages, one way or another.

And then, stomach twisting, she told them about the quarrel.

There was another sharp, indrawn breath around the room and then Annabelle reacted first, again.

Annabelle rose to her feet and came around the table to give Yvonne yet another hug, this one more lingering than the last, to the point where Yvonne could feel her heart beginning to race at the contact, wanting to be free. Just at the point of panic, Annabelle released her, wiping a tear from her eye, and returned to her place, lifting her glass.

"Quarrels are a blight on civilised society, and should always be eradicated. A toast, to Yvonne."

The rest of the room came to their feet, leaving Yvonne scarlet-faced, and echoed Annabelle's toast. Her skin prickled, discomfort at being the centre of attention even if it was in a heartfelt acknowledgement that warmed her. Talking of the quarrel, however briefly, had stirred up memories again, old and new. Memories no one should have to carry. Unable to defend herself. Teeth ripping. The crawl of dirt across her skin. And the quiet sounds of the quarrel in Kelton. The sobs. The pain. The limp bodies lying on the grass, too worn to move.

She had no time to linger in remembrance as, preliminaries over, serious discussion began around the table. Who could be behind this? How many people would be needed, would be involved in it? Where would they be gathering the children now? What possible use could there be for wagons full of children, being taken away from Three Falls city?

Pieris left the room briefly, returning with a map that made all of them gasp a little in envy. It spread across the table top, hastily cleared of glasses and plates and candles, Sillman sending a shower of magic light into the air above it.

"Where did you get such a beautiful thing?" Suanna asked, her naturally stern expression faded into open envy.

"Made it," Pieris said, his colour darkening under the astonished looks they sent him. "I've been in the northlands for a while. Not that many people, and winter was long and dark. Lots of time indoors," he added, a hint of defensiveness in his tone.

"It is exquisite," Yvonne told him. She had spent one winter in the northlands. She could well believe that a bright and capable mind like Pieris would have sought distraction. "I don't recognise half the spells you've used."

"It will fit to whatever surface it's opened onto," Pieris told her, a hint of pride in his voice. "And will focus on detail if I please. There's another layer I can make notes on."

"Extraordinary," Dundac said, eyes taking in the detail.

Yvonne frowned slightly, remembering another large and detailed map in a kitchen in Kelton, with several layers to it. "That layering is goblin magic, isn't it? I didn't think we could use that." It was a core part of their teaching, that Hunar could not use goblin magic.

"The original spells are goblin, yes," Pieris told her. He always seemed quiet until he was speaking about magic, then he came alive. "There was a bored Karoan'shae lord sent to review the mines. He was happy to talk magic with me." From the slightly unfocused expression that crossed his face, Yvonne was quite sure that they hadn't spent the entire winter simply talking about magic. Then his gaze sharpened, and he returned to her question. "But by studying the individual parts, I was able to make approximations using our magic. It took a while."

"You found a way of breaking down goblin spells and using them," Sillman echoed, shaking his head slightly, his face reflecting awe. "Impressive. Truly impressive."

"I had started making notes of the disappearances and abductions I heard about," Pieris said. He spoke a command word that Yvonne did not recognise. The surface of the map shivered, then an overlay appeared, points of brilliant sapphire appearing in areas near the northlands. "No abductions reported in the northlands. Or in the great forest. Although the darkin are hardly likely to tell humans that their children are missing."

Yvonne followed the sapphire points across the map, easily following the trail that Pieris had taken. He began marking more points on the map, shown in red, where the rest of the Hundred had heard of missing children and youngsters.

By the time they had finished, the map was a sea of red and blue. Hundreds of points. Each one someone's son or daughter.

Taken with no respect for boundaries, or whoever ruled the lands. She saw the grim realisation on the others' faces as she drew their attention to that. The mastermind had crossed borders.

"And that is why I called a Gathering," she told Sillman. "Because no one else travels like we do."

"Yes." Sillman's voice was heavy, face showing more lines than she remembered. He looked up, his eyes hard. "You did right. This must be stopped."

She looked back down at the map, her heart a little lighter. The Hundred were here. Between them they could tackle this.

The map shone faintly with the magic Pieris had woven into it, the bright points of missing children a scatter of stars across it. And, seen like this, Yvonne was struck, as she had been in Brea and Thort's kitchen, about the curious gaps in the reports.

"No abductions in or near the Karoan'shae lands," Sillman commented, returning to business.

"None near the Sisters," Suanna added.

No one was really surprised. The reports were all of human youngsters going missing. And there were very few, if any, humans brave or foolish enough to live among the Karoan'shae, or the dark elves. And no one, not even the most powerful king, wanted to incur the Sisters' wrath.

"And very few here," Yvonne pointed out. North of the territory around Hogsmarthen, which had seen very few missing children thanks to its proximity to the Sisters, there was a sparse line of markers, a few youngsters from farming towns, and then a blank. "That's Coll."

They all stared at the patch on the map for a while, then Pieris gave it another command and the area grew larger before their eyes, showing more detail. A few scattered, tiny towns, many of which didn't have names. A turn in the wide river that cut across the land, an easy crossing point which was a strategic advantage that the king of that land wanted looked after. And so, many years before, the Coll family had been charged with defence of that crossing point. So far from the Royal City they had a lot of autonomy, but still owed their fealty to the kings of Valland.

"I've never been," Suanna murmured, head tilted slightly to one side. She had a distant expression, someone trying to recall memories. "The old lord died, didn't he? A couple of years ago?"

"Something like that," Dundac agreed, frowning in his turn. "And the new lord hasn't turned up at the Valland Court to swear his oath of fealty to the King."

They all turned to look at Dundac. He shrugged, cheeks tinged with colour.

"It's a lovely Court. The kitchens are second to none. And there are people in need there, just as anywhere else."

It sounded perfectly reasonable, Yvonne thought, but also knew that was not the whole truth. Dundac was avoiding Suanna's gaze. Suanna had never had an apprentice longer than a few months, always finding fault with them. The others had stopped trying to get her to train any more after her last apprentice, Dundac, was taken on by Sillman and became a full Hunar a few years before Yvonne. It was no coincidence that Dundac chose to live in the Royal City, a place Suanna detested. They were cordial on the surface, but Hunar were adept at keeping secrets.

Mica drew a breath, eyes dancing with mischief.

"The Valland King has not sent for the new Coll lord?" Yvonne asked, before Mica could speak.

"More than once. He's not pleased," Dundac added, words slowing down as he realised what he was saying. "It's a near fortress."

Before he could continue, there was a sharp knock at the house's front door.

"I didn't feel the wards," Yvonne realised, hand going to her sword-hilt in reflex.

"Doesn't sound urgent," Joel commented, at her shoulder as she left the room. He drew a deep breath in, nostrils widening. "Smells like goblin."

"Guise," Mariah said in disgust, at Yvonne's other shoulder. "Why is he here?"

"He likely has more news," Yvonne told them, anticipation coursing through her. Guise's information usually led to action. "Go and see if the others want some more to drink or eat. Let me speak to him."

She opened the door to let in the cool night air and an impeccably-dressed goblin lord. He made a shallow bow, a reflex courtesy, as she closed the door.

"Mristrian, it is good to see you in health." He tilted his head, taking a sharp breath in, attention going past her. "My apologies, I did not realise you had visitors."

Yvonne's brows rose. His senses were generally far more acute than hers, and she found it difficult to believe he had missed the voices or the presence of other people in the house.

He shrugged, an uncharacteristic gesture, and in the faint light from the candles she thought he was blushing.

"I am not quite recovered," he explained.

From the poisoned arrow that an Abar al Endell assassin had shot into him. Yvonne tilted her head. She could well believe that the assassin's poison would have lingering effects.

"What do you need?" she asked him. It was blunter than she had intended, but he did not take offence.

"I've had word that one of the wagons was seen entering the territory of Coll. I wanted your help to track it."

"Coll."

She heard the word echoed and turned to find Sillman in the doorway of the dining room, eyeing Guise with a sharp, critical look.

"Yes," Guise answered, eyes widening a fraction as he saw the green symbol at Sillman's shoulder. "Hunar." He made another shallow bow.

"You must be Guise. I've heard a lot about you," Sillman added, tone suggesting that very little of what he had heard was favourable.

Guise smiled, eyes shimmering with green, the tips of his fangs showing. "I'm deeply flattered," he responded, with another shallow bow.

"He may have useful information," Sillman commented to Yvonne.

"It would be an honour to aid the Hundred," Guise answered, still smiling.

Yvonne glanced between the pair of them. They reminded her forcibly of Mariah and Joel, bickering over some trivial matter such as who'd had the largest helping of pie. She resisted the urge to roll her eyes.

"Guise, won't you come in? Mariah," she lifted her voice slightly, knowing she would be heard, "we need another glass. Have you eaten?" she asked Guise as an afterthought.

"Yes, thank you."

The faint smile faded as he stopped in the dining room doorway, taking in the people gathered there, and the map stretched across the table.

Another breath in, through his nose, as he studied the map, and he tilted his head slightly, eyes going unerringly to Pieris.

"Jaalam's work, I take it."

Pieris' colour rose and he ducked his head, smile tugging his mouth.

"Yvonne, you did not tell us about this one," Annabelle commented, eyes bright as she looked Guise up and down.

"He's not a toy, Annabelle," Suanna said, voice sharp. "Guise, is it? Come in and tell us what you know."

"Hunar." Guise made a slightly lower bow, directed to the room in general, and came forward, eyes travelling across the map which was still focused on Coll. "I see you have already identified Coll as a place of interest."

"Very few abductions," Pieris told him. He gave another command and the map moved, going back to its original size, showing all the red and blue points.

"Coll is not the only gap," Guise observed. He accepted a wine glass from Mariah with a murmured thanks, ignoring Mariah's sulky expression, and turned his full attention back to the map. "The Runacre Keep, near Ilfton."

"There's not much there," Dundac began, then frowned, "but you are right. There are not many reports around Ilfton, either."

"Or the other side of the mountain from the Sisters," Suanna added. She sighed, looking at the map. "We'll need to check them all."

"Runacre and the mountain are huge areas," Yvonne noted. "We'll need to split up."

"You and Guise follow the cart towards Coll, see what you can find," Sillman decided. "Annabelle, Dundac, Suanna, and Idal will go to Runacre. Pieris, Mica, Firon, and I will go to the other side of the mountain."

The rest of the Hundred nodded in agreement and Pieris folded his map away.

"We'll need to stay in touch," Pieris said, digging into his pocket and bringing out what looked like a series of small birds carved in stone.

"Just how many secrets did Jaalam give you?" Guise asked, eyes narrowing as he saw the birds.

"Not nearly enough," Pieris answered, mouth curving up again.

Guise shook his head slightly, but stayed silent as Pieris gave each of the Hundred one of the stone birds and then explained how to record a short message then send it back to him. All the birds were keyed to him, he explained, and would find him no matter how far away they were.

Yvonne took the stone bird with some scepticism. It seemed far too small, and too fragile, for the claims Pieris was making.

The weight of it surprised her. Despite fitting in the palm of her hand, with room to spare, it was heavier than a full bottle of spirits. Looking more closely she could see that although it appeared to be made of stone, it seemed in fact to be more like coils and coils of thread, each one sewn with spells.

"Just how long was this winter?" she asked Pieris, touching the bird with a fingertip. The threads stirred, wings fluttering. Like the map, it was exquisite work.

"Not long enough," Pieris answered, the soft look vanishing into sadness.

Yvonne felt an echo of his pain in her chest. Along with his quick mind, Pieris had a warm heart, and had not shared it with anyone for many years. There was little prospect of a settled home and family for most of the Hundred. The Hundred were rare enough. Rarer still were people prepared to stand alongside them. And goblins and Hunar did not generally mix well.

Chapter Twenty

A FEW DAYS' HARD riding, Yvonne's sturdy warhorse matching Guise's goblin-bred mount for stamina if not speed, had brought them to Coll.

The rest of the Hundred should be at their destinations soon, too, Yvonne knew, hand straying to her belt pouch where she had put the small bird. It had settled into the pouch and now felt as though it weighed nothing, although if she took it out to examine it, the weight returned. Remarkable magic.

There was nothing to tell Pieris, not yet. She was looking forward to having something to tell Pieris, so that she could see the bird's spells in action.

Quiet enquiries along the way, made by Guise of various individuals who had taken one look at the symbol on Yvonne's shoulder then found urgent business elsewhere, had confirmed that a wagon, or possibly two, had been seen on this route. Possibly ones from Three Falls. Possibly other completely innocent traders, going about their normal business. Guise wasn't sure, frustrated by the lack of information, even going so far as to complain at not being able to get straight answers from thieves, sending Yvonne a sour look as she laughed.

With no better information to go on, the trail had brought them to the castle itself, at the centre of the Coll lands.

It looked like a perfectly ordinary castle, sitting on a slight rise in the ground, a large moat dug around it. The wide river was shallower here, with a pair of sandbanks meaning that it was, just, possible to cross the river here rather than using one of the few bridges guarded by the king's men. The distance to the sandbanks was a short swim for a horse, and manageable for a human. The water between the banks was just deep enough for the river barges to pass by.

The crossing had been used by armies in the past. There had been no wars here, no invading armies, for far longer than Yvonne had been alive. But the

Valland kings had not kept a grip on these lands, and ensured its peace, by being complacent. The castle, and its watch over the river, were a part of the kingdom. Yvonne remembered Dundac's words and, not for the first time, wondered how the lord of the castle had got away with ignoring the King's summons for so long.

In the weak light of an overcast spring day, the castle was oddly still. There did not appear to be any guards on the walls, or at the open gates, which would earn the lord a severe reprimand from the king, even if he had been dutiful in his attendance at Court.

"He's going to lose the lands," she said, half to herself. The Coll family had held this castle, in the king's name, for generations, each one steadfast in their loyalty.

"Young fool," Guise agreed.

They were concealed in the last group of trees before the open ground around the castle. Discipline might be lax among the castle's inhabitants, but the boundaries were still maintained and this last group of trees was too far for any archers to attack the non-existent guards. Even if they had bows and arrows, and even with a bit of magic behind the arrow, it would have run out of any force by the time it reached the castle's walls.

"There's no easy way in," Guise commented. He sounded speculative rather than frustrated.

"But you have an idea?"

As far as Yvonne could tell, there were only two roads into the castle. There was the main route, on this side of the castle, that was a wide, well-maintained road leading up to a drawbridge over the moat and double doors, standing open, in the castle's walls. There was a smaller road leading from the back.

At least, those were the only ones that were visible. A castle like this, built when wars were frequent and this river crossing far more important, must have secret entrances and exits, usually only known to the family.

"I don't think you're going to like it," he said, still with that speculative tone in his voice.

Before Yvonne could tell him that she most certainly would not like it, whatever it was, and ask him to think of another plan, a soft sound behind them drew her attention.

The trees here were giants, worthy of places in the Great Forest, with deep shadows among them and in their canopies above. The resemblance to the Great Forest did not end there, she realised. What had looked like dark shadows underneath trees had become solid creatures.

"Darkin?" she said in disgust. "I didn't think there were any this far east," she added, hand going to her sword hilt.

"There shouldn't be," Guise confirmed, drawing his sword.

"Cousin. You are far outside your borders," one of the shapes said. They were creatures made up of shadow and bits of darkness, able to blend in with the shady depths of the Great Forest that they usually called home. Quite real, though, and deadly fighters. A match for goblins. Her heart sped up, body tensing, readying for battle.

"I was about to say the same thing," Guise answered.

Without speaking, Yvonne put her back to Guise's, and they stepped a little further towards the light. Darkin were not bound to stay in shadow, but it was easier to see them, and easier to fight them, in the light.

And there were four of them, Yvonne saw, disgusted with herself that she had not noticed them before. But they were, as Guise has said, far outside their borders. She could not remember the last time she had seen a darkin outside their own homeland. Her last experience with them had been almost cordial, as they had asked for her help. Not long after Elinor's funeral, when she had not really cared who asked for her help, as long as her mind and body were active.

"Hunar, what brings you here?" It was a teasing question, and she did not think that the speaker expected any response from her.

"Someone has been stealing children from their families and then selling them," she told the darkin. Children were rare, and prized, among their kind, like many of the rarer races. "And we think there may be information in the castle."

"There is," the darkin replied, a darker tone in his voice. His outline shimmered a fraction, became solid for a moment, and Yvonne saw that he had a metal band of some description around one of his wrists. "But we can't help you. We have orders."

"Someone bound them with iron," Yvonne told Guise. Most humans might scoff at legend, but some, like the Hunar, had been born out of truth. And this was another. Putting iron onto one of the darkin was torture for it, and bound the darkin to service.

"I can help you, if you ask me to," she told them.

"We have orders," he answered, and the four of them moved forward.

The approach of the darkin had concealed something else. There was something large and solid coming towards her. She caught movement out of the corner of her eye and turned her head, a cry of alarm stuck in her throat. The last thing she saw was a heavy object descending rapidly towards her head.

The world was shaking, moving in an extremely uncomfortable way. Her stomach twisted. Head was pounding. She tried opening her eyes and got a confused impression of light and dark and flickering shadows, quickly closing her eyes as her stomach rebelled at the motion and sight. She was upside down. Even as she realised that, whatever it was that was carrying her let her fall.

She hit stone with a force that made her grunt involuntarily, the cool, hard surface a momentary relief against the hot skin of her face. She tried opening her eyes again. The nausea was worse and, a moment later, she threw up whatever was in her stomach onto the stone floor. The smell made her retch again, and she scrabbled to her hands and knees, backing away from the sickness, trying not to breathe through her nose, turning her head away from the smell and the sight. It did not help much, her stomach lurching again. She did not think there was anything left in her to bring up and stayed kneeling, trying to breathe lightly, one hand going to her head and coming away sticky with blood.

"Humans are fragile, you know," Guise's voice said, in a conversational tone. He was not speaking to her.

She blinked, trying to clear her eyes, and turned her head away from her sickness, moving very slowly. He was standing near her. He seemed to have been in a fight. His clothes were torn, there was a spectacular bruise on one side of his face, and from the way he was holding himself she thought he might have broken ribs as well. He had also been stripped to his shirtsleeves, his weapons removed, and she did not need to look down to know that her weapons had gone as well.

More surprising was the identity of their captors.

"Vettr?" Her voice squeaked in astonishment.

The stone creatures explained her thumping head. They did not need weapons, when no sword could cut through their skin.

They were generally thought of as slow and stupid, but that was not always the case. They were, however, fanatically loyal. Obedient dogs, she had heard them called more than once. She thought that was insulting to dogs. Vettr were mean, and petty.

The one who had been carrying her bared its teeth in what she thought was a smile, small eyes gleaming with amusement. Pleased at her discomfort, she thought.

"I told you to be careful with them," a new voice said.

She forgot all about the vettr, her pounding head and her twisting stomach. That voice held far more power than it should.

Her eyes finally cleared and she saw who Guise had been talking to.

They were in the main hall of the castle, a giant room with high ceilings and walls that would typically be covered by tapestries and the coats of arms of the family who lived here and those who owed them service.

The walls were bare, only a few torches here and there, their light unnecessary in daytime. The focal point of the room was, therefore, a stone dais on which sat a massive, carved wooden chair.

The chair would easily have held four, but there was only one occupant, who managed to sit on it without looking stupid.

A young man, at least outwardly, he was strikingly handsome with clean, even features and black hair swept back from his brow, on which sat a simple gold band.

She forced herself to her feet, wobbling slightly. Guise made no move to help her.

"Lord Coll?" The age was right, and from what she remembered of the family, the face was right as well. But nothing else was.

He smiled, and where there should have been white, even teeth she saw darkened teeth that were slightly ragged. Even at this distance, she could see that his eyes were not the pale blue common to people of these lands, but a darker shade that did not belong on anything human.

"Not quite." He lifted his arm and turned his hand, palm up, and she saw that fingernails had been replaced by claws. "Human bodies are so limiting."

Her stomach twisted again and she swallowed against more nausea. There were very few things that could enter the human body and interfere with it to this extent. And none of them were good.

"Where is your master, young lord?" Guise asked, sounding bored. "I do not deal with underlings."

Yvonne tried to turn her head to look at Guise. A wave of pain and nausea had her crouching down on the floor again, eyes watering as she breathed lightly, waiting for the wave to subside.

Even through the discomfort she heard the lord's answer.

"I have no master." The voice held a sneer that spoke of contempt. But there was something else there, and if she had not been nursing her pounding head, she might have been able to work out what it was.

"Creatures like you always do," Guise answered, still in the same tone. "No imagination."

"I will grind your bones to dust." The voice had shaded further to dark, the mask of humanity slipping a bit more.

There were very few things that could take over a human body that way, Yvonne reminded herself, trying to keep her breathing steady so she could think. If she pretended she was calm, her mind might settle. Very few things, she repeated. There was a parasitic plant found in the Forbidden Lands. That did not fit, as the victims were usually immobile, unable to function once the plant had taken hold, releasing its spores. A small, vicious insect that was also found in the Forbidden Lands. Still, the host would not have black teeth and claws.

Her head swum again and her stomach twisted. She was running out of things. She went through another few possibilities, dismissing them at once.

None of them fit. Nothing she knew of would cause claws and darkened eyes and blackened teeth and the aura of crackling power the lord carried.

Nothing she knew of. But there were darkin outside, secretive and wary of contact beyond their own kind. And their distant cousins, the goblins, held onto their secrets with vicious determination. And there were unexplored territories beyond the northlands, and beyond the Great Ocean.

Arrogant to assume one knew everything. Elinor had said that often. She had found herself saying it to Mariah and Joel more than once.

"Why do you want bone dust?" Guise asked, cutting through her spiralling thoughts and rising panic.

There was a short, charged pause. Long enough for her to raise her head and see something in the lord's face. Something she was quite sure he had not meant to give away. Guise had touched a nerve. There had been what looked like fear in the lord's face. He had not meant to give that away. Bone dust.

In some small villages there was still a superstition about protecting your house by scattering the ground-up bones of murderers. And in at least one case when they had run out of murderers, the village elders had decided that petty criminals would do. There were always a few of those to be found.

But that was stupid human superstition.

Bone dust.

The way Guise had said it carried meaning. Goblin magic was quite different to human magic. It had taken Pieris an entire winter to break down some goblin spells for use in the Hunar way. And Guise had wanted to know how many secrets Pieris's goblin paramour had spilled. It had not been an idle question.

"Better question. Why does your master require bone dust?"

Bone dust. Graves. He is coming.

Her mind spun, making connections where there probably weren't any. She wanted to ask questions, find out information, work through the puzzle, but could not find the right words.

"Not your concern," the lord answered Guise, with a dismissive wave of his hand. "You will be dead anyway. You and your human whore."

Yvonne choked on an unexpected laugh. It was not the first time that the insult had been thrown in her direction. A lot of men seemed to have limited imagination when it came to describing women.

"And now you are offensive," Guise said, across her laughter. He did not sound amused. He sounded quietly furious.

"But it is funny," Yvonne managed to say, voice hoarse from being sick. She coughed to clear her throat. "Next he will probably say that I should be paying you for your company." That was a very common follow up. She choked on another laugh. "No imagination."

"How true," Guise agreed, turning his attention to her. "A very shallow little man."

There was a loud crack and a bang. They turned to find that the not-quite-human lord had flung his chair to one side, the vast throne cracking as it fell, and he was coming down the steps of the dais towards them. Her eyes were clear enough, and her head had stopped pounding long enough, for her to notice that he was wearing floor-length robes of a rich red fabric, over sewn with gold thread. They were clothes fit for a king.

"Lovely robes," Yvonne commented. She did not seem to be able to help herself, even though it simply made the lord more angry.

He stopped a few paces away and she had another shock seeing fine lines of darkness across his face, under his skin. Whatever corruption had taken him over, it was in his veins, tainting his blood. She was confident that if she opened a wound on him, he would bleed black.

His nose wrinkled, and he looked to one side, to where she had been sick. The smell doubtless offended him. She didn't like it much, either.

"Lick that up," he ordered the vettr that had been carrying her. "I told you to be more careful with her."

Yvonne's stomach clenched again as the vettr knelt on the stone floor and began licking up the sickness, its thick, great tongue scraping against the stone floor.

"A new look?" Guise asked, tilting his head to the bare walls around them.

"I have not decided yet," the lord answered, seemingly happy to be diverted into decoration. He was frowning slightly as he looked at them. "You are not as impressive as I thought you would be. The wastrel son of the Karoan'shae. The youngest Hunar. You are boring me."

Yvonne tensed. That seemed dangerous.

"Hold him," the lord ordered the other vettr. Guise tensed as the stone creature moved behind him and took hold of his arms, pinning them to his sides. The lord reached underneath his robes and pulled out what looked like a piece of folded paper.

"This should make things more interesting, though."

He opened the twist of paper and Yvonne had the briefest impression of a brilliant blue powder, before he flung the contents at Guise, the powder covering Guise's face.

None of the powder got onto Yvonne, and she was glad of it as Guise reacted violently, eyes widening in what looked like genuine horror. He tried to move his arms, to brush the powder off his head, and the vettr that held him did not move, absorbing his struggles with ease. "Oh yes, this should be much more interesting." The lord waved a hand at the vettr. "Take them away."

Chapter Twenty-One

Everything was black. Yvonne blinked, wondering for a moment if she was truly awake. Yes. There was the faintest suggestion, the barest sliver, of a lighter shade among the black. And she was so uncomfortable she had to be awake. She was on her side, lying on something cold and hard that felt like stone, her guess proved accurate when she put her hand out and pushed herself upright, into a sitting position. She wished she hadn't moved as her head thumped, pain making it impossible to think clearly. Her heart was pounding in counterpoint to her head, not helping matters.

The last thing she remembered was Guise struggling in the vettr's hold, face coated with blue powder.

The other vettr must have knocked her out again.

There did not seem to be any vettr here, at least. Despite being made of stone, they tended to be noisy, with loud, rasping breaths. It was silent around her. The only thing she could hear was her own breathing, too fast and harsh.

She seemed to be on some kind of a stone bench and, cautiously, moved until her feet were closer to the ground. Not quite touching. Her back was against a stone wall and she could feel damp seeping through her clothing. There was something wrong with that, although she couldn't work out what. Her head was a twist of pain. Running her hands across her hair, she found a hard knot behind one ear, which made her hiss involuntarily when she touched it. Besides that, both sides of her face were hot and sticky, swollen so that she could not feel the bones. No wonder her head hurt.

Her eyes must be clearing. She could make out more detail in the dark. Some faint, shadowed shapes. There seemed to be some kind of metal grate in the wall to one side that was letting in a small amount of light. It looked like it might be a barred window of some sort.

From the smell it seemed likely she was underground.

She was in a cell. The castle's dungeons, if she had to guess. Sadly, it was not her first time in a dungeon.

Worse. Far worse. She had finally worked out what was wrong with the damp seeping across her back. Her clothes were missing, lower legs and feet bare. She seemed to be just wearing her underclothes, a sleeveless tunic and knee-length trousers made of fine lawn fabric perfectly adequate with layers on top. Not suitable for a dungeon. It was cold as well as damp.

No clothes meant no resources, too. All the prepared spells she kept in a pouch at her belt. The small bird that Pieris had made, ready to fly back to him with news. All of it gone. Just her, and her pounding head.

She moved forward, slowly and carefully, until her feet touched the ground. She recoiled at once, the stone cold and damp, covered in some unknown substance. Cool air crossed her skin, unfamiliar and unwelcome. Her scalp was prickling. Perhaps from a sense of danger but, more likely, a reaction to the filth around her.

Dungeons were not known for being clean. Whatever was under her feet was a thick ooze and smelled rank. She wanted to draw her knees up to her chest, to make herself as small as possible, and to stay here, on this bench. She felt dirty enough without moving elsewhere. But she could not stay here. She had no weapons and she was getting truly cold.

Standing up on the dungeon's floor, or whatever it was on the floor seeping between her toes, took far longer than it should have done. She had to stay still for a moment, head swimming, pain making her hiss, letting herself adjust, breathing hard and rapid, heart thumping too fast in her ears.

At length, she was able to move. Slowly and carefully, keeping her feet close to the ground so she didn't stumble over anything, toes dragging through whatever-it-was on the floor, she moved towards the metal grate that she had seen.

It was a small, barred opening set in a wooden door that was bounded with metal. Not really expecting any success, she tried to find the door lock and see if she was able to open it. The lock fizzed against her fingers, a trace of magic making her step back quickly. Her head was still pounding too hard for her to conjure any spells, but somebody had put a powerful hex on the door. It had a flavour that she recognised, even with a pounding head. Goblin magic. Apart from Guise, she hadn't seen any goblins.

Although, it could be darkin magic. They were distant cousins, and there were definitely darkin about.

Thinking about it only made her heart beat faster, her stomach churn again and her headache worse.

The door was locked. She could not open it.

Instead, she started moving, slowly and carefully, around the cell, trying to be as quiet as possible. Sounds probably wouldn't carry outside the cell, but there was no point in taking risks.

The side wall of the cell, that joined onto the wall with the door in it, was covered in something sticky that she did not want to think about. There were also great iron stakes hammered into the wall, holding heavy iron manacles. Simple devices that fastened with an iron pin. They would hold most creatures, she thought, and wondered how many unfortunates had lost their lives in this cell.

Adding that to the growing list of things she did not want to think about, she continued on her exploration. She reached the far end of the cell, the wall opposite the door, when she realised that there was a darker pool of shadow in the next corner of the room, at the other end of the stone bench where she had been lying.

Her breath caught, and she took a hasty step back, bumping into the wall, one foot sliding on the floor.

She had not heard anything during her whole exploration of the cell, and had not realised that she was not alone.

She knew only one person who could be that quiet.

"Guise?" Her voice was too high, throat too tight to let enough air into her lungs. She sounded as panicked as she felt. Not enough air. Her limited vision wavered. Her back was still against the wall, skin prickling at the contact.

He gave a soft grunt in response. There were no words in it, but she recognised the tone.

"Are you awake? We're in a cell."

He made another odd, dark noise which sounded like agreement.

She was still breathing too hard and her heart was still racing too fast. She was trapped in a cell, in her underclothes, with a goblin. Old, old panic was rising up. She tried to tell herself that this was Guise, who had never shown any sign of wanting to hurt her, at least not physically. He was irritating, and frustrating, and had a really annoying habit of turning up when she least expected it. But he had never actually hurt her.

He moved slightly, a rasp of sound against the stone bench, and she let out an involuntary squeal, stumbling as she moved back along the wall, towards the door.

On the way, she bumped her head against one of the iron manacles, sending a fresh pulse of pain through her skull, and spit out a curse that she had not used for a long time. "Bloody manacles."

"Manacles?"

She froze at once. That did not sound like Guise. Not at all. She knew it was him but his voice was normally rich, a caress in her ears, drawing her forward. This sound was harsh, overlaid with something she did not recognise.

"Yes. There are manacles to hold the prisoner's hands."

"Feet too?"

She frowned in the dark, but knelt and, reluctantly, put her hand across the wall. She found matching manacles at floor level.

"Yes, hands and feet."

"Good. Bind me."

He moved, rising up from the bench as a blot of shadow and power, carrying with him an odd scent that caught something primitive in Yvonne's brain and told her that here was something incredibly dangerous. A predator. Far more dangerous than any wulf she had ever met.

She had her back against the door before she knew what she was doing, fingers scrabbling towards the lock. The frisson of magic against her fingers reminded her, and snapped her back to a moment of sense.

A sound outside the cell made her turn her head. Too fast. Her vision swam, white and red shards of agony shooting through her skull. She backed away from the door by instinct, moving towards the bench, not wanting to get closer to Guise.

Loud, dragging footsteps sounded outside. A stone floor.

The huge, unwelcome shape of a vettr stopped outside the cell. Their dark sight was better even than a goblin's and she could feel the small, mean eyes travelling around the cell.

"Still alive," the vettr grunted. "Pity. I was looking forward to licking your blood from the walls."

Her stomach turned, remembering the rasping of that tongue on the flagstones upstairs, every bit of her skin prickling in revulsion.

Guise made a sound she had never heard from a goblin before. A snarl close to one a wulf could make, carrying an unspoken and potent threat.

The backs of her knees hit the stone bench before she knew that she had moved. The bench bit into her legs and she sat down, hard, jarring every bone in her body and sending a fresh wave of white-hot, knife-sharp agony through her skull.

Breath hissed in, eyes damp with the effects, she was vaguely aware of words spoken over her head. Her mind could not unravel them, meaningless sounds, until the vettr moved and her attention sharpened. There were two predators nearby, and she was more afraid of the vettr.

"She'll be dead soon," the vettr was saying to Guise, sounding almost cheerful. "Then we will have fun with you."

The vettr made a noise like rocks grinding together and Yvonne realised it was laughing. Mean and petty. It was looking forward to her death, and whatever they had planned for Guise.

It watched them a while longer, but she stayed still on the bench, not sure if she could move, and Guise was holding himself too still at the other side of the cell.

With a grunt that sounded like disappointment, it moved away, heavy footsteps fading quickly from her limited hearing.

"I don't want to die," she told Guise, her voice a whisper. It was a pathetic statement. There wasn't much she could do about it, not injured and freezing and nearly naked in this dungeon that she could not escape from.

"I do not want you to die, either, mristrian," he told her. The weight of that wish stopped her heart for a moment. There was far more behind those words than she could guess at. "Manacles," he said, a change of subject that she could not follow until he moved.

She made an involuntary sound of panic, curling herself up on the bench. He might not want her to die, but she did not understand what was going on.

Guise was not moving towards her, though. He was moving to the manacles. With the uncertain light from the corridor behind her, she could see his darker shadow as he felt along the wall and found the first one. He got one foot into the manacles and she heard the small click as the pin went home, holding him in place. The restraints were designed to hold their captive at an awkward, spread-eagled pose across the wall, though, and he could not manage the second foot as well, instead making a low sound of frustration that carried savagery with it. He managed, somehow, to get one of his hands restrained and Yvonne heard the sound of the second pin clicking home.

"You'll need to do the rest," he told her. He still sounded savage, on the verge of some burst of destruction that she was quite certain she did not want to be anywhere near. "Mristrian," he went on, when she didn't move, drawing in a long breath that she could hear over her racing pulse. "Do this, please, then we can talk." That sounded more like Guise, the veneer of civility back.

Somehow, she uncurled from the stone bench and moved across the cell, wincing as more filth crept between her toes, and secured his other hand first, before kneeling to fix the restraint around his ankle, head swimming as she did so. The predator was confined. Even so, she checked all four restraints were in place before she straightened, stumbling as she realised that he was wearing even fewer clothes than she was, and she had been touching bare skin as she secured him to the wall.

She fell backwards onto the bench and hit her head again against the wall, letting out a small cry of pain. She did not need any more bruises.

"Are you alright?" Guise asked. He sounded fractionally less savage.

"Am I alright? I've been hit on the head twice, had my weapons taken away, and shoved in a cell with an angry goblin. A vettr wants to lick my blood off the walls. I'm supposed to die soon. And I don't know what that creature upstairs is. I am not alright."

Her voice had risen in pitch by the end, and even she could hear the note of hysteria. She drew her knees up to her chest and buried her face in them, hugging herself as tightly as she could. It did not help. Not much. She heard a low, harsh sob come out of her chest. Her head hurt. She was covered in filth. Her scalp was crawling. She could not even cleanse herself, unable to gather enough focus for magic. And she was getting cold. And hungry.

"I am sorry," Guise said. He sounded sincere.

"And what's wrong with you? Is it that powder?"

The low sound of fury he made had her backing up against the wall again, heart racing, throat tightening. She wished she had a weapon to hand. She had some energy, enough for a spell or two, if she could only think straight to use them.

"I don't know how he knew about it. It is a well-kept secret," Guise said. He was definitely more like himself, despite the growl of fury. She could hear the arrogance of generations of the Karoan'shae behind him in those words.

She bit out an unexpected laugh. "You think you're the only one who likes secrets?"

"A fair point, mristrian."

"What does it do? This powder?"

He made another low sound that had her freezing in place, terrified.

"It releases inhibitions. In small quantities it's like a drug."

"Like a human having a drink or two?"

"No." The growl was back. "More like a grain or two of terras root."

Her throat closed up in panic. Small quantities of terras root were often added to soldiers' meals before battle, giving them a harder edge in combat.

Larger quantities of terras root had shocking effects and could turn even the most mild-mannered human into a violent killer. She had helped Elinor investigate a village where one single person had slaughtered most of the rest of the villagers, killed by four brave youngsters who had somehow managed to get the man pinned down and cut his throat. She still remembered the hollow-eyed faces of those youngsters, the absolute lack of comprehension as they stood among the bodies of their friends and family.

"Terras root," she repeated, voice still too high. "Why haven't you killed me yet?"

The pitch of her voice made it sound like a complaint, making the question sound ridiculous.

It prompted an unexpected laugh from him. "You are far too valuable," he answered, the weight of that resonating through her entire being. She turned that over in her mind. Valuable. It was an odd choice of word. She was missing something, her mind too clouded with pain. "And I do not want to give in to that..." He drew a breath and said a word in his native language that she was glad she did not understand. The quality of his voice had changed, shading back to violence.

The goblin equivalent of terras root. And Guise had been given an enormous dose.

Her breath was shallow and rapid, too little air getting into her lungs, pulse racing so fast she could not make out the individual beats.

Goblins were savage by their nature. Like wulfkin, it took them many years to learn self-control, to learn to command themselves. They did it exceptionally well. They did it so well, in fact, that most people who met goblins thought of them as highly civilised beings, with their fancy clothes, impeccable grooming and elaborate manners.

There was nothing civilised about Guise just now.

Even as she thought that, she realised that she was no longer shivering. The temperature in the cell had risen, and not from any outside source.

"It's eroding your control," she realised.

"I do not want to hurt you, mristrian," he said. She believed him.

Neither of them needed to finish that thought. He did not want to hurt her, but he very easily could, and probably would, if the powder continued to run its course.

"Will the powder simply fade over time? Do we just wait it out?"

"No. That will not work. It's in my lungs."

Her throat closed again. In his lungs, his every breath coated with the stuff.

Guise moved, the clank of iron awaking old fear. Trapped. In a locked cell. Unwanted memories that she had carried for too long rose up, and she put a hand to her throat in reflex, expecting to find it torn and bloodied. There was no wound. It was in her mind. All in her mind.

There was not enough air again. Lungs burning. Sight fading. Breath too fast. An odd, keening sound coming from her throat. Trapped. She had to get out. Get away. Leave here. But there was a locked door, hexed with goblin magic in her way.

"Yvonne." The one word, that he rarely spoke, stopped her breath long enough for her to realise that she was not suffocating.

She drew a long, ragged breath, and wiped more tears from her face, smearing the blood that had crusted there.

Trapped.

Panic rose up again, choking her.

She was trapped. With Guise. She could not get out on her own. She needed his help.

Another wave of panic.

This was Guise. And however little she knew about him, she did know he had excellent survival skills. She needed his help.

Her mind sharpened. "I can't deal with the door. Goblin magic. Maybe darkin. You'll need to open the door. Is there anything that can counteract that powder? An antidote?" Another ridiculous question. They didn't have their belongings. Unless they could fashion an antidote from whatever sludge was on the floor, or the fabric they were wearing, there wasn't much they could do.

"In my coat. Not here," he answered, as though he had followed her line of thought. And yet. There was something in his voice that meant, for the first time, she did not think he was telling her the truth.

"No substance. Not here." She tested the words. They sounded right and felt right. The pounding in her head faded a little, the heat of the cell oddly soothing. "Something else? I can't work magic just now."

"It's not appropriate," he said, and she could almost see him shaking his head.

"Guise, there's a madman upstairs. He's tainted with something I've never seen. He's got vettr and darkin. He's put us here for fun. You heard that vettr. They want me dead, and then they're going to play with you. Whatever that means. We need to get out of here."

She was babbling again, unable to help herself, on her feet by the time she had finished speaking, moving closer so that she could see him better in the poor light of the cell. The air around him was as warm as standing near a fire, his eyes glowing. Red tinged, but mixed with the colour she had rarely seen among goblins. A pale yellow.

He bared his teeth at her, not answering, and she took an involuntary step back before remembering he was bound in iron. The snarl had been a warning. A deterrent. There was something he was not telling her.

"Guidrishinnal de'laj Krejefell." She made her voice as stern as she could, calling his attention.

There was a short pause, his head jerking up, red in his eyes fading. More yellow taking its place.

"What did you call me?"

"Guidrishinnal de'laj Krejefell."

"I didn't realise you knew my name. Who I was."

"Not at first," she told him. "But I like to know who I'm dealing with, and you do keep turning up."

He gave a soft laugh, humour directed at his own expense.

"We need to get out of here. What can we do?" she asked.

"I do not think it is right," he said. There was red back in his eyes again and a low, growling sound in his throat.

For the first time, she was not afraid of his bad temper. He was hiding something. "We need to get out. And you thought of something."

He snarled, teeth fully extended, and she stumbled back a step, before recognising the tactic. Her head thumped and she winced, putting a hand to her forehead. Her skin was hot, too. A bad sign.

They were neither of them in good shape.

She heard a soft sound, a sob, and realised it came from her as Guise snarled again, his eyes shading fully to red.

She stumbled back across the cell, onto the bench again, as far away from him as she could, and watched, wide-eyed and horrified, as he struggled against the bonds. She heard a distinct, grating sound and her throat closed, a high-pitched whimper emerging before she could prevent it. The restraints might be iron, but they had clearly never come across an enraged goblin, fuelled by whatever substance Coll had given him.

"Guise. We need to get out of here. I can't open the door. You can. You need to focus." Babbling again. Words too fast, voice too high. Breathing hurt. Head hurt. Every part of her skin crawling at the filth in the cell. Heart pounding far too fast. It was not just Guise in danger of losing control. "What do you need?"

He snarled again, but the red had faded, yellow shade reappearing.

"There is a bond that goblins can create. It means that, of all people in the world, I will never hurt you."

"That doesn't sound so bad," Yvonne heard herself saying. She had jolted her head in her retreat back across the cell, and her vision was wavering. A very bad sign. She really needed the attention of a healer, not to be in this filthy and now too-warm cell with a goblin on the edge of losing his control.

"It's not a bad thing," he agreed. The red was fading from his eyes, visible even across the cell.

"What do we need to do?"

There was a too-long silence which made her skin prickle with unease, wondering if he was losing control. He moved slightly, and she heard the unwelcome sound of the manacles grating against the wall again. They were definitely not designed to hold an enraged goblin. He could get out of them. Soon, if that noise was anything to go by. And then he would kill her. Perhaps not immediately, as he still seemed to have some control left. But control was fading, the poison settling into his system.

That rapid, harsh sound was her breathing. Far too fast. There was no air in her lungs. The world turned, her vision flickering in and out, bright pin-point stars appearing across the black of the cell. She clenched her jaw, forcing a slower breath. There was air. It just didn't feel like it. And she could not afford to collapse. Not now.

There was no sound or movement outside the cell door that she could sense. It was only a matter of time, though. The vettr would doubtless be back and disappointed that she was not dead. And the castle's lord had put them here for a reason, and may want to check on them personally. They needed to be away before he came looking for them. As far away as possible so she could find some way of contacting the rest of the Hundred.

The Hundred. They needed to be warned. That meant getting out of this cell.

"Guise," she prompted, keeping her voice low and calm with an effort that made the pain in her head tighten around her skull. "We need to get out of here. What do we do?"

"Mristrian, kof le maisre, Guidrishinnal de'laj Krejefell, ertre mies vej lorstra. Yvonne. Maisre." The words made no sense to her, spoken in a low, harsh voice that did not sound like Guise at all.

She stared back at him across the dark space of the cell, another scatter of stars crossing her eyes. There was not enough light for her human eyes to make out any detail. All she could really tell was that his eyes were no longer red. The stars faded and her vision blurred. She closed her eyes to focus better. The stars were there, behind her eyelids, waiting for her. She opened her eyes again.

"I don't understand," she told him baldly. "What do you need me to do?"

"If you accept, say your name, and then say. Maisre. Mies vej lorstra maisre Guidrishinnal de'laj Krejefell."

She turned the words over in her mind. Apart from the names, it was an ancient goblin language she did not know. Like mristrian, which he insisted on calling her, even as he avoided explaining its meaning.

Her vision blacked completely for a moment and her heart skipped, mouth dry. She could not remember how many times she had hit her head. Her stomach twisted, a gnaw of hunger and nausea combined.

They needed to get out of the cell. And Guise had a plan. His control might be fading, yet she still trusted his survival instincts. This would work. Their only chance.

"Yvonne. Maisre. Mies vej lorstra maisre Guidrishinnal de'laj Krejefell."

Her skin flushed, head to toe, warmth and magic washing over her. Goblin magic, with none of the hard edge she was used to. This felt like lifting her face to the sun after the rain had passed, warmth enveloping her with the same care and softness as a fine wool blanket.

Guise made a soft sound, a sigh of tension being released. Her eyes cleared for a moment and she could see his outline, relaxing against the restraints. His head bowed for a moment, normally sleek hair tangled. When he lifted his head and opened his eyes, she saw they were a colour she had never seen before. The yellow tint from before had deepened to a luxurious gold.

"My head doesn't hurt quite as much," she said in wonder, touching the side of her face gently. Her skin was still sticky, hot and swollen. There were no stars across her sight anymore.

"Will you free me?" Guise asked.

"Is it safe?" she countered.

"I will not hurt you, mristrian."

There was something under those words. Another layer she could not understand. The echoes of the goblin magic were still wrapped around her, holding her safe. The one person in the world that he would not hurt. Would never hurt.

She was caught for a moment in the familiar push and pull of his presence. That voice that drew her forward. The secrets that held her back and the memories, of wulfkin not goblin, that made her want to run.

But he would not hurt her.

She believed him.

That belief got her up from the bench and across the cell. The air was cooling rapidly, and she shivered slightly as she freed his hands, then knelt to take the pins out from the manacles at his feet. The stars returned as she knelt and she swayed slightly as she rose to her feet.

"The door?"

Yes, he definitely sounded more like himself.

"Goblin or darkin magic," she reminded him. She was not sure how much she had said, or he had heard, before. "The unpleasant sort."

She stepped back as he moved towards the door, going back to the bench while he inspected the lock.

By the time he made a soft sound of discovery, she was truly cold, her teeth chattering together. She barely noticed the soft sound as he undid the lock's magic, lifting her head only when the cell door swung open. Silently. However filthy the floor was, someone kept the doors in good working order.

"Shall we?" he asked.

"Clothes," she answered, moving to stand near him, "and my sword." More than likely she would not be able to hit anything with the sword, but she wanted a weapon.

"As you wish, mristrian," he answered, the greater part of his attention seeming to be on the corridor outside. He tilted his head back to her for a moment. "You are cold."

"I'm freezing, now that you've calmed down."

"I am sorry," he answered, sounding sincere. There was not enough light yet for her to judge properly.

"Clothes," she reminded him.

The corridor outside looked like any other castle dungeon. A short corridor with a few cell doors on either side, and a torch set in a sconce at the end where the corridor opened onto a larger, better-lit space. They crept along the dungeon corridor to the shadows near the torch.

The open space was a guard room of some kind. A few plain wooden tables and chairs, more torches along the walls, and a bundle of things carelessly thrown against the wall, spilling out into an untidy pile. Yvonne recognised her shirt sleeve poking out from among the items.

Apart from their belongings, the room was empty. Guise moved past her on silent feet, going to the only other doorway.

Yvonne did not wait for his return, moving across to their belongings, tugging her shirt out. It was not all that warm, but it had more weight than her underclothes.

"I hope they are dead." Guise's voice was low, menacing. She stilled, half-way through putting her sleeves the right way about, heart skipping, skin crawling. He sounded on the edge of violence again.

Moving as slowly as she could, she turned her head. He was a few paces away, eyes fixed on her neck.

The scars.

The scars that she kept hidden, that even her children had only seen once or twice in their lives. The ones she would always carry, that would not heal with magic. Not hers, not Elinor's. The scars that were a permanent reminder of a past she would dearly like to forget.

"Long dead," she answered, swallowing hard. It was one of the few things that made the scars bearable. "They burned." And now that she had started talking, the memories too fresh and too raw, she found she could not stop. "They didn't realise that one of the girls they had taken was not just a pretty little thing. She killed the first wulf who approached her." Yvonne shook her head in memory, pulling the shirt over her head, covering some of the scars across her shoulders. "Then she set a fire." She swallowed, remembering the horror of that night. "Most of the cages were locked, still. She didn't really care. She wanted it all to burn. But one of the other girls was a thief. Got her lock open. And a few of the others." Her throat closed for a moment, the faces rising in her mind's eye. "A few of us managed to get out." Amid the fury of the wulfkin, a few muffled screams from the others who had been caged. The worst memories were the girls who simply lay, waiting for the flames to reach them. Too battered to care if they lived.

"Mariah and Joel were in a pen at the end," she went on, eyes blind, remembering the tiny faces looking up at her. "Old enough to walk. Just about. No words." Her voice cracked in memory, the two filthy faces, with tangled hair, looking across at her, teeth bared in near-identical snarls. "I could not leave them." Her voice fractured again. They had looked absolutely bewildered and lost. Innocents caught up in something vile. And, as damaged as she had been, she had not been able to walk away. Neither Mariah nor Joel had wanted to go with her at first, but they had been afraid of the fire, and the screams.

"I am sorry, mies maisredayenni."

His voice was softer than she had ever heard it. She blinked, coming back to the here and now, and found him still standing a few feet from her. He was holding out one hand. She stared at it for a moment before she put hers into it. He gave one gentle squeeze, then opened his hand again, as though understanding that even that contact was difficult. Taken by surprise, she left her hand there for another heartbeat, the unfamiliar texture and sensation of another's skin against hers oddly distracting.

"Thank you," she said, not entirely sure what she was thanking him for.

Sound overhead drew both their attention to the door.

"We need to hurry," he said, moving past her to the pile of belongings.

As he moved past her, her breath caught at the sight of his back. As well as more recent bruises, dark blots across his skin, his back was bisected with long, wicked-looking scars.

He heard her intake of breath, of course, and glanced across, following the direction of her eyes.

"A tale for another time, perhaps. My scars were not as hard-won as yours."

And there was something overhead that needed their more urgent attention.

Chapter Twenty-Two

Yvonne had never been more glad that she kept prepared cleansing spells on her at all times. Before she put any more clothes on, she emptied a vial of cleansing spell over her head, not daring to look at her feet before she did so, and felt the magic wash down her body from head to toe, scraping away all the dirt and grime. She had three more spells left, and offered one to Guise, who accepted it with an oddly courtly bow considering he was simply dressed in his trousers.

Her scalp was still itching, but there was movement and noise overhead and they did not have time for her to perform more thorough cleansing. Besides, her head was still pounding.

Getting dressed required sitting down quite a lot of the time and by the time she was fully dressed, and all her weapons in place, she had to pause, resting her elbows on the table and her head in her hands, careful to avoid the bruises.

"You are badly injured. Do you have a healing spell with you?" Guise asked.

Healing spell. What a brilliant idea. She was annoyed with herself for not thinking of it before now, but she had been so desperate to be clean and warm again.

She searched through the pouch she wore at her belt and found the necessary vial.

"Only have one," she told him.

"I will manage."

She wasn't sure she believed him. She had seen the bruises, and there was something not right about the way he was standing. But she could not think straight, and her vision was wavering again with the effort of getting dressed.

The healing spell coursed through her body with a scorching heat that made her hiss in a breath and then rest her head in her hands again as the magic set to work. She had not realised how badly injured she had been, hearing and feeling a snap at the side of her face as her cheekbone set back in line. No wonder her head had ached.

She put a hand to the pouch at her belt that held the small bird Pieris had created. She might be able to summon help. But that required magic. Active magic, not simply releasing a prepared spell, and she could not summon enough focus for it. A defect in the design she would have to mention to Pieris.

"I will lead," he told her.

Looking up, she found him fully dressed and armed, ready for a fight by the looks of it. He was tucking what looked like an empty vial of his own back into a pocket, a red tint to his eyes that did not bode well for whoever they met on their way up the stairs that she could see through the other door.

"Are you alright?" she asked. "The poison?"

"For the moment," he answered, baring his teeth in a silent snarl. "I have potions of my own," he added, patting the pocket where he had put the vial. "It's a temporary fix. It will hold for a while."

She did not know why she was surprised. Of course Guise would carry an antidote, of sorts, to a remarkably rare poison.

"It sounds like fighting overhead," she realised. It wasn't just her sight that had been affected, apparently all of her senses had been compromised. She decided she was happy about that, as it meant she had not been able to smell how bad the cell really was, and had managed to avoid looking at her feet, so she did not have that memory to carry as well.

"I wonder who has been foolish, or brave, enough to attack a castle with the corrupted lord and darkin guarding it," he said, a note of speculation in his voice and a gleam in his eyes that suggested he would very much like to meet whoever it was who was leading the charge.

"Hopefully it's the Hundred," Yvonne said, managing to stand up without wobbling too much. She had forgotten that she was hungry, as well as injured, and swayed for a moment before getting herself under control.

"Sillman doesn't seem like the type to just attack," Guise commented, and headed off up the stairs before she had time to ask him what he meant.

She managed to get her sword out and held in more or less the correct position in front of her and then followed him up the stairs, far less quietly and with occasional pauses to put her hand on the wall. She could still feel the healing working through her body and knew that her headache would lift further very soon. At least, she hoped so. Fighting darkin was hard enough without the added handicap of a thumping headache and wavering vision. And she could not even imagine facing a vettr in this condition.

In the end, she did not need to fight anyone.

Guise was putting away his sword by the time she arrived at the top of the stairs and, looking past his shoulder, she could see why. The Hundred were there. And so were about a dozen corpses. Too-still bodies lay on stone flagstones, pools of blood around many of them. Even the vettr were dead, with Idal using a sledgehammer to break the final one's fingers into pieces. Vettr had extraordinary regenerative powers, and he was taking no chances. Yvonne approved.

The rest of the Hundred were standing in a loose circle around a pool of red robes on the floor, careful to keep out of the way of the blackened blood that was seeping out from underneath the robes.

Yvonne saw the robes, and an odd pang of disappointment rang through her. The castle's lord was dead. She had questions for him. Had wanted to know why he was involved with slavers. What his purpose was. What had taken hold of him, to turn his blood that colour. And she had wanted to be there at his end, she realised. To see for herself that he was gone from this world.

Sillman looked up as Guise moved forward and Yvonne sucked in a breath. When had he got so old? Oldest of them, by far, she had never seen him show his age before. It was only for a moment, before he straightened his shoulders and inclined his head a fraction to Guise.

"We wondered if we were going to have to rescue you. Is there anyone else in the dungeons?"

"We didn't check," Guise answered. "We heard the fighting, and thought it best to investigate."

"Annabelle, take Idal and investigate the dungeons," Sillman ordered. It was a definite order, rather than a suggestion. To Yvonne's surprise, Annabelle simply nodded, gathered up her apprentice, and left, going back down the stairs far more easily and quickly than Yvonne had come up them.

"You look terrible," Suanna said.

"I feel terrible," Yvonne told them. "I don't suppose anyone has some food? It feels like days since I've eaten."

"It probably is," Pieris answered, dropping his backpack at his feet and crouching to rummage through it. "None of us found anything. We came here as fast as we could." He tipped his head up to her for a moment. "We hadn't heard from you."

The bird. She had almost forgotten the little object. It seemed more effort than it was worth to try and find the thing now, her attention narrowing on whatever Pieris was hunting for in his pack.

"We caught a trace of darkin as we came in," Sillman said. "Tricky things."

"There were at least four of them," Guise answered. "You didn't see them?"

"No sign of them," Sillman confirmed, frowning.

Yvonne looked around the room and saw that, apart from the two vettr, the rest of the corpses were humans. They looked like ordinary castle servants, even if they were heavily armed.

The rest of the Hundred moved away from the robes on the floor, and the body underneath.

The lord was dead. Whatever corruption had taken hold of him was dead, too, the still pool of blackened blood around him testament to that.

The relief of it, of being safe, among those she trusted, of being clean and out of the cell made Yvonne light-headed for a moment.

She might not have been there for his end, but the lord was gone.

There was a distant sound. Someone calling her name. And then darkness.

Whatever was all around her was deliciously soft and smelled faintly of lavender. She moved slightly, curling into herself. She could not remember the last time she had been so warm and so comfortable.

"Yvonne." A familiar voice that she could not place for a moment. It did not sound quite right.

And she was comfortable where she was. Warm. Safe. Hungry.

"Yvonne." The voice was definitely one that she knew.

Her stomach grumbled.

"I know you're waking up," the voice continued. Annabelle. That was it. "We're in one of the king's taverns on the highway."

That explained the softness. The king's taverns were all well-equipped, and priced accordingly. The only times she had stayed in a king's tavern before were when travelling with Guise and even then, out of sight of the goblin lord, the tavern keepers had given her one of the small attic rooms, cramped and far less comfortable than this. The rooms had still been far more comfortable than she could have managed alone, so she had not complained. But now, having tasted this luxury, she might not be quite so willing to be shown to the attics again while Guise stayed in comfort.

Guise. Her mind snagged on his name. There was something she needed to remember. The thought slid away as she turned her face into the pillow. Lavender. The scent worked through her, drawing her back towards sleep.

"You've slept for most of a day," Annabelle added.

Yvonne made an inarticulate sound that might have been trying to be words.

"The others are comparing notes downstairs," Annabelle went on. "We got here last night." There was a short pause. "I'm sorry," she said, voice soft, almost as though she wasn't sure she wanted to be heard. "None of us realised how badly you were injured. You were walking and talking. I don't know how you managed it. Your skull was in pieces."

Yvonne considered that information, nose full of lavender. Skull in pieces. No wonder her head had hurt.

By all rights, she should not be here. That much damage was almost impossible to repair, even for a sorcerer or sorceress.

She opened her eyes, finally, to the brightness of a spring day, the heavy curtains across the window parted to let in light. Late in the day, she thought. Perhaps around noon.

Annabelle was settled in an armchair near the window, positioned to catch the light on a piece of embroidery in her hands. She set aside the cloth as Yvonne blinked at her, getting to her feet and coming across to the bedside.

"Here," Annabelle held out a wooden cup. "It's water with a bit of healing in it. You probably still feel awful."

Yvonne managed another inarticulate sound. Now that Annabelle had mentioned it, she did not feel herself. It took a great deal of concentration to sit up in the wonderfully soft bed, only then realising she was wearing a nightgown. Not hers. She did not possess such fine clothing.

"Suanna's," Annabelle told her, mouth lifting. "Apparently my nightclothes are too scandalous for you."

Yvonne's mind shied away from imagining scandalous nightwear. Suanna's nightgown was long-sleeved and high-necked, in keeping with the lady herself.

"Suanna and I undressed you," Annabelle added, perhaps guessing Yvonne's next unspoken question. "Suanna has left you this," she said, picking up a small jar that Yvonne had not noticed on the bedside table. It was an ordinary clay pot, covered with waxed cloth. "For your scars," Annabelle said, voice soft.

Of course. None of the Hundred, apart from Elinor, had seen her scars before. And knowing that she had been in a quarrel, long enough to be damaged, was quite different from seeing the evidence. Yvonne ducked her head to the cup, stomach uneasy. She had been undressed while she was unconscious, moved here without her knowledge. These were the Hundred. But still. She hated being vulnerable.

The water was cool and clear in her mouth, the slight mint taste of healing familiar.

"You healed me?" Yvonne asked, seeking a safer topic.

Annabelle shook her head slightly, going back to the armchair.

"We all did. You were almost dead." Annabelle's voice cracked. "We've lost too much."

Yvonne felt an echo of that pain in her chest. Too much lost. Far too much.

"Thank you," Yvonne answered. "I wasn't ready to go." Not yet. Not nearly ready. There was still too much to do. Mariah and Joel still to settle. Missing youngsters to find. The nagging sensation of an unfulfilled promise in her chest.

"Good. Now, your clothes have been cleaned. Although, they seem to mostly be repairs rather than original fabric. Excellent repairs." Annabelle gathered her embroidery up.

"Mariah. She is very skilled."

"She is indeed. There's a bath through there, and we'll be waiting downstairs when you're ready." Annabelle took a step to Yvonne's side, squeezed her wrist where she was holding the cup, and then left the room.

The bath had been kept warm with a small preservation spell that carried Annabelle's signature. A short while later, Yvonne was clean and dressed in her own clothes, tying her hair back into its normal, single braid down her back. Her arms ached by the time she was finished, satisfied that the plait was smooth, fingers closing around the end of it for a moment, feeling the weight of it. She remembered the girls in Kelton, dazed in the sunlight, wounded and fractured, with their crudely shaved heads, and wondered how many of them, even when their hair had grown back, would also live with the phantom sensation of scissors too close to their scalps and wulf claws digging into their shaven heads.

The bedroom had a small mirror on the wall near the door and she paused there, looking at her reflection for a moment. The only mirrors in the house were in Mariah's room, neither Yvonne nor Joel really caring about their appearances.

The mirror told her that there was no sign left of the bruising and damage that the vettr had inflicted. She could feel the echo of the Hundred's healing through her head, the slight itching sensation of bones knitting back together again. Nearly dead.

Her reflection was paler than usual, with dark smudges under her eyes, hollows where there shouldn't be any. She still looked nearly dead, she judged.

Her stomach grumbled again before she could think about it too much longer, and she went downstairs to find the others.

A wide, carpeted staircase took her from the hushed quiet of the sleeping floor down into the usual bustle of a king's tavern. The highways were busy year-round, only quieting a little in the worst of the winter weather when even the efforts of the king's men could not keep the roads clear.

The common room at the front was full of travellers and a roar of sound that made the bones of her skull itch again, healing not yet finished.

She moved past the public room, drawn by instinct and familiarity with her fellow Hunar. There would be one or more private rooms behind the public one, and the Hundred were most likely in there.

The first room she came to with an open door held only one occupant, a tall figure standing silhouetted in the window, facing outward. She was about to move on when she recognised him.

Something held her in the doorway for a moment, just outside the threshold. There was a gap in her memory. Somewhere between waking up in the fetid dungeon cell and finding the Hundred in the castle's great hall, with Idal methodically and viciously smashing the vettr into tiny pieces.

Guise was staring out the window with the same kind of intensity he usually reserved for questioning suspects, a single-minded focus on something inward, and unpleasant, by the pull of his mouth. For the first time, she had the odd sensation that he did not know she was there, and she was observing a private moment, a face that he would not usually show to the world.

The thought made her uncomfortable, and she stepped into the doorway.

The moment she crossed the threshold, his attention shifted. He turned, face tightening a moment, expression smoothing to polite attention, and inclined his head when he saw her, his eyes their normal green shade. For some reason she had been expecting them to be a different colour, and could not work out why, or remember what colour she had been expecting to see.

"Mristrian. I am glad to see you on your feet and healed."

"Not quite healed, I think," she answered, coming into the room to find that although he was the only other person there, the Hundred had been there. There was a circular table big enough to seat a dozen or more people, chairs pulled out at some places, and a row of familiar backpacks propped against the waist-high wooden panelling at one side of the room.

"Do you need to sit?" he asked, brows drawing together.

"No. Not just now. I ..." She closed her lips together and shook her head a fraction, the movement sending fresh itching across her scalp. "I have a blank space," she told him candidly. "We were in a cell together. Then we were with the Hundred."

"You don't remember anything between that?" he asked.

Yvonne paused before she answered. He was too still. A predator's stillness. Waiting for her answer.

"Nothing." She touched her forehead. "I remember having a pounding head."

"Your skull was badly damaged," he told her. There was a pale line around his lips as he closed his mouth, and the shade of his eyes had deepened, flickers of red appearing. Still not the colour she had been hoping to see.

Red in a goblin's eyes was a clear sign of danger. And yet she did not feel threatened. Rather, she felt oddly safe in his presence. He would not harm her.

Her breath caught. That phrase. She could almost hear it, spoken aloud in his voice. And then it was gone.

There had been something, though. In that gap in her memory, something important, if only she could remember what it was.

"Memory loss is common following head injuries," he told her, voice calm and even. She had the strangest impression that he felt anything but calm, that he was torn between relief and disappointment. "You may recover the memories in time." He tilted his head slightly. "The Hundred should be back soon. They went to order food. At least most of them did. Some went to check on the horses." His lips twitched. She almost asked why it took almost the entire Hundred to order food, and then remembered who they were. And where they were. King's taverns had excellent kitchens. Doubtless they each had their own requests to make.

"There was something before the dungeon. Powder. Are you alright?" she asked, remembering his struggles against the vettr's hold. It seemed important.

"Quite well, thank you." He inclined his head, the red fading from his eyes. "I was able to make an antidote." As with so many times before, she had the distinct impression that he was not telling her the whole story. There was far more to this than a simple antidote. Very little could poison a goblin.

"That's good. But can't you tell me? About the cell?" she asked.

He hesitated, and her eyes narrowed.

Before she could press for more information, movement at the door drew both their attention.

Sillman came into the room and did not pause until he had dragged Yvonne into a hug, eyes suspiciously damp-looking when he pulled back.

"Please don't frighten us like that again," he said, releasing her before the panic could rise.

"Thank you," she answered, and looked around the room as the rest of the Hundred came in. "Thank you all. I didn't realise I was that badly injured."

"Head injuries," Suanna answered, voice tight. "Tricky things. And Guise tells us that a vettr knocked you unconscious at least twice. It's a miracle you survived even one blow."

"Stupid creatures," Idal muttered, face tight. He was staring out the window. Yvonne's brows lifted in surprise. Outwardly, he was normally as carefree as Annabelle. He seemed to sense her eyes on him, looking across and pasting a smile on his face. "I don't like vettr," he explained.

There was far more to it than a simple dislike, but every person around the room had their own secrets. She respected his privacy, as the others also respected hers.

"It's a very good thing we were all there," Dundac added, giving her a hug. "It needed all of us to save you."

The rest of the Hundred were abruptly there, all wanting their own hug, so Yvonne found herself passed around the room, her eyes stinging at the evident relief of her fellow Hunar and the care that they all took, every one, to keep their hugs brief, not pushing her anywhere close to panic.

Then Sillman rapped his knuckles on the table.

"Food is on its way. There is much to discuss."

A half dozen servants arrived through the doorway, not even blinking at the odd assembly in the room. The servants put a series of dishes onto the long sideboard, and left plates and cutlery, bottles of wine, tankards of beer and pitchers of water. The scents made Yvonne's stomach growl and her mouth water.

When the food and drink was all set out, in mere moments, the head of the staff bowed slightly to Sillman.

"Put it on his tab," Sillman said, tilting his head towards Guise.

Guise's eyes, their normal green shade, lit with amusement and he nodded once when the servant turned to him for confirmation.

Firon closed the door behind the servants and spoke the necessary spell for privacy, then moved with the rest to help himself to food.

Yvonne found herself settled between Pieris and Firon, the pair of them the quietest of the Hundred, and she was content to sit, eat and listen.

The rest of the Hundred and Guise were clearly continuing a lively discussion that had been started while she was healing. She recognised the circular pattern of the discussion, and the edge of frustration to some of the voices. They had a lot of questions, and very few good answers.

It wasn't just the lord of the castle that had been corrupted. Some of the castle servants had been showing signs of it, with blackened teeth and fine lines of darkness across their skin.

The Hundred had searched the castle from the dungeons, all empty, to the highest tower. There was no clue as to what had put the corruption into the last of the Coll family. There were no youngsters or children, either. The slavers' wagons had not left any of their passengers behind.

Yvonne sipped her water and absorbed the information that was being exchanged.

"Are you going to leave that?" Dundac asked, peering around Firon's shoulder, eyes on Yvonne's plate. She glanced down to find she had left more than half of the plate untouched, but her stomach was uncomfortably full.

"No. Do you ..." She did not get a chance to finish, as the Hunar stretched across Firon and lifted the plate away.

"You are too thin," Suanna commented from across the table, frowning.

"I cannot eat any more just now," Yvonne said, biting her lip against a smile as Suanna turned a disapproving scowl on Dundac.

"You'll need to sleep again soon," Firon commented unexpectedly. Despite sitting next to her, he had been so quiet he was almost forgotten around the table. "Healing is exhausting."

Whatever she might have said in answer was overtaken as the others cleared the dishes away, making space for Pieris' map, Sillman commenting that he would wish to have such a map for himself.

Pieris shook his head slightly as he set the map on the now-empty table, dishes piled haphazardly on the large sideboard in the room.

"It would take another winter," Pieris told Sillman.

"But you have the knack of it now," Sillman pressed.

"Leave him be," Suanna interrupted. "It is an extraordinary piece of magic. And a lot of hard work. Be glad it exists at all. If it was easy, we'd all have one."

Yvonne wondered how long it would be before Sillman suggested that he should have the map, as the leader of the Hundred. Despite the fact that they had no official leader, and were all supposed to be equal in their tasks.

"It's also only cued to me," Pieris added, smoothing the part closest to him. He was looking at the surface of the map as he did so, carefully avoiding Sillman's eyes.

Yvonne bit her lip against another smile, and was sure she was not the only one.

"Very well," Sillman said, with remarkable grace. "We were trying to work out where the wagons could have been going, once they left Coll Castle," he explained to Yvonne.

Pieris gave the map a series of commands that had the image focused more tightly on Coll and the surrounding land. The road from the back of the castle was not on the map, as a local route. It could lead almost anywhere. Yvonne could understand the Hundred's frustration.

"I may be able to track them," Yvonne said. It felt like half a lifetime ago that Guise had come to her with that request. She was about to go on when an enormous yawn caught her by surprise.

"Tomorrow," Suanna said firmly, before Sillman could say anything. "Another night's rest will do us all good," she added, sending a frowning look to Sillman. "And the horses need it, too."

"I'll make sure they get some extra feed," Idal promised.

Yvonne yawned again, eyelids heavy, and left them to their planning, making her way back upstairs before falling back into the lavender softness and into sleep. She needed to heal. The castle's lord might be dead, but they still did not know what had happened to the wagons, or the children.

Chapter Twenty-Three

They started their journey at the castle. The rest of the Hundred wanted a final look to make sure nothing had been missed. The bodies were gone, of course. There were many ways of disposing of bodies, but the broad area of scorched earth outside the castle's entrance suggested that magic fire had been used. It burned everything, reducing bones to ash in moments. The Hundred had been busy while she slept.

The great hall looked odd with the bare walls, the fractured throne carelessly thrown across the room and the stone floor blotted in places with old, dried blood, some of it much darker than it should be, particularly where the lord of the castle had fallen.

Yvonne's stomach twisted with the memory of the vettr's tongue rasping against stone.

She also remembered the body on the floor, surrounded by the Hundred. A spike of irritation rose. There were so many questions unanswered. Not least, what had actually turned the lord's blood so black.

With the lord gone, she wondered how they were going to get answers.

And she felt cheated. The rest of the Hundred had defeated the lord, not her. The rest of the Hundred had not been the ones in the dungeon.

There was no time for her to go through the entire castle, but Guise, who had also been back here while she healed, had identified one of the rooms as the lord's study, and wanted another look. His information said that the slavers' wagons had passed through the castle, but there was no evidence of them anywhere.

The study was a wood-panelled room that had clearly been designed with comfort in mind, with a thick rug across the floor, a large desk and several comfortable chairs. It was an old-fashioned room, cluttered with objects. It did not match the bare walls in the main hall. Yvonne noted the contradiction and wondered how long ago the young lord of the castle had been corrupted.

She spotted a flaw in the wood panelling, a point that did not quite line up, jarring against the fine craftsmanship. She moved across to it. Castles this old tended to have a lot of hidden places. Guise followed her, and she was somehow not surprised when he managed to get the secret door opened in moments. Not the first study he had searched.

The wood panel opened to reveal a small space in the stone wall that was filled with a leather-bound strongbox heavy enough that Guise struggled to pull it out of the space into the room. The box was unlocked, which surprised both of them, and held a collection of leather pouches that made Yvonne's eyebrows lift.

"That is a lot of money."

"Not just money. There are gems here. Jewellery," Guise added, lifting a couple of the pouches out of the box to look underneath. He rose to his feet and set the pouches on the desk, opening them to reveal a spill of coins that made Yvonne's brows lift again.

"That is a lot of high-value coins for the lord of a small castle to have."

"Indeed." Guise was frowning as he tied the pouches off again and set them back in the strongbox, returning the box to its place in the wall and putting the panel back. "I can have people watch the place," he said in response to Yvonne's silent question. "See who comes back for the money."

It was a fair plan.

Too many questions, Yvonne thought, turning her back on the money and searching through the papers in the study. What had corrupted the lord? What possible connection could there be between an old, remote castle and the slavers? What use did the lord have for all those coins?

"Well, this is interesting," Guise said. He was standing by the window, holding what looked like a nearly-new ledger to the light.

Yvonne went to stand by his shoulder and read the entries his finger was resting next to.

"Your associate." Her brows lifted. "Interesting, indeed."

"It's a connection of sorts." Guise turned the next page, a low sound of irritation escaping as he saw they had reached the last entries. "That was about a month ago."

"He must have been here before he went to Three Falls," Yvonne speculated, turning back to the desk to see if there was anything they had missed. There was a letter from the Valland King, the ruler of the land, carelessly discarded on one corner of the vast surface. "And then on to Fir Tree Crossing."

"Yes." Guise still sounded annoyed. "That is not where he should have been. He was supposed to be in the Royal City before Three Falls."

"He lied to you?" Yvonne looked up from the letter she was reading, surprised.

"Found something?" Mica asked, coming into the room, followed by Sillman and Suanna. "The rest of the place is empty. Even the stables."

"There's a lot of money hidden in the room," Yvonne told Mica, most of her attention still on the letter. "Too much for this castle."

"So you re-hid it?" Mica asked, looking around.

"We could use that money," Sillman said, his eyes also travelling around the room.

"Really?" Yvonne's attention shifted, brows lifting in unfeigned surprise. "We don't know if it does belong to the lord. It could be stolen."

"What's that?" Sillman asked, nodding to the letter in her hand.

"A summons from the King. He was not pleased that the lord had failed to attend." It was confirmation of the information Dundac had given them. Yvonne wondered how long it would have been before the King had sent soldiers to drag the lord of Coll to his Court.

"One of my associates seems to have done business with the lord here," Guise said, before Sillman could ask more questions.

"Good. Let's find out what he knows," Sillman said.

"He's dead," Guise said, voice dry.

"Did you kill him?" Mica asked, simple curiosity on his face.

"No. Someone got to him before me," Guise answered honestly.

"It looked as if Ubel had been dealing with the slavers," Yvonne added. "He was at one of the warehouses in Three Falls. And his barge at Fir Tree Crossing had been used for smuggling."

"So, there's a connection of some kind between Guise and Coll?" Sillman asked, frowning. Yvonne's brows rose. It sounded like a simple question, and might be a logical deduction, but she could not help feeling there was more to it. Sillman was being deliberately provocative.

"No," Guise answered, his voice flat. "Between Ubel and Coll. He was a trader with many connections."

"Have we learned everything here?" Yvonne asked. "I haven't tried to find the track yet, and it's nearly midday."

"I agree. We need to be moving," Suanna said, frowning at Sillman. "You can snip at Guise on the road just as easily as standing here."

Sillman's colour rose even as Guise's lips twitched.

"Very true," Guise agreed.

Yvonne shook her head slightly, casting one final glance over the lord's desk before leaving the room, heading for the rear of the castle where they had left the horses near the smaller but no less fortified entrance.

She stayed on foot while the others mounted their horses, leading Lothar as she walked out under the thick walls and raised portcullis. The space between her shoulder blades itched as she left. Her skin had been prickling with unease the whole time they had been in the castle and she was not quite sure why. It might have been the odd echo of an empty building around them, one that should be bustling with life and the day-to-day business of both running the castle and managing the surrounding lands.

As soon as her foot landed on the wooden bridge across the moat, her tracking sense woke up, a surge of power sending another wash of unease across her entire body. There was a well-defined path. She could only hope it was the one they were looking for.

Still, she stayed on foot until they had crossed the bridge and were almost at the tree line, letting herself absorb the traces she had found. More than one wagon had passed this way, leaving a tear through the world and the impression of fear and misery behind. Only when she was quite sure she had the full trace in her mind did she get on Lothar.

"Can you follow them?" Mica asked, for once not in jest.

"There's a very strong trail. I think it's the right one. This way," Yvonne turned Lothar and moved him on to his smooth-striding trot that he could keep up for hours at a time. The others might be able to move faster, but she would back her old warhorse's stamina against any of theirs.

The roadway vanished almost as soon as they crossed the tree line, becoming little more than a grassy track, marked by wagon wheels.

And the track continued, on and on, for the rest of the day.

They camped a little away from the trail, stopping only long enough for a few hours' sleep, all of them up and ready with the dawn to keep going.

About mid-morning the next day, the narrow trail they had been following through the woods widened out, the trees thinning to give way to small fields and a village beyond them. A typical sight in this fertile land, where ancient forest was broken up by small villages, with a few fields and livestock to support the population. Most of the villagers who had settled here had been born far away, Yvonne knew, disillusioned with life in the big cities, and wanting a simpler, quieter existence.

Her first thought on seeing the village was that if quietness was what the villagers had wanted, they had certainly found it. The prickling up her spine told her that something was wrong even before her conscious mind had identified the source.

This village had once been a prosperous place. The houses had glass in their windows, and all the roofs were well-maintained. Mostly thatch, none of them sagging or rotten.

And it was completely empty.

There was not even a stray cat or dog wandering between the buildings. The doors were closed, windows shut and shuttered. No one had left in a hurry. There were no signs of struggle. It was just empty.

The sense of unease spread from her spine across the rest of her body. She sent her senses out, seeking any trace or sign of life. Nothing. Around her she could tell that the rest of the Hundred were doing the same, exchanging uneasy glances as they came to the same conclusions she had. There was no one here.

"My sources report similar villages nearby," Guise told them. He was the only one who did not look uneasy, but Yvonne knew that he was exceptionally good at hiding his feelings. A necessary survival skill among the Karoan'shae.

She remembered the maps that they had discussed. The seemingly impossible reach of the slave merchants, who had been gathering children and young people far and wide. And the odd, blank space around Coll Castle that had raised their suspicion. No reports of missing children or abductions. No reports at all, in fact.

They were in the middle of that blank space. She wondered what they would find as they moved through it, and shivered lightly.

"Daylight's wasting," Annabelle said, her voice serious for once.

"We should look around a little," Sillman proposed, normally genial expression replaced by a scowl. "See what we can learn."

They left the horses together, just outside the perimeter of the houses, and split up, moving through the dozen or so houses in ones and twos, opening the shut doors and checking inside each one.

Nothing.

None of the doors were locked.

All the interiors were neat and tidy. There were no signs of disturbance anywhere. No rotting food. Everything was in its place.

There was just no one here.

Sillman observed that from the amount of dust gathering in the houses the occupants had been gone a while. A matter of months, perhaps.

Idal reported that the fields all had their gates open, pinned back so that any livestock had been able to leave of their own accord. The farm buildings were the same. Any animal feed had been eaten already.

Firon observed that there were no signs of scavengers.

Yvonne's flesh crawled. No people. No animals. No scavengers. And the village had been empty for months.

Even after their search through the village, they had no better answers as to what had happened. Not until Idal, glancing back towards the horses, checked in his movement.

"What's that?"

It was something that they had all ignored until now. A sturdy pole in the town's centre. Yvonne was used to seeing them in farming villages across the lands, and doubtless the others were, too. Villagers flung canvas over the pole and stretched it out to make a basic tent that was used for festivals, or twined ribbons around it for other celebrations.

And occasionally pinned notices to it, for everyone in the village to see. Or, at least, those able to read.

There was a sheet of parchment pinned to the wooden pole, edges fluttering slightly in the breeze.

As they walked towards it, Yvonne could sense the crude preservation spell laid on it.

"A circle mage," Annabelle commented, lip curling.

Yvonne made a low sound of agreement, Elinor's words playing through her mind. Circle mages liked elaborate robes. They thought that being able to create flashes of lightning and pretty colours made them true sorcerers. And did not bother to learn the finer points of magic. They also despised Hunar. Apparently quiet use of magic, and helping people, was beneath the circle mages.

"I know this one," Sillman said, face reflecting distaste. "He was peddling his services to the highest bidder, last I heard."

"Well, it seems he found a new master," Guise said, eyes on the parchment.

The ink was fading despite the preservation spell, but it was still possible to read the proclamation.

"This place is now the property of the King of the ... What is that word?" Idal asked, peering more closely.

"Made up kingdom," Yvonne said, folding her arms across her middle.

"That's not what it says," Idal began, then turned and saw her expression, eyes widening slightly in comprehension. "Oh. Not really a kingdom."

"No. That's the old name for what's now Coll Castle," she told him. "Seems like the lord had extraordinary ambition."

"So, the lord proclaimed he was king of this land?" Suanna sounded sceptical.

"The King would never have stood for it. If he had known," Dundac added, voice shading to thoughtfulness.

"It does explain why Lord Coll did not come to the King to swear his oaths," Sillman agreed. "Although how the King could not have known …"

"The village is empty," Yvonne reminded them, arms still folded across her middle. Her skin was crawling again. "There's no one here to tell the King what the lord was doing."

"More questions." Annabelle sighed.

By silent agreement, they returned to their horses and rode forward, Lothar prancing in unease as he crossed the perimeter of the town, snorting and swishing his tail all the way until they crossed the invisible perimeter on the other side when he abruptly reverted to his normal, placid self. Too busy keeping her own seat, she barely noticed that the others were having similar difficulty with their own mounts. Whatever magic Lord Coll had performed here, whatever the circle mage had done, it had left a powerful residue, and they had still not reached the end of the trail.

Chapter Twenty-Four

The path that they had been following led from the village through the fields beyond, and on into the forest, giant trees rising high above them. As they rode among the trees, Yvonne noticed that the forest on either side of the ill-defined path had been allowed to run wild for some time. Forest edges around villages usually had some kind of cultivation. Lower branches taken for firewood, fallen branches cleared for kindling and firewood, paths cleared to allow livestock to roam, patches of earth turned over for some plants and to make mushroom foraging easier. The tangle of undergrowth here suggested that nobody had been far into the forest for quite some time.

The proclamation, declaring the village the property of Coll Castle, had been undated, the preservation spell a piece of low-level magic that could last quite some time. This village could have been empty for months.

There was an itch between her shoulder blades again as they rode on. The path was not natural, too clear a space among the wildness around them. More magic had been done here. She wondered how much the circle mage had been paid for his services, if indeed he was still alive.

They paused under the trees after a few hours' riding, when the path took them close to a stream that the horses could drink from, then continued riding at the steady pace Lothar had set, the others keeping pace behind him. Yvonne heard the occasional snort from one of the other horses, doubtless knowing they could go faster. No one offered to take the lead, though.

A while later, when they were all settled into the steady rhythm of travel, Lothar snorted, tossed his head and danced sideways in springy strides that belonged to a much younger creature before coming to a halt, the tension in his body clear even through the saddle.

"Easy," Yvonne said, stroking his neck, peering ahead to try and work out what had spooked him. The other horses had stopped, too, and she could see the whites of several pairs of eyes.

Warhorses were trained to go forward through fear, and although he threw up his head again, haunches gathering, he moved forward at her request so she could see what had startled him.

The wagon trail ended a few paces ahead, running directly on to an extraordinary sight, in this dense forest. There was a wide, well-maintained road cut through the forest. As smooth and wide as any King's Highway, although the forest grew right up to the road's edge, with some of the larger trees overhanging the road's surface, providing leafy shade from the spring sunshine. Branches had been cut to give clearance enough to allow wagons to pass underneath.

It looked perfectly innocent. Except that it was nowhere a road should be. And none of the horses wanted to go near it.

"This is new," Guise commented. "A year, perhaps a little more."

"Around the time of the earliest reports of children disappearing," Sillman said, voice heavy.

Yvonne remembered the map, the earliest reports scattered across the lands, across the black lines of the borders. The slavers had been careful, to start with, travelling distances to avoid detection.

"More magic," Yvonne noted. Her skin was prickling with the residue of it. No wonder Lothar was standing stock-still under her, all his muscles tense.

"Bloody mages," Suanna said, lips tightening as a few of her fellow Hunar sent her looks of surprise. "What? They are despicable. Selling their work to the highest bidder."

Yvonne winced, thinking of the few occasions she had accepted work from Guise, knowing that the pay would be good and not questioning the task at hand too closely.

"Everyone needs to eat," Pieris said, voice mild. "We don't all have your resources."

Yvonne's curiosity spiked. There had been hints over the years that Suanna came from a very privileged, wealthy background, more than enough to support whatever she wanted to do. It was to her credit she worked so hard as a Hunar,

Elinor had said more than once. But no one had ever said anything more, which Yvonne found equally frustrating and admirable. They all had their secrets, Elinor had told Yvonne. And that had been the end of the matter.

Suanna sniffed, clearly not convinced.

Mica slid off his horse, going towards the road, hand held out, murmuring the words to a spell, his voice too low for Yvonne to hear which one. Moments later the surface of the road shivered, shadows writhing along its length. Some kind of reveal spell.

"Death," Sillman said, voice heavy. "Too many dead."

"The road is built from the dead?" Guise asked, frowning. "Bone dust?"

The words echoed oddly in her head. She remembered him asking someone else about bone dust, but could not quite remember the conversation.

"No," Dundac answered, cutting through her frustration. "A lot of people died building it, though. That's why the horses are so worked up."

"We'll need to bind their hooves to move on," Idal said, sliding off his horse.

Guise looked confused, but dismounted with everyone else, watching with interest as Idal drew a set of leather boots out of one of his saddlebags, then raising a brow at Yvonne.

"Our horses are sensitive to magic, and to death," she explained. "It's part of working with a Hunar. Where we can help it, we do not ask them to walk on graves." She scratched Lothar behind his ear, and he turned and shoved his nose into her chest, demanding a scratch at the other ear, too. She almost smiled, giving him an extra scratch, the familiarity settling her.

At length all the horses had their boots fitted, apart from Guise's goblin-bred mount, which danced sideways, throwing up its head as Guise rode onto the road. A few more sideways steps and the horse settled.

"I suppose goblin horses must get used to dealing with death," Suanna commented. Her tone was quite matter-of-fact, as though stating something obvious.

"It depends on the horse," Guise answered, seemingly amused.

"And the rider," Pieris added, expression slightly unfocused again for a moment.

"Shall we go?" Annabelle suggested, acid in her tone. "Our horses aren't the only ones who don't like death."

"Keep following the road ahead," Yvonne told them.

With a clear, smooth road ahead she was not surprised when Sillman took the lead, his horse moving at a fractionally faster pace than Lothar. She was happy to move to the back, letting Lothar find his own pace, drifting a little bit behind the others. It had been another long, hard day's riding and she judged he was twice the age, or more, of all the other horses. Guilt twisted in her stomach. She was asking too much of him.

She put her hand on his dark neck, tangling her fingers in his mane for a moment. He had taught her more than she thought possible, and given years of faithful service. Overdue for retirement. Grazing in the fields around the house. The occasional, steady journey into town. She would need to find a companion animal for him, as he hated to be alone.

A soft sound of discovery ahead snapped her out of her plans, and she looked up to find that the forest was thinning, the others turning off the road, spreading out through the forest, looking ahead.

Sillman was off his horse when she reached the others. "We need to go ahead on foot," he said, face and voice grim.

Curiosity piqued, Yvonne left Lothar with the other horses and crept forward. All of them were skilled in moving quietly when they had to, and the whole group made barely a sound as they made their way to the edge of the forest. For a while, all she could see was that the forest came to an abrupt end a short distance ahead, suggesting that there was some kind of settlement.

They were spread out in a line so they reached the edge of the trees more or less at the same time and took a sharp, collective intake of breath that would have given their position away to anyone on watch.

For a long moment, her eyes refused to make sense of what she saw.

The forest gave way to an open swathe of what looked like dry grass, undulating ground that at length rose to mountain peaks, the tops shrouded in cloud.

Between the edge of the forest and the mountain slopes, the ground had been destroyed. The smooth lines of the grassland broke, giving way to an enormous crater in the world, a great, circular wound that led down into the earth. From where they were standing, they could not see easily into it, just enough to see some of the sloping sides.

It was no natural phenomena. Even as they watched, she could see things moving at the sides of the wound and realised that they were people, tiny specks against the sheer size of the thing. She looked back to the road and saw that it led to the edge of the wound. Following it, she realised that there was a roadway leading from what had been the natural surface, working its way slowly down in a giant spiral, around the edge of the circle, disappearing from view as it went deeper into the great hole. Even as she watched, she saw a wagon, drawn by a pair of oxen, moving slowly up the roadway, along the gentle slope that it formed up the other side of the wound.

"What is it?" Annabelle asked, voice soft.

"It is an open mine," Guise told her, voice equally soft. His face was grim. "There should not be anything here. There's nothing on the maps."

"What could they be mining here?" Yvonne asked, her stomach twisting. A mine that should not be there, with a road leading up to it that was clearly designed to carry heavy traffic.

An odd quality of the silence around her made her turn. The rest of the Hundred were looking at Sillman who was glaring, in apparent fury, at the mine ahead of them.

"Sillman?" she asked.

"They should not be here. No one should be here," Sillman said. He was not really speaking to her. Or to anyone. He seemed lost in some realisation. Not a pleasant one. He was pale, fists clenched by his sides.

"It's just a mountain," Idal pointed out.

Just a mountain. A remote place, days' travel from any major settlements. Outside Coll Castle territory. Great peaks rising up, providing an effective barrier most of the way around the mine, the deep swathe of ancient forest providing another barrier. So easy to get lost in a forest, Yvonne knew.

She exchanged a few glances with her fellow Hunar, apart from Sillman who was still staring ahead, face drawn.

They had received the same training she had. There was no such thing as just a mountain, or just a village, or just a road, or just a stream, or just anything else. Everything had a purpose, a meaning and a place, even if it was not clear.

Yvonne looked back at the scene ahead of them, at the wagon slowly ascending the spiral road. At the tiny figures moving. There were ladders up the sides of the mine, she saw, and a few figures moving up and down.

On the other side of the mine's vast, open mouth were buildings. They looked like hastily put together, single-storey buildings. The kind that might be put together as temporary shelter. She looked from the buildings back to the mine and thought there seemed nothing temporary about it.

"We should search the buildings," she said, before she really knew what she was saying. "We need more information."

"Good idea. We'll go," Guise said. He looked about, taking stock of the surroundings. "We can follow the trees most of the way if we go in this direction." He pointed.

He was right. As usual. When it came to sneaking around and making illicit entry to property, she did not know anyone better than Guise. He would have made an excellent thief. If he had not been too busy collecting secrets, that was.

"We'll go the other way," Annabelle suggested, glancing around the rest of the Hundred. "See what we can find."

To Yvonne's surprise, there was no protest from Sillman at the plan to split up. He still seemed lost in whatever realisation had gripped him. She found herself looking over her shoulder as she and Guise left the group, uneasy. It was not like Sillman to let someone else take charge. Or to keep matters to himself when information could help them.

Guise led the way and she attempted to stay close behind him, following his footfalls. They were far enough away from the lip of the mine that she did not think they would be heard. But there was no telling what else was in the forest, or even if the miners had set guards. Guards would be logical. The only things she knew of that came from mines were precious stones and precious metal. Definitely things worth stealing.

"This has been here for a while," Guise commented, stepping to one side so they could walk together for a moment. "To get to this size, mined by hand."

"There is no magic residue that I can sense," Yvonne told him. The high mountains, where Joel and Mariah's horses came from, were renowned for their sturdy people that spent a considerable part of their lives carving into the unforgiving mountain rock, in search of the precious gems and metals that were so prized and brought them what was rumoured to be fabulous wealth. She had never seen the mines, though, and had nothing to compare the great open space before her to, taking Guise's word for it. His education, and his travel, had been quite different to hers.

They continued in silence for a while until they were at the very edge of the trees. Whatever grass had been on the ground was long gone, along with whatever other plants there had been, and the space in front of them was simply packed earth. On a dry day, like now, it was sandy, but she could see the ruts from wagon tracks and thought that in winter it would probably be sticky and heavy to walk through.

"That looks like clay soil," she commented.

Guise made a low sound of agreement, eyes intent ahead of him. Figures were coming up from the lip of the mine, moving slowly with what looked like sheer exhaustion. Their shoulders were bowed as they reached the top of the ladder and scrambled to their feet, then paused for a moment before they moved forward, towards the buildings that she and Guise had seen on the far side of the mine.

Yvonne's breath caught in her throat. Not just people. Youngsters.

"Sturdy and strong," Guise murmured, hints of fury in his voice. He was remembering the descriptions that they had been given in Three Falls. The slavers who had not wanted the pretty children, but had wanted strong ones. Brought here, it seemed, by the wagon load.

Closer to the mine, they could not see quite as far into it, but she could see a dozen or more figures making their way up or down ladders that were strapped to the sides. They were all moving with the slow pace of exhaustion.

Captured, gathered up, sold, then forced into labour.

Even as she thought that, a familiar and unwelcome scent crossed her nose. Decay. Something, or more likely someone, had died and been left to rot nearby. And if she could smell it, then the children who were shuffling, shoulders bowed and heads lowered, would also be able to smell it as a constant backdrop when they were at ground level.

One of the youngsters stumbled in their slow walk away from the ladders. A few glanced over. Apart from that, no one reacted. She could not make out expressions at this distance, just see the subtle shift in their bodies. No one wanted to be near the one who had stumbled. No one reached out to help, or asked if he was alright. He stumbled again, paused, straightened his spine, and walked on even more slowly, but carefully upright, body tense with absolute focus on the ground ahead of him. Heading for what Yvonne assumed was a dormitory building. The curve of his shoulders and back suggested he was far too thin, exhaustion clear. A chill spread under her breastbone. He would not survive the night.

Not just sold into labour, then, but worked to death.

She clamped her jaw shut against a torrent of words and cry of outrage. The symbol at her shoulder brightened. The outline of the Firebird, the first Hunar's mythical companion. The bringer of justice, whose fury would scorch the earth clean before her. Yvonne wished, more than ever, that the Firebird was real. Some of her vengeance would be useful just now.

"They're dying," she said to Guise, her voice tight with emotion. "This needs to stop."

"We will stop it, mristrian," he promised, the weight of that promise ringing through her. Somehow she knew that he was as angry as she was. "First, we need to find out what they are doing here." There was a paler shade around his mouth and hints of red sparks in his eyes. He despised slavery. They had that in common.

"Miners are often well paid," she said slowly, her mind turning over that puzzle. Well paid, and subject to severe punishment if they were caught stealing. A skilled miner, or a crew of skilled miners, would surely be more use than wagon loads of unskilled and terrified youngsters.

"Quite so," Guise said.

Yvonne turned that over in her mind for a moment, nausea rising. Miners needed to be paid. Slaves didn't. She remembered those ledgers with the entries. She had no idea what a miner's pay was, but she suspected it was more than the cost of one of these children.

She said as much to Guise and saw the red flicker in his eyes, a low sound of anger in his throat before he turned his attention back to the buildings.

"I can draw some shadow around us," she told him. It was not a spell she used often, and had its drawbacks. "It will not hide any sounds we make, or our footprints, but it will encourage people to look away from us. We should be able to get to the buildings."

"Good. I think those two buildings are offices," he said, and pointed. Most of the buildings looked like they were barely standing, hastily constructed and poorly made. She guessed those were the dormitories for the slaves. The two buildings that Guise had pointed out were far more solidly constructed, and had actual windows in front of them, facing the mine itself. The doors were also facing the mine, though, and were both firmly closed.

"There may be a way in the back," Guise suggested.

She nodded and spent a moment mentally reviewing the requirements of the spell before speaking the necessary words, drawing a slight shimmer over them both, feeling the pull of energy from her as the spell rose.

Stepping out into the open with just the tentative protection of the shimmer always felt odd, and she had not got used to it, the few times she had used the spell before. Guise seemed fascinated, walking calmly and quietly by her side as they made their way across the open expanse of packed earth, round the back of the nearest dormitory building, and along to where the offices were.

Yvonne nearly drew attention to them, an involuntary sound in her throat, as she glanced away from the mine and buildings and saw the source of the smell of decay. A short distance from the buildings was a shallow, open pit into which bodies had been thrown. There was no attempt at burial, no attempt at dignity or respect. The dead had simply been flung in on top of each other. She could see tangled arms and legs, all covered in dust, eyes open in slack faces, staring up at the sky. The pit was nearly full and, looking along the line of buildings, she could see two more great mounds of disturbed earth that doubtless marked the presence of further mass graves.

And, in the pile of bodies, the trace of someone she had promised to find. Rebecca's brother. Long dead, by the trail she could sense. Her eyes stung, remembering Rebecca's desperation and fear.

A poor end for her brother, casually discarded along with the others.

Taken from all over the lands. Youngsters worked to death. And until Guise, Brea and Thort had plotted the missing on Guise's map, she had not realised the scale of it. She wondered how many law keepers across the lands were searching for children that were lying here, piled in careless heaps.

The symbol at her shoulder flared. Too many dead. They needed justice.

A grip at her wrist made her jump. Reacting on instinct, she turned her arm, twisting out of the hold and whirling to face her attacker.

Guise was quiet and still, red sparks in his eyes as he looked at her.

"Not now," he mouthed, near silent. His voice was deeper than normal, darkened with fury. "Soon."

She wanted to scream at him for being so uncaring, drawing in a deep, ragged breath to do just that. The stench of decay choked her and she hastily covered her mouth with her sleeve, breathing in for a long moment.

Time enough for her to realise that they were standing in the open, protected only by the slight shimmer of her spell. If she screamed at him, they would be discovered. And they did not know how many guards there were. Or what was going on. Why there was a great hole in the earth carved by hand by children. They needed to know these things before the children would be safe.

She dropped her arm, released her grip on her weapon and nodded, once, setting off towards the nearest office building again with rapid strides, Guise keeping pace with her.

Chapter Twenty-Five

The shimmer of the spell held until they were in the shadows of the first office building. It was quite a small building, barely bigger than the dining room at her house. There was, indeed, a back door. She kept watch, trying not to look back towards the graves, while Guise took a comprehensive set of lock picks out of one pocket and made quick work of opening the door.

He went inside first, moving with silent, lethal grace and she followed, closing the door behind her, just in time to hear a dull thump.

She whirled, one hand going to her sword hilt, only to find that Guise had knocked the occupant of the office unconscious and then caught him before he could fall to the ground. He was busy using the man's shirt sleeve as a gag, stuffing one end into his mouth, then binding it around his head before using the rest of the man's shirt to tie his hands and feet together, leaving his captive in an undershirt and trousers.

"We should search him," Yvonne said, reluctantly. The man was unconscious and no threat. She just didn't want to touch him, or anyone who was willingly at this place.

Guise made a swift and thorough check of the man's pockets and patted him down, producing a brace of knives, some chewing tobacco, and a few coins. Not a wealthy man, judging by the few coins and the well-worn clothes.

"He'll be out for a while," Guise said, dragging the man by his belt to an empty corner of the room.

Trusting his judgement, Yvonne turned her attention to the rest of the room. The whole building was, indeed, just one room, a little bigger than the dining room at her house. And it was an office, as they had suspected.

There were detailed drawings of the mine pinned to the walls, in various stages of its development, and a series of symbols that made no sense to her eyes. The mine was far deeper than she had imagined, even seeing the vast opening. She memorised as much as she could and turned to find Guise sifting through the man's desk, leafing through the ledgers that were lying on the writing surface.

"Records of some kind. It looks like slave records. Goes back at least a year."

She looked over his shoulder and saw the briefest of notations recording the slaves. Gender, approximate age, and date of purchase. A lot of the entries had lines through them. Date of death was not recorded, but the casual striking out of the bare information was clear.

Her stomach twisted, trying to imagine how many bodies the mass graves held. How long the slavers had got away with collecting and selling youngsters. How many had not been reported missing.

All those wagons. Youngsters bundled up in Three Falls, and perhaps other places. Shoved into wagons, transported here. Worked to death.

The symbol at her shoulder flared again.

"Any idea what they are mining?" she asked.

"No. But there are some letters here." Guise scowled. "Awful writing. We'll need more time with these."

He looked around the room and spied a large messenger's satchel, picking it up and checking it was empty before he started shoving the ledgers and letters he'd found into it.

Yvonne had spotted a large wooden box under the desk, hidden from casual view, held shut by a large lock. Guise made quick work of opening it, revealing a few pouches that clinked when he lifted them up.

"Not much," he assessed, checking each one in turn before passing them on to her to look at.

Not much. She shook her head slightly. The contents of one of the pouches would feed her whole family for a year. But she knew what he meant. For a mine, the lock box was poor pickings.

"Wages?" she suggested. "But for who? I haven't seen any guards."

"Excellent point," Guise agreed, taking the pouches and adding them to the messenger bag.

"If we're taking things, we should take the maps, too," Yvonne suggested, frustrated when she discovered that they were actually drawn on the walls.

"There are some sketches in here." Guise patted the satchel.

"He's still out?" Yvonne tilted her head to the man in the corner.

"Yes." Guise went across and stood over the man for a moment then nudged him with his boot. The man did not react. "It will be a while."

"We'll come back if we need to," Yvonne suggested. "The other office?"

"Can you do that spell again?"

She covered them with shadow again before they left the office through the back door, making their way to the second building.

The other building had a back door which also yielded quickly to Guise's lock-picks. It was a fraction larger than the other building, and not an office. A laboratory of some kind, filled with a pungent odour that made her nose wrinkle.

She covered her nose with her sleeve and looked around. There was a long workbench across the centre of the room, a waist-high structure covered with an unfamiliar apparatus. Clear glass bottles and small vials, what looked like short lengths of glass pipe, and a pair of oil burners, set close together, with small metal pots on each. And a large chopping board at the other end of the bench with a pile of reddish-hued leaves on it and a large knife and pestle and mortar sitting next to the chopping board.

The side walls of the building were covered in shelves, floor to ceiling, full of packing crates and spare glass bottles and vials, and more of the reddish leaves as well as large, clay jars that were usually used for liquid.

She turned from side to side, noticing a curious difference between the two walls. The stoppered bottles to one side all had a heavy black mark on the glass. The other side did not, even though both sets of bottles looked like they were filled with the same slightly pink liquid.

She had seen a setup like the bench only a few times before. Advanced healers used similar equipment to brew powerful and complex medicines.

It seemed unlikely that a healer would be working here. She turned to Guise, raising her brows. The smell was beginning to make her nose itch. She wanted to be out of here, working out how to free the slaves from this place and to find out who was in charge so she could ask them some questions. Probably at the sharp end of one or more of her knives.

"Well, now we know why there are no visible guards." Guise was staring at the apparatus on the bench, his eyes pure red, fangs fully visible. Any sensible person would have backed away slowly.

Yvonne stayed where she was, hand on her sword hilt, confident that he would not hurt her even though she could not say why she was so sure, and wondering again where the guards were. This much equipment, and the fine glass ware, was expensive. Highly unlikely it was unguarded.

"Explain, please."

"It's poison. Of a sort."

"It's either poisonous, or it's not," Yvonne protested. Her eyes were beginning to itch as well.

"Not always true," he told her, but tilted his chin, acknowledging the point. "We need those bottles." He indicated the full bottles with no mark on the side "In fact, we need most of this. I'll explain when we've burned the place to the ground."

Yvonne silently approved the idea of setting the place on fire as she looked around the room at the extent of the bottles they needed to take.

"We're going to need a lot of packing material. And a wagon or two," she told him. "And help getting this all onto it."

Even as she was wondering how easy it was going to be to commandeer one of the wagons and sneak all the bottles out past the guards, the front door to the building opened and a slender man stepped in, fine clothes suggesting immediately that he was not one of the slaves or, indeed, one of the guards, wherever they were.

He stopped in astonishment, one hand still on the door handle, and opened his mouth to either challenge them or call out for help.

Guise moved with speed that a wulf would envy and clamped a hand over the man's mouth, dragging him inside and shutting the door with the same precision.

"This one looks like he belongs in a city," Yvonne commented. "Not in an open mine in the middle of the forest."

"Scientist, I think," Guise said, nose wrinkling. He still had a hand over the man's mouth. "He smells."

"So this must be his workplace?" Yvonne looked around the room. The man's eyes followed her gaze, and she caught the tiny, almost imperceptible flinch as his gaze passed across the bottles with the black marks on the side. "I'm guessing that's the poison," she said to Guise, going across the room and reaching up to take one of the bottles from the shelf.

"Be careful, mristrian. He seems extremely worried by whatever is on those bottles."

"Good. I was thinking we should ask him to drink it," Yvonne said, voice hard.

The man's eyes bulged, and he shook his head as much as he was able to under Guise's grip.

"Perhaps he would like to answer some questions instead?" Guise suggested, hiding his smile as the man nodded. "Stay quiet, keep your voice down."

"Hunar, help me," the man said as soon as Guise took the hand away from his mouth.

Yvonne's lip curled. It was not the first time a criminal had appealed to her for help, and would not be the last. There was no pull inside her. Whatever magic aided the Hundred, it did not consider this man worthy of help.

"It does not work like that," she told him. "Hunar help those in need. Why should I help you?"

"They made me do it."

"How?" Guise asked, exchanging glances with Yvonne over the man's shoulder. Doubtless remembering, as she was, that Rebecca's brother had been captured to secure her aid.

"They threatened me."

"Just that?" Yvonne asked, oddly disappointed. Her eyes narrowed. "You are too well-dressed to have been coerced," she told him, ignoring the lack of logic, listening to her instincts. "He is stalling."

"I agree." Guise held out his hand for the bottle Yvonne was holding. She took the stopper out and handed it across. Guise backed his captive against the wall with a hand at his throat, and put the open mouth of the bottle against his lips. "I will make you swallow this unless you tell us what we want to know. Who are you? Who is in charge? What's being done here? Answer the questions, and you may live."

The man's eyes were fixed on the open mouth of the bottle, so near to his lips, and his mouth opened and shut a few times before his voice came out.

"Niall. Of Three Falls."

Yvonne watched as Guise's hand tightened around Niall's throat. She did not know the name, but he clearly did.

"I have been looking for you," Guise said, in a tone which suggested that their meeting would probably have ended up this way anyway, with him threatening the human.

"Really? What for? I can offer you very reasonable rates," Niall babbled.

Guise made a low sound that made Yvonne's hand twitch towards her sword hilt.

"Keep talking. You might still live," Guise suggested.

"The master here had heard about me. I don't know how. They offered me a job. All very secret. I didn't know. I didn't know they would be children. But then I was already involved. And there is nothing for miles around. Where would I go?"

"Keep talking," Yvonne said. She moved across to the window. Niall might be a coward, and greedy, but she sensed he was telling the truth. She was also certain that he was stalling, playing for time.

"The master should be here soon. He likes to inspect progress."

Niall's voice had changed slightly, growing in confidence, despite the open mouth of the bottle still in front of his face.

"And you think he will help you?" Guise asked, his tone conversational. "Interesting."

"He's not here now," Yvonne pointed out. "Finish answering Guise's questions."

"I don't know what's happening here. All I know is that we are not deep enough yet. And the master is furious about it."

Not deep enough. From the little she had seen, the depth of the mine outside was greater than the highest building in Three Falls, although the true scale of it was hard to tell. She could not think what was found so deep into the earth that was worth the slaves outside, the mass of bodies in the ground nearby and the sheer effort that had been put into the mine.

Movement outside the window caught her attention. There was a trio of men headed their way. Mercenaries, by the looks of them, with the hard edge and twitching movements that she associated with mercenaries in combat situations. They did not look like they were particularly skilled, mismatched clothing suggesting they weren't well paid, but she was not minded to take any chances. This whole place was making her skin crawl.

"Mercenaries on their way," she told Guise.

"Then we don't need this one anymore," Guise commented, and tipped the bottle closer to Niall's mouth.

Niall squealed, a high-pitched, keening sound, and somehow wriggled out of Guise's grip. Guise snarled, fangs bared, eyes sparking with red, and reached for him again. Niall sprinted for the door, faster than Yvonne would have believed possible.

Niall flung open the door just before Guise reached him and sent out a cry of alarm as he ran out. Beyond his shadow in the doorway, Yvonne could see the three mercenaries picking up their pace. Just as the mercenaries reached Niall's shoulder, Guise threw the bottle of poison. It broke against Niall's shoulder, spraying its contents over him and the three mercenaries.

Niall let out a wail of fury and despair and turned back to Guise, face distorting. "You've killed us, you goblin filth," he screamed at Guise.

"There's an antidote," Guise answered, apparently calm apart from the red in his eyes.

"Only if it's swallowed," Niall said. His knees gave out and he folded to the ground, a stunned expression on his face, limbs twitching.

Yvonne watched in horror as the three mercenaries collapsed as well, all four men twitching in what looked like agonising seizures before their bodies convulsed, spines arching up from the ground, and they went still and limp.

Dead. In a few heartbeats.

Her feet were locked to the ground, unable to move from the doorway of the laboratory.

"That was interesting," Guise commented, just in front of her. She glared at his shoulder. Somehow he felt her stare and turned back, his eyes still sparked with red. "He fed poison to children," he reminded her, "and took money for it. And the mercenaries were paid to work children to death. I do not think they deserve your sympathy, mristrian."

"You're right." She blew out a breath, revulsion rising. He was right. There were mass graves not that far away. And all four men had continued working, taking money, while the bodies piled up. "It would have been helpful to get more information," she said, trying to focus on more practical matters. "He said the master was on his way. None of these look like they are in charge."

"And the other one," Guise tilted his head towards the office and the bound man, "did not seem to be in charge either."

Yvonne looked at the corpses.

"We can't search them," she said. "Not if the poison is that dangerous."

"We still have one to question, though." He moved out of the doorway towards the office, careful to avoid the bodies.

"Assuming he wakes up," Yvonne pointed out, voice sharp. "You were not very careful when you hit him," she added at his sideways glance.

"Would you rather he had raised the alarm?" he asked, tone one of genuine curiosity.

"I'd quite like to stab someone right about now," she told him.

He turned to face her, feet continuing to move towards the office, his face lit with amusement. "You're very welcome to try, mristrian," he offered, a hint of fang at his mouth. The red was gone from his eyes, though, a swirl of a paler colour among the green.

Yvonne shook her head, refusing to answer. As skilled as she was with her weapons, goblins had turned swordplay into an art form, taught from the cradle in most cases. And Guise was exceptionally skilled, even for a goblin.

"I'll even stand still," he added.

She glared at him, mouth opening to tell him exactly what she thought of that idea, but before she could say anything the ground beneath them shook so violently she staggered sideways, hand going to her sword hilt in reflex.

"That came from below us," Guise said, all humour vanished.

"We need to get down there," Yvonne said, turning to go back towards the great gap in the world.

She paused as she turned. There was a group of slaves standing near to the corpses they had left, their eyes travelling from the corpses to Guise and Yvonne. About a dozen there so far, with more arriving. The youngsters were mostly dressed in rags, rough cloth trousers and tunics, coated with dust from the ground, many of them with no shoes.

"You're Hunar," one of the youngsters said, shoulders straightening. She seemed less worn than the others. Probably a more recent purchase, Yvonne thought bitterly.

"I am. I'm Yvonne. This is Guise."

"Help us, Hunar," the girl said, echoed by a dozen or so voices around her.

The pull of magic made Yvonne's knees buckle and her vision waver. She fell to one knee, hissing a breath as the magic woke in her, the symbol at her shoulder flaring with blinding green light, destroying what was left of her vision for long moments.

"I will help you," she managed to say, the weight of that promise a hard knot in her chest, "but I need some information from you first."

"What do you need to know?" A different voice. Male, she thought, her sight still blank.

"How many guards are there?"

"About fifty." That was the girl again, voice hard. "Although we're not sure. They are spread out. Some below. Some around here."

"And what about the one in charge? Where is he?" Yvonne asked.

Her vision cleared slightly as a ripple of unease travelled around the group. Whoever the master was, the slaves were frightened of him.

"He's not been here for days," a different voice answered, sounding reluctant to say even that much. "He brings the guards their wages."

"And we always have to work harder when he's been," another one added, voice a bare thread of sound.

So, the master controlled the guards by withholding their wages, even as the slaves were controlled with the poison. Yvonne's stomach was in a knot, disgust and anger tied together.

"What does he look like?" Guise asked.

"We're not supposed to speak about him," one of the slaves whispered. A murmur of agreement rose.

"We need to know what he looks like so we can kill him," Guise told them, gentle tone at odds with his hard words.

There was another murmur among the crowd, Yvonne's sight returning as she rose to her feet to see the youngsters' faces pale with worry underneath the coating of dust.

"I will help you," she said again, "but we need to know these things."

The reassurance opened a flood of comments, all overlaid.

"He's a tall lord."

"Wears red robes."

"Black hair."

"Black teeth."

"His skin is weird."

"He has vettr with him."

The comments went on and on, the same information being repeated. Yvonne and Guise exchanged glances. She doubted very much that there was another person with red robes and blackened teeth in the area. They were describing the lord of Coll Castle.

"He's dead," Yvonne told them baldly. "We met him a few days ago in his castle. Not far from here."

"How did you kill him?" the girl, the original speaker, asked, eyes narrow in suspicion. Yvonne approved. It was a good thing to be wary.

"The Hundred killed him," Guise answered, nodding past the group.

The slaves turned, some more slowly than others, wary of turning their attention away from a goblin, no doubt, turning more quickly as gasps filtered through the group.

The rest of the Hundred were on their way over, horses in tow.

Sillman looked from the worn, exhausted slaves to the four dead on the ground, to Yvonne and Guise and lifted a brow.

"I can't believe you started without us," Mica protested, cutting across whatever Sillman might say.

"There are more guards, apparently," Yvonne answered dryly.

"Oh, good." Mica tapped his sword hilt, eyes travelling over the exhausted youngsters. "Someone needs to pay."

"Th-there are more Hunar," one of the group said, voice shaking.

"Did you really kill the master?"

"How did you kill him?" the girl asked, sharp tone cutting through the babble of questions. Yvonne saw her own approval reflected on Suanna's face. A questioning mind was always encouraged.

"We stabbed him with our swords," Mica told them, keeping his tone light. "Several times."

"And then Idal smashed the vettr to pieces with a hammer," Annabelle added, matching the light tone, "so you don't need to worry about them, either."

"Are you really all Hunar?" the girl asked next. Yvonne bit her lip against a smile. That girl would go far, once she was free of this place.

"I am not," Idal answered her, expression serious. "I am training to be one, though. And Guise is not, either."

"Of course not," the girl said, sniffing. "Goblins can't be Hunar."

"Very true," Guise agreed, eyes gleaming with mischief. "Piety is so dull."

The girl scowled at him and he smiled, making a slight bow in her direction. Yvonne suppressed a sigh. Now was really not the time.

"Goblins think that helping people is dull, and pious," she said, rolling her eyes.

"It really is," Guise added, in a tone that suggested he was trying to be helpful. Yvonne rolled her eyes again. The girl's expression didn't change as she looked between Yvonne and Guise.

"She says she will help us," the girl said to the rest of the Hundred. "Will you help us, Hunar?"

The weight of the request was just as forceful as the first time, the Hundred staggering where they stood as the magic coursed through them.

"We will," Sillman answered for the group.

Before he could go on, the ground shook again.

"It's been doing that most of the day," one of the boys said, voice higher than it should be.

They were frightened. And no wonder.

"Will you get everyone together?" Yvonne asked the girl. "We need to know you will all be safe."

"There are still some of us in the mine," the girl protested.

"How do you get everyone out?" Annabelle asked, eyes narrowing. "There must be a way."

"There's a horn," one of the other girls said, turning and pointing. Not far away, at the lip of the mine, there was an odd contraption that looked like a chair on stilts, with a long object hanging to one side. "There's usually a guard sitting there."

"Probably gathering his friends," Mica suggested, tapping his sword hilt again.

"Fifty, give or take," Yvonne told him.

"Oh, good, that will leave some for the rest of you."

"Care to wager on that?" Guise asked.

"Hunar do not bet," Mica told him, lifting his nose slightly, "we execute."

Yvonne shook her head and saw several of the youngsters beginning to smile at the exchange. Not completely lost, then. Not all of them.

"If we deal with the guards, will you find a wagon, some packing crates, and packing materials?" Yvonne asked the girl.

"I thought you were going to help us?"

"We will. But it will be much faster if you help us, too," Pieris said.

"What are we packing?" Dundac asked.

"Look in there," Yvonne pointed to the open door of the laboratory.

The rest of the Hundred exchanged glances and made their way into the building, careful to step around the corpses.

"Poison. And an antidote," Suanna summarised when she came back. She was white around her mouth, brows lowered. She glanced at the corpses. "Was this thing responsible?"

"Niall from Three Falls. Yes," Yvonne said.

"I've heard of him." Suanna looked at the corpse, assessing the position of the body. "A fitting end, I think. Did he swallow the poison?"

"No. I threw it at him," Guise told her.

"Ah. So, we should be careful not to spill any."

"Very careful indeed," Guise agreed, voice dry.

"Mercenaries on the way," Idal said.

"Get the horses out of the way," Sillman ordered. "What's your name, girl?"

"Lily."

"Lily, gather everyone up and take them into the forest edge while we deal with the guards," Sillman ordered. "When we've done that, we'll get everyone out of the mine, and you'll need to get the wagons as Yvonne said."

"Alright," Lily answered, jaw set.

That one would lead armies, if she chose to, Yvonne thought, as in very short order Lily had gathered up the twenty or so slaves around them, hustling them along towards the tree line.

With the slaves and horses out of the way, there was nothing but four dead bodies between the Hundred and the oncoming mercenaries.

"Perhaps we should go around the bodies?" Yvonne suggested. "We don't know how long that poison is deadly."

"Last one buys the drinks!" Mica cried and surged forward, sword aloft.

Chapter Twenty-Six

"Idiot," Suanna muttered, drawing her sword and following Mica at a much more sedate pace.

Yvonne was not surprised when Guise outpaced them in a few strides, so that he and Mica were the first to meet the oncoming mercenaries.

"There aren't fifty of them," Sillman observed.

At most, thirty men were heading towards them, in the same mismatched clothing and armour of the mercenaries lying dead outside the laboratory. Second-tier swords for hire. The highest paid mercenaries tended to have better equipment. Yvonne's lip curled. No need to pay more to guard poisoned children. Second-tier was good enough.

"There might be more elsewhere," Yvonne suggested. "It's a big mine."

"Plenty for all of us," Dundac said.

Yvonne had never been to war, but she thought this might be what it was like. Utter chaos. The thin line of the Hundred, and Guise, met the greater number of mercenaries. The mercenaries might be second-tier, but they were scarred and wily, veterans with plain, serviceable weapons and swift, sure moves. They met Mica and Guise's initial charge as one unit, co-ordinated and deadly.

The Hundred were not soldiers, but they were trained to better skill than most soldiers could aim for. Messy, uncoordinated, they held against the mercenaries.

Dust kicked up from their boots made it hard to see. The air was full of the clash of steel on steel, heavy footfalls as bodies shifted position, grunts of effort.

A flicker of steel came out of the dust towards her. She met it with the flat of her sword, impact ringing up her arm, and changed position, long dagger sweeping down to catch her attacker's second weapon. With weapons locked together, she shifted her weight, kicked forward, and found a softer target than she had been aiming for, the man grunting in pain and staggering backwards.

Before she could press ahead, another flicker of steel was coming towards her and she had to defend herself again.

"That's three!" Mica's voice rose over the cacophony of noise, cheerful and carefree as ever.

"Five," Guise answered.

"I got one," Dundac added, sounding out of breath, "but who's counting?"

"Shut up and fight," Suanna snarled.

However many the rest had managed to defeat, Yvonne abruptly had three mercenaries closing on her, one of them moving at a shuffle thanks to her boot. Second-tier or not, three were a serious threat. She sheathed her long dagger and grabbed a prepared spell from her belt pouch instead, speaking the command word as she threw the vial.

A concussive force threw the mercenaries off their feet, several paces away from her.

"Nice," Mica commented, darting in from one side, ready to attack as the mercenaries got back on their feet.

"Do you have any more of those?" Guise asked, coming up behind the mercenaries.

"A few," Yvonne answered. A footfall behind her had her turning, bringing her sword up to meet the killing blow, holding firm as the mercenary spat a curse at her. The fury and revulsion were still twisted inside her, lending her the strength to push the man back.

"Using magic in a sword fight. Very unsporting," Dundac commented, panting as he came to stand by her shoulder. "But an excellent idea. Stand back."

The Hundred and Guise moved away from the mercenaries as Dundac threw his own spell. The impact was smaller than the one Yvonne had used. Enough to disrupt the mercenaries' co-ordinated attack again.

She moved to stand back-to-back with Dundac, the clash of steel now overlaid by his laboured breathing. He would not last much longer, she realised. There were still too many attackers for him to fail now.

"You're out of condition," Pieris observed, coming to stand with them. "Watch our backs, old man."

"Who – are you – calling old?" Dundac demanded.

Pieris didn't answer, taking a step forward towards his latest attacker and making a complicated move that had the attacker's sword on the ground and Pieris' sword in the man's throat in moments.

The mercenaries were dying. None of the Hundred, or Guise, showed any mercy. Even as the air thickened with the scent of blood, Yvonne did not blame them, remembering the mass graves.

Eventually, the dust slowly settled, coating the fallen bodies, the blood sinking into the dry ground.

"And we get to do it all again soon," Mica commented, moving forward.

For a moment, Yvonne could not work out what he meant, then saw that he was heading for the horn. Of course. There were more guards, and if the noise of fighting hadn't alerted them, the horn would.

A low, keening note rang out, bouncing back from the sides of the mine. There were a few panicked cries from the slaves nearby, and across the other side Yvonne could see small figures moving, heading towards the ladders that led up to the surface.

Mica blew the horn again, another long note, then stopped, staring down.

The rest of them moved across to join him, in a line along the edge.

Yvonne's breath caught. She had known the thing was big, but could not have imagined anything so vast. It was deeper than she had believed possible, width narrowing as it descended into the earth. And it was full of people. Mostly slaves, the threadbare clothes giving them away, but there were more mercenaries, riding horses up the twisting spiral path that led around the sides of the mine, driving wagons pulled by oxen, plodding along despite the mercenaries' urging.

"That's a lot more than fifty," Annabelle commented, eyes narrowed.

"We'll need the horses," Suanna said.

When no one answered, Yvonne turned and saw that everyone's attention was moving from the extraordinary sight of the mine ahead of them and to Sillman.

The Hundred's leader was staring into the mine, face chalk-white, lips moving in what looked like a silent prayer, visibly trembling.

After a moment, Yvonne realised it was not a prayer. He was saying the same words over and over.

It cannot be.

It cannot be.

It cannot be.

"What cannot be, old man?" Mica asked.

Sillman's head snapped around towards Mica and he blinked, as if he had forgotten that anyone else was there.

"I will not speak it," he said, voice shaking. "We need to go down."

The first of the slaves reached the surface and stopped, swaying on their feet, staring. Yvonne wasn't sure if they were more surprised by the symbols that gleamed faintly in the light, or the sight of a goblin lord among humans. Lothar shifted under her, shaking his head. There was the scent of blood in the air, and he knew that meant work to do.

"Go with the others," Suanna ordered the slaves. Settled on her tall, dark horse, sword hilt ready to hand, hair pulled back into a tight knot, Yvonne thought that her fellow Hunar looked entirely capable of leading an army to war. The slaves looked past the Hundred to where Lily was organising her group with the sort of brisk efficiency any army officer would envy.

"And don't worry, we'll be back soon," Mica added. He had his sword out, his horse prancing sideways as he urged it forward. The first of the wagons was nearing the surface, the end of the path a short distance ahead of them.

Yvonne caught Sillman and Suanna shaking their heads slightly, almost identical expressions of disapproval on their faces.

"He's never going to change," Dundac commented, in no hurry to move ahead. He was sitting with his hands folded on the high pommel in front of him, his reins loose. His horse was resting a leg, seeming half-asleep.

"It's going to be a difficult journey down," Idal commented. He had one hand on the hilt of his war hammer, ignoring the sword at his side, his body taut with some inner excitement betrayed by the gleam in his eyes. Yvonne remembered him breaking the vettr to pieces in Coll Castle, the same expression on his face.

"We'll never get to the bottom if we don't move," Pieris said.

Yvonne was not surprised to see Guise ahead of them already, joining Mica, his goblin-bred horse moving with the dancing strides of a creature ready to spring in any direction, neck arched and tail held high.

Before she could follow Mica and Guise, there was a scream ahead of them. One of the mercenaries had been thrown from his horse, falling down the side of the mine, bouncing off the sloping sides all the way down the bottom, cries cut off as he fell. It was a long way down.

Her insides twisted. A long way down if any of them fell.

The mercenary's horse ran past them, whites of its eyes showing.

The Hundred's horses snorted in disgust at the trail laid out before them. Yvonne did not blame them.

Many of the religious orders across the lands talked about an after-world, a place where evildoers would receive eternal punishment. Looking down into the mine, Yvonne thought this might be what an after-world would look like. The sheer scale of it was impossible to grasp. If she looked down, at the drop next to her, she could see the return of the spiralling road below them.

The surface of the path and the sides of the mine were packed smooth, the path showing the occasional rut from a wagon wheel, the sides as smooth as any plaster wall. It was the colour that held her attention, though. A dull, uniform grey, rather than the clay soil or earth she had been expecting. There were no roots or rocks scattered through the soil that she could see. No sign of life at all. Just that grey soil.

Looking back at the ground around the mine, she could see traces of the grey showing there, too, fading gradually to a more normal colour of soil nearer the mass graves.

A place for evil, indeed.

"Odd colour of soil," Idal commented. "I've never seen it before."

No one spoke for a moment, but the quality of Sillman's silence drew Yvonne's attention again. He was still pale, lips pressed in a thin line as though he was holding something back. For the first time in their dealings, a prickle of unease crept along her spine. He was Hunar. They had sworn the same oaths, undergone the same training. It was one of the fundamental truths of her life that her fellow Hunar would support her, as she would support them. And now, for whatever reason, Sillman was hiding something.

It chilled her, that one of the Hundred would not tell them all he knew.

"We need to go down," Sillman said at length, perhaps sensing her gaze on him, seeming to ignore the fact that Guise and Mica were ahead of them, doing just that, another riderless horse running past them, ears flat to its head as it fled the mine. The horse was followed at a far slower pace by a wagon, laden with soil. Just soil. Nothing else.

Yvonne frowned after the wagon. Surely no one would make something this enormous just to get some unusual soil?

There were no answers here, though. They needed to go down.

Whatever Sillman feared, he seemed to have communicated it to his horse, which refused, point-blank, to set foot on the path. The other horses were picking up on the unease, digging their heels in and refusing to go forward. Yvonne pressed Lothar forward, trusting the old warrior to obey her. Unlike the others, he was trained to charge ahead where no sane creature would go.

Even so, he shivered nose to tail, arching his neck. He might be trained to war but, like her, he was not eager for it. After the minor protest, he moved forward with his normal, smooth stride, ears flicking as they moved down, lengthening his stride to catch up with Mica and Guise without Yvonne's prompt.

They had ridden what Yvonne thought was one full circuit of the mine, descending steadily, when Yvonne realised that there were no more mercenaries in front of them. Another pair of wagons had lumbered past, oxen moving steadily toward the surface. But no more armed men.

"They're gathering at the bottom," she realised, looking ahead and down.

If the mine itself looked like something from an afterlife for the damned, the bottom of it was surely where the worst offenders would be sent. It was shadowed by the enormous sides of the mine, making it difficult to see, the darkness resembling a wide open mouth of some giant and awful creature.

In the dark below, people were moving. The mercenaries were grouping together in greater numbers than she had expected.

"Definitely more than fifty of them," Guise noted. He did not sound worried.

"And no slaves left," Mica said, looking around. "That's something."

It was something, Yvonne agreed. No more innocents caught up.

Lothar snorted but kept moving, the others with them. Down into the mouth.

As they rode, a knot of tension gathered in Yvonne's stomach, getting heavier and tighter as they rode. Mercenaries ahead. And they still did not know what the mine was for. What all this effort, the enormous hole in the world, was for.

"It's getting warmer," Guise commented. He sounded calm. She was not fooled. His shoulders were square and straight and he had one hand on his sword hilt.

She had been so distracted in trying to figure out where she was, and understand what this place was, that she had not noticed the rise in temperature. Now that he had mentioned it, it was noticeably warmer. It had been a slightly chilly spring day at the top. Closer to the bottom of the mine it was more like a warm summer evening, when the sun had faded.

Her vision wavered for a moment. Something about a rising temperature reminded her of the dungeon, and that missing bit of her memory.

"Looks like they're ready for us," Mica said, snapping her out of the almost-remembrance.

They were at the final turn to the floor of the mine, and there were no more wagons, just the mercenaries, many of them on horseback. Waiting, as Mica had said. Spread out in some kind of formation that Yvonne did not recognise. And these were not all the second-tier mercenaries they had met above. These ones wore matched armour, weapons made by master craftsmen. Apprehension sent static across her skin. Formidable opposition for their small group.

"There is no sign of any precious stones, or precious metal. In the wagons, or the ground," Guise said. He checked his horse slightly so that Yvonne could ride beside him.

"Is this soil valuable?" Yvonne asked. It was the only thing she could think of. This far down, the soil was darker than it had been closer to the surface. The same colour as the soil in the wagons.

"Even if it is, they would not need to dig so far down to harvest it. It is easily accessible from the surface."

"Do you know what soil that is? I've never seen it before," Yvonne asked.

"No. It's almost like potters' clay, but not quite." Guise was frowning, as puzzled as she was.

"It is corrupted," Sillman said unexpectedly. His voice was heavy and, when Yvonne turned slightly to look at him, his expression had not changed from the surface, lips still set in a firm line.

"You need to tell us, old man," Annabelle said, voice tight.

"I don't want to say," Sillman said. "It may not be true."

"Aren't we better off prepared?" Mica asked, tone belligerent. "You've always taught us that the more information the better. And we've got mercenaries to fight, too."

"We need to focus on our enemy," Sillman said. It was an accurate observation, but it sent another prickle of unease through Yvonne. Hasty words rose in her throat and she clamped her mouth shut against the impulse to shout, to demand answers. He was still hiding his knowledge, keeping secrets from them. And she had a conviction, which sent a further chill through her, that Sillman would not answer her.

"We need to know what we're facing," Suanna objected. "Talk, old man."

"We are not alone," Sillman protested.

Annabelle produced a snort of derision worthy of her horse. "Just tell us. Guise is already here, and proved his usefulness."

Even in the circumstances, Yvonne had to bite her lip to hold in a smile at the thought of Guise being relegated to simple usefulness.

"I'm glad to be of service," Guise said mildly. "You should tell us what you suspect, Sillman. I like to know when I'm riding into a trap."

Yvonne couldn't help lifting a brow at that, eyes straying to the mercenaries waiting for them, not that far away. Out of earshot. Only just. More than fifty mercenaries, most of them elite. Less than a dozen in her group. They were not good odds, even with a goblin on their side and the Hundred's skill with magic. Her mouth was dry, pulse too fast.

"Not a trap. Not precisely. Well, not for us," Sillman said. It sounded like the words were being dragged out of him.

Yvonne's mind snagged on that little snippet of information. A trap, but not for them. The corrupted soil. The depth of the mine. The increasing warmth.

"You think there's something buried here?" she said slowly, keeping her eyes on Sillman's face. He flinched as she spoke. "Something evil." He twitched again, face even paler against the backdrop of the dark earth. "He is coming." The words were out before she knew she had spoken, and she saw uneasy glances from the rest of the Hundred. "The messages from the sight."

He is coming.

"The enemy," Suanna murmured, face pale, shaking her head in disbelief. "But he's dead. The first Hundred made sure of it. Dead and buried."

"He should be," Sillman answered, voice harsh. "He should never have been found. The location was known only to a few living back then, and no one alive just now."

"The enemy of the Hundred? You mean the first Hunar's brother?" Guise said, drawing uneasy glances and a murmur of surprise from many of the Hundred. Yvonne was not surprised. The Hunar and the Karoan'shae were not enemies. Not quite. But the goblin philosophy was to see everyone as a potential threat, and learn as much as possible about them. The Karoan'shae took great pride in their education and the extent of their knowledge, and Guise's business was secrets, after all. "I thought they killed each other, the first Hunar only surviving a bit longer thanks to the first Hundred. That's what the legends say," he added, with a pointed glance at Yvonne. She remembered telling Rebecca the same thing, what seemed a lifetime ago.

"Quite so," Annabelle answered him, shaking her head slightly. Idal was looking bewildered. She tilted her chin to him. "You've not reached that part of your training yet."

"You mean the legends are true?" Idal asked, voice rising in pitch. "The legends say that the Hunar and his brother nearly destroyed the world."

"Stories often have some basis in truth," Suanna commented.

"I know. But ... Destroy the world?"

"She said some basis in truth," Annabelle reminded him.

"Still, he's been buried for, what, four hundred years?" Mica said. "How dangerous can a rotting corpse be?"

"I think we are about to find out," Yvonne said.

"We must find out if he is here, and make sure he stays buried," Sillman cut across whatever anyone else might say.

The rest of the group looked at him, and Yvonne saw everyone else come to the same conclusion as she did. Whatever else he knew, Sillman was not going to say anything more. And there were enemies ahead. Mercenaries who had worked slaves to death in creating this mine, digging into corrupted earth.

The knot in her middle tightened again.

"I think you're behind on the count," Mica told Guise, unsheathing his sword.

"Your arithmetic is lacking," Guise answered. There was red in his eyes, and his fangs were out. "But who's counting?"

"The Hundred!" Mica yelled, and pressed his horse into a forward charge across the flat surface of the mine's floor.

"Idiot," Suanna muttered, sword ready in her hand.

"Not quite," Sillman contradicted, watching Mica's charge. He was not heading for the centre of the group, as it had seemed. Instead, he had veered off to one side and three mercenaries on horseback had come forward to meet him.

"Divide and conquer. Good plan," Pieris approved. "Yvonne, do you have more of those spells?"

"A few, yes."

"Good. Can you throw one in the middle?"

"I can't throw that far," Yvonne told him, measuring the distance. "Does anyone have a bow or crossbow?"

"Of course." Annabelle produced a very delicate looking crossbow from somewhere under her riding skirts. "What?" she asked, arching her brow at Dundac's astonishment.

"That's the first time I've seen one kept there," Dundac answered. "What else –"

"Enough," Sillman cut across the question. "Annabelle, fire Yvonne's spell into the middle."

Even with him withholding information, following Sillman's orders was as natural as breathing.

The first of Yvonne's spells, wrapped around one of Annabelle's crossbow bolts, split the group of mercenaries. The bolt had struck home in one mercenary's shoulder, the concussive force of Yvonne's spell blowing the man's arm and body apart. She felt sick, but handed Annabelle another spell when asked, powered with the command words.

Annabelle fired the second bolt at the larger group, directing it at the ground in front of the horses' hooves. The horses screamed and reared back, unharmed, as soil spurted up in front of them, then threw their riders and ran off, heading for the upward path as fast as their legs would take them, leaving their riders on the ground, some of them still and unmoving.

By this point, the rest of the Hundred were in the middle of the mercenaries, Yvonne not surprised to see Idal on his feet, swinging his war hammer, his horse standing out of the way, ears flicking back and forth as it watched the fight.

Lothar arched his neck and pranced sideways, tail flicking. Yvonne looped the reins around the pommel, leaving them loose enough for him to move, and guided him forward with her legs and heels.

He shoulder-barged the nearest horse, using his greater bulk and training to simply brush the horse aside while Yvonne stabbed the heavily muscled mercenary trying to cut her head off. The mercenary fell, trampled under his own horse's hooves.

Lothar was already moving, seeking his next target. A mercenary was trying to creep up behind them. A swift, sure kick and the man was on the ground, unmoving.

Another concussive spell detonated a short distance away. Much less powerful than hers, it still unseated riders, leaving them vulnerable to Idal's hammer.

A sword flashed at the edge of her sight, someone trying to cut underneath her. Sword down, catching steel. Leg against Lothar's side. He turned, reared up and kicked the swordsman in the head with deadly accuracy.

Four feet on the ground again, hindquarters turning. Another kick. Another fallen mercenary.

Another spell detonated. More horses loose, getting in the way. Before she could move, Dundac was there, grabbing reins and leading the riderless horses away, sending them up the path out of the mine.

Then Guise was there, his war-trained mount sidling up to hers, still springing on its hooves. Amid all the chaos, she knew where he was, moving Lothar to work with his horse.

A mercenary ran at her. She deflected his charge with the flat of her sword, Lothar moving them out of the way, and Guise took the man's head off with a single sweep of his blade, flicking the blade at the end of the cut to shed some of the blood.

"They're retreating," Pieris observed, on Guise's other side.

"No. They are regrouping," Guise contradicted, voice flat. "What is that?" He used his second sword to point.

The mercenaries were gathering again. Despite the number of bodies and body parts on the ground, and the pools of blood, there were still more mercenaries than Hunar.

"Bloody, sneaky cut-throats," Suanna said, in a furious, bitter voice. One of her arms was hanging by her side, blood dripping down to the ground below. "Lost my sword," she said, with a grimace.

"Here." Idal handed the sword to her. She took it in her other hand, grip awkward, and grimaced again.

"Not sure how much use I'll be," she admitted.

"Any other injuries?" Sillman asked.

Yvonne shook her head silently, eyes going back to the mercenaries. She could not see what it was that Guise had pointed to.

Then one of the mercenaries moved, and she caught a glimpse behind him of a deeper, blacker hole in the mine's floor. Beyond the mercenaries, away from the path that led down, was a bank of that darker soil. Almost black. It was piled nearly as tall as the mercenaries, an effective guard for their backs.

"It's a hole," she answered Guise's question. "And the soil is darker."

She expected a sarcastic retort. It was a very obvious thing to say.

When he stayed silent, she glanced across to find he was frowning at the hole, and even in profile she could see that his eyes were red, fangs extended.

"Everything gets darker and warmer towards that spot," Idal observed.

"That must be what they've been digging for," Suanna said.

They all turned back to the deeper hole, guarded by the mercenaries. Perhaps they were expecting something to emerge. Some sign that Sillman's guess was right, or that there was indeed some purpose to the mine.

Nothing happened.

The mercenaries were ready, weapons out. Warriors, with the battered, plain armour and weapons of seasoned veterans, awaiting the approach of their enemy.

The Hunar were tired and worn, although Guise showed no sign of fatigue and Idal looked as eager as ever for battle. Yvonne swallowed nausea. So much death. More to come.

The mercenaries waited.

Chapter Twenty-Seven

Moving by instinct, Yvonne slid off Lothar, sending him away with a gesture and a word. He danced around the dead, staying within calling distance, eyes on the mercenaries, ears forward. He knew an enemy when he saw one.

She took a few steps forward, not close enough to be in danger, and looked down. The soil did darken towards the hole, but that was not all. Closer to the ground, she could see faint trails of darker soil among the grey, as if veins of black were growing. It reminded her of the Coll lord's face.

"Look at this," she said.

Guise was first, followed by the rest of the Hundred while Idal kept watch, his eyes on the mercenaries.

"It's coming from that hole," Annabelle said. She crouched down, careful not to touch it. Her nose wrinkled. "It stinks. Something dead."

"He's here," Sillman said, his voice heavy. "And still powerful."

"Still alive?" Guise was astonished.

"If he was really alive to start with," Sillman answered.

The hole in the ground looked perfectly innocuous, apart from the black soil and the ring of armed men guarding it. There was nothing immediately visible to suggest that the first enemy of the Hunar was buried there.

"He's been buried for centuries," Yvonne said, thinking aloud. She looked up at the mine, at the extraordinary depth that had already been dug. "If it's taken this long for the soil to be corrupted like that, he could still be very far down."

"We should just bury him again," Annabelle said, ignoring the mercenaries in their way.

"Yes. Stop him from rising," Yvonne agreed. It sounded almost insane, speaking her fear aloud. The ancient enemy, buried for hundreds of years. He should be long dead. And yet, there was this vast mine around them, and the darkened soil. And the blackened tendrils stretching out from that rotten hole.

"Between us, we should have enough power," Suanna commented.

Yvonne realised that she did not feel particularly powerful at the moment. Her skin was sticky with the heat, the back of her neck prickling as though something was standing behind her. She glanced over her shoulder, the sensation was so strong. There was nothing immediately behind her. The horses were gathered together a short distance away, watching their riders.

Looking down, she realised that she was standing on one of the black veins amid the grey. She did not think it had been there a moment before. She took a step back, shaking her feet as she did so, and felt some of her energy return.

"Don't stand on the black," she said, hand going back to her sword hilt.

They all looked at the ground and a couple of the Hundred moved hastily back, out of the way of the black.

Even as she looked, the black line she'd been standing on moved. She blinked. No, she had not imagined it. It had twitched in the ground, stretching out.

Looking along the line of black, she could see more lines snaking out from the hole, underneath the mercenaries' feet. The lines were stretching beyond the Hundred. Towards the dead. The lines twitched as they moved, circling around discarded weapons. Stopping only when they reached the abundant pools of blood soaking into the soil.

"It's after the blood," she said, voice hoarse.

She saw similar shock on the others' faces as they followed the trails of black.

As they watched, the first seeking tendrils of black reached the first body. The blood pool dried, soaked into the earth, before the soil itself moved, creeping up around the man's body, covering it for a moment. When the soil receded, the body was cloud-white, the soil darker. Carrying the blood, Yvonne realised. No wonder there was no life down here.

"We need to bury him again," Sillman said, voice shaking, "keep him contained."

The lines of black were thicker now, coiling in on themselves, spiralling into a knot that grew larger as she looked.

Yvonne took a step back, careful to make sure she was still on the grey. The rest followed, another pace away from the dark hole and the mercenaries, who were holding their ground despite the black lines.

"It is getting warmer again," Guise commented. His eyes were red tinted and he had a sword out in his hand, ready and waiting for the enemy.

Yvonne opened her mouth to tell him that the enemy would not likely be defeated by steel, interrupted by a cry of discovery and alarm from one of the others. She was not sure who. Then it did not matter who. All around the dark hole in the ground, the tendrils of black were curling back on themselves in tighter and tighter bundles, the knots of black rising up from the ground, tentacles stretched out.

The first tentacle whipped around one of the mercenaries' throats, the man dropping his sword to clutch at the black strand, scrabbling frantically as it tightened before the tip of it disappeared into his mouth.

The other mercenaries panicked, moving away from the black, a few of them caught by tentacles that struck with snake-like speed and precision, trapping the men in black strands, dragging them back toward the hole.

The few mercenaries who had escaped kept running, heading for the path up the side of the mine and the ladders there.

"Let them go," Sillman ordered. "Does everyone have cleansing spells ready?"

"You think cleansing will work?" Guise asked, apparently genuinely interested.

"If it's powerful enough, it should stop the corruption," Sillman answered, rummaging in his belt pouch.

The rest of the Hundred had their own spells ready, Yvonne included. She hoped that no one asked her just how many prepared cleansing spells she carried. She might not remember everything about the dungeon, but she could clearly remember the sensation of something putrid between her toes and had used a few moments alone in her tavern bedroom to prepare as many spells as she could manage.

"Give them to me," Annabelle said. She had her crossbow ready, quiver of bolts across her shoulder. She tied the spells to a few bolts, two spells at a time, and readied her bow.

"Mercenaries first," Yvonne suggested. An easier target than the wriggling black in the ground.

The tentacle-wrapped bodies were still on the ground, hands still at the throats, mouths wide, eyes staring at the sky.

Annabelle lifted a brow at Yvonne's suggestion, but fired the first cleansing spells, her own, into the nearest body.

The body twisted and arched with a scream that would haunt Yvonne the rest of her days, the black unravelling as fast as it had taken the man over, sliding back into the ground, leaving a hardened mercenary huddled over and crying, clutching his throat, eyes wide as he spied the Hundred, one hand reaching out in a plea.

"Hunar, h –"

His words were cut off as his head parted from his body.

The other black-wrapped bodies had risen while the cleansing spell had been working, swords ready, bodies moving with odd, jerking movements, no whites showing in their eyes.

"Again," Sillman ordered.

Annabelle was already firing, another pair of spells twisted around the bolt. Dundac's this time, the Hunar activating the spells as they flew.

The cleansing magic cascaded over the shuffling form, the mercenary falling to his knees, eyes and mouth wide. A torrent of black flew out of him, soaking back into the ground, and he toppled over, sightless eyes staring at the sky.

Annabelle fired again, Idal moving to her side as the mercenaries drew closer. There were only five of them left. But the Hundred only had one crossbow.

"Give me a spell or two," Guise said to Yvonne. He had a throwing dagger in one hand.

She handed over a pair of spells without protest, watched as he twisted the parchment around the hilt, and then spoke the command words as the knife flew, straight and true, to its target.

Another knife, another pair of crossbow bolts, and only one was left, within a few paces of Sillman. Sillman raised his sword, only to be beaten by another dagger from Guise.

Sillman looked at the body in front of him, at the black creeping back to the hole in the ground and visibly shivered.

"That was too easy," Guise commented.

"Easy?" Dundac's voice rose an octave on that one word. Yvonne saw the astonishment reflected on other faces.

She agreed with Guise, though, and kept her sword ready as she moved forward, careful to keep her feet on the grey, to stand near the last fallen body.

"He looks similar to the Coll lord," she commented. The mercenary's pale skin was lined with dark veins.

"The same corruption," Sillman said, voice heavy. He seemed shaken, staring at the dead, at the evidence of what the corruption could do.

"How did the Coll lord become infected?" Suanna asked. An excellent question.

"What's that?" Idal asked, voice rising, cutting across further speculation.

The black lines in the ground were reforming, tentacles thickening, rising out of the ground, becoming human-like shapes, with what looked like a head, legs and arms. Formed out of the black, they were not tied to the ground, moving across the grey earth.

"Suggestions?" Yvonne asked, voice clipped. Her heart was pounding, too hard and too fast. She had her sword out and did not remember drawing it.

"More cleansing spells," Sillman answered, an edge to his voice she had not heard before. Panic.

"Here." Yvonne handed Guise another cleansing spell.

He threw another knife. It struck the black creature in its centre, the creature letting out a wordless howl that grated the bones in Yvonne's head, the mass writhing until it faded back into the ground.

"That works," Guise said, with grim satisfaction. "Again."

"We're running out of spells," Annabelle commented, loading another bolt into her crossbow.

And the creatures were moving faster than the mercenaries had done, covering the short distance with easy strides.

Annabelle let loose another bolt, reducing another creature to black ash.

The first of the creatures reached Idal, standing guard before Annabelle, and swiped out with one long, misshapen arm.

Idal danced sideways, out of reach, hammer lifting, smacking the tentacle away. It made a flat, dull sound as it came into contact with the creature. The creature shuddered but did not fade.

The rest of the creatures paused, at some invisible signal, just out of reach of the Hundred. The rest of the Hundred were equally still, staring wide-eyed at the things before them.

"They're solid," Guise commented. "If they're solid, they can be destroyed."

It seemed logical.

"Will you keep watch while I prepare a spell?" Yvonne asked. The words sounded strange in her mouth, the whole situation strange. She had thought that the Hundred could take on anything, and yet they were standing still facing an unknown enemy.

"Of course," Guise answered, and took a careful, deliberate stride forward, putting himself between her and the creatures.

She put her sword away for the moment, drew a strip of blank parchment from her belt pouch, and called the spells she needed to mind. Cleansing and fire. Combining spells was never straightforward, but she had mere moments to speak the necessary words, the spell forming on the parchment. She balled the parchment up so that she could throw it, then stepped up to Guise's shoulder and cast the spell out, aiming for the nearest creature.

The fire bit into the black substance, whatever the thing was made of, and the creature lit up like a torch at Mid-Winter Feast, the grating sound coming again, vibrating through the bones of her head. The fire burned the creature to the ground, then took hold of the black and spread out, catching another of the creatures as it spread.

When the fire had died down, there was nothing but ash left, the creatures gone.

"Fire spells, everyone," Sillman ordered, snapping out of his motionless state. "Yvonne, Guise, Idal, keep watch."

Yvonne moved forward with Guise and Idal, all of them with their swords ready, while the rest of the Hundred made their own fire spells. It would not be enough. Even as they threw the first volley, Yvonne realised it would not matter. There were more creatures forming in the black near the hole in the earth.

Sillman ordered another round of fire spells, his voice grimmer than before, and Yvonne knew that he had seen what she had seen. There were more of the creatures coming and they were more cautious now, and more cunning. They were beginning to circle around the group, using their greater numbers to gain the advantage.

She felt hollow, all her energy used up in the cleansing fire and the battle before it. There was not even the pull of an unfulfilled promise.

The Hundred moved, standing shoulder to shoulder, with Idal and Guise in their circle, facing their enemy. Weapons ready. Magic all but done.

It was not enough.

They needed the unique power of the Hundred. The energy that came from helping those in need.

But there were no supplicants here.

Her breath caught. No ordinary supplicants, true. But there was a chance.

"Guise, we are overrun. Is there something you would ask of me?"

Everyone and everything around them stilled. Hunar could not choose who they helped, not really, and they could not help themselves. The magic decided.

But goblins and Hunar had an uneasy relationship at the best of times, and goblins rarely managed the humility or sincerity that would trigger the magic.

Guise lifted a brow, red dimming in his eyes. He looked at the enemy around them, and then back at her. Her breath caught. He was one of the most arrogant people she knew. He put his sword away and, of all things, made a shallow, formal bow.

"Hunar, we are overrun. Hunar, help me." There was no humility in the words. There was, though, absolute sincerity.

It was enough. The magic woke in her, and she could see the others straightening, too, as the pledge that they had all made took hold. To help those in need.

And there were more promises to keep. To the slaves on the surface high above them.

Around the circle, green light flared as the symbols of the Hunar lit up. The magic had accepted Guise as a supplicant and remembered the promises made above.

Power rose inside her. The same crackling, intense power she had used in the quarrel. A Hunar's power.

"Stand inside our circle," Sillman ordered Guise. The old man looked taller than he had done for many years, voice carrying traces of the crackling power that was cascading over Yvonne's skin in static sparks.

Guise moved into the circle of Hunar with no complaint, Idal joining him a moment later when Annabelle gave her apprentice a hard shove. Idal looked belligerent, jaw thrust out, knuckles white holding the war hammer.

"Send the horses away," Suanna said, her voice carrying the same power as Sillman's.

Lothar was moving before she gave him the command, running up the path around the mine with determination, the other horses flying after him, even Guise's goblin-bred horse straining to keep up with the headlong pace.

"Form a circle," Sillman ordered. There were a few indrawn breaths. Practised, on the rare occasions when they were together. Never used.

The Hundred moved closer together, so they could each put their right hand on the next person's shoulder, leaving their left hands free.

"Fire," Sillman commanded, speaking his spell at once.

The circle blazed with magic, fire cascading out over the black creatures, rendering them into ash, the shrieks of fury and agony carrying into the air above.

"And now, we will bury him," Sillman said, breaking the circle and striding over the ground to the deeper hole and the blackened earth.

Yvonne's breath caught as she saw the black retreating from Sillman's approach. She followed him, moving to one side as they reached the hole.

The black kept creeping back away from their feet as they approached, Idal and Guise following, the Hunar circling the hole so that they were standing on a ring of grey, looking down into black.

The hole was empty. It was deeper than she had expected, even with the evidence of the piled earth around them. But there was nothing there. No sign of life. No bones. No cloth. Nothing that she would expect to see in a grave.

"He's still buried," Annabelle whispered, voice shaking with relief.

"And we must make sure he stays that way. Circle," Sillman ordered again.

They faced inward this time, in a tight ring around the hole, stretching to touch the nearest shoulder. Another body would have made this much easier, Yvonne thought, missing Elinor.

But they were here. Eight of them. And the symbols they each carried were blazing with power, still.

"Guise, Idal, make sure you have hold of one of us," Suanna ordered without looking away from the hole.

Somehow Yvonne was not surprised when Guise's hand landed on her right shoulder. She stayed still under the contact. Guise would not hurt her. Her hand was on Pieris' shoulder, Dundac's hand on her other shoulder. Her throat tightened, breath quickening. Too much contact.

Before she could give in to the panic, Sillman spoke.

"We are the Hundred. We are the ones who protect those who cannot protect themselves. And we will not let him rise." Sillman's voice rang through the mine, bouncing off the earthen walls, rattling off the ladders and the metal bits on the horses' harnesses as they reached the surface.

Following the horses' path, Yvonne saw a row of tiny figures along the lip of the mine. The slaves. Making sure the Hundred kept their promise.

The power of the Hundred rose, brought with Sillman's words. The static crackle of lightning cascaded over all of them, growing brighter and stronger as they stood, gathering their power, until Yvonne could not see anything or feel anything or hear anything apart from the crackle of lightning. And then, when they were all blind and deaf, the crackling lightning formed a shape. Outlined in brilliant green light, the shape of the Firebird rose in the middle of the circle, over the deep hole. The first Hunar's mythical companion. A creature of magic and fury, her symbol worn by the Hunar as their commitment to justice.

Yvonne gasped, lifting her head to follow the bird's rise, the power of the circle still flowing, all that static charge and magic pouring into the creature that rose above them. Details were impossible to see through the light, just the merest outline to start with. Then the green shivered, the outline growing clearer, the Firebird formed of orange and red and white and yellow and blue and green, long feathers of her tail and wings shedding lightning as she rose, flames bursting into life around her, the heat of them scorching Yvonne's face.

Her heart was in her throat, mouth dry. The Firebird. Present and real. The great eyes, golden-hued and rimmed with green, seemed to stare straight into her soul, judging her. Yvonne wanted to scream and cry and rage. She was not worthy, she knew that, but she did her best.

The Firebird blinked and her gaze softened, Yvonne's throat closing up. She had been judged. And was still alive.

The Firebird rose over them and beat her wings, once, sending the lightning and power of the Hundred out around the mine. The walls of grey earth, so carefully and meticulously carved and crafted by slave labour, the path, the ladders, the mass of earth, all came surging towards the circle, flowing beneath their feet as though it was water, lifting them up, the earth continuing to flow inwards as the Firebird beat her wings again, lifted her head, beak wide as she shrieked her fury with a sound Yvonne was sure would be heard across all the lands.

They were picked up, tossed in the earthen sea, carried on the wild tide far from where they had started, the Firebird still there in the air above them, her great wings spreading to cover the whole of the mine, her focus downward, to where the blackened earth had been.

She raised her head again, screamed her power and triumph to the sky, and then faded as swiftly as she had arrived.

Leaving the Hundred scattered on the ground, covered in grey dust, staring at a vast, shallow depression in the ground where the mine had been. A year or more of work. The labour of countless slaves. The corruption of the soil. All destroyed and buried.

The soil was still settling as Yvonne watched, ripples of the earth from the outer edges to the centre, dust slowly dying down.

Her ears were ringing with the after-effect of the Firebird. When she blinked, she could see the after-image of the Firebird behind her lids. And her skin felt scorched, as though she had stood far too close to a fire.

"You did it."

The voice was faint, as though from a very great distance. She looked up, only then realising she was sitting on the ground, to find Lily next to her, face slack with amazement.

A familiar scent crossed her nose a moment before there was a nudge at her shoulder. Lothar was there, ears flicking forward and back as he looked at the space where the mine had been.

She stroked his nose, resting her head against his for a moment as she stared at the changed landscape, blinking several times to make sure it was real. It was.

The mine was gone.

There was no sign of the black.

And she felt hollow. As though every bit of energy and life she possessed had been scraped out and used.

"Here." The voice was still faint. Lily was back, with a waterskin. It looked familiar. "I got it from your horse," Lily told her. "He's lovely."

As she took a long, much-needed drink, Yvonne's ears popped with a sharp pain that made her wince. She handed the waterskin back and struggled to her feet, limbs weak, leaning against Lothar for a moment.

The rest of the Hundred were settled on the ground around her, looking as dazed as she felt. Idal was crouched next to Annabelle, waterskin in his hand. Guise was on his feet. Of course he was. He was checking over his horse and, as she watched, he took a pair of waterskins and moved across to where Pieris and Dundac had ended up settled near each other.

"We got the wagons ready," Lily told her.

"Good," Yvonne said. "And thank you for the water."

"Is it over?" Lily asked, voice softer. She was trying to look as though she didn't care, as though it were not the most important question in her world just now. Yvonne was familiar with the look from Mariah.

"Yes. The man who paid the mercenaries is dead. The mine is gone. And we're going to see you back home, if that's what you want," Yvonne told Lily, pitching her voice so that her words would carry more widely.

More promises to keep, the rightness of them settling into her chest.

Chapter Twenty-Eight

Yvonne struggled to hold on to the sense of wonder and relief over the following days. She could still hear the echo of the Firebird's scream now and then, and feel the fan of heat against her face from the downbeat of the bird's wings.

The mine might be gone, but there had been hundreds of youngsters in slavery, some of them too weak to stand. It had taken the rest of that day and far into the night to get everyone organised to move, raiding the mercenaries' sleeping quarters for blankets and finding a locked room stocked floor to ceiling with food. More food than the slaves had been getting.

And then there had been the laboratory to empty, Guise taking charge of that with Lily and the boy who had organised the wagons, slowly and carefully dismantling the equipment and packing everything away, making sure there was enough antidote for all the slaves for several days.

It had been first light before they had left the mine, moving slowly. Even with every wagon they could salvage, and as many horses as they could catch for the former slaves who could ride, and even with the wide, smooth road, it was slow going.

The seemingly unending supply of mercenaries' food was finished within a few days, the youngsters starving after limited rations and hard labour. Better food, and rest, and some of them had energy back, glimmers of mischief appearing among a few. The ones who hadn't been there as long. The longer-serving slaves were mostly still hollow-faced and hollow-eyed, not paying that much attention to anything around them, sleeping most of the days and nights. They did not cause any trouble, following the instructions they were given, silent and watchful.

Pieris and Mica had ridden ahead, as fast as their horses would take them, to their destination so that, when they finally arrived, with no food left and a dwindling supply of antidote, the way was ready for them.

The Stone Walls rose ahead, a phenomenon strange enough to draw the attention of even the most hollow-eyed child. As they came out of the forest and the wagons moved onto the wide, cobbled road that led up to the gates, the chatter gradually died down and all attention turned ahead.

The Stone Walls were higher than most buildings and seemingly made from single sheets of stone. Yvonne knew that was an illusion, carefully crafted and maintained by the Sisters, to deter any ignorant travellers from thinking this was an easy place to get into. Even the gates appeared made of stone. Another illusion.

The amount of magic required to maintain the illusion of the walls and gates was staggering, but many of the Sisters, those who made their life here and chose to remain, were powerful sorceresses, powerful enough to rival the Hunar, with a few extremely competent witches among them. They had more than enough power to maintain the walls, and their borders.

Even though Pieris and Mica had gone before them, Sillman asked Yvonne to go first. Of all Hunar, Elinor had the closest ties to the Sisters and, of all living Hunar, Yvonne knew them best.

Even without Pieris and Mica, Yvonne knew that the Sisters would have been prepared. She had tried to tell the rest of the Hundred, but Sillman had wanted the reassurance of an in-person message. Not wanting the frightening responsibility of the youngsters longer than he had to, Yvonne thought. She did not blame him. She had two youngsters within her care, and that was more than enough for any one person. As troublesome as they could be, she wanted to get back to her children. She just hoped the house would be in one piece when she did.

As Yvonne rode ahead, Lothar's ears pricking forward and his strides picking up as he recognised the walls ahead, the great gates split in the middle and swung open, smoothly and silently. The Sisters had seen them.

Yvonne could not remember the last time she had seen both gates open. The land that was revealed looked like paradise. Fertile, rolling farmland stretched as far as the eye could see, dotted here and there with cottages and barns which, she knew, held livestock and animal feed.

Foolish and boastful kings and princes might like to say that the Stone Walls was just an elaborate garden, but Yvonne was quite sure that none of them had actually seen the extent of the land that the Sisters occupied. It was bigger than many of the kingdoms whose leaders mocked the Sisters. And the Sisters had chosen their home well. The lands nestled among a jagged ring of impenetrable mountains. Many had tried to scale the mountain peaks, never to be seen again. The Stone Walls, and their gate, were the only entrance and exit.

There was a delegation approaching the gates from the inside. A few wagons, drawn by sturdy, patient ponies, and a large gathering. Men and women both. The Sisters did not discriminate.

"Yvonne!" One of the women in the lead group raised a hand, smile evident from this distance.

Yvonne brought Lothar to a halt a few paces away and slid off, allowing the woman, and a few of the other Sisters, to give her brief, hard hugs. Like the recent meeting with the rest of the Hundred, each face brought back bittersweet memories. The last time she had seen most of them had been at Elinor's funeral, none of them bothering to hide their tears.

"It is so good to see you again," Adira added, brushing away a tear of her own.

Yvonne's throat tightened, remembering the last time she had seen Adira before the funeral. Early morning in Elinor's kitchen, the two older women sitting at the table in their nightclothes, giggling like teenagers, hair loose, their feet tangled under the table, Yvonne pretending not to hear the whispers between them as she made a morning meal, the room full of love and laughter.

Adira shook her head a little, perhaps shaking off memories of her own, smile chasing away the sadness, white teeth startling contrast to her bronzed skin. "Thank you for all the gifts you have sent us."

Yvonne found an unexpected laugh inside her and let it loose. Only the Sisters would see additional residents in their valley as gifts.

"And you have more for us, I see," another Sister said.

"Yes. Did Pieris and Mica tell you?"

"We had heard the rumours of the missing," Adira said, all joy faded. "Terrible." She put a hand on Yvonne's shoulder, pressing lightly. "But you found them."

"Too late for many," Yvonne said, remembering the mass graves. "And for Rebecca's brother. There were graves at the mine."

"Ah. Poor child," Adira closed her eyes for a moment, lips moving in a silent blessing for the dead. "She has a good heart, that one, and will have a home here as long as she needs. We will tell her," Adira added.

"I had hoped for a better answer for her," Yvonne said.

"She is expecting the news," Adira answered, shaking her head slightly, then tilted her head to the wagons. "And we have enough here to keep her busy."

"They have been badly used," Yvonne told her. "We ran out of food yesterday and, as Pieris and Mica will have told you, they were poisoned. There's not much antidote left."

"Do you know what it is? The poison?" It was one of the older members of the group who spoke, a woman who had been here every time Yvonne had visited.

"I don't, but Guise might. He's been working on it."

"Ah. The infamous Guidrishinnal. I have long wanted to meet him," Adira said. "Is he as handsome as Elinor reported?"

Yvonne felt her spine stiffen slightly, conscious of Guise not that far away, and perhaps within hearing distance for sharp goblin ears. And her mind echoed with Guise's proper first name. She had the oddest feeling she had said it herself, and quite recently, but was unable to remember. The only blank space she had was the dungeons at Coll Castle. For the briefest moment, she had a vivid memory of her heart in her throat, body rigid with fear, and then the impression was gone, leaving her unsettled and no closer to knowing how to answer Adira.

"Handsome? What's the point in that? Never thought I would see that idle layabout actually working," the older Sister said, cutting across whatever Yvonne might have said. The sharp words imperfectly disguised the affection she clearly felt for Guise. Yvonne did not know why she was surprised.

She took a quick glance across her shoulder and saw Guise's face light in a smile. Sharp goblin ears indeed.

"We don't have room for so many in the houses at the moment. We're making as much room as we can, but we'll take them to the barns first," Adira said, squaring her shoulders. "I hope that staying together for a while will help them adjust. Will they want to go home, do you think?"

It was a question which had troubled Yvonne over the past few days, too. A few of the youngsters had ventured the question. Most had stayed silent, whether through exhaustion or something else, she did not know.

"Most of them, yes, I think so. Some have asked already. We know that most of their parents are worried."

Yvonne did not need to say the rest of it. That, for some of them, there would be no worthwhile home to go back to, and the parents would have been relieved, more than anything else, that their children were missing. Or annoyed because they had lost their free labour. For a lot of the children, as with a lot of the people that Yvonne had sent behind the Stone Walls over the years, life with the Sisters was far preferable to the one that they had left behind. And if they did not want to stay behind the Stone Walls, the Sisters would not hold them but send them on their way, more often than not with a few coins in their pockets.

The wagons had arrived, along with the horses, animals lifting their heads slightly, nostrils flaring, as they caught the scent of green growing things beyond the gates. Yvonne moved to one side to let them pass and to let the Sisters, and those they had brought with them, make greetings. The group was larger than she had thought at first. There was a pair of Sisters for every wagon and a few more besides to take charge of the riders. They were used to greeting newcomers, and it was not long before even the most hollow-eyed child was showing better signs of life.

While the Sisters made the children welcome and comfortable, and shared some snacks that they had brought with them, all carefully outside the walls, the elderly Sister took Guise to one side with the wagon that held the laboratory equipment and dwindling supply of antidote. The pair had their heads together for a long while, going through the wagon's contents and the ledgers that they had found.

Enough antidote for at least two days more, Guise had thought that morning, even if he still did not know how to cure the poison. Making the antidote should be relatively easy, he had said, and she could see from the Sister's reaction that she agreed, even as she shook her head. Giving poison to children to force them to work was despicable, even among the horrors that the Sisters dealt with on a daily basis.

At length, the pair were done talking, and all the former slaves were looking ahead with curiosity. Only when they were comfortable did the sisters move the horses and wagons forward.

Adira stayed behind, just outside the walls.

"We will look after them for as long as they need to be here," she told Yvonne, unnecessarily. "Are you going to Hogsmarthen?"

"I think so. I need a bath, at any rate," Yvonne said, wrinkling her nose. She received a brief hug from the Sister again.

"You are better than you were last time I saw you," Adira said. She and Elinor had shared a direct way of speaking that many people found rude. The Sister smiled, sadness in her face again. "But you are still too hidden. You have so much to give the world."

"I am quite content. And kept busy enough," Yvonne answered. It was the same answer she gave every time Adira, or Elinor, pressed her.

"Give my love to the children. Peace be with you."

"And with you," Yvonne answered.

Adira turned to follow the last wagon in.

One of the youngsters from the last wagon turned his head as they passed the Hundred and Guise.

"You not coming with us?"

"Not this time," Yvonne answered.

"The Hundred have their tasks out in the world. You will be safe here," Sillman added.

Moments later, the great gates shut with a dull thud that echoed through Yvonne, making her wish, as she did every time, that she could go back within the walls. There was no time, though.

The gates closing left the group facing a seemingly impenetrable sheet of stone that stretched almost as far as they could see to either side, the only clue that there might be an entrance the cobbled road that led straight up to the wall.

"Did someone mention a bath?" Annabelle asked, nose wrinkling.

"An excellent idea. Come on, we should be able to make Hogsmarthen by nightfall," Dundac said.

Yvonne watched as the rest of the Hundred rode ahead. She followed more slowly, aware of Guise nearby.

"You have been behind the Stone Walls," Guise said. It was not a question and for a moment she did not answer, caught up in memory. Injured and terrified, with two wide-eyed, near-feral wulfkin toddlers in tow, she had somehow found her way here. And the Sisters had opened the gate for her, as they did for every wounded or lost soul that asked for admittance.

Within the Stone Walls she had found some badly-needed healing and, more than that, she had found Elinor, whose loss still echoed through her. The Hunar had seen something in the younger Yvonne that made her take her on as an apprentice, even with two orphan wulfkin in tow.

"Two seasons," she answered him at length, voice rough. "After the fire." She did not need to tell him which fire.

"It looks like a beautiful place," he said.

She found another unexpected laugh and let this one loose, too.

"You should ask the Sisters for a tour. They would be delighted to have you within their walls," she told him.

He laughed in turn, shaking his head.

The Sisters did not take in visitors, as such. If you went within the walls, you were expected to stay there for at least a season, and do whatever work you could whether tending the animals, working the fields or preparing meals. It was the price of the Sisters' aid. A fair one, Yvonne had always thought. But she could not imagine Guise willingly stepping out of the world for an entire season. She remembered the map he had created. Behind the walls, he would miss gathering all those secrets.

Chapter Twenty-Nine

Saying goodbye to the Hundred after a pleasant evening in Hogsmarthen had been hard. It always was. They might only gather for solemn or awful occasions, but they were an extended family, the clashing personalities and long history set aside as soon as they were needed.

They could not stay, though. None of them. There were too few Hunar in the world, and too many people in need of their help.

There had been no lingering goodbyes, just brisk farewells and promises to write.

Then she had made her way back to Fir Tree Crossing, passenger on a river barge that Guise had commandeered. He had been oddly quiet since they left the Sisters, and left her at the docks, saying he had family business to attend to. She was used to his abrupt arrivals and departures. It might be months before she saw him again. Or it could be a few days.

She felt hollow as she left him. Too many farewells.

She arrived at the house just as the sky was beginning to darken, Lothar's ears sweeping forward as they crossed the bridge.

No screams this time. The house looked intact as she rode up to it, and then around the side to the stables.

As she slid off Lothar's back, the kitchen door opened and Joel and Mariah tumbled out, hugging her one after the other. Brief, hard hugs.

"You're home," Mariah said, voice high with excitement and something that sounded like relief.

"I am," Yvonne answered, putting a hand out and briefly touching Mariah's arm. "What's wrong?"

"Nothing."

"We were worried about you," Joel said, taking Lothar's reins. "All of you. It sounded serious."

"It was. It is," Yvonne told them, frowning at his back as he led her horse into the stable.

"Is everything alright now?" Mariah asked.

Yvonne watched Joel unsaddle Lothar for a moment, trying to think of the right way to answer that, to reassure her children.

"Yes." She tried to put as much conviction into her voice as possible. "We helped a lot of people." It was a poor summary of what had happened, and yet she did not want to say more, did not want to relive the memories of the mine and the black tendrils. Those memories did not belong here, with this quiet house, serene in the evening light. This was becoming their home and she wanted to defend it, however impossible that might be.

"Good," Joel said, giving Lothar a final pat and coming out of the stable, taking the saddle and bridle to the harness room at the end of the block. "We went to the bakeries earlier," he told her as he came out of the room and back towards her, her saddlebags over his shoulder. "Plenty for all of us."

"Bakeries?" Yvonne's brows lifted. More than one. Perhaps every baker in Fir Tree Crossing. Knowing her children, that was entirely possible. "Did you set the kitchen on fire?"

"No, not this time," he answered, smiling.

"Nothing went on fire," Mariah added, doubtless trying to be helpful, but making Yvonne wonder instead what had gone wrong while she had been away.

She used the excuse of wanting a change of clothes to sneak a look around the house before they ate. Everything was intact, and she came back to the kitchen to find that Joel and Mariah had set out a feast for them. Her children had, indeed, been to every bakery in town, spending some of their wages.

Joel had poured her a glass of wine, and they settled around the table, Yvonne demanding all the news since she had been away, Mariah more than happy to tell her.

It was the perfect end to the journey. Settled in her family's kitchen, listening to the news of the town, a glass of wine next to her. Far, far away from the misery of the mine, the slaves even now under the Sisters' care, and the corruption of the ancient enemy.

Another day passed and she found herself with that rarest of things, an afternoon off.

Mariah was at the dressmaker's, and had left almost skipping that morning, so Yvonne was not expecting to see her back until after dark. It was always a wonder to her that Mariah found such joy in putting clothes together, but she excelled at it and worked hard, and seemed satisfied with Yvonne's words of praise, even if they were probably ill-informed.

Joel was at the docks. A few of the other young wulfkin in town had discovered that they, too, could earn good money loading and offloading river barges. The dock hands who usually took on such jobs, and who had been moaning about the work and the poor pay, were suddenly faced with competition from much stronger wulfkin, who could clear a barge in half the time it would take the same number of humans. Yvonne could foresee trouble ahead. For now, though, there was a good-natured competition being set up between different crews. Four wulfkin against ten humans seemed to be about right, and the wulfkin had somehow negotiated to be paid the human equivalent, so four wulfkin were splitting the equivalent of ten humans' pay. That would not last long, she was sure. Joel was fully aware of the potential for trouble, and had mentioned, too casually to be an accident, that Sephenamin himself was taking an interest, along with Grayling. So, Yvonne set her worries aside.

It was an unfamiliar feeling, to have both children out of the house and employed. And to have the house to herself. The horses were out in the field, enjoying a warm day. There had been no supplicants at the gate.

Time off was rare. On previous occasions she had taken an extra-long bath, read a book or written some long-overdue letters.

This afternoon she could not be still, turning instead to the well-stocked kitchen and some recipes she had been wanting to experiment with.

She was in the middle of measuring ingredients for a beetroot cake, hands stained with the purple juice, when one of the wards tripped, alerting her to a visitor. She looked around the mess in the kitchen, and down at herself. Despite the apron, she was covered in flour, as well as having stained hands. For once, she did not care. There were far more important things in the world.

She washed her hands quickly, hung up the apron and went around the side of the house to meet the visitor, brushing flour off her clothes as she did so.

Guise was the last person she had expected to see at her house. He was usually meticulously careful at arranging their meetings in public spaces, somehow sensing she did not like to have people in her house. He was also dressed with unusual care, even for him, and she felt even more shabby than usual by comparison.

He got off his horse and led it to a convenient spot under a tree where a water trough had been set up before turning to her. He made an odd bow before he moved towards her and when he came close enough, her brows lifted at his expression. It was a similar expression that she had seen on Joel or Mariah's faces when they had done something they knew she would not approve of. Eating the rest of the cake. Sneaking out after dark.

It was not an expression she expected to see on a goblin's face, let alone Guise's. Guilt at being caught out in some mischief or other.

"Good day, mristrian," he said, his voice apparently calm.

"What have you done?" she demanded.

He shifted on his feet from side to side, reminding her even more of a guilty child.

"I don't think there is enough time to explain fully," he began, "as we are about to have visitors."

"What do you mean visitors? And what do you mean we?"

"Do you have your memories back? From the dungeon?"

She opened her mouth, then clamped her jaw shut against angry words and shook her head instead.

"Occasional flashes. Nothing more." She looked away for a moment, swallowing hard. "I remember fear."

"I am sorry," he said, sincerity bringing her eyes back to him. He bowed slightly again. "I was not myself." He stood silent, frowning for a moment, then shook his head slightly. "I do not think it is right that I simply tell you what happened. It would be better if you remembered it."

"Does this have something to do with how we got out of there?" she asked, eyes narrowing. His gaze slid away, and her eyes narrowed further. "It does. What happened?"

"You remember the bond?" he asked instead. He was not meeting her eyes. In fact, he was looking everywhere but at her.

Bond. Something stirred in her memory. The grating sound of metal on stone.

"I'd been hit on the head at least twice," she reminded him. "I don't remember. Something about ... Poison?"

"Yes."

There was a snarl in his voice that a sane person would back away from. She stood her ground. He would not hurt her.

The certainty of that echoed through her. He had not wanted to hurt her. He had not hurt her.

"The lord put us in the dungeon for you to kill me," she remembered, feeling the colour drain from her face.

"Yes."

"But you didn't. Somehow." She frowned into middle-distance, trying to remember.

"Do not try and force the memory. It's likely to come back."

"Before these visitors arrive?"

"No." His face closed.

"So, you were poisoned. And there was a bond. And we escaped," she concluded.

"Somewhat. And not quite."

She resisted the urge to roll her eyes, unease creeping into her, knotting her stomach. He would not hurt her. It was a core-deep truth. Of all the people in the world, she was safe with him.

"Guise, you are worrying me. I do not like to be worried. Just tell me what I need to know for these visitors."

"I think you may want to sit down."

And he insisted that she did, walking with her over to the bench outside the front of the house, remaining standing while she sat in the sun and glared up at him, waiting for an answer.

"It doesn't translate well," he began, and she almost interrupted him, annoyed at the further delay. Something in his manner kept her still and quiet, though. He was not delaying anymore. He seemed to be struggling for words to try and explain what he needed to tell her. "Goblins create bonds. There are family bonds, which we are born with, although we can choose to reject them. And there are bonds that we create through our lives. Something like, and nothing like, the contract humans enter into between each other."

Yvonne sat back against the wall of the house, the sun-warmed bricks a welcome support, not really feeling the warmth as her whole body chilled. She thought about what he had said, and not said, and clamped her jaw shut. He had more to say.

"I did not intend to make such a bond with you," he began, hesitating, and fleetingly met her eyes. He looked ashamed. "I intended to speak a temporary bond, that would let us get out of the dungeon. But I was not quite myself." That was an understatement. She remembered the fear. The sound of metal restraints grating in the wall as he struggled, and almost pulled them loose. "So I gave you the words for a much more serious bond. A lifetime commitment."

She was abruptly glad she was sitting down as the world seemed to spin. The chill that had been creeping over her numbed her nose and toes and her face froze, her mouth half-open.

"I am sorry." He sounded sincere.

All at once, she was on her feet, hands on hips, furious and disbelieving at the same time.

"Married? We are married? Actually married? This isn't a joke?"

"In human terms, marriage is the closest equivalent. But it's not quite the same."

"You said visitors?" Her mind would not comprehend the idea of being married, let alone to Guise, so she turned to something more understandable.

"I had family business. My mother sensed a change in me, and –"

"Your mother is coming here?" Yvonne interrupted, breath running out of her. "Helgiarast se'laj Krejefell, the current star in the Karoan'shae, is coming here?" The Karoan'shae were the corona, ruling the goblin nation, and at their centre was a star. A king, or queen, in human terms.

"You seem well-informed about my family's position in the Karoan'shae," he commented. It sounded like a compliment, from someone who valued secrets and information.

"Your mother is coming here?" she said again, her mind stuck on that one fact. "I'm covered in flour and beetroot juice. There is nothing in this house to serve her. I haven't cleaned the house." Her voice had risen in pitch by the end, hysterical, and she closed her mouth against further babbling.

"You are beautiful, mies maisredayenni," he told her. It was said in the most matter-of-fact tone possible, as if he was commenting that the sky was blue or the grass was green.

She was staring at him, open-mouthed and uncomprehending, when the sounds of carriage wheels drew her attention past his shoulder.

"Your mother is here," she said. She looked down at herself and, for the first time in a long while, wanted the ground to open up and swallow her. Her clothes were old and worn, perfectly appropriate for an afternoon in the kitchen, even though she was also wearing her weapons. She could feel wisps of hair around her face. Her fingers were still tainted pink, despite the quick wash.

Lifting her head, she tried to judge the distance between the carriage and the house, and whether she would get away with using a quick cleansing spell to take the worst of the day's activities off her person. The carriage was too close, though. And goblins had exceptional eyesight, hearing and sensitivity to magic. There was no way that whoever was in that carriage would miss her attempt to tidy herself up.

"You are perfect as you are," Guise told her, in the same matter-of-fact tone.

"Have you hit your head?" she asked. "What have you been drinking?"

His mouth curved up in a smile, eyes shading to gold for a moment before he shook his head. Her breath caught, attention snagging on that gold shade. She had seen that shade before, but could not remember when or where. And then she realised it must have been in the dungeon, in that missing space in her memory.

The carriage drew to a halt before she could follow that thought further. The driver jumped down from his perch, landing lightly on the ground with the grace of a cat. Another goblin. Of course. He was dressed in navy, head to toe, which was an unusual colour but, if she recalled correctly, the house colour of the Krejefell, Guise's family. He might be a carriage driver, but he was armed, and his beautifully crafted clothes were decorated with enough gold thread to feed her family for a year.

He ignored her and Guise, going instead to open the carriage door and put out a hand for the occupant to lean on as she descended.

Guise's mother stepped out of the carriage with the same lithe and easy grace that her son possessed. Doubtless she also excelled at weapons and swordsmanship. She was not dressed for combat, though. Instead, she was dressed in a gown that Yvonne was quite sure would make Mariah's eyes pop out of her head. All Yvonne could tell was that it was well fitted and of a smoky, pinky grey shade that should have looked strange against the lady's dark grey skin, but which instead almost glowed in the sunshine.

"You must be Yvonne. I am Helgiarast. I am delighted to meet you."

Of all the greetings Yvonne might have expected, in the few moments she had been given to realise that Guise's mother was on her way, this was not at all what she thought would happen. She froze, realising she didn't know if she was supposed to bow or curtsy, or how she was supposed to address the current star of the Karoan'shae.

"I'm pleased to meet you," she managed to say. "Be welcome to my house."

"Mother," Guise said, his voice dry, "you must have raced all the way here."

"I was impatient to meet my new daughter," Helgiarast answered, a light note in her voice that might have suggested playfulness but, Yvonne was quite sure, was anything but, making her even more wary. The wrong word in the Karoan'shae could get someone killed.

"I regret I did not know that you would be coming," Yvonne said, with as much grace as she could muster, "so the house is not prepared well for you. But I do have some excellent wine and I've just finished baking, if you'd like to come inside for some refreshment?"

"That would be most pleasant. My lady in waiting can deal with the refreshments, if you will give her directions to the kitchen," Helgiarast said.

Feeling like a visitor in her own home, Yvonne looked past Helgiarast to find an elderly goblin lady standing patiently by the carriage, awaiting instructions. She gave her a brief description of where to find the kitchen and then led Helgiarast through the front door of the house and into the sitting room. It was clean, at least, as it was rarely used, but it was a cacophony of mismatched furniture and clashing prints that even Yvonne knew was hardly the sort of thing that Helgiarast was used to.

To her surprise, Guise's mother looked around the room with an attentive expression on her face and made a low sound.

"Rented properties are so difficult, aren't they?" she said. "One never knows what one is going to get."

Yvonne recognised an attempt to put her at ease in her own house and had to bite her lip to stop an unexpected smile. She was quite certain that the current star of the Karoan'shae had never done anything as pedestrian as occupy a rented dwelling.

Continuing to display the exquisite manners that were expected of the Karoan'shae houses, Helgiarast somehow managed to allow Yvonne to sit down, with Guise not that far away, and subtly take over so that when her lady in waiting arrived with a tray of refreshments, she was gently dismissed and Yvonne found herself waiting for Helgiarast to reveal the real purpose of her visit.

It took half a glass of wine being consumed by all, and Helgiarast's effusive compliments on Yvonne's baking, before the lady approached her point.

"I was so surprised when Guise told me about the bond," she commented lightly.

In fact, her tone was so light that Yvonne almost missed the real meaning behind the words.

Helgiarast was waiting for a response, but Yvonne thought she was getting the measure of her now. A wrong word now would have implications that Yvonne did not understand. And she still could not remember what had happened. But she knew the effect of it. She and Guise had escaped the locked dungeon, both in one piece, and it had taken the efforts of the entire Hundred to heal her, putting her skull back together. She could afford to take a little bit of time to find out what was going on, and what she wanted or needed to do about it.

Yvonne lifted her brow slightly in response.

"He's never been one to settle down," Helgiarast added, slanting a glance at her son. For some reason, Yvonne thought of the faceless Abar al Endell assassin.

"Mother," Guise said, "you are making a poor first impression."

"I am being rude. You're quite right. Is this what you want?" Helgiarast asked Yvonne directly.

"This is you being polite? She can hardly answer that now," Guise said, tone exasperated.

"Can't she?" At the pointed question and lifted brow, Yvonne realised that the barbed question had not really been for her, but to see what reaction she would get from her son. "I do hope that Guidrishinnal explained to you that it is a lifetime bond. It is almost impossible to reverse while both parties are alive."

Yvonne's skin pickled. Her fingers twitched, wanting to move for a weapon. She held herself still with effort. Even if she drew a weapon, either of the goblins in the room with her would be able to kill her before she had done so much as scratch them.

"You said almost impossible," Yvonne said. She was quite certain that those were the words that Helgiarast had wanted her to pick up on.

"Well, yes. There is a way of reversing the bond. If you were tricked into it. If Guise lied to you."

"And do you think that your son lied?" Yvonne asked, genuinely curious. She did not really care that it was a rude question.

Helgiarast gave a short bark of laughter, genuine surprise on her face for a moment.

"Mother has a very low opinion of me," Guise said, his voice as light as his mother's had been. Yvonne did not think that reflected his true feeling on the matter.

"And what would happen if I said he lied?" she asked, keeping her eyes on Helgiarast. She was not being told the full story.

"Nothing you need worry about, mristrian," Guise told her, his voice calm.

"Well, quite," his mother agreed, tone still light. "I mean, we can't have you going around creating bonds with just anybody you meet."

Yvonne looked between mother and son and saw, despite the light tone both had adopted, the banked fury in Guise's face along with a hint of colour, and a reflection of that in Helgiarast's face. Her curiosity spiked, and she wondered what the story was and whether Guise would tell her.

If she said he had lied, the bond would be over. And she had bone-deep certainty that she would not see Guise again. The thought of that hurt more than she would have imagined. Although she never felt she quite understood him, she enjoyed his company. The world would be somehow flatter without him around.

Puzzling through the behaviour and manners of the Karoan'shae always gave her a headache. Luckily, she had only needed to try a few times in the course of her life. Trying to work out what was going on between the two of them, and what the implications might be if she said Guise had lied was making her head hurt, and giving her a strong wish for the rest of the bottle of wine. That would not solve anything, though.

"Presumably, if there is one bond in place then another cannot be created," Yvonne said. It was mostly speculation, but she saw that she was right by Helgiarast's reaction. And Guise had stilled nearby, going almost completely motionless in a way that told Yvonne that the answer was vitally important to him.

So, whatever this bond was that had been created in the dungeon, it stopped him creating any other bonds. And that was a source of rancour for Helgiarast. The star of the Karoan'shae would be used to getting her own way. And doubtless had her own plans for her son's future that did not include shabbily-dressed Hunar.

"He's not the most obedient of children, is he?" Yvonne said, acid creeping into her voice. "I know that feeling."

She saw surprise on Helgiarast's face again. Whatever the star of the Karoan'shae had expected, it was not this ill-mannered, poorly-dressed, blunt-spoken, human female. Yvonne had an unexpected impulse to smile.

"I'm afraid I cannot oblige you," she told Helgiarast. "Guise did not lie." It was another core-deep truth. He would not hurt her. He had not lied to her. He had not told her the whole truth, he rarely did, but he had not lied, and she would not say that he had.

Helgiarast's brows lifted almost to her hairline, and her mouth opened slightly.

"You are most unexpected," she said. "If you change your mind, you have only to let him know. At least, for a little while, before the bond has fully settled."

Helgiarast rose to her feet as she spoke, said a brief farewell and made her way out of the house.

Yvonne found she was frozen to the spot, listening to the carriage wheels leaving and, moments later, feeling the slight vibration in the wards as the carriage passed through her perimeter.

"Why did you do that?" Guise asked her. "You could have been free of me."

Free of him. Yvonne's mind turned the words over. She shook her head slightly. He was arrogant and frustrating, and yet she would be sorry to never see him again. And did not want to tell him any of that.

"I do not lie," she said, giving him the absolute truth. "It's one of the core principles of being a Hunar. And you did not lie to me. So I cannot tell the Karoan'shae that you did." She shook her head again, looking around for her wine glass, suddenly exhausted.

"The matter will not end here," Guise said. He was standing perfectly still, with his hands folded behind his back and Yvonne knew that, if she could see his hands, his knuckles would be white, fingers laced together.

"I don't want to be married," she told him bluntly. "Not to you. Not to anyone. I never have. I don't understand why you created the bond you did."

"It is the highest and most profound honour among my people," he told, voice low, "and anything less than that would be an insult to you."

"I don't understand you," she told him plainly, having nothing apart from the truth to offer him.

"I know," he answered, the faintest trace of a smile on his face, which faded as he went on, "but I would very much like it if you did."

Chapter Thirty

Yvonne was not sure what to say to that, or how to react. She felt strange. Breathless, with a strange impulse to laugh, as though at the end of a long, joyous gallop on Lothar. At the same time, she was bruised all over, as though from a fight. She wanted to laugh, and cry, and shout in anger. She did not want to deal with any of it.

She did not have to react, though, as light footsteps sounded in the hallway and she realised that her children had returned to the house without her even noticing.

"Kalla," Mariah's voice sounded, high and excited. "We saw a carriage leaving. With goblin horses."

"And there's a horse outside, Mariah," Joel added, clearly following his sister.

They came in through the room's open door and stumbled to a halt in an almost comical fashion when they saw Guise.

"What's he doing here?" Mariah asked, lip curling. "He's not welcome in the house."

"Mariah, your manners are appalling," Yvonne said, voice calm. Dealing with rude children was extremely familiar.

"Well, it's my house too," Mariah answered, lower lip sticking out in a clear sulk.

"It's not just your house," Joel told his sister, tone scornful. "And if we cut out everyone you didn't like, there'd be no one to talk to."

"Be that as it may," Yvonne interrupted before the two of them could descend into a flaming argument that would take the rest of the day, "Guise is here, and you were rude, Mariah."

"Does he have something?" Mariah asked, ignoring Joel and Yvonne's attempt at discipline.

"My mother," Guise answered. He did not seem offended by her. He always seemed to find Mariah more amusing than anything else, which usually infuriated her. Having now met Guise's mother, Yvonne could not help wondering about Guise's family, and what passed for polite conversation there.

"The star of the Karoan'shae was here?" Mariah's eyes widened. "And I missed it? What was she wearing, Kalla?"

Yvonne shook her head slightly. Trust Mariah to focus on the things that mattered to her most, and ignore the more extraordinary thing, that the star of the Karoan'shae had actually been in their house.

"Does it matter what she was wearing?" Joel asked his sister, distinct growl in his tone. His eyes lit with wulf power, showing how unsettled he was. "Are you all right, Kalla?"

"I am fine, thank you," Yvonne told him, although she was not sure it was quite the truth. "It has been quite an eventful afternoon." She sent a sideways glance at Guise as she spoke, and he inclined his head, a hint of colour in his face.

"I should leave," he said. "I have business that takes me elsewhere for a few days. I will call on my return."

"Probably a good idea," Yvonne agreed. A few days was time enough for her to think about what she had learned this afternoon. Possibly enough time for her patchy memory to restore itself, and certainly time enough for her to research goblin bonds. Neither Guise nor his mother had been telling her the entire truth, which she found both irritating and worrying.

Ignoring her open-mouthed children, she showed Guise to the door and watched as he got on his horse and rode away.

As he cleared the boundary wards, she became aware of shadows behind her, standing in the house's hallway.

"Something's changed, hasn't it?" Joel asked. He sounded a little bit sad.

"It seems so," Yvonne answered. "We were locked in a dungeon together in Coll Castle. It seems that Guise … That we created some sort of bond in order to escape the dungeon. I had a head injury. I don't remember much." A bond. The words sounded strange, awkward and clumsy on her tongue. Even the phrase was wrong. We. As though there was some connection there.

"Bond?" Mariah looked blank for a moment, then her eyes sparked. Anger or humour, Yvonne could not tell for a moment.

"Yes," Yvonne answered with stiff lips. The disparate parts of her body wanted to move in separate directions. Her legs to run. Her arms to find Lothar to hold on to. Her head to dive under a pillow, or a blanket, and not emerge until the world made sense again.

"A goblin bond," Joel said slowly, head tilted. "Like a marriage?"

Trust her children to get to the heart of it more quickly than she had.

She could not bring herself to speak, so she nodded instead, trying not to look at them. She hated not understanding, and not remembering.

They looked at each other for a moment, then giggled. It was not the reaction that Yvonne had expected and she lifted her brows.

"Married. Do we need to call him Papa?" Joel asked, eyes dancing.

"Papa Guise." Mariah's lips twitched.

"Papa Guise," Joel echoed, and they both collapsed into laughter.

"You are both horrible," Yvonne told them, colour surging up her neck and face. She went back into the living room to fetch the tray, looking longingly at the wine bottle. For a moment, she considered curling up on one of the comfortable chairs and finishing the wine. But that would not solve anything. There were no answers to goblin bonds, the behaviour of the Karoan'shae or her laughing children in that bottle. So, she added the bottle to the tray and took everything back to the kitchen.

The children's laughter accompanied her on the way. It was a better reaction than some, she supposed. But her face was burning.

"Papa Guise," Joel muttered and choked on another laugh.

"Horrible," Yvonne repeated, grabbing the apron again. There was a half-finished cake to keep her hands busy.

"Kalla," Joel said, voice almost serious. She looked up across the table and met his eyes. "This is not necessarily bad. He's been sweet on you since you met. Years."

"I don't like him," Mariah said, before Yvonne had a chance to react.

"I know," Yvonne told Mariah. "You never hide your feelings." She frowned at Joel, opening her mouth to say something. What, she had no idea.

"Yes," Joel said, quite serious, holding her eyes. "All this time. He hides it well," he added, "because of who he is. Still. Years."

"Horses," Yvonne said the first thing that came into her head. It was drawing towards evening. Time for fresh feed and water to be laid.

Joel came around the table and gave her a brief, warm hug, before grabbing Mariah's arm when she protested, dragging his sister out into the early evening, leaving Yvonne in her kitchen, hands covered in beetroot again. She looked down at the vegetables she was chopping and realised that she had forgotten the recipe and what she needed to do next.

Then she realised that her eyes were hot with tears. She rarely cried. Anger. Confusion. An overwhelming sense of embarrassment. How had she ended up in this situation?

Years, Joel had said. How had she missed that?

Because you did not want to see it. Elinor's voice crossed her mind, as vividly as if she had been in the room. Yvonne turned her head, looking for her old mentor and finding only blank space. She closed her eyes and tears fell. Too much change. Too much loss.

She wanted peace and quiet. A home. A place to settle, for her and for her children, after so long displaced.

And she could see that here. The beginnings of it, at least. The house was theirs for a while longer. The town was more than she had hoped for. A place for Joel and Mariah to finish growing, to find friendships. Perhaps more. And somewhere for her, too. A place to belong. Safe. Or, at least, as safe as a Hunar could ever be.

And she also wanted to have her memory back. To know what, exactly, she and Guise had promised each other in that dungeon. To remember what he had told her. And perhaps to solve the puzzle of why she was so reluctant to let him go. Goblins were not safe. And she could not imagine Guise ever being content to settle, here or anywhere else.

Before she could do anything more, Joel came back into the kitchen in a rush.

"Sillman and Suanna are coming, with Mica," he said, slightly breathless. "You didn't tell us."

"I didn't know," she answered, wiping her eyes with her flour-dusted sleeve, pulling the apron off, and then digging a cleansing spell out of her belt pouch.

At least she was finally clean, the staining gone from her fingers, no more flour on her. And her fellow Hunar were here.

She went through the house to meet some of her oldest friends, feeling the world settle again with each step. The Hundred only met on solemn or awful occasions. There must be something requiring her aid.

By the time she reached the front door and stepped out to meet them, they had crossed the bridge and were riding towards the house. She raised her hand in greeting, everything settling in her, waiting to hear about whoever was in need, and the task they had for her.

Whatever else was true, she was Hunar.

THANK YOU

THANK YOU VERY MUCH for reading *The Gathering*, The Hundred - Book 1.

It would be great, if you have five minutes, if you could leave an honest review at the store you got it from. Reviews are really helpful for other readers decide whether the book is for them, and that also helps me get visibility for my books - thank you.

Yvonne's story continues in *The Sundering*, The Hundred - Book 2, also available at Amazon.

If you want to know what I'm working on and when the next book will be available, you can contact me and sign up for my newsletter at the website: www.taellaneth.com.

CHARACTER LIST

NOTE: TO AVOID SPOILERS, some names may have been omitted, and some details left out.

Adira - human, senior head Sister in the Stone Walls
Annabelle - human, one of the Hundred
Brea - goblin, wife to Thort and mother to Jesset
Brias - wulfkin, second in the range at Ilfton
Caroline - human, daughter of Viola the herbalist
Cressin - human, tanners, from Silverton
Dundac - human, one of the Hundred
Elinor – human, deceased at start, formerly of the Hundred
Ella - wulfkin, in Sephenamin's range
Firon - human, one of the Hundred
Frida - human, dressmaker, from Fir Tree Crossing
Grayling - human, head of law keepers at Fir Tree Crossing
Guise - goblin
Handerson - human, potter, from Fir Tree Crossing
Idal - human, apprentice Hunar
Jesset - goblin, Brea and Thort's daughter
Joel - wulfkin, one of Yvonne's wards and Mariah's brother
Keffle - human, potter, from Fir Tree Crossing
Kraig – senior law keeper, reporting to Grayling
Lothar - Yvonne's horse

Mariah - wulfkin, one of Yvonne's wards and Joel's sister

Mica - human, one of the Hundred

Modig - mixed heritage, hotel manager in Three Falls

Niall - human, chemist, from Three Falls

Orla - human, clerk in the mayor's office, Fir Tree Crossing, Priadan's sister

Pieris - human, one of the Hundred

Priadan – human, mayor of Fir Tree Crossing, Orla's brother

Rebecca - human, from Hogsmarthen

Sephenamin – wulfkin, cerro in Fir Tree Crossing, owns The Tavern

Sillman - human, one of the Hundred

Suanna - human, one of the Hundred

Thort - goblin, Brea's husband, Jesset's father

Ubel - human, merchant

Viola - human, herbalist in Fir Tree Crossing

Willa - wulfkin, works at The Tavern, Fir Tree Crossing

Yvonne - human, one of the Hundred, legal guardian of Mariah and Joel

PLACES

Abar al Endell – southernmost city, at the edge of the desert, near the Forbidden Lands

Coll Castle - part of Kingdom of Valland

Fir Tree Crossing - busy trading town on the Great River

Forbidden Lands - desert territory beyond Abar al Endell

Hogsmarthen - closest city to the Sisters in the Stone Walls, on the Great River (upriver from Fir Tree Crossing)

Ilfton - mountain town where Yvonne lived before Fir Tree Crossing

Kelton - artists' town on the Great River between Hogsmarthen and Fir Tree Crossing

Royal City - home of the Valland Kings, furthest upriver on the Great River

Runacre Keep - small fortress not far from Ilfton

Silverton - small trading town upriver from Fir Tree Crossing

Stone Walls - home of the Sisters in the Stone Walls, a high-sided mountain valley not far from Hogsmarthen

Three Falls - city state near Valland

Valland - largest Kingdom in the lands, holds the Royal City, a lot of the Great River and Coll Castle

ALSO BY THE AUTHOR

(as at July 2024)

Fractured Conclave
A Usual Suspect, Book 1
A Broken Contract, Book 2 – expected to release October 2024

The Grey Gates (complete)
Outcast, Book 1
Called, Book 2
Hunted, Book 3
Forged, Book 4
Chosen, Book 5

Ageless Mysteries (complete)
Deadly Night, Book 1
False Dawn, Book 2
Morning Trap, Book 3
Assassin's Noon, Book 4
Flightless Afternoon, Book 5
Ascension Day, Book 6

The Hundred series (complete)
The Gathering, Book 1

The Sundering, Book 2
The Reckoning, Book 3
The Rending, Book 4
The Searching, Book 5
The Rising, Book 6

The Taellaneth series (complete)
Concealed, Book 1
Revealed, Book 2
Betrayed, Book 3
Tainted, Book 4
Cloaked, Book 5

Taellaneth Box Set (all five books in one e-book)
Taellaneth Complete Series (Books 1–5)

ABOUT THE AUTHOR

Vanessa Nelson is a fantasy author who lives in Scotland, United Kingdom and spends her days juggling the demands of an elderly, spoiled cat, two giant dogs and her fictional characters.

As far as the cat is concerned, she is in charge and should always come first. The older dog lets her know when he isn't getting enough attention by chewing up the house. The younger dog's favourite method of getting her attention is a gentle nudge with his head. At least, he would say it's gentle.

You can find out more information online at the following places:

Website: www.taellaneth.com

Facebook: www.facebook.com/taellaneth

Made in United States
Troutdale, OR
07/01/2025

32564123R00177